GOD SAVE THE QUEEN

Books by Kate Locke

The Immortal Empire

God Save the Queen
The Queen Is Dead
Long Live the Queen

GOD SAVE THE QUEEN

KATE LOCKE

THE IMMORTAL EMPIRE

orbit

www.orbitbooks.net

Orbit
Hachette Book Group
237 Park Avenue, New York, NY 10017
www.HachetteBookGroup.com

First Edition: July 2012

Orbit is an imprint of Hachette Book Group, Inc.
The Orbit name and logo are trademarks of Little,
Brown Book Group Limited.

The Hachette Speakers Bureau provides a wide range of authors for
speaking events. To find out more, go to www.hachettespeakersbureau.com or
call (866) 376-6591.

The publisher is not responsible for websites (or their content)
that are not owned by the publisher.

Library of Congress Control Number: 2012934770
ISBN: 978-0-316-19612-3

10 9 8 7 6 5 4 3 2 1

RRD-C

Printed in the United States of America

This book is for my sisters: Heather, Linda and Nathalie.
I could list the reasons why,
but that would be a book in itself.

PICCADILLY
CIRCUS

DOWN STREET
GOBLIN ENTRANCE

BUCKINGHAM
PALACE

XANDRA'S
HOUSE

WELLINGTON
ACADEMY

PALACE GUARD

VICTORIA
STATION

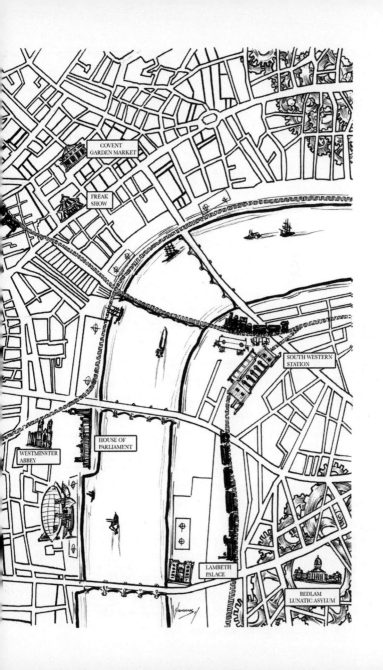

AUTHOR NOTE

God Save the Queen is set, obviously, in an imaginary world – an alternate timeline. Some of its history, however, is exactly what you'll find in the textbooks. In my world, history began to diverge in the late eighteenth century, when "mad" George III was still on the throne, and his son "Prinny" ruled as Regent. In reality, George III suffered, it is believed, from porphyria, a blood disease that is thought to also have affected Mary, Queen of Scots. The disease has many symptoms, including hallucinations, confusion, red urine and sensitivity to sunlight.

In my world, George III was simply the first of the "aristocrats" to show the effects of the Prometheus Protein, which was caused by a mutation of the bubonic plague. By the time Victoria was born in 1819, the aristocracy was beginning to display more and more vampiric and lycanthropic traits. It's around this time that history as we know it begins to dissolve a little more. Certainly by the late 1800s, it was a different world entirely. America and Canada broke away from English rule and banded together. Britain kept many of her other colonies, and was still ruler of one of the largest empires in the world.

Enter the twentieth century and things change even more drastically. The Russian royal family was never assassinated. Anastasia is a vampire. World Wars I and II never happened. This is a world without Hitler, without the Blitz. Without the Beatles. Without *Doctor Who*. A world where Bram Stoker had to flee the UK after writing *Dracula*. Air travel is done in ships that, while modern, still look a lot like Zeppelins. Music and movies are stored on cylinders. Cell phones look nothing like what we're accustomed to using. But technology is still there, though perhaps not as streamlined as it is in this world.

There is, however, one notable similarity between our world and that of *God Save the Queen*, and that's hope. Everyone's looking for a better tomorrow, and just trying to make the best of what they have.

And oh yeah, vampires don't sparkle. ☺

GOD
SAVE
THE
QUEEN

CHAPTER 1

POMEGRANATES FULL AND FINE

*London, 175 years into the reign of Her Ensanguined Majesty
Queen Victoria*

I *hate* goblins.

And when I say hate, I mean they bloody terrify me. I'd rather
French-kiss a human with a mouth full of silver fillings than pick
my way through the debris and rubble that used to be Down Street
station, searching for the entrance to the plague den.

It was eerily quiet underground. The bustle of cobbleside was
little more than a distant clatter down here. The roll of carriages, the
clack of horse hooves from the Mayfair traffic was faint, occasionally completely drowned out by the roar of ancient locomotives
raging through the subterranean tunnels carrying a barrage of
smells in their bone-jangling wake.

Dirt. Decay. Stone. Blood.

I picked my way around a discarded shopping trolley, and tried
to avoid looking at a large paw print in the dust. One of them had
been here recently – the drops of blood surrounding the print were
still fresh enough for me to smell the coppery tang. Human.

KATE LOCKE

As I descended the stairs to platform level, my palms skimmed over the remaining chipped and pitted cream and maroon tiles that covered the walls – a grim reminder that this . . . *mausoleum* was once a thriving hub of urban transportation.

The light of my torch caught an entire set of paw prints, and the jagged pits at the end where claws had dug into the steps. I swallowed, throat dry.

Of course they ventured up this far – the busted sconces were proof. They couldn't always sit around and wait for some stupid human to come to them – they had to hunt. Still, the sight of those prints and the lingering scent of human blood made my chest tight.

I wasn't a coward. My being here was proof of that – and perhaps proof positive of my lack of intelligence. Everyone – aristocrat, half-blood and human – was afraid of goblins. You'd be mental not to be. They were fast and ferocious and didn't seem to have any sense of morality holding them back. If aristos were fully plagued, then goblins were overly so, though such a thing wasn't really possible. Technically they were aristocrats, but no one would ever dare call them such. To do so was as much an insult to them as to aristos. They were mutations, and terribly proud of it.

Images flashed in my head, memories that played out like disjointed snippets from a film: fur, gnashing fangs, yellow eyes – and blood. That was all I remembered of the day I was attacked by a gob right here in this very station. My history class from the Academy had come here on a field trip. The gobs stayed away from us because of the treaty. At least they were *supposed* to stay away, but one didn't listen, and it picked me.

If it hadn't been for Church, I would have died that day. That was when I realised goblins weren't stories told to children to make us behave. It was also the day I realised that if I didn't do everything in my ability to prove them wrong, people would think I was defective somehow – weak – because a goblin tried to take me.

I hadn't set foot in Down Street station since then. If it weren't for my sister Dede's disappearance I wouldn't have gone down there at all.

Avery and Val thought I was overreacting. Dede had taken off on us before, so it was hardly shocking that she wasn't answering her rotary or that the message box on said gadget was full. But in the past she had called me to let me know she was safe. She always called *me*.

I had exhausted every other avenue. It was as though Dede had fallen off the face of the earth. I was desperate, and there was only one option left – goblins. Gobs knew everything that happened in London, despite rarely venturing above ground. Somehow they had found a way to spy on the entire city, and no one seemed to know just what that was. I reckon anyone who had the bollocks to ask didn't live long enough to share it with the rest of us.

It was dark, not because the city didn't run electric lines down here any more – they did – but because the lights had been smashed. The beam from my small hand-held torch caught the grimy glitter of the remains of at least half a dozen bulbs on the ground amongst the refuse.

The bones of a human hand lay surrounded by the shards, cupping the jagged edges in a dull, dry palm.

I reached for the .50 British Bulldog normally holstered snugly against my ribs, but it wasn't there. I'd left it at home. Walking into the plague den with a firearm was considered an act of aggression unless one was there on the official – which I wasn't. Aggression was the last thing – next to fear – you wanted to show in front of one goblin, let alone an entire plague. It was like wearing a sign reading DINNER around your neck.

It didn't matter that I had plagued blood as well. I was only a half-blood, the result of a vampire aristocrat – the term that had come to be synonymous with someone of noble descent who was also plagued – and a human courtesan doing the hot and sweaty. Science considered goblins the ultimate birth defect, but in reality they were the result of gene snobbery. The Prometheus Protein in vamps – caused by centuries of Black Plague exposure – didn't play well with the mutation that caused others to become weres. If the proteins from both species mixed the outcome was a goblin, though some had been born to parents with the same strain. Hell, there were even two documented cases of goblins being born to human parents both of whom carried dormant plagued genes, but that was very rare, as goblins sometimes tried to eat their way out of the womb. No human could survive that.

In fact, no one had much of a chance of surviving a goblin attack. And that was why I had my lonsdaelite dagger tucked into a secret sheath inside my corset. Harder than diamond and easily concealed, it was my "go to" weapon of choice. It was sharp, light and didn't set off machines designed to detect metal or catch the attention of beings with a keen enough sense of smell to sniff out things like blades and pistols.

The dagger was also one of the few things my mother had left me when she . . . went away.

I wound my way down the staircase to the abandoned platform. It was warm, the air heavy with humidity and neglect, stinking of machine and decay. As easy as it was to access the tunnels, I wasn't surprised to note that mine were the only humanoid prints to be seen in the layers of dust. Back in 1932, a bunch of humans had used this very station to invade and burn Mayfair – *the* aristo neighbourhood – during the Great Insurrection. Their intent had been to destroy the aristocracy, or at least cripple it, and take control of the Kingdom. The history books say that fewer than half of those humans who went into Down Street station made it out alive.

Maybe goblins were useful after all.

I hopped off the platform on to the track, watching my step so I didn't trip over anything – like a body. They hadn't ripped up the line because there weren't any crews mental enough to brave becoming goblin chow, no matter how good the pay. The light of my torch caught a rough hole in the wall just up ahead. I crouched down, back to the wall as I eased closer. The scent of old blood clung to the dust and brick. This had to be the door to the plague den.

Turn around. Don't do this.

Gritting my teeth against the trembling in my veins, I slipped my left leg, followed by my torso and finally my right half, through the hole. When I straightened, I found myself standing on a narrow landing at the top of a long, steep set of rough-hewn stairs that led deeper into the dark. Water dripped from a rusty pipe near my head, dampening the stone.

As I descended the stairs – my heart hammering, sweat beading around my hairline – I caught a whiff of that particular perfume that could only be described as goblinesque: fur, smoke and earth. It could have been vaguely comforting if it hadn't scared the shit out of me.

I reached the bottom. In the beam from my torch I could see bits of broken pottery scattered across the scarred and pitted stone floor. Similar pieces were embedded in the wall. Probably Roman, but my knowledge of history was sadly lacking. The goblins had been doing a bit of housekeeping – there were fresh bricks mortared into parts of the wall, and someone had created a fresco near the ancient archway. I could be wrong, but it looked as though it had been painted in blood.

Cobbleside the sun was long set, but there were street lights, moonlight. Down here it was almost pitch black except for the dim torches flickering on the rough walls. My night vision was perfect, but I didn't want to think about what might happen if some devilish goblin decided to play hide and seek in the dark.

I tried not to imagine what that one would have done to me.

I took a breath and ducked through the archway into the main vestibule of the plague's lair. There were more sconces in here, so I tucked my hand torch into the leather bag slung across my torso. My surroundings were deceptively cosy and welcoming, as though any moment someone might press a pint into my hand or ask me to dance.

I'll say this about the nasty little bastards – they knew how to throw a party. Music flowed through the catacombs from some unknown source – a lively fiddle accompanied by a piano. Conversation and raucous laughter – both of which sounded a lot like barking – filled the fusty air. Probably a hundred goblins were gathered in this open area, dancing, talking and drinking. They were doing other things as well, but I tried to ignore them. It wouldn't do for me to start screaming.

A few of them looked at me with curiosity in their piercing yellow eyes, turning their heads as they caught my scent. I tensed, waiting for an attack, but it didn't come. It wouldn't either, not when I was so close to an exit, and they were curious to find out what could have brought a halvie this far into their territory.

Goblins looked a lot like werewolves, only shorter and smaller – wiry. They were bipedal, but could run on all fours if the occasion called for additional speed. Their faces were a disconcerting mix of canine and humanoid, but their teeth were all predator – exactly what you might expect from a walking nightmare.

I'd made it maybe another four strides into this bustling

netherworld when one of the creatures stuck a tray of produce in my face, trying to entice me to eat. Grapes the size of walnuts, bruise-purple and glistening in the torchlight, were thrust beneath my nose. Pomegranates the colour of blood, bleeding sweet-tart juice, filled the platter as well, and apples – pale flesh glistening with a delicate blush. There were more, but those were the ones that tempted me the most. I could almost taste them, feel the syrup running down my chin. Berry-stained fingers clutched and pinched at me, smearing sticky delight on my skin and clothes as I pressed forward.

"Eat, pretty," rasped the vaguely soft cruel voice. "Just a taste. A wee little nibble for our sweet lady."

Our? Not bloody fucking likely. I couldn't tell if my tormentor was male or female. The body hair didn't help either. It was effective camouflage unless you happened upon a male goblin in an amorous state. Generally they tried to affect some kind of identity for themselves – a little vanity so non-goblins could tell them apart. This one had both of its ears pierced several times, delicate chains weaving in and out of the holes like golden stitches.

I shook my head, but didn't open my mouth to vocalise my refusal. An open mouth was an invitation to a goblin to stick something in it. If you were lucky, it was only food, but once you tasted their poison you were lost. Goblins were known for their drugs – mostly their opium. They enticed weak humans with a cheap and euphoric high, and the promise of more. Goblins didn't want human money as payment. They wanted information. They wanted flesh. There were already several customers providing entertainment for tonight's bash. I pushed away whatever pity I felt for them – everyone knew what happened when you trafficked with goblins.

I pushed through the crowd, moving deeper into the lair despite every instinct I possessed telling me to run. I was looking for one goblin in particular and I was not going to leave without seeing him. Besides, running would get me chased. Chased would get me eaten.

As I walked, I tried not to pay too much attention to what was going on in the shadows around me. I'd seen a lot of horrible things in my two and twenty years, but the sight of hueys – humans – gorging themselves on fruit, seeds and pulp in their hair and smeared over their dirty, naked skin, shook me. Maybe it was the fact that pomegranate flesh looked just like that – flesh – between stained teeth. Or maybe it was the wild delirium in their eyes as goblins ran greedy hands over their sticky bodies.

It was like a scene out of Christina Rossetti's poem, but nothing so lyrical. Mothers knew to keep their children at home after dark, lest they go missing, fated to end up as goblin food – or worse, a goblin's slave.

A sweet, earthy smoke hung heavy in the air, reminding me of decaying flowers. It brushed pleasantly against my mind, but was burned away by my metabolism before it could have any real effect. I brushed a platter of cherries, held by strong paw-like hands, aside despite the watering of my mouth. I knew they'd split between my teeth with a firm, juicy pop, spilling tart, delicious juice down my dry throat. Accepting hospitality might mean I'd be expected to pay for it later, and I wasn't about to end up in the plague's debt. Thankfully I quickly spotted the goblin I was looking for. He sat on a dais near the back of the hall, on a throne made entirely from human bones. If I had to guess, I'd say this is what happened to several of the humans who braved this place during the Great Insurrection. Skulls served as finials high on either side of his head. Another set formed armrests over which each of his furry hands curved.

But this goblin would have stood out without the throne, and the obvious deference with which the other freaks treated him. He was tall for a gob – probably my height when standing – and his shoulders were broad, his canine teeth large and sharp. The fire-light made his fur look like warm caramel spotted with chocolate. One of his dog-like ears was torn and chewed-looking, the edges scarred. He was missing an eye as well, the thin line of the closed lid almost indistinguishable in the fur of his face. Hard to believe there was anything aristocratic about him, yet he could be the son of a duke, or even the Prince of Wales. His mother would have to be of rank as well. Did they ever wonder what had become of their monstrous child?

While thousands of humans died with every incarnation of the plague – which loves this country like a mother loves her child – aristocrats survived. Not only survived, they evolved. In England the plague-born Prometheus Protein led to vampirism, in Scotland it caused lycanthropy.

It also occasionally affected someone who wasn't considered upper class. Historically, members of the aristocracy had never been very good at keeping it in their pants. Indiscretions with human carriers resulted in the first halvie births, and launched the careers of generations of breeding courtesans. Occasionally some seemingly normal human woman gave birth to a half or fully plagued infant. These children were often murdered by their parents, or shipped off to orphanages where they were shunned and mistreated. That was prior to 1932's rebellion. Now, such cruelties were prevented by the Pax – Pax Yersinia, which dictated that each human donated a sample of DNA at birth. This could help prevent human carriers from intermarrying. It also provided families and special housing for unwanted plagued children.

By the time Victoria, our first fully plagued monarch – King George III had shown vampiric traits – ascended the throne, other aristocrats across Britain and Europe had revealed their true natures as well. Vampires thrived in the more temperate climes like France and Spain, weres in Russia and other eastern countries. Some places had a mix of the two, as did Asia and Australia. Those who remained in Canada and the Americas had gone on to become socialites and film stars.

But they were never safe, no matter where they were. Humans accounted for ninety-two per cent of aristocratic and halvie deaths. Haemophilia, suicide and accidents made up for the remaining eight.

There were no recorded goblin deaths at human hands – not even during the Insurrection.

I approached the battle-scarred goblin with caution. The flickering torches made it hard to tell, but I think recognition flashed in his one yellow eye. He sniffed the air as I approached. I curtsied, playing to his vanity.

"A Vardan get," he said, in a voice that was surprisingly low and articulate for a goblin. "Here on the official?"

Half-bloods took the title of their sire as their surname. The Duke of Vardan was my father. "Nothing official, my lord. I'm here because the goblin prince knows everything that happens in London."

"True," he replied with a slow nod. Despite my flattery he was still looking at me like he expected me to do or say something. "But there is a price. What do you offer your prince, pretty get?"

The only prince I claimed was Albert, God rest his soul, and perhaps Bertie, the Prince of Wales. This mangy monster was not *my* prince. Was I stupid enough to tell him that? Hell, no.

I reached into the leather satchel I'd brought with me, pulled out the clear plastic bag with a lump of blood-soaked butcher's paper inside and offered it to the goblin. He snatched it from me with eager hands that were just a titch too long and dexterous to be paws, tossed the plastic on the floor and tore open the paper. A whine of delight slipped from his throat when he saw what I'd brought. Around us other goblins raised their muzzles and made similar noises, but no one dared approach.

I looked away as the prince brought the gory mass to his muzzle and took an enthusiastic bite. I made my mind blank, refusing to think of what the meat was, what it had been. My only solace was that it had already been dead when I bought it. The blood might smell good, but I couldn't imagine eating anything that . . . awful . . . terrible . . . *raw*.

The goblin gave a little shudder of delight as he chewed and rewrapped his treat for later. A long pink tongue slipped out to lick his muzzle clean. "Proper tribute. Honours her prince. I will tell the lady what I know. Ask, pretty, ask."

The rest of the goblins drifted away from us, save for one little gob who came and sat at the prince's furry feet and stared at me with open curiosity. I was very much aware that every goblin who wasn't preoccupied with human playthings watched me closely. I was relatively safe now, having paid my tribute to their prince. So long as I behaved myself and didn't offend anyone, I'd make it out of here alive. Probably.

"I want to know the whereabouts of Drusilla Vardan," I said quietly, even though I knew most of the goblins had keen enough hearing to eavesdrop without trying. Their sensitivity to sound, as well as light, kept them deep underside.

The prince raised his canine gaze to mine. It was unnerving looking into that one bright eye, seeing intelligence there while he had yet to clean all the blood from his muzzle. "The youngest?"

I nodded. My father had gone through something of a mid-immortality crisis about two and a half decades ago and done his damnedest to impregnate every breeding courtesan he could find. The first attempt had resulted in my brother Val, the second in me and the third and fourth in Avery and Dede. Four live births out of nine pregnancies over a five-year period – pretty potent for a vampire.

"She's missing." He didn't need to know the particulars – like how she had last been seen at her favourite pub. "I want to know what happened to her."

"Nay, you do not," the prince replied cheerfully. "Pretty wants to know where her sibling is. The prince knows." He petted the little goblin on the head as he bared his teeth at me – a smile.

Sweet baby Jesus. Even my spleen trembled at that awful sight.

Trying to hide my fear was futile, as he could surely smell it. Still, I had to give it a go. "Would you be so kind as to share my sister's whereabouts, my lord? Please? I am concerned about her."

If there was one thing goblins understood it was blood – both as sustenance and connection. Offspring happened rarely because of their degree of mutation, and were treasured. No decent goblin – and I use "decent" as loosely as it can possibly be construed – would turn down a request that involved family.

"New Bethlehem," he replied in a grave growl.

I pressed a hand against the boned front of my corset, and closed my fingers into a fist. I would not show weakness here, no matter how much the prince might sympathise with my plight – he was still a goddam goblin. "Bedlam?" I rasped.

The prince nodded. "She was taken in two nights ago, in shackles."

Albert's fangs. I blasphemed the Queen's late consort to myself alone. My mind could scarcely grasp the reality of it. "You're wrong," I whispered. "You have to be wrong." But goblins were never wrong. If he hadn't known, he wouldn't have said. That was their way – so I'd been taught. "Honourable monsters", Church had called them.

"Alexandra."

I jerked. I shouldn't be surprised that he knew my name. Of course he knew it. It was the posh way he said it – his voice sounded almost like my father's.

He stood before me – I was right, he was my height. The little one remained glued to his side. I had the sudden and inexplicable urge to reach out and pat her on the head, just as I had wanted to do to a tiger cub I once saw in a travelling exhibit. The comparison kept my hand fisted, and at my side. I wanted to keep it.

"Your prince regrets telling the pretty lady this news."

I turned my attention back to him. The pity in his eye almost brought me to tears. Why should a monster pity me?

"There was an incident at Ainsley's. The Vardan get tried to stab the earl, she did."

That I believed, and therefore I had to believe my sister really could be in Bedlam – where all the special barking mad went to die. Dede and Ainsley had history – a painful one.

The goblin held out his furry hand, and etiquette demanded I take it. The prince was offering me friendship, and my getting out of there alive just might depend on my taking it, treaty or no.

I nodded, my throat tight as his "fingers" closed around mine. He was warm. For a moment – and only one terribly mad one – I could have hugged him. "Thank you."

He shook his head. "No thanks, lady. Never thank for bad news."

I nodded again and he released my hand. The goblins watched me as I turned to leave, but no one spoke. They didn't even try to tempt me to stay; they simply let me go. I think I despised them most at that moment, especially that little one who waved goodbye.

My sister was essentially in hell and goblins felt sorry for me. As far as I was concerned, things couldn't get much worse.

I stumbled cobbleside on shaky, numb legs. The heavy door closed with a thud behind me as I braced a palm against the closest chipped and pitted brick wall. Scorch marks and faded maroon paint marred part of the once impressive frontage. The two buildings flanking the old station had been empty since the fires of '32, their derelict state a blemish on the formerly opulent neighbourhood. This end of Down Street looked like it belonged near the docks rather than within the walls of Mayfair. It was still the most exclusive neighbourhood in London, but for the past eighty years it had existed behind high walls of stone and wire, guarded against the possibility of another human uprising. Broken lamps kept this part of the street, unaffectionately nicknamed "Gob Lane", in the dark. Further up, just past Brick Street, the lamps retained their bulbs, casting a golden glow over the worn cobblestones. Here, grass and weeds poked up from between the cobbles, and someone had propped a broken carriage wheel against the side of the building to my right. Mayfair had its share of ruins, but this was the only one with ABANDON ALL HOPE above the door in flaking white paint, and the only one that still had bloodstains on the threshold.

My ride was waiting for me where I'd left it – no worries about theft on Gob Lane. I swung my leg over the Butler 1863 motorrad and started the engine. The machine roared to life, and I tore off down the street on three hundred kilos of rubber and steel, my frock coat whipping out behind. I stopped at the gates because I had to, but I couldn't remember anything John or Mick, the Royal Guards on duty, said to me. I must have given the correct answers because they let me go.

It wasn't until I neared Wellington district, and my part of it – the area formerly known as Belgravia – that the numbness eased and I began to feel like myself again. I'd entered the plague den and survived, and now I knew where Dede was. It did nothing to make me feel better, but at least I knew.

Bedlam. Fang me.

Why couldn't she have run off with one of the wolves who were down from Scotland for the season? That was what other Peerage Protectorate girls – and boys – did. Shagged the hairy brutes and protected them at the same time – not that weres needed an abundance of protecting. The Scots were looked down upon by some aristos for being a little too physical, but they were impressive in their strength.

I pulled the Butler to the kerb outside the house my sister Avery and I shared on the upper west side of Belgrave Square. The closer to Buckingham Palace and Mayfair you got, the older the neighbourhood appeared. In the East End they'd repaved some of the streets, and even had tall buildings, but here almost everything looked as it had two centuries ago. Even the parts that were new had been made to look old.

It was the same in most cities across Europe with a strong concentration of aristo citizens. The plague had spread across trade routes, taking the Prometheus Protein with it. There were vampires and werewolves all across the continent – halvies too, though the first of my kind had been born right here in London. Or at least, the first halvie in historical record had been. Aldous James was born in 1900. His father was Devonshire, but this was before we took titles as our surnames.

My house had been built in the 1820s. It was a large town house that used to be part of a huge mansion. My father had bought it for his children, but only Avery and I lived there now. Val had his own flat, and Dede had moved out six months ago, claiming she wanted her own space as well.

I unlocked the door, slipped inside the darkened foyer and punched the code into the alarm. That was as fancy as we got. When you were half-vampire, and trained to survive and protect at any cost, you didn't really need much outside security.

I ran straight up the winding staircase to my bedroom. So far my night off had been a nightmare, but it wasn't over yet. There was one person who would try to help me if what the goblin prince said was true. I had to get changed and haul my arse to a party in Curzon Street before sunrise in order to find him.

I had several decent gowns in the walk-in off my bedroom. I had to – Queen V didn't like what most of us considered fashion, so at fancy aristo functions the Royal Guard and the Peerage Protectorate had to dress to code, females in gowns and men in black tails. Sometimes it was a bit of fun, but other times – like now – it was an exercise in frustration. It wasn't that the aristocracy fought progress; just that time moved so slowly for them, it took change longer to take hold. They clung to that which was familiar.

I grabbed the easiest to get into – a pewter-coloured silk with tiny sleeves and long concealed slits on either side of the skirt in case I needed to move quickly or fight.

My shower took exactly four minutes, including waiting for the water to get hot. I didn't have time to wash my bright red hair, so I dusted it with shampoo powder, gave it a bit of a back-comb and twisted it up on to the top of my head.

The hair thing was often copied by humans looking to emulate halvies, but wigs and dye couldn't quite get the same shine. Aristocrats had gorgeous hair – thick and rich, with extraordinary highlights due to the plague's mutation of the pigmentations that determined hair colour. The only way I can describe it is to say that the plague seemed to make everything "more". With halvies, this pigmentation was often sent into overdrive by our unique maternal genetics. It didn't happen in all halvies, but the brighter colours were something of a status symbol amongst our kind. My colour, the same red as Christmas barley candy, was highly unusual.

Clean undies and a fresh corset that hooked up the front went on as quickly as I could manage, followed by stockings, boots and then the gown. I was still fiddling with the zip on the side as I raced back downstairs. I had to get to Curzon Street. I had to find Church.

It was quarter past three in the morning. Most aristo functions ended around four to give everyone time to get home and into their dark chambers before the sun rose, so that gave me forty-five minutes. Luckily, my destination was less than a mile away.

I thought of Dede – not of her locked up in Bedlam, but as she had been when we were younger. She'd always been tiny, sprite-like. Shiny and sweet and full of life. Our family, especially me, had been so protective of her, but even we couldn't save her from herself. She'd fallen for Ainsley's charm as though her bones were made of lead. I'd held her after she lost the baby, crying myself as she sobbed as if the world was ending. I suppose for her it had. I thought she was done with the bastard.

I turned on to Grosvenor Place. Checking the traffic, I saw something in the park to my right that made me put my foot down to stabilise the Butler and look again.

"Fang me," I muttered. Why now, of all times? I had some-where to be. I did not have time for betty-bashing.

I lifted my foot and whipped the machine between two cars – the space from the boot of one to the bonnet of the other was just large enough for my ride. I kicked the stand and jumped off. Skirt hitched, I raced along the pavement, wishing I'd worn my arse-kicking boots instead of the pointy-toed, hourglass-heeled ones that matched my gown. Still, I was fast and quickly caught up with the people I was chasing.

There had to be at least a dozen of them. From their swagger and their cricket bats I pegged them as bubonic betties – humans who injected themselves with aristo hormones. Eight male and four female, dragging what appeared to be two unconscious people along the dimly lit path. Despite the dark I could see the two of them very well, see the blood on their faces and the jacked-up state of their captors. And I could see their hair – the girl had blue and the bloke's was purple. They were halvies, and they were in trouble.

"Oy!" I shouted as I approached. I didn't even have a weapon in my hand. My ID I'd shoved inside my corset as soon as I jumped off the motorrad.

The men didn't listen to me, of course. I hadn't expected them to. The females at least glanced in my direction. I yelled again and picked up the pace, running past them to cut them off. "Let them go," I said as I stood before them. I had no delusions of getting out of this unscathed, but defeat wasn't an option.

"Sod off," retorted one in a deep, low-brow voice.

They were all in the vicinity of six feet tall and wore black clothing. In the sparse light I could see the sores on their faces, the blackened tips of their fingers. Aristo hormones gave them heightened senses and strength, but the price was an early and painful death. Sometimes they cut the drug with silver nitrate to lessen the harmful side effects, but it weakened the potency and increased skin-blackening.

That was what the plague did to those not of royal blood.

"Let them go," I repeated through clenched teeth. I had somewhere else to be, damn it, and these fuckwits were taking up minutes on my ticking clock. Still, wouldn't have been right of me not to intervene.

One of the males from behind came forward. The breeze that carried his scent to me brought the smell of unwashed flesh, stale sweat, blood and the early whiff of decay. "It's another one," he said in a cockney accent so thick I could have spread it on toast. "Another dirty half-blood."

Well, at least I now knew that these Samaritans weren't simply helping two sick halvies home – as if the thought had even crossed my mind. Fucking humans. They hated us, tried to kill us, but poisoned themselves so they could be more like us. "Hand them over to me and there won't be any trouble," I said.

The betties laughed. They always did – like the laughter track on those American sitcoms broadcast on the pirate box stations. With my bright hair and my expensive gown I obviously didn't look like much of a threat.

The chuckles stopped pretty abruptly when I slammed my shin into Stinky's wedding tackle. The breath rushed out of him in an animalistic moan. As he sank to his knees, I jobbed him between the eyes – twice – and laid him out cold.

"You beauties going to let them go now?" I asked sweetly as the betty crumpled at my feet. "Or do I have to humiliate each and every one of you?"

Of course they didn't oblige me. I'd just relieved their mate of his manhood and my taunting only made them further obligated to exact a little revenge. Two of them came at me – one straight on and the other sneaking around behind.

Albert's fangs. I was still shaky from the goblins, hungry, tired and I'd forgotten to take my supplements – again. All I wanted was for them to leave the halvies alone so I could get to the bloody party on Curzon Street and talk to Church. They were standing in the way of me getting help for Dede and I did *not* have time for this shit. Those limp halvies had better hurry up and metabolise whatever the betties had given them, because I was on a schedule.

The betty up front came at me swinging. I ducked, but not enough. He caught me on the right jaw with a solid blow that knocked my head back and pissed me off. I came back with two quick punches to his gut, and when he bent double, the wind knocked out of him, I brought my knee up and broke his nose.

Then I pivoted, whipped that same leg up – thank God for my split skirt – and brought the back of my heel down on his skull. He hadn't hit the ground when I whirled around to take on the next betty. She wasn't expecting me, so she went down a little faster than her friends.

Somebody really ought to tell them that bubonic-derived steroids might make you faster and stronger, but that wasn't much help up against someone even faster and stronger and better trained. It would be like me taking on Church – no contest.

Three down. Only nine more to go. *C'mon, halvies, wake the hell up*.

Two more came at me. These two actually had weapons. No matter how strong you are, a crowbar to the temple *hurts*. I tried to shake it off, but while I was recovering from that, another betty punched me hard in the stomach, and I wasn't wearing a re-inforced corset. When he attempted to break my nose as I had his friend, I kicked him hard in the side of his opposite knee. He screamed, but he didn't go down immediately. That required a tap or two on the noggin with his own crowbar, which I then used to render his companion incapacitated. She went down a bit easier than he had.

Seven more. My head hurt – enough that I couldn't quite ignore it. I would probably bruise.

One of the women came at me. Her lips were grey, and the skin on one side of her neck was patchy and black – swollen. She wouldn't live much longer than a fortnight. I could be merciful and kill her here and now, but I wasn't feeling overly merciful at the moment. She'd taken the plague willingly; let her ride it right to its ever-suffering end.

My knuckles split those cadaverous lips. Infected blood splat-tered across the backs of my fingers, soaking through the thin silk of my gloves. I had the sudden urge to suck the coppery warmth out of the fabric, but I ignored the craving as the bleeding betty recovered and came back swinging. I grabbed her raised arm with one hand and twisted hard.

It's an odd sensation, feeling bone break beneath your fingers. She crumpled with a scream. I backhanded her with my other hand, hard enough to knock her backwards and end all that nonsense.

The other betties didn't seem to know what to do. Out of the six remaining, only two of them had their hands free – the others were supporting the dead weight of the battered halvies.

One of the female halvie's eyes was swollen shut. The fact that she hadn't woken up yet worried me. And then, as the next goon stepped up, I saw her foot move. One boot came up, the sturdy sole planted firmly on the pavement. She was waiting for me to dig in before she caught her captors unawares. Smart girl. Lazy, though, letting me do the brunt of the work. How long had she been awake? The male was coming round as well. This was going to become knobbed-up very quickly.

I didn't have any more time to wonder about it as another girl betty came at me, brandishing a cricket bat as though I was the only thing standing between her and total victory. She swung and I ducked, the edge of the bat bouncing off my shoulder.

"Fucking hell!" It hurt – but only for a couple of seconds. Adrenalin is a wonderful thing.

I didn't have much time, as the rest of them had finally begun to think with that one dim-witted brain they seemed to share, and had realised that if they ganged up on me they might stand a better chance. Thankfully, the halvies chose that moment to jump into the fray and began battling it out with the betties who had been holding them. The humans never saw it coming.

Blood screamed through my veins, my heart thumping wildly. Fang me, but I loved a good punch-up. At the Wellington

Academy – where all halvies were educated and trained – I'd excelled in violence. Church held me up as an example to other students of how to fight. No goblin was ever going to take me down without a struggle again.

As if to prove that point, I delivered a walloping kick to the betty's head with the side of my boot. She was a little tougher than the last, however, and came staggering back at me, bat held high above her head as though it was a claymore and she was William fucking Wallace. I rolled my eyes.

"Bored with this," I said, at the same time whipping my arm up to smash the heel of my hand into her nose.

She dropped the bat behind her, and then fell to the ground. She didn't move. For a second I wondered if I had killed her. I'd never killed anyone before.

Any remorse I might have felt was eclipsed by the large bulk blocking out the street light. The other halvies were making sport of their opponents, leaving me just this one last betty.

He was big – the biggest of the lot. And he was much faster than the others – graceful as well. Anticipation hummed inside me. He was a real fighter, an actual challenge. Smacked me a hard one on the jaw before I was ready for it – same side as the crow-bar, bastard.

I shook off the stars dancing before my eyes and came back with a few shots of my own. His head flew back, but he didn't fall. He hit me again in the same spot. The pain made me grit my teeth and want to make him eat his own spleen. Enough of this. I caught him with two quick jabs to the stomach and then one between the eyes. He staggered backwards, then came back at me with a solid punch to my mouth. I tasted blood as I pulled my dagger out of its sheath.

That was when what I always referred to as my "aristocratic genes" kicked in, and the vampire half of me really woke up. It was something I kept to myself, because it wasn't a typical halvie reaction to blood, and it didn't matter whetherit was my own or someone else's, and it was the equivalent of flicking a switch inside me – like going from low to high. It was why blood-sharing was more of an intimate thing for halvies. It made sex incredibly intense – switching off our humanity and making us all instinct and sensation. Appetite.

I had planned to gut him if necessary, but now . . . I wanted to eat this betty – and not in a sexy way. Fangs extended from my gums with the sweetest of aches, eager to pierce some flesh regardless of how diseased and disgusting it was.

I smiled, enjoying how his eyes widened.

Then I pounced – straight at his jugular.

CHAPTER 2

IT RUNS IN THE FAMILY

Strong hands grabbed my shoulders just as I was about to take a bite out of my reeking victim, who trembled beneath the blade I pressed against his heart.

"Don't," said a low female voice. "He probably tastes like shit, and you don't want to go there."

I thought about turning on her and maybe taking a bite out of her instead, but she was right. He *would* taste like shit, and I *didn't* want to go there. I'd never bitten anyone, and I didn't want to start with this piece of filth.

It was a struggle to clear the haze in my mind – the need. It was like having chocolate pressed against my lips and fighting the urge to take a bite, only multiplied by a thousand. I released the betty. As soon as I let go, his hands clutched at me, trying to pull me close again. Albert's fangs. He *wanted* me to bite him. He even had a hard-on. *Humans.*

Up on my knees, I punched him in the face – hard – with the fist wrapped around my dagger, and knocked him senseless. His hands fell away, landing with a dull thud on the ground.

"Good choice," said my blue-haired companion, offering me a hand up, which I gratefully accepted after sheathing the knife.

"Thanks." I swiped my knuckles across my lip – it had stopped bleeding.

"I should be thanking you." She smiled at me as though this kind of thing happened to her every day. Maybe it did, because I sure as Sunday wouldn't be smiling if my face looked like that. "They probably planned to toss us in front of the next tourist bus."

I glanced at her purple-haired friend, whose battered face was expressionless. "That would have made some Yank's trip."

She laughed. "Wouldn't it, though?"

I stared at her. There was something familiar about her pale face. Her eyes – the one that was open – were almost the same greenish blue as her hair. She was about my height and I was certain I didn't know her, and yet . . .

"Thanks for saving my arse," she said, squatting down and rooting through the big betty's pockets. Her search turned up a wad of pound notes. She quickly counted through them and offered me several.

"Not necessary," I said, holding up my hands. It wasn't that I was morally opposed to her robbing the bastard; I just didn't need the money.

She shrugged, and I noticed dirt on the back of her black satin coat. Her companion's too. "Did they . . . hurt you?" I asked.

She stood up, stuffing the money into the pocket of her tight black leather bloomers. Not sure how she managed to fit her hand in there, let alone all those notes. "Did they rape us, you mean? Nah."

I frowned. "Why not? This one" – I kicked the still motionless betty near my feet – "obviously wanted a tickle. I'd have thought if he had a couple of unconscious halvies in his possession he'd take advantage." Both of them were pretty. Her friend was downright gorgeous, even with a faceful of bruises. He had very fine chiselled features, dark green eyes and a nose that could cut butter. I took a second to appreciate his loveliness as he shoved his rotary into his trouser pocket. I hadn't even noticed that he'd made a call.

Blue-hair pulled a pack of fags from her cleavage and offered me one. I refused. She lit up and took a deep drag before responding. "Fang fetish, most likely." The clove-scented tang of her smoke drifted around her head. "You were just another filthy halvie till you fanged out, then he got all tingly for your aristo bits."

I'd heard of humans like that before, but had never met one that I knew of – until tonight.

"Why did they nab you?"

She cast a glance at her friend, who shrugged. "Wrong place at the wrong time," he said, but I could hear the lie in his voice. Fine by me. It wasn't my business, and it wasn't as though I'd side with the betties anyway. Every half-blood and aristocrat knew that humans couldn't be trusted – not after the Great Insurrection. They despised us and wanted to see every one of us dead. Dede used to tell me I was a bigot, but it wasn't prejudice. It was truth.

"You should at least let me pay for dry-cleaning." She gave me a good look up and down. "Those stains will never come out."

I glanced down. "Fuck it all." She was right. My gown was ruined. Blood soaked the silk in a six-inch splodge, and there was dirt and grass stains from the Nosferatu impersonation I'd tried to pull. My face was bruised and bloody and my hair was probably a mess by now too. Lord knew my gloves were beyond repair. There was no way I could show up at Curzon Street looking like this. Vardan would be humiliated, but besides that there wasn't any point – already the streets were filling with carriages and cars heading deeper into Mayfair. I was too late.

I wouldn't even be able to catch Church at home. By the time I got there he'd be underside. The lore about vampires despising the sun was true. Their skin was super-sensitive, just like their eyes and their ears, and would blister under ultraviolet light. They weren't undead, though. The Prometheus Protein affected them on a cellular level, putting their bodies in a sort of stasis. They aged, but at an incredibly slow rate. No one knew just how long a vamp could live. Queen V had been born in 1819 and looked like she was in her late twenties, early thirties. The Church condemned all of us with plagued blood as demons, but science deemed us *Homo Sapiens Yersinia*. Rumour has it Her Majesty ate the previous Archbishop of Canterbury when he made the announcement, and had the Prime Minister appoint his successor over his still warm corpse.

Even if Church was still awake when I got to his house, he would be in lockdown for several hours. He was one of the many aristos who took to sleeping in an impenetrable, vault-like room as protection against attack after the Insurrection. As much as I wanted to talk to him about Dede, I had no choice but to go home and try to get some sleep.

"I'm sorry," Blue-hair said. I'd almost forgotten that she was there. "If not for us, you'd be wherever it was you were supposed to be."

I shrugged. "It's not your fault." Of course I had the uncharitable thought that if I had just minded my own business I could be with Church right now, but that was just wrong. I didn't regret stopping to help them. I regretted not being able to do both.

I glanced up as the headlamps of an arriving motor carriage washed over the scene. "Is that for you?"

"Yes. Can we give you a lift?"

Her friend had already left us, gone to speak to whoever the car belonged to. Bit rude, but I was intrigued by the whole scenario.

There was something surreal, slightly off about the whole thing. "No thanks . . . I'm sorry, I don't even know your name."

She smiled, and the familiarity of her features struck me once again. I knew her from somewhere. "My friends call me Fee."

The name didn't ring any bells. I offered her my hand. "Xandra."

"Yeah," she said, an odd light in her one good eye. "I know. Thanks again for helping us out. I owe you one."

I probably should have been more surprised that she knew who I was, and at the weird way she looked at me, but I was thinking of Dede and her having to spend more time in Bedlam because I'd fucked up. I shrugged. "You would have done the same, I'm sure."

She arched a brow. "Are you? I appreciate the confidence." Then she touched the brim of an imaginary hat. "I'll bid you adieu, for I suspect our friends are waking up."

She was right about that – the betties were stirring, and I had no desire to tango with them again. "Night, then. Don't spend those funds all at once."

A quick grin flashed in the darkness, and then she was off, running east across the grass. I turned on my heel and was hauling arse back to where the Butler sat waiting when a tickling sensation in the centre of my back had me glancing over my shoulder.

Fee and her friend stood beside the motor carriage – an antique Swallow, silver and sleek, engine a low purr. They were watching me, but it was the sight of the tall, well-built man with them that made the breath catch in my throat: Vex MacLaughlin – alpha of the UK wolves.

The halvies climbed into the vehicle, leaving me pinned under the weight of glowing yellow eyes. His presence was overwhelming even at this distance. Wolves were one step down from goblins on the ferocity scale. Many vampires, my father included, thought them barbarians, but I'd always been a sucker for a boy with fur. And the MacLaughlin, as he was known, was no boy. He was in the vicinity of two hundred years old, and had been made alpha after the Great Insurrection, when he'd continued to fight despite being wounded, and saved the lives of half a dozen aristos.

He'd apparently carried the former alpha to hospital during the attack only for the wolf to die under human care. No one knew if he was murdered or not, though most thought the latter. It was the MacLaughlin who, after the funeral of Prince Albert, decided there needed to be hospitals specifically for aristos. That was when the noble world saw the benefit of halvies as protection, and as professionals in aristo-friendly establishments. Scads of research went into growing my race. There were still three humans for every halvie, but we were doing all right.

I'd seen photographs of what the humans did over those few days. I saw the bodies and the destruction – violence that only fuelled my prejudice. The only human I ever trusted was my mum, and she wasn't a regular human – she'd been a plague carrier. A courtesan. They were special.

Vex MacLaughlin had yet to breed any halvies, but he certainly seemed to consider them part of his pack. He came to the rescue when they called. I couldn't imagine my own father doing that. What were Fee and her friend to him that he'd come personally to fetch them?

I shook my head. None of my business. I'd turned to climb on to the Butler when a growl tore through the weakening dark and raced a cold finger down my spine. I looked up to see the alpha grabbing the betty I had almost bitten by the throat. For a second I thought he was going to kill the bastard, but he tossed him into the boot of the Swallow instead. The betty was big, but MacLaughlin lifted him like he was nothing more than a rag doll.

He slammed the boot shut before walking around to the driver's door. He paused, and turned towards me once more, his rugged features impassive. Our gazes locked. He inclined his head – a slight nod – before sliding into the vehicle and tearing off down the street as the sun began to shove pale fingers across the sky.

What was that all about? I'd never know, and I had more important things to worry about.

Dawn was coming. Nothing for me to do but get the hell home, which I proceeded to do.

I dragged myself over the threshold with a sigh. Suddenly, I was very tired. I hadn't eaten in hours and I needed my supplements. Our fast metabolism mean that half-bloods need to eat more often than humans. Sounds fun, but it ain't. Try being in the middle of a tango with a bunch of betties and losing your momentum because your blood sugar's bottomed out. Not pretty.

I locked the door behind me and fought a bout of dizziness. I wanted a steak, rare and juicy, but that would take too long. Instead, I settled on a sandwich – a big one – and bed. In fact, I'd eat the sandwich *in* bed.

I made straight for the kitchen, the rustle of my skirts the only sound. I washed the blood and dirt from my hands and went to work scrounging for food. I found thickly sliced bread in the cupboard and loaded it up with meats and cheese, vegetables and a thick layer of spicy mustard. While creating my masterpiece, I nibbled on stale shortbread biscuits. Starving halvies couldn't be fussy.

Plate in hand, along with a small glass of creamy milk, I made my way back through the dimly lit house to the staircase. I'd taken a huge bite of the sandwich before I left the kitchen, so I was still chewing as I tried to negotiate the stairs without lifting the hem of my dress. I got all the way to the top before I realised I wasn't alone. The smell of food had made me oblivious to other scents.

By the time I noticed, it was too late. I saw bright pink toenails two steps above me on the landing and came to a dead stop. I looked up, and swallowed.

"What the bloody hell happened to you?" my sister Avery demanded, hands on the hips of her snug black bloomers. "And why does your bedroom smell like a wet goblin?"

I've often thought my sister Avery resembled a walking mound of candy floss, with her pink hair and penchant for the same colour, but beneath that sweet exterior lived the soul of a fishwife.

"Yersinia?" she said, using the goblin name for their underground city. "Xandy, what the sweet hell were you thinking?"

I winced as a mug was slammed on the table in front of me. Delicious-smelling Darjeeling sloshed over the side. Avery had dragged me to the kitchen to interrogate me, and if she was breaking out the Darjeeling, it was bad indeed. "I was looking for information on Dede," I replied, wiping up the spill with a napkin. I had finished my sandwich and was thinking of dessert. Not more shortbread, that was for certain.

"Albert's fangs," my sister muttered, joining me at the table with her own cup. She rubbed her fingers violently across her forehead. Her nail varnish matched her toes. "That chit runs off, and every time you chase her like a damn puppy, but going to the goblins is beyond mental."

Facing her across the table, I looked for some indication that we were even related. The matching green of our eyes was the only sign. How could she be so cold? Yes, Dede had always been something of a hellion – a handful – but that didn't mean we shouldn't worry, did it? Flighty she might be, but never cruel. For shit's sake, she still slept with a stuffed bear.

"She's never been gone this long before," I defended. "Not without ringing me."

Avery arched a brow, looking at me as though she thought she knew the inside of my head. "So this is about you, then? Dede hasn't checked in with mama bird so something has to be wrong. Face it, Xandy, she's selfish and spoiled and right now she isn't thinking of anyone but herself. She'll show up in a few days wondering what all the fuss is about."

"Something *has* happened to her," I protested. "The goblin prince—"

"You spoke to the prince?" Avery's eyes were huge, cheeks chalk-white. "Were you trying to get yourself eviscerated? I swear on Albert's grave, when Dede comes back I'm going to smack her senseless. And you . . . I don't know what to do about you. You're not our mother, Xandy, it's time you stopped acting like it."

My hands tightened around the mug. "Dede's in Bedlam."

My sister went still. "You're lying." And there was our family resemblance: instantaneous denial.

"That's what the prince told me. And you know they don't lie."

"We need something stronger than tea." Avery left the table to open a cupboard by the sink. She took out a bottle of whisky, and two glasses from the cupboard above. She returned to the table, uncapped the bottle and poured a double for each of us. Neither of us spoke until we'd each taken a deep swallow. It burned, but it cleared the last of the shock in my system. Unfortunately, we metabolised alcohol quickly.

"Was it because she went hatters on Ainsley?" Avery asked, rolling her glass between her palms along the tabletop.

I stopped toying with my own glass. "You knew?"

She nodded, not quite meeting my astonished – and pissed – gaze. "I was there with the Ashworths. I was the one who pulled her off Ainsley." Both she and Dede were part of the Peerage

Protectorate – privately contracted guards for aristo families. They were different from the Royal Guard in that it was the RG's job to protect *everyone* of rank, with emphasis on the royal family and their guests. We covered gatherings and events – such as the Queen making a public appearance – while the PP were private guards who made themselves available whenever their clients wanted.

"You knew and you didn't tell me?" I could have slapped her, but I didn't seem to have any fight left in me. I'd used it all up betty-bashing. I was tired right down to my bones.

She shrugged. "Val and I thought it was for the best not to tell you about it."

"Val knew too?" I could believe Avery keeping this from me, because she thought I stuck my nose too far into her business – Dede's too – but Val? My brother was only a year older than me and we were usually unified when it came to family.

"He was the arresting officer."

My shoulders sagged. "Bollocks." Val was Special Branch, a division of Scotland Yard that dealt with aristo- and half-blood-related crimes. Of course they would have been called. "It must have killed him to take her in."

Avery made a scoffing noise just before slugging back the rest of her drink. "Not to mention how humiliating it must have been for a chief inspector to have his sister behave in such a manner."

I bristled. "I doubt that was foremost in Val's mind."

My sister shrugged. "You can bet he thought it later. It's an embarrassment for all of us." Then she sighed, and it was as though all the anger drained out of her. "I never thought she'd end up in Bedlam."

There was something in the way she said it that made my jaw clench. "No. Of all of us, I'm the one you'd expect to go hatters."

She shifted uncomfortably, even as she rolled her eyes. "Don't be stupid."

It was no secret that my mother had been hauled off to Bedlam when I was ten. I'd grown up knowing that insanity ran in my blood. Sometimes I felt as though it nipped at my heels. So maybe I was overly sensitive to the subject, but not this time.

I pushed back my chair. "I'm going to bed." I didn't wish her a good day, or even take my dishes to the sink. Sod her.

"Xandy!" Avery called after me. "Xandy, come on. I didn't mean it!"

I waved her off, but didn't stop, didn't speak. I just kept walking. Of course she meant it – she just hadn't meant for me to realise it.

The Wellington Academy, the school where all half-bloods were trained and educated, was located in the St James's sector, not far from the gates of Buckingham Palace. Some of the old-timers still referred to it as the Old Admiralty, but it hadn't been used as such for almost eighty years. A statue of the great man stood high on a pedestal in the courtyard, flanked by the Academy and the Royal Guard House.

I stood a moment before this statue, peering up at it from beneath the brim of my brolly. Wellington was a legend not only for his victory over Napoleon, and his tragic death during the Great Insurrection, but for being one of the few human nobles to be turned into an aristocrat. Not just any human can be turned – a fact that continues to elude many of the betties running around the city. Being "made" takes a great deal of physical and psychological strength, not to mention a genetic inclination towards the aristocracy on the part of the plaguee. Only a powerful full-blood can do it. Noble crypts are filled with the dusty remains of those who failed to survive the change.

I wished I had known him. Hell, just to see him in the flesh would have been amazing. Church used to tell me stories of Wellington and his bravery during the Insurrection. Those stories were what so many of us aspired to.

I knew halvies who had gone on to do amazing things. I wasn't one of them. My father was disappointed that his only child to make the Royal Guard had yet to earn a commendation – not that he'd ever come out and be so cruel, but he couldn't hide it from me. I was very strong, and one of the best fighters to ever emerge from the Academy, but I had yet to distinguish myself. We lived in a time of relative peace, so the chances of me doing so were slim.

But thinking about it only served to make me pouty and disagreeable, so I stopped staring at the likeness of a long-dead vampire and walked the short distant to the Academy entrance.

James, the yellow-haired guard at the desk, smiled when he looked up and saw me. "Hello, Miss Alexandra. What brings you by this gloriously wet Wednesday?"

"It is lovely, isn't it?" Unlike aristos, half-bloods could stand in the sun and not get fried, but most preferred a grey day to a sunny one. Lucky were those of us who lived in Britain. "I'm here for the old man. Do you know where I can find him?"

He consulted his computer. "You're in luck. He's got a group in the gymnasium. Do you recall the way?"

"Unless you've moved it," I replied with a grin. I'd spent fourteen years of my life at this place; I'd know my way blindfolded. "Best to the wife and offspring, James."

The gymnasium was on the ground floor. All teaching rooms and the cafeteria were on the first two floors – the floors that didn't have windows, but were illuminated with artificial daylight. When the building was renovated in 1933, it was decided to make the basement, ground and first floors light-tight as a safeguard should the humans ever attack again. This not only protected the few aristo professors on the staff, but in the event of an emergency could provide shelter for London's entire nobility.

That absence of daylight was the only reason Church, being fully plagued, could teach here. On days that he taught, he arrived via the school's private underground railway just before sunrise. He was yelling at a couple of wrestling young halvies when I entered the gymnasium. The place smelled of sweat and blood, both fresh and old. It wasn't exactly a pleasant scent, but it was a familiar one that awakened many good memories – like the first time I bested Rye in a fight. Thinking of Rye was bittersweet, though not nearly as painful as it once had been. He had been my friend, my mentor and my first love, and then he'd been taken away from me by a mob of murderous humans. But thinking of him hurt, so I pushed thoughts of him out of my head, and approached the ginger-haired dictator barking out orders to his students.

The first time I'd seen Churchill I'd been a little girl, and he had seemed a giant to me. In reality he and I were about the same height. He had a strong, unyielding face that was as quick to grin as it was to scowl, and though he was of a fairly lean build, he was the deadliest aristocrat I'd ever met. His only weakness was a slight speech impediment that one daft Year 8 kid always seemed to mention within the first three days of class.

His mother was American – one of the wealthy heiresses who had bought their way into the aristocracy in the late 1800s. There wasn't a high population of plagued on the other side of the pond, but aristo men had a bit of a reputation for carousing, so that genetic material made its way into many human women over the centuries. The plague was strong, and could exist quietly for generations within a family, just waiting to be exposed to similar genes.

Many of the heiresses who came over didn't survive the change – they hadn't known about the biological factors necessary for it to take – and of the few who did turn, only a handful managed to carry full-term pregnancies. Of those, only two had been born alive.

Church obviously had been one of the healthy births, but Queen V decreed that 'making' aristos only muddied the bloodline, and that was the end of the American heiresses. He had the glowing pale skin of a vampire, the thick, shiny hair and bright eyes, but he wasn't quite one of them because his mother hadn't been born to the blood.

A small group of halvies watched their classmates fighting. It was a good-size class for a senior year – seven bright-haired, bright-eyed half-bloods full of piss and vinegar and ready to take on the world. They stood straight and eager in their training uniforms of loose trousers and tunics. The girls all wore flexible corsets that allowed them to move without restriction.

"Marlborough, you fight like a human," Church growled, his rich voice reverberating through the gym as he berated the student. "Where's your pride, man?"

"Still building strength through belittlement, I see," I said as I drew close.

My mentor's back stiffened beneath his dark green waistcoat and pristine linen shirt. His head slowly turned towards me. His charges watched me with open mouths – even Marlborough and his sparring partner had paused in their exercise to see who dared speak to the old man in such a way.

Churchill's scowl turned to a grin when his gaze met mine. "Aren't you a sight? Class, meet the best student I ever had the privilege of training – Leftenant Alexandra Vardan of the Royal Guard." The way he said it made me sound like something special and I preened under the compliment.

I waved at the kids, who were staring with open awe now. I might not have a commendation, but I had broken records during my time at this place, and held them to this day. "Hullo." Then to Church, "Sorry to interrupt your class, sir. I wonder if I might have a word?"

A twinkle lit his pale blue eyes. "Of course you may."

"Thank—"

"Right after you help me show this lot how to really fight."

That shut me up – for a second. Suddenly I was quite aware of myself. "Are you serious, sir?"

"Couldn't be more so. Come on now, put your outerwear in the corner and help me demonstrate."

He had no dominion over me any more. I was no longer his student, but I did what he told me without protest, and quickly. I draped my long leather coat over the back of a chair and rejoined the group. There was nothing special about my clothes – snug black and white striped bloomers with a vest-like black corset, and my usual arse-kicking boots, but the kids continued to stare. My hand went self-consciously to the fading bruises on my face that I'd tried to cover with make-up.

Churchill chuckled – not at the barely discernible marks, but at me. "I believe my students noticed your tattoo, Alexandra."

When I graduated from the Academy, Rye had taken me out and we'd got matching tattoos of fanged skulls with crowns on the back of our right shoulders. We thought we looked so bad-ass.

"Did it hurt?" one of the girls asked, nodding at my shoulder.

I was an unfortunate victim of what Avery referred to as "spastic brow syndrome" but I managed to keep my amusement hidden despite raising a brow. The girl could survive being hit by a lorry and she wanted to know if a tattoo hurt?

"It was more annoying than painful," I replied honestly. "I had to sit still for a long time."

"Something Alexandra's never been very good at," Church informed them with a smile. "Enough stalling, Vardan. Let's fight."

Churchill was one of the few peers who didn't use the Protectorate when he went out, although he sometimes had a halvie accompany him for show. It was considered gauche for an aristo to fight, which made it even stranger that Church taught halvies. What was the point of being so powerful when you couldn't be bothered to defend yourself?

It didn't really matter, I supposed. No amount of physical strength was going to do you any good against sunlight and silver. That was where halvies came in. We weren't as strong, but neither sunlight nor antibiotics would kill us. The latter might make us sick and weak, but it wasn't deadly.

I stepped on to the mat with Church, who had removed his cravat and rolled up his sleeves to reveal muscled arms dusted with ginger hair. I was still smarting from the fight with the betties the night before, and as an aristo, Churchill was a lot stronger than I was.

I was about to get my arse kicked well and good.

"Alexandra, show the class the correct way to bring someone down when they charge you," he instructed before lowering his upper body to do just that.

I didn't think of my training, I thought of fighting. Instead of trying to throw him or deflect, I pulled back my fist and jobbed him hard and fast between the eyes just before he could grab me. He went down like a stone.

The class gasped. So did I.

I moved to stand over him, lying on his back on the mat. "Are you all right, sir?"

Churchill grinned. "That was unexpected. Well done, Alexandra."

I barely had time to enjoy my self-satisfaction. He grabbed my ankles and pulled my feet out from underneath me. I hit the mat with a loud "oomph", the breath knocked right out of me. Served me right. I should have known better than to assume he wouldn't retaliate or to believe I'd bested him.

Once he had me down, it was a pretty short fight. Grappling was not my strong point. Vampirism aside, my opponent was male, better trained and stronger than me. As a woman I had to be more than strong and skilled. I had to be fast and limber, both of which were much easier to achieve on my feet. On the floor, I was no match for Church.

I had to take pride in the fact that I had at least knocked him down. Once.

"You've improved." He delivered the compliment with a bit of a frown. "I actually had to work for it."

I grinned at the genuine surprise in his voice. "You're the one who taught me, old man." It was odd, but when I fought Church, I felt like I was stronger than I'd been before, when in actuality I was most likely weaker. I'd forgotten to take my morning dose of supplements. This forgetfulness wasn't like me – proof of how preoccupied I was with Dede. Did they give halvies their supplements in Bedlam, or were they allowed to weaken, making them easier to control? I didn't want to think about it.

Afterwards, when Church had dismissed his students and we were alone, he gave me biscuits and made me coffee in his office – a large oak-panelled room stuffed with books and trophies, photos and stacks of papers needing to be marked. An old stained-glass lamp stood in the corner behind his desk. I picked up a framed photo taken on my graduation day. In it he had his arm around me, both of us grinning like idiots, while I held up my diploma and letter of acceptance into the Royal Guard. It had been the happiest day of my life.

I was the only student he had a photo of in his office. He used to have one of Rye, but put it away after the murder.

"You didn't come all the way here just so I could show off to my students," he remarked good-naturedly, giving my shoulders a squeeze before seating himself in the brocade wing-back chair behind the sturdy desk. "What's wrong?"

He knew me too well for me to bother trying to sugar-coat it. I put the photo back and took a chair on the other side of the massive desk. "I heard a disturbing rumour and you're the only person I can think of who will tell me whether or not it's true."

He steepled his fingers against his mouth. "All right. What is it?"

I cradled my coffee in my hands. The caffeine and sugar were already dancing in my blood. "Is Dede in Bedlam?"

He stared at me a moment, his expression suddenly grave. There was no need for him to speak – I could see the answer in his eyes – but he chose to do so regardless. "Drusilla's predicament is something you should discuss with His Grace."

I hated it when he used my father's higher rank as a way of avoiding talking to me. He did it when Rye died as well – even though he had been the one who had been there when it happened.

"I want to discuss it with *you*. You won't diminish or leave out details you think I'm too fragile to hear."

He glanced away, but almost immediately turned his attention back to me. Church always looked me in the eye. "This isn't how I wanted you to find out, but yes, I'm afraid your sister is in Bedlam."

It wasn't a shock. Inside I had known he'd reiterate what the goblin prince had already told me. And it pissed me off. "Apparently I'm the only person who knew nothing of her arrest. What a relief to find out now, after days of worrying."

He winced. What I lacked in grappling skills I made up for in bite.

"Your father thought it best if we waited a few days to tell you." Of course he had. "He knew you would want to see Drusilla, and what the poor girl needs right now is rest."

Meaning what? That I would agitate her? "What she needs is her family." And by that I meant she needed *me*.

Church leaned across the desk, placing his hands over my icy ones. Contrary to popular belief, vampires ran hot rather than cold. "Listen to me," he commanded in a gentle tone that nevertheless would not be refused. "Your sister attacked a peer of the realm in front of witnesses. Not only that, but she began to insist – in front of these witnesses – that Ainsley's heir was her child. She humiliated Lord and Lady Ainsley in addition to the physical violence."

Oh, Dede. I thought she had given up that nonsense. "Did you see this first hand, or is it hearsay?"

He looked at me with pity – much the same way the goblin prince had gazed upon me the night before. Nausea writhed in my stomach. "Yes," he said softly. "I was there. You must believe me when I tell you that Drusilla was not herself. She was like an animal, Alexandra. A wild animal. They had to shock her to remove her from the premises."

I closed my eyes. Shocking was pretty much the only sure-fire way to incapacitate a halvie without doing any physical damage.

"She's not hatters, Church. She just wants to believe her baby didn't die." I think she also clung to the hope that Ainsley would leave his wife for her, but I wisely didn't mention that.

Strong hands squeezed mine. "But it did, and she must accept that if she ever hopes to return to the world."

I scowled. "If? Is there some question as to whether or not she'll be released?"

He nodded, mouth grim. "Alexandra, Lord and Lady Ainsley only agreed not to press charges if Drusilla submitted to treatment.

It's obvious the poor girl is deluded and needs professional help. She will get that at Bedlam."

I swallowed, throat unbearably tight. "She'll die in there."

A second's silence. Gentle fingers tenderly brushed one of the bruises on my face before sliding down to cup my shoulder. "You say that because of what happened to your mother, but there's no reason to believe that Drusilla won't recover with the proper treatment. If you go raging in there spouting how a travesty of justice has been committed, you won't be helping your sister."

He knew me so well, but not as well as he might think. If I managed to make myself enter the nightmare that was Bedlam, I'd only rage to disguise my pants-pissing terror. My mother had been swallowed whole by that place. They never cured her.

I was wary of humans. I was afraid of goblins. I was *terri-fuck-ing-fied* of Bedlam.

"What if they can't help her?" I asked, my mother's face lingering in my mind.

He squeezed my fingers again. "You cannot think that. You must remain hopeful. Drusilla is a Vardan, with all the strength that comes with that lineage. She will persevere."

This reminded me of after Rye had been killed. I'd been nigh-on inconsolable. Church had looked at me with that same loving determination and told me that I would get through that awful time, that I would mourn and eventually recover. I hadn't believed him then, but the years had proven him mostly right. I could only trust that he would be right about Dede as well.

"Thank you," I said.

He nodded. "Meanwhile, why don't I ring the hospital tonight? See what I can find out for you?"

I liked that he hadn't called Bedlam an asylum. "You don't have to do that."

Church's face took on a vaguely amused expression. "I'm well aware of that fact. Perhaps I *want* to do it for you – and for Drusilla."

A sudden knock at the door kept me from replying. We both looked at it in surprise – like the last two people on the planet discovering there was a third.

"Come in!" Church bellowed.

The heavy oak door swung open, and the last two people I expected to see entered the office. It was Avery, and with her our brother Val, who was tall and smart in his black uniform. People were always amazed that we were related, as Val favoured his mother's Japanese heritage more than his English. His indigo hair was slightly mussed – an oddity for him – and his Asian eyes the same green as mine, were rimmed with red.

One look at the pair of them and I knew something wasn't right. They looked so... crushed.

"What is it?" I asked, rising to my feet. My chest felt tight, as though my heart hadn't enough room to beat.

"It's Dede," Val said, his usually stoical expression marred by sorrow.

"What of her? Christ, Val, don't lead with something like that and then make me wait."

"She's ... " He stopped on a sob.

Avery put her arm around him as she stepped forward. She looked me dead in the eye – hers were as red as Val's – and I knew then that I didn't want to hear what they'd come all this way to tell me.

"No," I said.

A tear trickled down Avery's smooth cheek. "She's dead, Xandy. She killed herself."

CHAPTER 3

A HOST OF FURIOUS FANCIES

I demanded to see the body.

Val tried to put his arms around me. "Xandy, you don't want to do that."

I pushed him away. "Yes I do. She's not dead until I see for myself." I stomped to the door of Church's office. "I'm going to Bedlam." All thoughts of my own fear disappeared, replaced with an odd sense of determined desperation.

Avery grabbed my arm. "Xandy, no. She . . . she set herself on fire."

I froze, the tension of her hold threatening to pull my shoulder out of joint. "Dede wouldn't do that." I jerked my arm free. "She was afraid of fire." And just how was that even possible? Where would she have got the tools necessary for such a macabre feat? Didn't places like Bedlam take precautions to make sure its mad denizens didn't give into the demons riding them?

The three of them – my siblings and Churchill – stared at me as though I were as delusional as Dede was accused of being.

They looked as if they felt sorry for me that I couldn't accept the death – and madness – of my youngest sister.

Did they not understand that no one with even a shred of their right mind would set themselves on fire? Then again, when you're bred to be hard to kill, suicide options are limited.

I could accept it – if it were true. But it wasn't. If Dede was dead I would know. When she was eight Dede became hung up on the idea of "blood sisters". She had seen it on the box. I explained to her that we were already related, but that didn't matter. She wanted to mix our blood. For some reason she was obsessed with it. I indulged her – even then I would do anything she asked – and allowed her to make a small cut on the pad of my right index finger. She did the same to herself and then we pressed the wounds together. Ever since she'd maintained that she felt closer to me because of that. Maybe it was bollocks, but it was sweet, and a part of me wanted to believe it.

If Dede was dead, I would feel it in my blood.

"Alexandra," Church began in a tone that I suspected was supposed to be soothing, "the hospital wouldn't have notified the family if it weren't true."

"Yeah?" I challenged. "No one notified me and I'm listed as her next of kin!" I turned to my siblings. Avery's pink frock coat was buttoned up wrong, and one of her stockings had a tear. She had dressed in a hurry. "Now the two of you can either come with me or not, but I'm going to Bedlam."

Avery looked horrified at the prospect – which was exactly why neither Dede, Val or myself had her listed as an emergency contact. Me, the one who had nightmares about Bedlam Asylum, I was going to walk through its doors to prove that the charred corpse in their possession was *not* my baby sister, but Avery would rather tear off her own fingernails than visit a morgue.

It was my brother who stepped up. "I'll come." As soon as the words left his mouth, his rotary rang. He swore, and accepted the call. "Vardan," he said in a clipped, hard tone that I teasingly referred to as his "big boy" voice.

"Right ... Now's not a good ... " He turned his back, walking to the other side of the room. We could all hear him, however. "Of course ... Yes, of course, I understand, sir ... I have a family emergency, sir ... I'll be there as soon as I can, of course." He hung up, his expression pinched as he turned back to us.

"Jesus, Val," Avery spat around a sob. "Your sister's dead. Can't you leave the job for a few minutes at least?" I would have corrected her about Dede, but she was right about Val, so I kept quiet. He worked too hard – and spent too much time kissing his superintendent's arse.

"Someone broke into the PAH last night," he told her, as if to justify himself. "Stole the records of every halvie born between November 1990 and December 1991. Looks like it was a halvie who did it."

Prince Albert Hospital was where all half-bloods were born and received any medical attention needed throughout the course of our lives. Someone stealing records was a big deal – but not more important than family. Still, it took me a second to realise that my own records would be amongst the ones stolen.

"Halvies stealing half-blood records? That's a little dodgy, isn't it?"

He shrugged. "I've heard of stranger things." He straightened his shoulders and shoved his wireless into the leather sheath on his belt. "Right, so let's get to Bedlam and get this over with."

"Don't tell me you believe Dede's not dead just because Xandy doesn't want to believe it?" Avery's cheeks were flushed the same colour as her hair. "I don't want to believe it either, but that doesn't make it less true."

"No harm in checking. We owe Dede that much." Val's expression was sadly resolute as he put his arm around me. "Come on. Let's go. See ya, Church."

I glanced over my brother's shoulder at my sister and former professor. Avery looked like a sad and angry child with her red-rimmed eyes, but she stood her ground. Church raised his hand in sad farewell. He didn't say anything – he didn't have to. He knew me well enough to know that he'd be the first person I rang once I saw the truth with my own eyes.

I just hoped that truth wouldn't be that my blood didn't know fuck-all, and that my sister really was dead.

Val and I didn't speak the entire drive to Lambeth Road. I sat in the passenger seat of his vintage Triumph motor carriage and watched parts of the city go by, blurred by the increasing rain. The carriage was lower to the ground than its horse-driven counterpart, and it was a rich auburn colour, with cream wheels turning beneath metal arches. The long snout was curved, narrowing toward the front where the wide headlights sat like startled eyes. To be honest, I was surprised that my brother had his precious baby out on such a wet, thankless day. He usually treated it as though it was made of sugar.

Rain didn't just fall from the sky, it stomped down like the feet of a child in the middle of a tantrum, spraying up around the tyres as we raced across roads that were a mix of cobblestone and modern ashphalt. The city was grey; it looked as though a giant hand had dipped the spires and stone in pewter. It was exactly the kind of day it should be when you got news of your sister's suicide.

Alleged suicide, I corrected myself as I dry-swallowed the supplements Val had forced upon me after telling me I looked feral. He had plenty of his own script left, so I didn't mind taking a couple.

My brother had his A-cylinder plugged into the Triumph's audio system. The small metal tube stored hundreds of songs on its internal memory – a vast improvement from the wax cylinders used a century and a half ago. Like so many other blokes I knew, Val had a thing for electronics, and he liked to play loud music when he drove. Today he had the noise at a decent volume – I could still hear the rain on the roof. I only half-listened as Sid Vicious warbled a slightly off-key, yet strangely melodic version of "Luck Be a Lady" from the Frank Sinatra tribute album he'd released last month.

I couldn't get Dede out of my head. I still didn't believe she was dead, but a lump of dread sat like cement in the pit of my stomach. What if I was wrong? What if all the trust I put in my instinct and blood was nothing but ego?

"Did you ring Vardan?" I asked, rejecting the doubt in my mind.

Val didn't take his eyes off the road. "Avery did on the way to find you."

"How did he take it?"

He shot a dry glance in my direction. "How do you think? He was stunned, just like the rest of us."

I may have imagined the slight barb in his voice, but I ignored it regardless.

It took us almost half an hour to reach our destination. The Triumph was fast, but traffic was heavy, the road stuffed with motor carriages much like the Triumph, horns blaring and engines revving. It never failed to grate upon my nerves. I was more accustomed to Mayfair, where horsedrawn carriages were more the norm, and motorists were much more relaxed.

Eventually, we reached our destination. Of course there were no open parking spots on the street when we arrived – all the pay posts were taken. Fortunately Val had brought his Scotland Yard permit, which he placed on the dash so it was visible through the windscreen. Normally I would have teased him for such a cheeky abuse of power, but not today.

"You don't have to do this," he said to me as I opened my door, umbrella in hand.

I looked at him and didn't feel any conflict between my head and my heart. That was how I knew I was doing the right thing. My gut was another matter – it rolled and churned as though trying to digest itself. Just the sight of this place was enough to make me want to puke. "Yes I do."

We braved leaving the dry warmth of his carriage at the same time, both of us as protected as our gear allowed. We ran together through the opening in the wrought-iron gate topped with lengths of metal twisted and formed to spell out the name Bedlam. Water splashed up my boots as I hurried up the paved walk to the impressive columned portico.

The asylum formerly known as New Bethlehem Hospital didn't look like a house of the damned. It wasn't dark and monstrous, falling down upon itself. In fact, it was quite the contrary – a fact that only served to make it all the more intimidating. It was a long, sprawling red-brick building with white trim and a dome on top. Three storeys high, it had to have six dozen windows along the front of either wing – most of those were barred.

"Almost looks like a country house, dunnit?" Val remarked, his words echoing my thoughts.

"Mm." It was as much conversation as I could offer through my clenched jaw. My palms were beginning to sweat and there was a hot, prickling feeling in my torso. When we reached the shelter above the steps, we stopped running.

And then my feet didn't want to move at all. I stood there, just beyond the rain mark on the stone, frozen like a fucking statue.

Val shook the water off his umbrella and turned to me. "You coming, Xandy? Xandra?"

I blinked and met his gaze. The pins and needles inside me had grown insistent. I could feel them in my head now. "I need a little help, Fetch." That was what I'd called him when we were still in the courtesan house, so long ago now that I didn't even remember how the moniker had come to be.

His face softened and for a moment I thought he might actually break down, but he came towards me, holding out his hand. "Then I'll help you." He didn't just mean at this moment, he meant inside as well, and I loved him even more for it.

I've always prided myself on being a bit of a kick-arse, confident – perhaps overly so – in my ability to fight and win. There wasn't much that scared me other than goblins – and you had to be a special kind of stupid not to be afraid of them. Even then, Bedlam terrified me more.

Because I honestly believed that one day I would be an inmate here. This was where I would die if some Human League zealot, whose mission was to ensure that humans were the last race standing, didn't take me out first. This place was my destiny. Sounds like bollocks, but I felt it in my bones.

"You're going to break my fingers," Val whispered as we crossed the threshold into the awful place.

I eased up on my grip, but didn't let go of his hand. I wasn't even embarrassed – that's how freaked out I was. Inside we found ourselves in a small but impeccable foyer, separated from the rest of the building by gates and a security station. Val was right: if it weren't for all the tech, this place would look like a country house, right down to the oak panelling, ornate plaster ceiling and Axminster carpet.

There must be good money in madness.

We were greeted by halvie guards, both in black trousers and red frock coats with "ASYLUM SECURITY" stitched on the left breast. Val and I flashed our respective official identification. Neither guard looked terribly impressed; they simply nodded and gestured for us to move on to the hounds – machines fitted with sensors that smelled the person walking past the "nose" posted on either side of the frame. It could tell in a few seconds if a visitor had a weapon, drugs or anything else that might be considered dangerous.

I'd left the Bulldog at home, but Val had to give up his hand-gun. They told him he couldn't take it inside, not unless he was there to arrest someone.

Fortunately, lonsdaelite had no odour, so the dagger hidden in my corset didn't register. I wasn't about to sashay on into Bedlam without some kind of weapon beyond my own hands and teeth. Although I was fairly certain I could chew my way out of this place if necessary.

"Are we done?" I asked, standing toe to toe with the rougher-looking of the two guards. "We'd like to see if a body in your morgue is our sister."

The guard's eye twitched. What do you know, a hint of remorse. "We're done. My associate will escort you to the morgue."

The guard who'd searched Val led us to the lift. Behind us I heard the other bloke radio ahead to let them know we were coming. I stepped inside the antique cage, turning so I faced the front. The guard inserted a key into the control panel, turned it and pressed a button marked "B". The gate crept shut and the floor beneath my feet shifted, dropped.

The morgue was underground. It was a well-known fact that London, nicknamed the "Necropolis", was built on graves ranging from pre-Roman times to historically preserved plague pits to nineteenth-century tombs. Dig deep enough almost anywhere in the city and you'd find bone fragments of some kind. So it seemed only natural that this place associated with death should, like the pits and ancient graves, keep its dead like a dirty secret, buried deep.

There was a bit of a draught – I felt it along my hairline where my skin was damp with perspiration. The place made my flesh creep, my breathing shallow and my heart race. Silly to be so afraid of somewhere I'd never set foot before, but I was. A little fear was a good thing – it made you sharper – but too much made you a wreck. Made you weak.

I was not going to let this pile of stone and madness make *me* weak.

The lift jolted to a stop, wavering beneath our feet before stilling enough for the gate to jerk open. The corridor was dimly lit, with a low ceiling and a worn floor that looked shabby compared to the maintained grandeur of above stairs. I stepped out into the unknown at the same moment as our escort, looking right and then left. We were totally alone – the only sound the hum of the grainy lights.

"This way, please," the guard said, setting off down the shorter part of the corridor on the left. Val and I followed without looking at one another, him with his hands behind his stiff back, me with mine curled at my sides. The guard's shoes made soft clipping sounds as he walked, but Val and I moved as silently as ghosts, as we were trained to do.

At the end of the corridor was a scarred metal door with an obscured window and the word "MORGUE" in chipped black paint. The guard punched several keys on a security pad to the left of the door, and when the light turned green, he twisted the knob and led us in.

I went first. Now that I was here, I was determined to get this over with as quickly as possible so I could get the hell out again.

I walked into a sterile-looking room – all white with surgical green and stainless steel. The overhead lights were bright, flooding the room with artificial brightness. The concrete floor was dull, sloping downwards to a drain in the centre. I smelled formaldehyde, the charcoal-coppery scent of scorched blood, the faintly musky-sweet odour of burnt spinal fluid and charred meat. My stomach churned as my throat tightened.

Val reached out and took my hand. I squeezed his fingers.

A man in a lab coat came out of a room in the back. He looked to be part Indian, with thick, wavy black hair and a spine so straight you'd think it was made of steel. Pale blue eyes regarded us from behind square-cut glasses. "Inspector Vardan?"

Val stepped forward and offered his hand. "Yes, and this is my sister Alexandra. Thank you for seeing us."

He nodded, not a hint of expression on his handsome face. "I'm sorry for the circumstances." He sounded about as sorry as someone returning a bowl of cold soup. "If you will come this way, we can get this unpleasantness over with."

Val and I exchanged a look as he walked away. "His empathy is overwhelming," I remarked drily.

My brother's expression was strained, but his green eyes held a flicker of warmth. "Manners, Xandy."

I shrugged, and followed the doctor. Any other smart-arse remarks I might have made disappeared under the lead weight that seemed to have settled in my stomach.

The doctor stood beside one of the walls of refrigerator units. When we approached, he opened one and pulled out the slab. The body on it had a black sheet over it – it wasn't a sign of mourning; it was because black didn't show stains like white. A little consideration to the family, I supposed, and to the laundry.

Pale eyes flickered from Val to me. The doctor held my gaze a little longer than necessary, as though looking for the answer to something in my eyes. I didn't blink, but I arched a brow.

"I apologise for this," he said, looking away from me as he took hold of the sheet. "There's nothing I can say to make it easier for either of you."

Val gave a quick nod. "We appreciate that."

The doctor hesitated just a moment, as though girding himself against the sight of what was beneath that sheet. I took those few seconds to do the same. Then he peeled back the fabric.

Black. Cracked. Monstrous. The thing on the slab didn't look like a person at all. It looked like something out of a movie – a prop. It smelled real, though. Too real. But it didn't smell like Dede – though that didn't prove anything. Burnt didn't smell like anything but burnt.

I looked away from that face that was no longer a face, a surreal kind of detachment taking hold of me. The corpse was the right size to be Dede. It was obviously half-blood, given the sharp but small fangs in its gaping mouth where the gums had receded, shrunk. It even had her ring – the Vardan signet – melted on to her finger.

"It's her," Val whispered hoarsely.

I shot him a sharp glance. "We don't know that."

"Xandy." He took my arm and pulled me aside. "It's Dede. You know it and I know it."

I didn't know it. One thing I did know, however, was that this "doctor" was watching us closely – too closely. He was listening to us as well, even though he pretended to be very interested in his clipboard. Someone wanted us to believe this poor soul was our sister – and they'd done a good job of selling it. Only not quite good enough.

"Whatever you say, Val," I murmured, turning away to examine the body once more. Dede was a natural copper-head – hair the colour of a brand-new penny, and just as shiny. But there wasn't any hair left on this poor thing.

My gaze drifted downwards. There was a small hoop in the corpse's right nostril, just like Dede had. The surgical steel was slightly warped, the curve scorched. My stomach clenched, bittering my mouth. Could it be . . . ?

Then I looked at the teeth. Enamel would burn, same as bone – it just took longer than flesh and hair. Halvie bones and teeth were especially strong. The body's teeth were in full view, the lips having been charred into ash. My heart kicked me in the ribs.

This wasn't Dede.

A few years ago, when Dede had been a teenager, she'd had a huge crush on the lead singer of the halvie band Diamond Dogs. The singer – he was called Rufus or something – had a diamond embedded in his right front tooth. Dede had gone out and had a diamond put in hers as well. It hadn't been all that noticeable unless the light caught it.

The body on the slab did not have a diamond in its tooth.

I lifted my gaze to the doctor's. He was watching me, his broad shoulders rigid. I could sense his anxiety almost as though it was my own. There was something devious going on here. Something secretive enough that it was worth putting me, Val and Avery through hell thinking our sister was dead. And that meant it was something I wanted to get to the bottom of.

Burning a corpse was the only way to destroy its scent as well as ruin any distinguishing features. It was a fantastic way of concealing identity. As efficient as it was, it was also very drastic. Someone truly wanted us to believe that Dede was gone. I hoped this poor girl had already been dead when they did this to her.

"It's her," I said, low and careful. "It's our sister."

Val put his arm around my shoulders and squeezed, turning slightly so that he held me against him. I hugged him back, but I kept my peripheral attention locked on the doctor and caught his barely perceptible sigh of relief.

If I pounded his skull into the floor would he tell me the truth, or would he take it to his grave? I was tempted to find out, and I wasn't bothered that murderous thoughts occurred to me with such careless ease.

I stood back as Val thanked the doctor for his time and he went through all the motions of a professional. The more I watched him, the more I was convinced he was lying. I didn't say anything to Val as we were escorted from the lab by the same security guard. I didn't want anything to get back to the doctor – either via the guard or through listening devices that might be concealed nearby. Plus, Val wouldn't believe me. He thought Dede was exactly the weak and broken kind of girl who would go mental and set herself on fire. Avery thought the same. Even if I told them about the tooth, they would fight me.

They believed she'd killed herself because they'd seen her headed in that direction for years, and now they didn't have to worry about her any more. They'd tell me I was the foolish one for thinking differently. They'd argue that she had had the tooth fixed.

We took the lift back up to the ground floor. Val stopped at the security desk to retrieve his gun and I took a few moments to look around and get an idea of just how secure the building really was. I would be coming back soon. It still scared the child inside me, but now it pissed me off as well. These walls held the truth about Dede, and I was going to find it.

Val's rotary buzzed as we stepped outside. It had stopped raining and the day had that slightly warm dampness I often associated with spring. It was going to be a humid night.

We paused so he could check the message. "Digigram," he said, referring to the electronic telegrams sent between wireless devices. "The Yard has new information on a member of the Insurgent Army who they think was involved with the theft at PAH."

The IA was like the Human League, but was made up of half-bloods as well as humans. They didn't believe in the superiority of any race, but held that the aristocracy was a dictatorship ruled by fear and that Victoria should be forced to step down as monarch. They wanted a democracy where half-bloods weren't bound to the peerage, while the Human League's goal was to obliterate anything that wasn't human.

I had more respect for the League than I did for the IA. Going against your own kind was just ... wrong.

"Good," I heard myself reply, though my thoughts were still on Dede. What could anyone hope to gain by falsifying her death? Had it something to do with our father? The Duke of Vardan was an important man, but any villain would be better served by kid-napping Dede and demanding a ransom rather than pretending she was dead. "If you see this halvie, ring me asap," Val said, bring-ing me back to the moment. "She's dangerous." He handed me his mobile so I could see the photo.

My breath caught in my throat as I gazed at the person captured by hospital cameras. It was a bit grainy, but I recognised the face – and the blue hair.

It was Fee, the halvie whose life I'd saved the night before.

Avery made me wear black to work that night. She told me I should call in and take my bereavement leave, but the last place I wanted to be was stuck at home with her and Val as they pored over old photo albums and drank too much wine. They might be in mourning, but I wasn't. So I slipped into a black satin evening gown that had enough give for me to fight, and tugged on matching gloves and a pair of pointy-toe boots before setting off on the Butler.

I was right – it was a humid night. Warm, damp air tugged at the pins in my hair as I drove toward the gates of Mayfair. They would have cool air circulating at the party to keep all those fast metabolisms comfortable. That was another reason why it made more sense to me to move the Season to the winter months, when it not only stayed dark longer, but was cooler as well. But Queen V was a stickler for tradition in many ways, hence why I was in a gown rather than my usual kit.

Tonight's party was at the Duke and Duchess of Somerset's home. Theirs was one of the houses rebuilt after the Great Insurrection. The next house down the street had been left a ruin, the family who owned it destroyed in the fire. It stood as a memorial to all the aristos lost that awful day, and had been turned into a beautiful garden, filled with night-blooming plants and vines that climbed over the charred stone. I took a deep breath of floral-scented dampness.

It was just after 11.30 p.m., and the guests were due to arrive shortly. My task this evening was to prowl round the perimeter of the party and make sure all was secure. Of course, each couple or individual would have their Peerage Protectorate detail lurking nearby, but the Royal Guard had to be wherever a royal might show up, and Bertie, the Prince of Wales, was on the guest list.

Mayfair parties hadn't changed much since Victoria took the crown. They were still overcrowded and overheated. Fortunately sweat was more prevalent amongst humans than aristos, and hygiene was considered a friend to all, so the smells of the evening stayed relatively pleasant. Supper was put out, mostly for the halvies, though some aristos nibbled on the fare. There was also a variety of blood on hand, as well as rare beef for the weres, who often preferred to eat, rather than drink, the protein their evolved bodies craved.

The blood came from willing donors – often humans related to aristo families. Mandatory blood donation for healthy humans over the age of eighteen had been put into place fifty years ago. Every three months, British citizens were required to give a pint. Some of this blood went to human hospital blood banks. The rest went to aristos. There was also a supply of foreign blood – purchased from America, Canada, Mexico and other human-rich countries. China was a huge supplier. I had no idea if the rumours were true, but it was said that foreign blood tasted more exotic than domestic.

Some of the other RGs came up to me and offered their condolences – news of Dede's death had travelled fast, all the more so because of the scandal attached. I took each well-meant word as it should be taken, and thanked my colleagues, even though I wanted to scream from the rooftops that it wasn't true. I held myself together well, until my father approached.

The Duke of Vardan wasn't an overly tall man – somewhere in the vicinity of six feet. His thick wavy hair was dark and his eyes were the same clear green as mine. He was as handsome as he was intimidating.

"My dear Alexandra," he said, giving me a quick, loose hug. I wanted to lean into him and hold him a little longer, absorb some of his strength, but he moved away before I could. "I heard you went to New Bethlehem today. I'm so sorry you had to go through that ordeal."

It was a sign of his age that he referred to Bedlam by its proper name. "Thank you, Father, but it had to be done."

He shot me a sympathetic look. "The burden should have been mine, child. Not yours."

Tears prickled the back of my eyes at that simple admission. I blinked them away.

He stepped closer, so that his arm almost brushed mine. Not a speck of lint could be seen on the fine black wool of his jacket. His cravat was impeccably knotted. He was the perfect gentleman in every respect.

"Are you certain it was Drusilla?" he asked me softly.

I started. Did he have the same misgivings as I had? Or was he simply clinging to the hope that his child was alive? Regardless, something inside me stopped me from answering truthfully. He was regarding me in a way that made me paranoid that maybe he thought I was delusional. Val or Avery – or Church – must have said something to cause him concern about me.

"As certain as I can be, sir." The lie slipped off my tongue with all the ease of butter gliding across a hot dish.

He seemed almost relieved, and I knew my suspicion was right.

"You look pale, my dear. Are you taking care of yourself? Getting your injections, making certain you eat properly?"

Anyone else and I would have rolled my eyes, but it warmed me knowing he was so concerned about my welfare. In addition to individually prescribed supplements, halvies got vitamin shots once a month. Every three months I had to get an extra shot because of some deficiencies I'd suffered since childhood. It was certainly no great scandal, but it added to how freakish I'd felt when I was younger. "I'm well, sir. Only mourning the loss of my sister."

"Of course you are." He patted me on the shoulder. "Make certain you take the full amount of leave. You are a good girl, Alexandra."

I preened, though I knew he'd probably say the same to Avery – or to Dede. "Thank you, Father."

He left me shortly after that, so that I could return to my duties. First, I paid a visit to the refreshment room. All manner of delicacies and sustenance was laid out for the guests' pleasure, including a platter of live Russian leeches raised on a diet consisting solely of the blood of virgins fed the best beef and the purest vodka. Apparently aristocrats of vampiric nature considered them a delicacy.

I didn't share the sentiment. Wiggly, slimy little buggers.

I stole several slices of ham from a plate and wrapped them in a bun before ducking out to do my usual checks. I ate as I walked.

At the end of the corridor was a set of French doors that led out on to a terrace. There were similar doors upstairs in the ballroom on to a balcony that not only overlooked the garden but had stairs down to it as well. It was a perfect place for someone to gain entry into the house, especially during a busy party.

Chewing the last bite of my crude sandwich, I opened one of the tall doors and slipped out into the night. It was warmer out here than inside, but I didn't mind it so much. The darkness smelled of jasmine – Dede's favourite – and I sucked in a deep breath.

I will find you.

Sighing, I lifted my skirts and walked down the shallow steps to the gravel path. Nearby, shrubbery rustled, though there wasn't much of a breeze. I reached behind me and took the Bulldog from the holster secured beneath the bustle of my gown. I didn't expect any trouble, but I would rather have a gun in my hand that I didn't have to use than not have one when it was needed.

Of course, the gun wasn't needed. There was no sign of human activity, nor whiff of stink on the air – other than that of horse. I finished my patrol and was coming back around the terrace – near the stairs up to the first-floor balcony – when I smelled a familiar tobacco. I turned towards it and saw Church standing by a stone pillar, smoking one of his specially blended fags that smelled slightly of clove and cardamom. He was not alone. Vex MacLaughlin was with him, also smoking.

Both of them watched me as I approached. The MacLaughlin's luminescent gaze was almost academic in its studiousness. I lifted my chin, determined not to be intimidated, or reduced to girlish flutters, no matter how tempting the latter was. Did he know what Fee had done? Was he protecting her, or had he turned her over to the Yard?

These were not questions I would get the chance to ask. He murmured something to Church as he casually flicked his cigarette into the night. It landed not far from me on the path – I could see the burning tip. Then the tall alpha straightened, rolled his broad shoulders and walked away without giving me so much as a second glance.

Though my ego insisted he had wanted to do just that.

"Patrolling, Leftenant?" Church enquired. There was nothing overt in his tone, but something told me not to ask about the wolf, no matter how much I wanted to. It was none of my business.

"Just finishing, sir," I replied as I joined him. He eyed me with a mixture of stern appraisal and vague amusement.

"Have you time for a break?"

"I'm due." I took the cigarette he offered me. He was the only person I ever smoked with. It made me feel like we were part of a secret club. As far as I knew, I was the only former student he spent any amount of time with – since Rye's death, that was.

He flicked his thumb over his lighter and offered me the flame that jumped up. I stuck the end of my fag into the fire and took a drag.

"I never got the chance to express my condolences," he said, staring out into the night. "I'm sorry about Drusilla – more than words can express."

"Thank you." My throat was tight. I might be able to carry on this charade with Avery and Val and even my father, but not with Church. "Sir, I don't think Dede's really dead."

He turned his head towards me as he exhaled a thin stream of fragrant smoke. "It's not unusual for people to feel that way after the loss of a loved one. It's part of grief, my dear girl."

"I saw the body," I reminded him before inhaling deeply on my own cigarette. "It wasn't right."

"Not to be morbid, but intense heat can do strange things to a body."

"Maybe," I agreed, "but I don't think so in this case. The corpse didn't have a diamond in its tooth."

He frowned, turning his body towards me as well. "You think someone purposefully burned the corpse so you'd think it was your sister? Xandra, that sounds like something out of a novel."

"I don't know what to think, except I'm certain the body in that morgue isn't Dede, and someone went to a lot of trouble to make me believe otherwise."

"Your brother is a detective, Alexandra." He eyed me carefully. Plague me – did everyone think I was barking hatters? "How is it you noticed what he didn't? Are you certain you saw what you saw?"

Was it possible I didn't? No. "To Val, Dede is capable of killing herself, but I know better. I know my sister is still alive and I'm going to find her."

A half-smile curved Church's lips. "I have no doubt that if Dede is out there you will find her, but promise me you'll entertain the notion that you might be wrong. I don't want to see you sacrifice judgement to hope."

I nodded, swallowing hard. "I promise."

"Good girl. Let me know what your investigation uncovers – you've intrigued me."

"I will." I took another puff and we stood there for a few moments in silence, smoking. Finally I tossed the smouldering butt to the flagstones and ground it beneath my heel. "Duty calls. Enjoy the rest of the evening, Church."

"You as well." He wrapped his arm around me for a quick squeeze and then let go. "Oh, and Xandra?"

I'd already begun to walk away, so I had to turn to look at him. "Yes, sir?"

"Vexation MacLaughlin was asking me about you tonight. Is there something I should be aware of between the two of you?"

Only that I saw him toss a human into the boot of his vintage 1971 Swallow before he drove off with a wanted criminal. "Not to my knowledge, sir."

He nodded, seemingly satisfied. "Keep it that way. That's one dog you don't want sniffing around your door."

"I'll remember that." But as I walked away I couldn't help but realize that if the MacLaughlin decided to come "sniffing around" there was nothing I could do to stop him. Thankfully, I could kick my way out of a boot, should the situation arise.

CHAPTER 4

DEATH IN THE FAMILY

At three o'clock the following afternoon, I stumbled out of bed, threw a dressing gown over my knickers and tank-top, and staggered barefoot downstairs to the kitchen, where I found Avery and Val at the table, talking in low voices over coffee and a box of doughnuts.

They shut up when I walked in, both turning their gaze towards me.

"You know, I can tell when you're talking about me," I growled at them, as I headed for the cafetière on the stove top. I was in fine form today. I hadn't slept well. I kept thinking of Dede, and the way Vex MacLaughlin had looked at me.

What the hell had I done to attract his notice, other than help a couple of his halvies? He had no way of knowing that I knew about Fee's criminal extracurricular activities. "We weren't talking about you," Avery replied unnecessarily. I grunted in response, breathing in the scent of hot, fresh coffee as I poured myself a large mugful. I dumped in milk and sugar until I had a hot, sweet, beige confection and took a satisfying slurp.

Fang me, it was good. I smiled in pleasure, and joined them at the table, feeling a little more awake – and decidedly more chipper. I plucked a chocolate-glazed doughnut out of the box and took a big bite. Bliss!

Avery watched me as though I were some kind of bug. "Christ, Xandra, how can you smile when Dede is dead? Have you no heart?"

I hit her before I even realised I'd moved – backhanded her across the face so fast my hand was a blur. A loud crack filled the air, and her head whipped around. A bright red splotch blossomed on her otherwise pale cheek. "Fucking bitch!" she snarled, but she didn't retaliate physically.

"Fuck you," I shot back, itching to hit her – anyone – again. The back of my hand stung. I didn't know what was wrong with me, but violence thrummed in my veins. "Don't you talk to me like I don't care about Dede. I'm the one who was with her when she lost the baby, remember? I'm the one who took care of her after. I'm the one she called whenever she was in trouble, you cow."

Avery glared at me. "She didn't call you this time, did she?"

That struck the right nerve. Val spoke but I didn't hear him. I was out of my chair in a flash, diving across to knock my sister out of hers as well. We fell to the tiles like a couple of spitting and snarling cats, only instead of using my claws I used my fists.

It didn't last long – we both managed to land a couple of good blows before Val pulled us apart.

"Stop it!" he shouted. "Both of you!"

I climbed to my feet with the taste of blood in my mouth, satisfied to see crimson trickle from Avery's perfect nose. Her lip was going to get fat too. I sat down at the table once more and went back to my doughnut and coffee as though nothing had happened. My hands didn't even tremble as I popped the lids off the bottles containing my supplements. I palmed them into my mouth and swallowed them with coffee.

"What the bloody hell's wrong with you?" Val demanded, as he took the seat across from me.

I looked at him. "I don't have a heart," I replied drily, before taking another bite of doughnut.

He pinched the bridge of his nose. "Avery, sit down."

She did as she was told – generally we always did what Val said. He was the eldest, after all.

"Apologise," he commanded. "Both of you."

Avery and I looked at each other. "Are you sorry?" I asked.

"No," she replied, dabbing at her bleeding nose with a napkin.

I shook my head. "Neither am I. You don't tell me how I choose to mourn or not mourn our sister, got it?"

To my surprise she nodded. "Got it."

And that was that. It was the way it had always been with me and Avery. The matrons at the Academy always said we were more like brothers than sisters in that regard. We'd get mad at each other, have a knockdown and then all was right with the world once more.

Val stared at us – looking back and forth like he couldn't believe his eyes. "You're both mental," he admonished. "Completely hatters."

I shrugged and snatched another doughnut from the box – custard this time. De-lish. I wanted to eat until I puked, but that was pretty much an impossibility. So I'd have to settle for just eating.

I chugged more coffee. "What were the two of you talking about when I came in? Other than me, of course."

"Of course." He pulled a face, but not before I saw how tired and pale he was. I really should be more careful with the two of them. They thought Dede was dead, and as much as I wanted to curse them for being so stupid and easily fooled, I had to remember that they truly believed we'd lost a member of our family. They were mourning her, while I believed that rumours of her demise had been, to use a well-known phrase, greatly exaggerated.

"Bedlam released Dede's body," Avery informed me, her voice cracking, tossing aside her ruined napkin. Her nose had already stopped bleeding. "The funeral's tonight."

My spine snapped rigid. "Tonight? Isn't that a little soon?"

Val picked at the doughnut on the napkin in front of him. "We could hardly have a viewing, could we?"

I glared at him. "It's still soon." A funeral made it final. I had no time to prove the corpse wasn't Dede.

"Take it up with Father. He was the one who insisted she be interred in the family crypt right away. I think he reckoned if we took care of it quickly enough the press wouldn't be so hard on us."

Ah, the press. I'd forgotten about them. They'd already got hold of the story – nothing stayed private for long, not with the way gossip spread across this city.

As if reading my thoughts, Avery set a copy of the *Sun* in front of me. There, on the front page, below the crease, was an old photo of Dede with the caption "VARDAN DAUGHTER'S SUICIDE". The story went on to inform readers that a "source" said that the body was in such an "alarming" condition that DNA and dental records had to be used to confirm that it was in fact Drusilla Vardan.

Obviously they *hadn't* compared dental records or they would have known it wasn't Dede.

"Christ," I muttered. How did they find out these things so soon? Had someone at Bedlam called them as soon as Val gave a positive ID? I could only imagine what the headlines would scream when it was revealed that Dede was really alive.

When they started talking about her "alleged" affair with Lord Ainsley, I tossed the paper aside. Alleged my arse. The bastard had told her he loved her, pretended that he was going to leave his wife for her, and my sister, bless her naïve little heart, had fallen for it. She'd gotten pregnant, and he tossed her aside when the baby died shortly after its birth. Went crawling back to his wife, the weasel.

"You're coming with us, right?" Val looked me dead in the eye. "Tonight, to the service."

I didn't want to, but someone had gone to a lot of trouble to make us think my sister was dead – enough trouble that even though I'd seen proof to the contrary with my own eyes, I still had moments where I wanted to cry. That kind of effort wasn't done for nothing, and I didn't want to give the people responsible any reason to doubt their ruse had worked.

"Of course." I added a little indignation to sell it.

From there the conversation turned maudlin. It started with Avery tearfully remarking that she missed Dede and dissolved from there until we were all weeping and reminiscing about things the four of us had experienced, and trading favourite Dede stories. All of them were from before the baby, back when she'd been happy and silly.

It broke my heart. How could I have been so blind to what Val and Avery had seen? No wonder they believed that body was Dede's – they'd seen how depressed she'd been these past three and a half years. What they hadn't seen was the one thing that had blinded me to everything else – Dede determined to make herself whole again. And that, I reminded myself, was why I knew she could never have done something like setting herself on fire.

Or perhaps I was the delusional one, wanting so desperately for her to be alive. Because if Dede was alive then I wouldn't have failed her.

That night I dressed in full mourning – head-to-toe black, complete with a long black mandarin-style frock coat that flared around my boots as I walked. My hair was up in a simple twist secured with an ebony stick. I put on just enough make-up so I didn't look washed out.

Avery's girlfriend Emma – a gorgeous halvie with café au lait skin and white hair – had arrived a few hours earlier and the two of them emerged from her room scant minutes before Val arrived, both dressed in a more formal mourning style of long black skirts, fitted black jackets and wide, veiled hats. My brother wore a long coat like mine with a jasmine bloom pinned to the lapel – a lovely tribute to Dede.

We couldn't take his Triumph to the service as it was a two-seater, so I rang for a motor carriage and driver – a perk of being a Royal Guard was having on-call transportation.

The driver, a middle-aged halvie of about five and seventy, took one look of the four of us – looking like a murder of crows – and his kind face fell. He took off his hat to reveal thinning blue hair. "I'm sorry for your loss," he said in a thick northern accent that sounded strange coming out of his mouth.

Val sat up front with the driver. I handed him a black handkerchief over the seat as we pulled away from the house. I gave one to Avery as well. That neither of them had thought to bring their own was no surprise to me – they never thought of these things, especially Avery, the one who would need it most of all. I offered a handkerchief to Emma as well, but she, smart girl, already had one. She smiled at me over Avery's bowed head and I smiled back, knowing she probably had more than one handkerchief in that bag of hers. She would take care of Avery. The only one I need concern myself with was Val.

There was a line of cars outside St Albert's Cathedral – a beautiful stone cathedral built in memory of the half-bloods who died in the Great Insurrection. Many of them were buried in nearby Kensal Green cemetery, and that was where the Vardan crypt was.

And where an impostor would be interred under my sister's name.

I had to let go of these thoughts – at least for the remainder of the evening. If I didn't look sufficiently like the grieving sister, there would be talk, and I couldn't afford that, nor did I want to embarrass my family by bringing more scandal upon us.

My father arrived shortly after we did, driven by his assistant in a stately lacquered carriage pulled by four glossy black horses. As I watched him approach, I had the uncharitable thought that he should have driven all of us here. We should have arrived as a unit. As a family. But Her Grace wouldn't like that. She despised my father's half-blood children. I reckoned she'd have liked us more if she'd managed to produce a healthy, fully plagued child of her own.

Father looked terrible – tired and anguished. I didn't enjoy his pain, but I was glad to know that it was for Dede. She'd always believed he didn't love her as much as he loved the rest of us. I believed he loved all of us as much as a man could love children he rarely saw and had never lived with.

He greeted the three of us with individual embraces, an oddly personal display for him. When he left me to embrace Avery, I caught sight of another arrival being admitted to the family room – Church. I left my father's side and went to greet him. He took me into his arms and held me so tight that I could have lifted my feet off the floor and not budge.

"Thank you for coming," I whispered hoarsely. Having him there made this charade feel so incredibly real.

"My dear girl, I will always be exactly where you need me to be." He kissed my temple. "Now, no weeping. Save that for when no one can see you."

I nodded, blinking away the tears his kindness had wrung out of me. He released me with a smile that gave me the strength I needed to get through the evening.

The attendant told us it was time, and Father led the way into the main body of the cathedral, where the service was to be held. Since we were family, we were the last to go in, and the entire chamber rose to its feet when the Duke of Vardan entered. It would be in all the papers tomorrow, how he looked, how we looked – and that Her Grace had not attended. They would bring up the child she had lost years ago as well, no doubt, just to add extra titillation to the story.

And they would mention that I walked in on Churchill's arm.

We sat in the first pew; directly in front of us was the coffin – rosewood with pewter accents. Avery dabbed at her eyes with the handkerchief I'd given her. Val stared at his hands, and Father spoke softly to Dede's mother, Lecia. Rather than see the anguish in the poor woman's expression, I stared at that highly polished box and wished I at least knew the name of the person in it. Church took my hand, and I held tight to it. He was reason in a sea of insanity.

Shortly, the vicar came in and began to speak. He went on and on about how good Dede had been and how her soul was now at peace – all the right things. By the time a lovely soprano began to sing "Amazing Grace", Avery was sobbing openly on Emma's shoulder, and I was ready to punch someone.

I was going to *kill* whoever was responsible for putting my family through this pain.

Finally it was over, and the coffin was carried out by members of the Peerage Protectorate – Dede's colleagues. Family followed. Avery and Emma walked behind, and Church escorted Lecia, the tiny little woman hanging on to his arm as if it was the only thing keeping her upright. Val and I flanked Father so he wouldn't be alone when the flash bulbs went off outside. They were blinding in the darkening night – especially to our sensitive eyes. The press – human – was here in droves. So much for the theory that we'd avoid gossip by having the burial quickly. A quick funeral was like a quick wedding – it had to be a cover-up for *something*.

"Your Grace, is it true that Drusilla vowed to kill Lord Ainsley?"

"What about allegations that your daughter was a transsexual?"

"What would you say to Drusilla if she could hear you?"

"Do you feel the asylum was negligent? Are you going to sue?"

We pushed through the crowd. I wanted nothing more than to bare my fangs – which had extended in my anger – and hiss at the pushy humans. The only thing that kept me from doing so was that it would end up on the cover of all of tomorrow's papers. Instead, we escorted Father to his carriage as quickly as possible.

"Get in," he commanded, sliding across the seat. "I refuse to give those hounds any more of my blood today."

I slid in next to him along with Val. Avery, Lecia and Emma sat across from us. Church sat up front. Father's assistant shut the door just as a reporter tried to get a shot up Avery's skirt, preventing me from grabbing the camera and smashing it over the bastard's head.

The carriage pulled away, hooves tempered by vulcanised discs. It was slow going, but at least we were going. My father pressed a glass of wine into one of my hands. "Drink this. You look positively feral."

That was the second time I'd been told that by a family member. I was beginning to get a complex. But then he patted the top of my thigh. "So fiercely loyal to those you love."

By the time we reached the cemetery I was almost myself again. This quick temper wasn't me, nor was this desire for violence. But these weren't normal circumstances, so I made a mental note to get a better hold on myself and let it go for now.

The Vardan crypt was only one of the many dedicated to the peerage. There hadn't been anyone entombed here in almost seventy years – those lost in the Great Insurrection, and that long-dead step-sibling before that.

One day they would bring my body here – not a thought I wanted to entertain. My only hope was that I lived a long life, but not so long that I was ancient and useless, relegated to squiring people around like the halvie who brought us to the cathedral.

Only family came this far – and Church, of course. Security at the gate would make certain no reporters got through. This was supposed to be our private time, when each member of the family could go into the crypt and have a moment alone over the coffin.

Except for me, of course. I stood outside and looked around – at anything but my grieving family. That was when I caught sight of a strangely familiar head of blue hair behind another crypt a short distance away. Fee? What was she doing here? Suddenly it didn't seem like such a coincidence that I had saved her from the betties a short distance from where I lived, or that the birth records she stole from the hospital would have included mine. And now here she was at my sister's funeral – uninvited – watching us.

Or maybe just watching *me*.

Call me paranoid, but there was something dodgy about all of it.

"Are you all right?" Church asked me, glancing in Fee's direction. Of course, she ducked out of sight before he could spy her.

"I'm fine," I replied, not quite meeting his gaze. "Just thinking."

He gave my shoulders a squeeze, and I fought the urge to lean into him as Vardan approached.

"Do you want to go in, Alexandra?" my father asked. He looked tired, but his eyes were clear.

"No," I replied with a shake of my head. "Dede and I always said what we needed to say to each other." It wasn't a lie so I didn't feel guilty about it.

He nodded absently. I'm not even certain he heard me.

Avery and Emma came out of the crypt a little while later, and my father gave permission to close the tomb up once more. He hadn't gone in either. Why not? I knew my reason – because that wasn't Dede in there – but what was his?

I wondered about this as the six of us walked out to the gate. I resisted the urge to look over my shoulder to check on Fee. I should have told Val, so he could arrest her, but I kept quiet. There was a mystery here, and squealing on Fee would only hand it over to someone else to solve. *I* was going to suss out this intrigue.

A few photographers and reporters waited by Vardan's carriage, having followed us from the service. Flashes went off, questions were yelled at us over the top of one another. I hesitated just inside the gate. Val glanced at me. Poor thing looked a wreck.

"Coming, Xandy? Father's going to take us home."

I shook my head. "I'm not ready to leave just yet. You and Avery go on without me."

He ran his hand up and down my arm. "I understand. You have your rotary?" At my nod he said, "Ring me if you need anything. See you tomorrow?"

Another nod. We hugged and kissed each other on the cheek.

Church embraced me as well. When he asked if I wanted company, I thanked him and told him that I really just needed a little time alone. I don't think he wanted to give me that, didn't want me to be by myself, but he respected me enough to do just that. He waved at me through the carriage window as it pulled away.

I returned to the cemetery, ignoring the shrinking number of reporters. It was darker here than out there on the street, and while I could see everything perfectly, the vultures couldn't see me. I don't think they even noticed I wasn't with the others; it was the Duke they were interested in.

I waited a few moments, until my family and the reporters were gone, before slowly making my way back to the Vardan crypt. I kept low, using the elaborate monuments and headstones as cover as I crept silently through the grass. It was slow going – I had to be quieter than usual, and stay downwind.

Crouched behind a stone sarcophagus, I peeked around the worn edge. From there I had a dead-on view of my family's final resting place. I wasn't surprised to see the door to the tomb was open again. I had a pretty good idea who was inside.

What the fuck was that blue-haired thief up to? Anger – no, aggression – bubbled inside me. I wanted to march in there and tear her head off, protect what was mine. But that would be foolish, and I wasn't that stupid.

I didn't see anyone else lurking about, but that didn't mean they weren't there. I moved fast, ducking behind another stone as I manoeuvred closer to the tomb. I approached from the side so that whoever was inside wouldn't see me coming, pausing long enough to pull the lonsdaelite dagger from the sheath sewn into my coat.

I slipped into the crypt. A lone figure was standing next to the rosewood casket, covered from head to toe in a long hooded cloak. It was Fee, judging from the size. And she was about to lift the coffin lid.

I pounced on her, using my body weight and strength to pin her to the coffin, which shifted on its shelf. She struggled, but I slammed her face into the casket before flipping her over so that she faced me. I pressed the edge of my dagger to her throat and tore her hood off with the other hand.

I was right. It was Fee. The dagger trembled, eager to slice through her skin and give me access to the blood beneath. I was so angry. So *hungry*.

"What the bloody hell are you doing here?" I demanded as saliva flooded my tongue.

"Paying my respects," she replied, glancing down at the blade as blood trickled from her nostrils to her mouth. "Could you put that away?"

I ignored the request. I wanted to lick her upper lip clean. "How do you know my sister? And why did you steal the records from the hospital?"

"I don't know what you're talking about."

A little pressure and the blade bit ever so slightly into the skin of her throat, drawing a bead of blood. "You tell me or I fucking end you right here." It was a lie, of course. I wasn't going to kill her – not while she had information on Dede. Though I couldn't promise I wouldn't take a bite.

"I'm really sorry," she said with a slight smile.

"For wha—" And that was all I got to say before I was struck by lightning and died.

I woke up a few seconds after my heart started beating again. Sprawled face down on the crypt floor, I was drooling on the dirt. Crypt dust tasted just like I thought it would. At least I hadn't pissed myself from the jolt. That was something to be bloody thankful for.

I spat out most of the grime coating my teeth and gingerly pushed myself to my feet. My muscles were a little twitchy, but otherwise I was all right.

Brushing the dirt from my clothes, I cursed myself. The bitch had shocked me good. She must have used a professional-grade machine – the kind usually only available to Scotland Yard and a few government agencies. Good shockers were hard to get, for the very reason I had just experienced – they rendered a half-blood useless.

I could only assume I was still alive because she felt she owed me for saving her life. The irony of her debilitating me the same way the betties had her was not lost on me. The next time we did this particular dance I would have to make certain I knew the steps a bit better. She'd got me because I let my guard down. I was so intent on finding answers I forgot to be vigilant.

My dagger was on the floor. I swiped it up and slid it back into my coat. Nice of her, I suppose, not to take my weapon. She couldn't have known what, or how valuable, it was.

Or, I thought, turning to the coffin, she'd got what she wanted and just wanted to get the hell out of there. Call it a macabre hunch, but I opened the casket. The crispy half-blood was still there, releasing a sweet charcoal smell into the air. But I smelled Fee as well, and when my gaze fell upon the corpse's hand, I realised what she had been there for – Dede's ring.

I knew Fee was a thief – Val had the surveillance photos to prove it – but why take a melted ring? She could try fencing it, but pawn shops were reluctant to take items that were obviously aristocratic – trouble tended to find those who bought and sold stolen aristo goods.

I had given Dede that ring for her birthday. I'd wanted her to know that she was a part of the family, even though she often felt left out. She'd cried.

There was a splintering sound as I slammed the casket lid shut. My breathing quickened and my heart began to pound as irrational rage bubbled up inside me. It raced up my spine, brought heat to my neck and cheeks. I felt like I was about to come out of my skin, the flesh over my cheekbones taut and hot.

I wanted that bloody ring back. I didn't know what Fee's game was, but I was going to find out.

I ran out of the crypt, causing debris to kick up and twirl in my wake. As I swung the door shut, I sniffed at the night air; I'd always had a very sensitive sense of smell, even for a halvie – another perk of my breeding. As with every sense, when it was extremely keen, you learned how to "tune" it and ignore those things on the periphery. It had taken me years to get so those industrial rubbish bins restaurants used didn't gag me – or worse, the whiff of sewers. Church used to tease me and tell me I had the senses of a goblin.

I hadn't taken it as a compliment.

But now, I had no such squeamishness. I sniffed my hands, digging past the dirt and wood and burnt flesh to find Fee's scent. It was there, as subtle and unique as jasmine amongst wood chips. I chased it to the street, whipping past tombstones so fast my eyes stung. But there, outside the gates, the scent faded, mixing with others – petrol and rubber and steel. She'd been picked up, or had a vehicle waiting.

I sniffed again. The scents were so familiar, trying to sort through them was like putting together a jigsaw puzzle that was all the same colour. When I finally found all the pieces, they'd faded to almost nothing, and I was certain one of them had to be wrong because the person it belonged to had been lost to me for a very long time. But the other . . . the other wasn't really dead at all.

Dede.

CHAPTER 5

MY SISTER'S KEEPER

Now I had proof the briquette in that coffin wasn't Dede – not if I could smell her this well. Scent can linger on things – clothing, skin – but not like this. This was full-flesh halvie smell. Living. Breathing.

And gone.

I could tell which direction the motor carriage went, but that was it. Wherever Dede was now it was east of where I stood. I could panic and rage, but neither of those would do me any good. So I made the conscious decision to keep my head firmly on my shoulders and *think* rather than go off on instinct. Trying to guess where Dede might be would be like looking for a goblin claw in a heap of offal – unpleasant, pointless and time-consuming. I'd drive myself absolutely mental chasing shadows all over London. My best option was to start at the places I knew she'd been.

Across the street was a Met station. I hurried down the worn stairs to the platform, where a scuffed oak-panelled train had just stopped, its faded red engine chugging puffs of steam that drifted up and out of the vents cobbleside. The lights were extremely bright down here – a naïve deterrent against goblins. Emergency cases held the standard axes and fire hoses, and then there were the ones that contained huge UV cannons – those might actually keep you alive if one or two goblins came a-hunting. You'd think the aristocracy would outlaw anything that might hurt their own kind, but none of us were safe from goblins, so it was an acceptable risk.

Besides, I could crack the bones of a human forearm in half before they could successfully break that case open, so unless there was a crowd of them already down here, with the cannon at the ready, I wasn't in much danger. No one paid me much attention anyway. I was a freak as far as humans were concerned, but I was the kind of freak most of them had grown up with. Halvies were part of their cultural lexicography, and aside from the odd wanker, they left us alone so we'd leave them alone.

The air was humid and smelled of wood polish, dirt, human and metal. I hopped on just before the doors slid shut.

I had to transfer at Baker Street for a train that would take me to Whitechapel, where Dede had moved barely six months ago. At the time I thought it was strange – not to mention dangerous – her wanting to live in a predominantly human section of London. Now I wondered if there wasn't more to it than rebellion and her excuse that her doctor thought she needed to be less dependent on family.

She'd given up living with Avery and me, to get a smaller place in an area that had once been the most notorious rookery in the city. Now it was a trendy neighbourhood of renovated town houses painted bright colours, home to artists, uni students and pretentious bohos. It was lovely, but not what I would call safe for a halvie, and hardly the kind of home befitting the daughter of a duke.

But it made her alone – no one to notice her comings and goings but humans who woke and slept by a different clock, and probably didn't care about the local "half-breed bastard", as we were often called.

She would have lived quietly, privately. No one to tell her nosy older sister what she might have been up to. And I was convinced she had been involved in something, because people didn't go around faking their own death – or having it faked for them – without good reason. Why else would Fee grab a melted, unpawnable ring if not to give it back to its rightful owner?

I had a set of keys to Dede's place, and I let myself in through the downstairs door of the red brick and white trimmed Georgian. The flat was suspiciously clean for a place inhabited by my sister. Not a speck of dust in sight. Barely any food in the fridge – nothing perishable. No rubbish in the bin either. Almost as though she had planned on being away. Although it could easily be argued that as a professional young woman living alone, she was hardly home and probably ate takeaways for most of her meals.

But I was tenacious by nature, so I sought out clues that would support my theory that Dede was alive, because nothing short of being visited by her ghost would convince me otherwise. Desperate, yes, but that didn't mean I wasn't right.

Her antidepressants weren't in the kitchen cupboard where she usually kept them. They weren't in any of the cupboards. She could have run out, though, and just hadn't picked up the new prescription. In Bedlam they would have doled them out themselves.

It wasn't proof that she was still alive.

Her toothbrush was still in the holder in the bathroom, but that kind of thing was easy to replace. I opened the cabinet. Nothing there but a box of tampons, toothpaste and dental floss.

I went into her bedroom. It looked pretty much as it had last time I was there, though there was one thing missing. The fanged teddy bear I'd given her on her eighteenth birthday was gone. It was something probably no one but me would notice.

Buoyed by the discovery, I yanked open the wardrobe door. There were clothes hanging there – a sight that would have depressed me if there weren't spaces throughout. Dede was a clothes horse. There was never a space in her wardrobe. No, clothes were missing. All her favourites, from the look of it.

There was no laundry in the hamper. I couldn't tell if any underwear was missing, or jewellery or make-up. I grabbed a lipstick she'd stolen from me and slipped it into my pocket before going out into the living room. The beige carpet, off-white furniture and oak accents had a very mellow feel to it, relaxing. Dede had worked hard to keep herself on the most even keel she could after the baby died. Her AC player wasn't in the dock and her favourite video cylinders were gone, as was the photo of the four of us from last Christmas. The player she might have had on her when she was taken in, but she wouldn't have been carrying movie cylinders, or a framed photograph. What more evidence did I need? I spent the most time with Dede. That was probably why Avery and Val got the call about her "death". If one of them had come here, they wouldn't have seen what was missing – I was the only one who'd even visited her here. Mostly Dede had come to us, which now seemed suspicious as well.

"I'm going to find you," I murmured to the empty flat before I walked out the door. "Whether you want me to or not."

Downstairs I knocked on the landlady's door. Mrs Jones was the only human I'd ever met and liked despite myself. When she answered the door she took one look at me and burst into tears. She pulled me inside and into her arms for a fierce hug. Pressed against her sugar-biscuit-scented self, I was suddenly aware that I hadn't got all the crypt dirt off me.

"I wanted to come to the funeral," she told me a few moments later, as she fussed about her kitchen making us a cup of tea, "but I had to wait for a plumber to show up – no getting out of it."

I didn't doubt her sincerity. "Dede knew you loved her, Mrs Jones. You didn't have to go to her funeral for that."

The grey-haired lady wiped at her eyes as she filled a teapot with hot water. "You're sweet to think of an old woman in your time of sorrow, so considerate."

Consideration had nothing to do with it. I wasn't thinking of her at all. Still, I gave her a slight smile, and sat with my back to the wall so I could keep my attention focused on her. I liked her, but that didn't mean I was stupid enough to trust her.

"Have you noticed if anyone other than me has been to the apartment?" I asked. I got up to help her when she tried to carry a tray heavy with tea, cups and biscuits to the table.

She gave up her burden with a smile. "Thank you, dear. Other than you and the folks from the hospital, I haven't seen anyone around Dede's place." She dabbed at her eyes again.

I had been in the process of pouring the tea, and sloshed a little over the side of my cup I'd been so startled. "People from the hospital?"

Mrs Jones smiled. "Yes, the nice young man and woman they sent to get some of Dede's things. Let me wipe that up for you."

Bedlam didn't send people to collect an inmate's belongings. That was the duty of family – if the inmate was allowed to have any personal items. It was an asylum, after all. And asylums hadn't changed that much during Victoria's seventeen and one half decades on the throne.

"Was one of them a woman with blue hair?" I asked, following my rising suspicion.

Mrs Jones's wrinkled face brightened. "Why, yes, it was! Had a very handsome gentleman with her – from India, I think."

I wasn't interested in the tosser with her. "Did you happen to see what they took? Just so I know when I pack the flat up."

The brightness drained from her features. "I'm afraid not. They had Dede's keys. And you needn't rush to tidy things up, dear. Dede paid up to the end of the month. Such a good tenant. I was so surprised when she gave notice."

I froze, biscuit poised halfway to my mouth. "She planned to move out?"

She looked surprised. "Why, yes. She didn't tell you? She said she was going to live with some friends." Surprise turned into guilty consternation. "Dear me, she did tell me it was a secret, but I didn't think she meant from you."

Like hell she didn't. I patted the old girl's hand. "Don't fret, Mrs J. No doubt she thought I'd try to talk her out of it."

Mrs Jones dabbed at her eyes again, but she smiled through the sheen of tears. "You're right about that, Xandra, yes you are."

I stayed long enough to finish my cup of tea and eat seven biscuits. Then I took my leave. It was after midnight now, and Mrs Jones was starting to yawn. I thanked her for her time and vowed to be back soon to take care of Dede's belongings. She gave me half a dozen biscuits to take with me.

I was going to keep all Dede's ACs and VCs just to piss her off. She had scads of American bootlegs I coveted.

Outside, I set out for the closest Met stop. I wished I had the Butler, but I had started this evening with plans to attend a funeral, not run about London. I hopped as few trains as needed to get me to Lambeth Road as quickly as possible. Soon I was standing on the street, looking through the locked gate at the sprawling asylum and chewing thoughtfully on a biscuit. I'd eaten almost all of them on the way here.

I could jump the fence, but that would set off the alarms – and it was so well lit and open in front that I wouldn't be able to conceal myself. Plus, there had to be video surveillance. I reckoned someone was watching me on a monitor somewhere.

I walked down the street and turned the corner. It was darker this way, and there were trees inside the wall. I was sure there were security measures in play here as well, but they'd been designed to keep people in, not out. No human would be able to get in without considerable effort, but I wasn't human – half didn't count.

This wasn't much of a residential area, and at this time of night it was very, very quiet. As I approached the shadows near the wall I heard voices – jovial voices – coming from the other side. Was Bedlam having a party? Dear me, I'd forgotten to RSVP. Maybe Fee put my name on the guest list.

The thought of how I'd helped her – felt a kinship with her – burned in my gut. If I'd known then that she'd had anything to do with Dede's disappearance, I would have beaten the truth out of her.

What was the connection? And what did the missing hospital records have to do with any of it? Why pretend my sister was dead? I had more questions than answers and it pissed me off.

That anger gave me the courage to do what I had to do next. I took a deep breath and ran for the wall, easily vaulting on to the top of it. Balanced precariously, I peered into the trees for a foothold. I jumped, grabbed a limb over my head and swung myself into the shelter of leaves and branches. My feet landed on what felt like a sturdy branch, and from there it was just a matter of climbing and swinging.

I dropped to the ground by the side of the building, where it was shaded and just out of reach of the floodlights and cameras. Slowly I moved towards the back of the asylum. I peeked around the corner, the brick wall cool and rough beneath my palms.

The back lawn of Bedlam was prettily landscaped. The far side bordered what I assumed was a parking area for staff vehicles. There was an ambulance there. The sight of it dried my throat. I remembered my mother being hauled away in a similar vehicle.

From there, I turned my attention to the people on the lawn. They sat on dilapidated chairs that were at least a hundred years old, chaises that weren't in much better shape, and overturned crates. A small fire burned in a nearby pit, and I could hear the occasional "tink" of glass as they chattered and laughed amongst themselves.

They were mostly half-bloods – I could tell by the hair. There were humans there as well, though. It made me uneasy seeing the two races mix so casually, so easily. Yes, I was bigoted and not in the least bothered by it. History taught that humans were not to be trusted. Were these people staff? Some wore lab coats and uniforms that made me think they were, but others looked like regular citizens.

Amongst the crowd I spotted Fee's blue head. She was talking to a man whose face I couldn't see – his back was to me. She laughed and smiled as though she hadn't a care in the world. I was so going to enjoy making a job of her. I should have brought my brass knuckles.

Partway up the wall there was a ladder – the sort used to escape during a fire, or slip out to meet mates at the club when you were underage. I took a step back, then threw myself at the building. Pushing against the wall with my toes, I leapt up and grasped the bottom rung. The metal quivered as I pulled myself up. Then it groaned. I heard a "ping" and something hit my cheek; it was one of the brackets holding the ladder to the wall. The bloody thing was going to snap loose, tossing me to the ground. It wasn't injury that concerned me, but rather the noise that would accompany it.

For security, I reached out and pressed the tips of the fingers of my left hand into a crevice between bricks. My grip felt strong, the wall sturdy. I frowned. I'd never really had to do much climbing before, but I enjoyed it. Still, it was one thing to climb a rope in class, or scale a rock wall. Could I pull myself up the side of this building?

Digging my fingers into the brick, I lifted my right foot and pressed the toe of my boot against the wall. Then I pushed up. I clutched at a window casing like an insect, heart beating hard enough to bruise my ribs, and slowly moved upwards, toward a better vantage point.

Using handholds caused by deteriorating mortar and bits of architecture, I worked my way up with surprising ease. When I reached the roof, I stepped over the low balustrade that ran around the entire perimeter and crept towards the centre, where I could crouch down and spy upon their do in a proper manner.

So many pretty hair colours mixed in with mundane blondes and gingers. Human hair wasn't as glossy as halvie, so once you knew what to look for, it was relatively easy to pick out those masquerading from the real thing.

The man Fee had been talking to had left her during my climb, but the blue-haired halvie was a freaking social butterfly, flitting around the gathering like they were flowers and she was trying to pollinate them all.

And then I saw her stop and speak to a young woman with black hair. I probably would have dismissed it if I hadn't caught a flash of gold as Fee handed her something. Was that a ring? The other woman raised her face with a smile – and that was when the breath caught in my throat.

It was Dede.

I watched her for what felt like hours but was probably only one, possibly one and a half. She looked happy – happier than I'd seen her look in a long time. It was heartbreaking to see her laugh.

I hated her at that moment. Her family and friends were in mourning and she looked so fucking happy. Was it possible she didn't know that we'd been told she was dead? No. She hadn't questioned the melted ring. She knew. To rub a little salt in, she was wearing a pair of my earrings.

The fires and lanterns were doused as the crowd slowly thinned and moved inside. I waited a little bit before trying to find my own entrance. The windows on the building were barred, again to keep people from getting out, but effectively preventing me from getting in without doing damage that was sure to be noticed. The windows on the chapel dome didn't have bars, but I reckoned I'd have to break the glass to get in, and that would undoubtedly set off alarms.

The answer to my problem turned up about quarter of an hour later, when the human security guards began their rounds. Patience wasn't one of my virtues, but it was easier to crouch and wait with anger and disappointment overwhelming me. I'd always been Dede's staunchest supporter, always believed in her. But I had to face it, there was simply no bloody way I could excuse her of all culpability in whatever kind of mess this was. It simply seemed too premeditated to me.

I glanced down at the guards and was glad that hueys were easy to sneak up on. I swung my leg over the side of the roof and quickly scampered three quarters of the way down, confidence in my climbing abilities coming easily this time.

The guards began their rounds – one coming towards me, the other going around to the other side of the building. I clung to the window frame until the nearest guard turned the corner to walk past where I hung like a spider. Slowly I eased myself down the wall until I could drop soundlessly to the grass. I crept up behind the guard. He had an ear bud in one ear – I could hear the melodic hum of music from his A-player. It wasn't enough to keep him from hearing his buddy if he called for help, but it was just enough to distract him from me. Obviously they didn't get much trouble round here.

The guard's key card was attached to one of those clips that latched on to a belt loop and had a little retractable cord so you could display and use the ID without having to look for it. My dagger slid noiselessly from its sheath. I caught the dangling card and pulled it down and back, the pressure so light the guard didn't notice. Then I severed the cord with one clean slice.

I froze when the guard suddenly stopped. My breath ripened in my lungs as he reached back and felt for the clip. If he turned around he'd see me and yell for back-up. I didn't want to hurt anyone tonight if I could help it. I didn't want any alarms to sound until I'd got what I came for.

Luck was on my side. The guard's blunt fingers only went so far as to determine that the clip was still attached to his belt. He didn't feel for the card. Success. When he eventually noticed it he'd think he'd snagged it on something. I'd drop it by the side of the building before I left.

Card in hand, I backed away as the guard kept walking, blissfully unaware. Once at the corner, I turned around and ran towards the door. I didn't know what the hell I was going to do when I got inside; I'd figure it out once I was there.

The light on the card port turned green when I inserted the card, and I quickly turned the knob and crossed the threshold. I was in a corridor that looked far more welcoming than it felt. It had the same dark panelling as the foyer and a carpet with a William Morris design. To my right was what looked like a drawing room and to the left a huge dining hall with large windows that overlooked the grounds.

At least my mother had been imprisoned in a nice place. The temptation to find out about her was strong, but my fear of discovering what this place might have done to her was greater. There wasn't anything I could do for her, but I could still save Dede.

Save her so I could fucking kill her myself.

I had to admit, with the exception of the morgue, Bedlam didn't look nearly as nightmarish as I thought it ought, a theory only reinforced as I tiptoed down the corridor into the spacious and welcoming great hall. There I stopped for a moment and sniffed the air. Dede's scent rushed to greet me, bringing the sting of tears to my eyes.

I don't think I'd realised just how afraid I'd been that she was actually dead – that somehow I'd imagined all evidence to the contrary.

My sister's scent led me to the right – what would be the west wing. Here oak wainscot contrasted with creamy walls. The ceiling above was white with embossed tiles, and on the floor there was more pretty carpet. The doors were curved at the top, and between each room was an ornate wall sconce emanating soft light. Little side tables held vases of fresh flowers that filled the wide corridor with the smell of spring. But Dede's scent remained.

I chased the smell, letting my nose lead me. I kept an eye and an ear out for company, but none came.

At the end of the hall was a hidden staircase – probably used by servants once upon a time. I climbed it, following my sister. On the next floor I paused, listening. Muted voices conversed behind closed doors. Someone was playing a guitar. Someone else was watching the box. Easily a dozen other scents reached out to me, daring me to put their puzzle together. I ignored them, because my head wanted to make them into something familiar, and I didn't have time for it.

My search led me to a room three doors down on the left. On

the other side of the door I could hear Sid Vicious warbling about the summer wind. It couldn't be that this was where the scent ended, not with Sid played inside.

I didn't knock. I shoved the guard's card in the lock, grabbed the brass doorknob and turned it, my heart pounding against my ribs. The heavy wood swung open and I crossed the threshold, alert to any possible threat. But nothing happened. No one jumped me or tried to shoot me. I turned towards the bed and the young woman sitting on it. A book was page-down beside her on the patchwork quilt. She wasn't reading it, she was staring at me. And I was staring at her black hair – so human and common-looking.

My sister smiled. "Hullo, Xandy. I was wondering when you'd turn up."

Killing her would be too kind.

She looked so at home here in this lovely room with its sage-green walls and white woodwork. Gauzy curtains with little green leaves covered the blinds at the windows, and a cream, taupe and sage rug sat in the middle of the hardwood floor. The furniture was white as well, but the focal point of the room was the enormous four-poster bed, on which my sister sat, dressed in white knee-length bloomers and a loose shirt, legs crossed like a yogi, smiling like a fucking idiot.

She must have seen murder in my eyes because her smile quickly faded. "You shouldn't be here," she said.

I closed the door and leaned against it, arms folded over my chest so she couldn't see how my hands shook. "Really? A moment ago you said I'd been expected."

"You were, unfortunately." She climbed off the bed and came towards me, looking more like a kid than a twenty-one-year-old woman. I couldn't look at that God-awful hair. "I told them you'd show up. That you wouldn't be fooled. I knew you wouldn't just let me go."

She sounded both pleased and disappointed – if that were possible. I couldn't look at her – I was too angry. But when I turned my head and saw the bear I had given her sitting on that bed, I whirled on her, barely containing the tempest of emotions that raged within me.

Fang me, but I really wanted to tear her apart. I also wanted to sob in relief that she was alive.

"Get your things," I commanded. "We're going home, and you're going to explain to your grieving family why a char-grilled stranger is interred in the family mausoleum. And don't forget my *fucking* earrings."

Thin arms crossed tightly over her slight chest, she glared at me with eyes so much like my own. "I'm not leaving. I'm sorry if I've hurt you or Avery and Val, but I'm not going back to that life, and if you have any love for me at all, you won't tell them the truth."

"Are you completely mental?" I straightened away from the door. "You must be to fake your own death. And a shit-poor job you did too. Fee stealing your ring back was bad enough, but you took things from your apartment, gave notice to your landlady. Did you think we wouldn't figure it out?"

"I knew Avery and Val wouldn't notice anything or even think to ask. They both think I'm hatters as it is. I also knew our father wouldn't bother to investigate, but *you* . . . " She smiled again and shook her head. "I knew you'd be trouble."

"You knew I'd find you, but now I have to leave? Without you?" I could practically taste the incredulity in my voice.

Dede nodded, her expression suddenly grim. "I'm glad you know the truth, but now it's best for everyone if you forget you saw me. Let me go."

"I can't do that."

Inky hair fell over her pale forehead. Her wide gaze met mine with stark sincerity. "You tell people I'm alive and it won't be long before I'm dead for real."

This was too much. She sounded paranoid and manic and ... mad. Mad as a bloody hatter. And yet I played along. "Who? Why?"

She rubbed a hand over her opposite shoulder, as though she was chilled. I had to fight the urge to find her a sweater. "I know too much. If it weren't for who I am, I probably would have been tossed to the goblins, hence my hasty admission to New Bethlehem. I suppose they figured this would be the one place you wouldn't come looking for me."

I still wasn't any closer to figuring out what she was doing here. "Start from the beginning." I didn't add that it had better be good. Dede could tell a story to rival Shakespeare. What it had better be was *true*, and not some wild conspiracy theory.

She sat down on the trunk at the foot of the bed. I stayed where I was in case anyone tried to interrupt our little family reunion.

Her eyebrows knitted. "Seven months ago I was approached by ... someone I knew. This person told me things that supported what I'd already presumed – that the aristocracy is not to be trusted."

"Albert's fangs, Dede!" I looked nervously around the room. What did I suspect was about to happen? Did I think Queen V would suddenly burst out of the wardrobe shouting "Treason!?"

"It's true, Xandy. You've never seen it because you don't want to."

No bloody way was I going to be the guilty one. "This isn't about me, Dee. It's about you." And what government was totally trustworthy? Really.

"It's about something bigger than the both of us," she informed me smartly. "Half-bloods were an accident, Xandy. And once they found out we were useful, they bred us and put us to whatever use they could find, but they don't care about us. They experiment on our minds and bodies – our reproductive organs. They're killing halvies and humans in an attempt to make their own lives better."

"Who are? Aristos?" Astonished, that was what I was – and somewhat alarmed that my sister might really be mad.

She shook her head. "I knew you wouldn't believe it. They were the ones who took my son, you know. When they discovered he was fully plagued, they took him and gave him to Ainsley to replace the one he lost. I've seen him."

A lump swelled in my throat. Reality had deserted my beautiful baby sister. "Your child died, luv. You know that. There's never been a fully plagued birth from a half-blood and an aristo."

"That you've been told about," she retorted.

"Because there's nothing to tell." Although, that was odd, wasn't it? If two human carriers could produce a fully plagued living child, why couldn't a halvie and an aristo?

She made a scoffing sound, staring down her pert nose at me as though I were an ignorant lout. "I've always envied your ability to blindly believe what you're told."

"I didn't believe you were dead," I countered with a little bite. "How could you do this to us? To your mother and to our father?"

She watched me for a moment as though I were some sort of odd bug and she was Charles bloody Darwin. "You can't imagine displeasing him, can you? Of course you can't, because you still hope that one day he might be a proper father. He's different with you. Church too. They both adore you. Why is that?"

I didn't like her tone. "I dunno. Maybe because I don't go running around attacking peers at parties?"

That took some of the fight out of her, but not all of it. The finger she pointed at me barely shook. "They took my son, and when I dared speak up about it – when I became a 'problem' – they sent me here, where they send all their unwanted halvies."

I made a show of examining my surroundings. "Doesn't seem such a bum deal."

She mocked me with a smile. "I can show you the locked ward."

The thought of that brought an acrid taste to my mouth. "I thought you wanted me to leave."

All traces of smile vanished. "I do. Promise you won't tell anyone you saw me, Xandy. Please, if you have any love for me, you won't tell anyone – not even Avery or Val, and especially not Churchill – that I'm alive."

I had already told Church my suspicions, but I trusted him with my life. "You can't ask that of me, Dede. It's not right."

"What they're doing to us isn't right!" she cried, then lowered her voice. "For the first time I feel as though I'm part of something good, something meaningful. I'm doing the right thing and I belong here."

It was as though the proverbial light switched on in my head – and I didn't like what it showed me. "Albert's fangs. You've joined the Insurrectionists, haven't you?" I had no idea how it had happened, or what they had to do with Bedlam, but the pieces suddenly fell into place with cruel clarity – Dede had turned traitor.

She lifted her chin as she toyed with the bottles on the dressing table. "You say it like it's something to be ashamed of."

"It is!" I threw my hands in the air, then pressed them against my head. "God, Dede. You'll be executed."

She smiled again. "Can't kill a dead woman."

And there was my answer as to why anyone would try to fake Dede's death. "Who is that poor soul in our family crypt?"

"A halvie who died at a horror show," came her hoarse reply. "She'd been tossed down a hole for the goblins to get."

My stomach rolled, partly from disgust and partly from the fact that I hadn't eaten in a little while. As though reading my thoughts, my sister opened one of the drawers, took out a Cadbury and tossed it to me.

"Horror shows are illegal," I said, taking a bite of the chocolatey goodness without thanking her. The term referred to spectacles where aristos drank from humans – and occasionally halvies – to the death. They had been terribly popular in Paris and Venice years ago. Often times the victims were people who sold their mortality to the show in return for money to support their families.

"Don't be naïve." Dede's tone and expression were harsh. "Go into the Freak Show sometime and ask them about their employees who have vanished over the last three months. Apparently a horror show involving freaks brings in three times the crowd. There was one in London just a fortnight ago."

"I never heard about it."

"No. Well you're not exactly listening to the *right* people, Xandy. You try so hard to be part of that world, you have no time for anything not aristo-related."

"That's not true."

This time her smile was sad – pitying really. "You never noticed what I've been up to these last six months. It was all about getting here. I won't let you ruin that."

"De—"

She held up her hand to cut me off. "Don't. Do not tell me you just want to protect me, or that you think I'm misguided. What if I could prove to you that the aristocracy is not as wonderful as you think? That people you trust are not to be trusted?"

I crossed my arms over my chest. "I'd say show me."

She stepped forward, stomping her little foot like she had as a child whenever she was frustrated. "I'm going to introduce you to the people in charge."

The people in charge? I licked a spot of chocolate from my finger. How could I turn down such an opportunity? I'd have names, faces. Good Lord, Victoria would probably declare me a hero if I delivered a cabal of Insurrectionists to her.

Wouldn't Father be proud? Church too. The praise and pride I imagined in both their eyes might just be worth Dede hating me for a while. She'd get over it once her sanity returned. Of course I'd tell them that she had helped bring the traitors in; I wouldn't let them know she'd been one of them.

"Lead on," I said, trying to keep the excitement from my voice. If she thought for a minute that I was going to essentially betray her, she'd change her mind. She wasn't stupid. And I wasn't normally this cold, but the Insurrectionists had killed Wellington. They'd killed Prince Albert too.

Dede tossed on a lightweight embroidered kimono. She regarded me as though I was a recalcitrant child and she was about to teach me a very important lesson.

As we left the room I took a good look at her. She did seem better than she had in a long time. She appeared rested – alive. Peaceful. All because of what she'd found in this godforsaken place.

It made me angry. "I hate your hair. It makes you look human."

She glanced at me over her shoulder. "It's supposed to."

"I still hate it."

She snorted and looked away. "This coming from a woman dressed like a Chinese undertaker."

"Sorry, I've just come from my sister's funeral and didn't have time to change."

She stopped dead so quickly I almost stepped on her. Her face turned, gaze darting to mine. "Was Ainsley there?"

Not family, not friends, but fucking Ainsley.

"Yes. He sat at the back." I should have lied to her and said he wasn't there, but I couldn't do it.

There were tears in her eyes as she turned away and resumed walking. She didn't say another word – not even to apologise for putting us through the pain of a funeral – until we'd descended that concealed staircase and stood in front of a large double door halfway down the corridor. "Here."

"Aren't you going to make me swear to secrecy?" I whispered – mockingly, I might add – as she knocked upon the polished wood.

She shot me a cool glance. "Don't have to."

"That sure of your new friends, eh?"

The corner of her mouth lifted. "I'm that sure of *you*."

Before we could enter the room, there was a shout, and the two guards from outside came running down the corridor towards us. I knew it was them from the ruddy-rage colouring the face of the one in front – and the security card missing from his belt.

"Stop right there!" he shouted. "Step away from the girl."

It was obvious that he was talking to me because I was the one he was pointing his gun at. I was fairly certain I could break both of his kneecaps before he shot me so badly I would require medical attention. Not sure about his friend, though.

Dede tried to intervene. "There's no need for this. She's my sister."

The guard didn't even look at her. "I said step away." Then to his partner, "Take the other one to the administrator."

Perhaps it was just me, but that sounded fairly ominous. "You're not taking her anywhere."

He reached for Dede, tried to push her towards his partner. All it took was that little push – nothing violent about it, but I reacted all the same. She stumbled towards the other fellow, her declarations that I was not a threat falling on deaf ears.

Still, she was all the distraction I needed. The sight of the guard's hand on her unleashed something in me, and suddenly I was like that green monster-man in the American comic books Val's aunt used to send him. I couldn't remember the name, but I knew people didn't like him when he was angry.

I was very, very angry. What else was new?

I ran towards the guard, and when he lifted his gun, I pivoted so that I ran partway up and along the wall. He fired at the spot where I had been standing just a split second earlier. But by the time he caught up, I was in front of him and the hand he had on the trigger was broken at the wrist. I disarmed him as he fell to the floor, screaming.

His partner forgot about Dede and obligingly came at me in a defensive rush, so that all I had to do was lift the pilfered weapon to the proper height and he rammed his face right into it. He jerked back and fell to the carpet in a graceless, boneless heap. Blood trickled from his nose.

Humans.

Someone began to applaud as I lowered the gun. I turned towards the sound. It was Fee, looking like she was about to lead a marching band, in a military-style red tail coat and snug black trousers tucked into wellington boots. But it wasn't the blue-haired witch who caught my attention – that belonged to the lovely woman standing next to her.

My brain stopped working. In fact, I think my entire body shut down. My knees felt like rubber, my ribs crushed my lungs and I was somehow hot and cold at the same time. I had to grab Dede's shoulder to keep from falling.

Standing before me was a woman I hadn't seen for twelve years. A woman I had been led to believe was forever lost to me.

My mother.

CHAPTER 6

THE LUNATICS HAVE TAKEN OVER THE ASYLUM

This couldn't be real.

"You're dead," I rasped. Pinpricks of hot disbelief assaulted the periphery of my mind. "You're supposed to be dead."

But Dede was supposed to be dead as well, wasn't she? I pushed aside my shock and concentrated on putting one foot in front of the other. My knees trembled as I moved forwards, towards the ghost in front of me. Fee stepped between us, as though to prevent me from getting any closer. I turned my head to look at her – dead in the eye. Whatever she saw in my gaze was enough to make her move aside, and I took another step.

Juliet Clare was my mother's name. She'd been one of the most sought-after breeding courtesans twenty-some years ago because her children tended to be strong and agile. No miscarriages on her record. My father chose her because those traits went well with his own sense of self-preservation and stubbornness. He wanted to breed a warrior. He got me – the only halvie ever to have been attacked by a goblin and lived to tell the tale.

I remember when my mother heard about the attack – it had been just before she was sent to Bedlam. She'd worn an expression much like the one she wore now. She looked as though she wished she could take this moment away from me, live my terror herself.

I hated her for it then and I hated her now.

She was about my height, perhaps a little shorter, and possessed the most flawless skin I'd ever seen – pale cream with just a touch of peach. Her hair was a mix of gold and flaxen blonde, her eyes cornflower blue. She was beautiful, and she didn't look a day older than I remembered her. Wearing an old-fashioned coral House of Worth gown that cinched her waist and fell to the floor in a froth of fabric, she looked like she should be hobnobbing with the Mayfair set, not here. Not in this place that had been the setting for so many of my nightmares.

Her fingers trembled as she raised them to my face. I flinched when she touched my cheek – not because it hurt, but because it had been so long since anyone ... well, I wasn't used to being touched that way.

"Alexandra." Her voice was light, a little breathy. She took a step forward and halted, as though she wasn't sure if it was safe to come closer. "I can't believe it's you."

"Ditto," I croaked. How was this possible? So many things I wanted to ask her and I didn't know where to begin.

A sob tore its way out of my tight throat. I pressed my hand to my mouth to stifle any other noises or words that might want to jump out, but I couldn't contain the sobs, nor could I seem to prevent tears from burning my eyes and running down my cheeks in scalding streams. I was choking and couldn't seem to get a breath. It was as though my body was too small to contain me, and I wanted out, frantically pushing against my seams.

Strong arms closed around me, wrapping me in a subtly perfumed embrace. She smelled like summer and roses, just as I remembered.

What the bloody ever-loving hell was going on? Now that some – just some – of the shock had worn off, I was able to think again. How could it be that two of the most important people in my life were here while the world thought them dead? Why hadn't I known? Why the lies?

And if my mother was full-on hatters, why was she walking about like she owned the place rather than rotting in a cell?

Sniffing, I withdrew from her strong – too strong – embrace. I didn't want to lean on her. My mind was slowly clearing and all that numbness was being replaced with something very much like rage.

For years I'd believed her lost – even dead. How could she be . . . this? And why was Fee so protective of her? What was the connection between my mother and a thief?

I turned my gaze on the wanted halvie. Fee stood beside Juliet like a bodyguard. That was when I noticed how much the two of them looked alike. Noticed the strange little similarities between myself and Fee as well. Probably the reason why I'd taken to her that night with the betties. Had she known who I was then? Probably, once I'd introduced myself. I kicked myself for not recognising her, but then I hadn't seen her for seventeen years, since she went off to Scotland to be trained up there.

Fee was Ophelia Blackwood, and she was my maternal sister. It was the final slap in the face.

At least I hoped it was the final slap, because I was afraid my poor brain couldn't take any more surprises. Not tonight. I already felt laughter deep inside me, wanting to spill out like a hyena's sinister cackle. I was on the edge of madness at that moment. At least I was in the right bloody place.

"Twelve years." I looked my mother dead in her pretty eyes. "Twelve bloody years. Did you ever think of me?"

Ophelia stepped forward, obviously reacting to the tension in me. Fangs distended from my gums. They felt huge in my mouth. I hissed at her, baring my teeth. "Step the fuck off, nutcracker." Her blue eyes widened but she didn't step back.

"Twelve years." I looked from Juliet to Dede, who'd gone paler than usual. All I knew was that these people had walked out of my life. Abandoned me in a way I would never have done to them. "You knew."

Dede held out her hands. "I can explain—"

"No," I interrupted, hands fisting at my sides. "You can't. Can you think of any possible reason good enough why you didn't tell me my mother was alive and well? How long have you known?"

She stared at me, eyes waif-wide, shrinking from my anger.

"*How long have you fucking known?*" My throat tore as I yelled at her. Oh yes, my hinges were coming undone.

"Leave her alone," came Ophelia's biting tone.

I ignored her, keeping my gaze glued on Dede. Let Ophelia come at me. I'd tear her and her epaulettes apart. My teeth clenched, fangs threatening to break through the delicate skin of my mouth. If I tasted blood, would I lose control as I had with the betties? "How long?"

"Seven months," she whispered. "Shortly after Ophelia first approached me."

"Seven months." I couldn't believe it. "On the last anniversary of her being taken away, I told you how I wished I knew what had happened to her. You knew then that she was fine?" Because there was no doubt that the woman was in good health.

Dede nodded. "Yes," she whispered.

I slapped her – hard enough that her head snapped back and she staggered under the blow. She was lucky I didn't go for her throat.

God help me, I wanted to. I was so far past reasonable anger it wasn't funny. At that moment I could have killed her – I felt the bloodlust rushing through my veins, demanding vengeance. My skin prickled with it.

"I went into the plague den for you," I told her, voice low and menacing, even to my own ears.

Dede turned even paler, if it were possible. Her eyes widened and she stared at me as though ... as though she finally realised the risks I had taken, the lengths to which I had gone to find her. As though she finally realised just how much I loved her – and how deeply she had cut me.

"That's it." A strong feminine hand came down on my shoulder. It was Ophelia, I could tell by her scent. I spun around, shucking off her hand and catching her by the throat with my own hand. She hit me but I barely felt it; I just kept squeezing. I could crush her windpipe if I wanted. She'd recover but at least it would shut her up for a while.

"Alexandra." My name seemed to echo throughout the room, delivered by a voice that was much more than human. My eyebrows shot up as I turned my attention to my mother, standing so still and preternatural. Just what had my mummy turned into during our estrangement? "Release her."

I glanced at Ophelia, gasping for air as she struck me again and again. Why couldn't I feel the blows? Was I so far gone that even physical pain couldn't permeate?

"Let her go, Xandy." This time it was Dede who spoke. "She's not the one you want to hurt."

"Actually, I kinda do," I replied casually, but I released her regardless. I was prepared for her attack, though. Were the situations reversed I would have gone after her as well. Family resemblance, I suppose.

Her fist struck me on the jaw. It bloody well hurt now. For a moment I wondered if she'd knocked teeth loose. I retaliated with a backhanded slap that knocked her head back. I whipped my dagger out of my corset, pushed the blue-haired girl up against the wall and put the razor-sharp blade to her throat.

I didn't want to kill her – I just wanted her to stand down, although I *could* have killed her at that moment.

A soft but firm hand came down on my shoulder. It was my mother. "Let her go, child. Violence won't make you feel any better."

Her words had a very soothing effect. I lowered the blade and released Ophelia. She glared at me – looking almost like my doppelgänger – but didn't strike back.

I turned my back to the wall and slid down it to the carpet, fingers still wrapped around the dagger as though it was the one thing keeping me from falling apart.

With my rage gone, all I had left was a sense of soul-deep betrayal. I didn't know reality. I didn't even know myself, my control was so frayed. My eyes stung, my knuckles hurt and inside me was this terrible wrongness I would do almost anything to be rid of. No one tried to comfort me, which was just as well.

I didn't want it.

Some time later – after I'd returned to the land of sanity and dignity – someone, I think it was my mother, decided I deserved an explanation.

No shit.

"In 1935 those who opposed aristocratic rule needed a place where they could hide and be safe from persecution. The administration of Bedlam was sympathetic to their cause and it's been a safe haven ever since. An asylum in the truest sense."

I stared at her, realisation penetrating the dense fog of my brain. "You're all Insurrectionists?"

Traitors to the Crown. The same Crown I'd sworn to protect with my life.

"You shouldn't tell her this," Ophelia advised our mother with a stern glance. "She's an RG. She's going to report us."

That was exactly what I was duty-bound to do. Exactly what I was *going* to do. Still, it burned that she was practically a complete stranger and knew me better than I knew her.

"Xandy's not going to turn on us," Dede spoke up, her voice strangely strong with conviction. She had a bit of a welt where I'd slapped her. "She knows they'd execute us."

That explained why she didn't seem to care that I'd found her – she knew I couldn't have her death on my conscious. I would do whatever I could to get her out of this. Her blunder, however, was in assuming I cared what happened to Juliet or Ophelia. Really, with names like those they had to know tragedy loomed for them both. I didn't know Fee, and my mother had essentially abandoned me. What did I owe either of them?

But Dede . . . I would remove her by force if I thought I could keep her away, but I would never turn her in and she knew it. There was nothing I could do for her. Even if I could cover up her plotting against the Crown, she had tried to kill a peer and faked her own death. Not to mention the fact that I was beginning to believe she might actually be mad.

"Not to mention the scandal," Ophelia remarked drily, watching me. There wasn't any mockery in her gaze, just simple truth. Our entire family would suffer for Dede's actions. Avery and Val . . . my father. It would affect and hurt them all so deeply. The tabloids would have a ball with the scandal. Dede knew that too.

I looked at my little sister and let it show in my eyes how

disappointed I was. "I wish you hadn't made it so easy to find you," I told her. "I'd rather have you dead than this."

Crimson stained her smooth cheeks, but she didn't look away. Her chin quivered ever so slightly. "And I'd rather be dead than under the thumb of a race who see themselves as superior and everyone else as servants to their whim."

"You should know that none of us chose this life lightly, Alexandra," my mother said, offering me a cup of the tea a human had delivered to us a few moments earlier. How very civilised. Her voice tore my attention away from Dede, which was just as well. I couldn't stand to look at my sister any longer.

There were four ginger biscuits set around the saucer at the base of the cup. My stomach growled at the same time Ophelia's did. I glared at her. She arched a brow in return.

"Then tell me why you did choose it," I suggested as I dunked a biscuit in my tea. I forced myself to appear calm, almost disinterested. The more they told me, the more I had to use against them. "Make me understand why you would let your children – *child*," I corrected with a bitter glance at Ophelia, "think you were dead." *And while you're at it, explain to me why you look like you could be my sister instead of my mum.*

"It chose me," she replied cryptically, a slight smile curving her mouth. "I was sent here to be got rid of. I was a dilemma the aristocracy – one aristocrat in particular – no longer wished to be concerned with. I was lost and angry and frightened, and then a lovely man took me under his wing and showed me the truth."

There went that eyebrow of mine again. I had no doubt the aristo she referred to was my father. She would try to make me doubt him. Took her under his wing? Was that a euphemism? "What truth would that be?"

"The truth about the aristos," Ophelia replied, biting into a biscuit. "And what they're doing to humans and half-bloods."

I had to admit, they were really selling this on a sincerity level. There was something in Ophelia's eyes that reminded me of the old-timers who'd been through the Great Insurrection. As though she had seen things I couldn't comprehend.

"What are they doing to humans and half-bloods?" I asked.

Ophelia turned her right arm so that her palm faced up. There, along the flesh of the inside of her wrist, tattooed in rusty ink, was a series of letters and numbers: S32FHWE12.

"Subject 32, female half-were, cell E12," came her emotionless reply. "I wasn't even good enough for a name. And I wasn't alone. There were at least a dozen of us. They used us, experimented on us. Told people we loved we were dead. Some eventually did die, but it wasn't quick."

There was no faking the flatness in her gaze. I'd seen something similar in the eyes of Insurrection survivors. "Who did that to you?"

"I don't know. The only name I ever heard was Churchill."

My heart gave a sharp thud against my ribs. "Church would never do that."

"Know him well, do you?" Her mocking Scottish burr grated on my raw nerves.

"Of course I do! We all know him." I turned to Dede. "Tell her."

My younger sister turned away. "He treats you differently from the way he treats the rest of us, Xandy. You're his favourite."

"Favourite, eh?" Ophelia shook her head. "He must be saving you for something good, then."

I blinked. "Church would never hurt me." Church had never been anything but a friend and mentor to me – more a father than Vardan.

Dede spoke up. "How often do you get sent for blood work, Xandy?"

"Every six months." What did that have to do with anything? And why did I all of a sudden feel as though I were the one who had done something wrong?

The three of them exchanged knowing glances. "What?" I demanded.

It was my mother who answered. "Half-bloods have an exam and blood work once a year, dear. Only the ones they're monitoring get tested more often."

A chill raced down my spine. She was either an extremely talented actress or there really was truth to this madness. "I don't believe you."

Ophelia snorted. She was slouched in her chair like she'd rather be anywhere but here. "You're not really that naïve to think they keep you close because they like you? Christ, even among freaks you're freaky."

"Ophelia!" my mother cried, shooting her a furious glance.

The blue-haired witch shrugged. "It's true. If she's that strong on their poison, what's she like without it? You saw her fangs."

I resisted the urge to conceal my mouth with my hand. My fangs had retracted and were now sitting normally in my mouth. What was wrong with them? Poison? "Did you find this out from the hospital records you stole?"

She didn't try to deny it. "Interesting fact, *sister*, there wasn't anything in your file but your birth certificate and a record of immunisations. Almost every other file was full of boring tests and routine work-ups. Even Dede's had a little information, but yours was as barren as an empty tea tin. Strange, what?"

Strange didn't even begin to describe it. I shook my head. "That can't be right." I'd gone to hospital a couple of times, once because of a knife stuck in my leg and another time to facilitate the healing of some particularly nasty burns after a huey sprayed petrol on a group of aristos about to enter a royal event and tossed in a match. Those things should be in my file. Results from all of my blood work should be in that file, along with dates of all my vitamin shots.

Ophelia laughed humourlessly. "No, it's not right at all, but it's true. So what's so special about you that your medical records aren't kept where they're supposed to be?"

"Maybe because I'm Royal Guard—"

She cut me off. "There were records for three RGs in the lot I took. Yours was the only one so obviously empty. Makes me think that somewhere there's a big fat file on you locked up real tight." Her tone was just a little too mocking for my liking. She smirked at me as though I was unnatural – a deviant whom she was delighted to catch doing something pervy.

"I should have let those betties have you," I said softly, looking her dead in the eye. It was an awful thing to say, but by God at that moment I meant it. My reward for being such a rotten bitch was the bitter satisfaction of watching her smirk disappear.

"That's enough." My mother was obviously a woman accustomed to being heeded. "The two of you are sisters, not enemies."

Ophelia and I glared at each other. Odd that I had liked her so much in the park that night yet despised her so much now. I'm not quite sure how she'd become the focus of my hatred, but she had.

Oh hell, who was I fooling? I despised the witch because she'd obviously enjoyed a longer and closer relationship with our mother than I had. She knew Dede in a manner I certainly did not.

"Churchill accused me of being mentally unstable," Dede said suddenly, her tone flat. "He told me to be quiet and accept my fate, that everything would seem better after some rest."

"How is that wrong?" I asked.

My sister didn't even blink. "Because someone sent an assassin after me the night I was to be transferred here. Why do you think we faked my death?"

"But ..." I simply could not reconcile my Church with this monster they described. "He's always been so good to me."

"You're useful," Dede countered. "They keep a watchful eye on you, monitor your vitals. Face it, Xandy, they've quarantined your records; they want you for something."

Ophelia shifted in her chair, the leather of her corset creaking. "Maybe they've experimented on her already. That would explain the missing records and her freakdom."

"No." My mother's blonde brows drew together. She looked like an angel sitting primly on a throne. "They're waiting."

"That's it," I announced, lurching to my feet. "I've heard enough. You lot are fucking mental."

Ophelia's chair fell over when she leapt out of it. "You stupid cow! You refuse to see the truth when it's right in front of your bloody eyes!" She snapped her fingers in my face. "Wake. The. Fuck. Up."

Slowly I turned my gaze to hers. It was hot in here and I was covered from head to toe in merciless black, still wearing my funeral garb. I felt a trace of sweat around my hairline. I was hungry for something more substantial than fucking biscuits, but I didn't know what it was. I hadn't taken my supplements in hours and I felt itchy.

"You're telling me to believe that people I've known and trusted are villains, that everything I hold dear is a lie, and you expect me to believe it simply because we share blood and you say so? Piss off."

We stood toe to toe, practically nose to nose. I imagined we looked rather like bookends, staring each other down as we were.

"She's right," my mother declared. She was on her feet now as well. Ophelia and I turned our heads towards her at the same time, but it was me she watched. There was something a little bit scary about my mother, and I didn't think it was because she was supposed to be full-on hatters. "Alexandra deserves something more than our *word*. Dede dearest, why don't you take your sister to the east wing and show her round?"

This was not open to negotiation and Dede knew it as well as I did. My mother wanted the two of us out of the way so that she and Fee could discuss us. Discuss *me*. That was fine. Maybe they'd decide to kill me to keep their dirty secrets. I wished them luck trying.

Dede beckoned, trusting and unsuspicious. "C'mon, Xandy."

I followed her from the room. The moment the door closed behind us, I grabbed her arm and propelled her down the corridor. Not a guard in sight. "We don't have much time. We've got to leave here now." I couldn't explain it, but the need to get her out of there – to get me out of there – was a pressing weight against my chest.

She dug in her heels – literally – bringing me up short. "I'm not leaving."

I laughed. "Oh yes you are." I'd put her on a passenger ship bound for America and go on pretending she was dead. And I would go on pretending my mother was dead too, because that was what she might as well be – what I wished she was, rather than a traitor.

"No." She yanked her arm free. "I'm not. This is where I want to be, Xandy. Take me away and I'll find my way back."

For someone like me, who needed to be in control and on top of a situation, this was vexation at its finest. When had she grown a spine and become so stubborn? She hadn't challenged me on anything since . . . since before she lost the baby.

This was how she used to be, and it broke my heart. I hadn't been able to fix her, but apparently becoming a traitor had.

"You can leave." She pointed way down the corridor to the

foyer I'd walked through with Val the other day. "Go back and pretend none of this ever happened."

"I don't think I can do that," I told her honestly.

Her pointy little chin lifted. "Are you going to turn us in?"

"I haven't quite decided." I shrugged. If I were smart I'd get the hell out of there. I'd haul my arse back to my comfortable home and genuinely mourn the loss of my sister, because once I left here she would be lost to me for ever. I would never see her again as family, but I might some day as an enemy.

Could I kill her if necessary? No, not a rutting chance.

"Show me the east wing," I said, reluctant to lose her just yet, and curious as to what my mother wanted me to see. "Make me understand why this is so important to you." *Give me something I can use as an excuse not to turn you over to Scotland Yard.*

She grabbed my hand. "Thank you, Xandy! I knew you couldn't walk away."

I stared at the ruined ring on her finger. "Don't thank me." I pulled my fingers free of hers. "This isn't good, Dede. Not by any means. Don't for a minute think I'm okay with it. I'm not."

She nodded, looking crestfallen, and turned away. What the hell did she expect from me?

We walked the rest of the way in silence, me trailing after her like a trained dog. It occurred to me that she could be luring me into a trap, but paranoia wasn't a good colour for me, so I kept my thoughts still and my senses alert, memorising every inch of the building we walked through. I ought to be ashamed of suspecting her capable of such deceit, but a week ago I wouldn't have thought her capable of treason either.

"You might find some of these patients shocking," Dede said as we went down one floor to the basement. "Some are in a very bad way."

So there were actual hatters here – the ones who believed

Victoria the root of all evil. "I don't think anything can shock me after seeing my mother."

"I'm sorry. I didn't mean for you to find out this way."

I nodded. I didn't really want to talk about it. "Where are we?" I asked.

"The subterranean ward," she replied, and gestured for me to follow her to a heavy steel door. "This is where some of the saddest souls you'll ever see live. Shit. I don't have a pass key."

Remembering the card I'd stolen from the guard, I pulled it out of my pocket. "Try this."

She stared at it, then at me; even the fingers that took it from mine seemed to express disbelief. "Fee's going to pitch a fit when she finds out you had this."

"She should. This place needs better security."

She shot me a wry glance as she swiped the card through the lock. "After tonight I reckon it will."

The light on the lock turned green and Dede turned the handle on the door. She did not give the card back to me, but tucked it into the pocket of her waistcoat.

It was darkish here – like a cinema during the previews. "Is it punishment?"

"Being kept down here? Nah. It's quieter down here and sometimes the light bothers them."

I peered around and felt a stirring of the fear I'd harboured for this place. "So the asylum isn't just a cover for the resistance?"

Dede shook her head, then tossed a glance at me over her shoulder. "Oh no. We have a staff of trained professionals who look after the patients. We keep to the west wing above ground and the patients get the east. Works out well – it's the last place anyone would want to look for us."

She had that right. "You don't find it a little bizarre hiding out in a madhouse?"

She stopped and turned to face me. Suddenly I found myself looking into the eyes of a woman, not the little girl I'd adored from the first moment I saw her. "For once I feel as though I have purpose – that I'm home."

I swallowed, throat tight. I didn't want to face the realisation that she hadn't found that happiness with us. I hadn't been able to give it to her.

We came to the first doors that lined either side of the corridor. Each was heavy and made of metal – iron, I suspected.

"They seem sturdy enough," I remarked.

Dede flashed a sideways glance in my direction. "Even if they weren't, the halvies on the other side wouldn't bother. They know they're safer here. Take a look."

I peered through the small shatterproof glass window. Inside the cell was dark as pitch, save for one small light near the floor. It gave enough light for me to be surprised. The cell was carpeted and the walls had been papered in a pattern reminiscent of the nineteenth century. The bed was small, but made of carved mahogany and covered in a thick quilt. It looked more like a guest room than a prison cell. Even the loo was partitioned off. A stack of books sat on a table by the bed.

And on that bed a half-blood lay on her side, watching me as I peered about her room. I almost jumped when my gaze met hers.

She had short yellow hair that stood out in soft spikes all over her head, and a sweet round face. I guessed her age to be early thirties.

"My head hurts," she informed me, in a flat tone. Her voice was amplified by the speaker on the outside wall by the door. A two-way intercom.

"I'm sorry to hear that," I replied.

Dede stuck her face near mine so that she could speak to the halvie as well. "It's all right, Georgianna. Your medicine will be here soon."

My sister pulled me aside, towards another door. "She's been here eight months. Her head hurts because they put bits of metal in her brain and we haven't been able to get them all out yet."

"Christ. Why would someone do that?" Her mind would try to heal around them – or worse, push them out.

"To see what would happen," came Dede's bluntly simple reply. "In the next cell we have Livia. She was rescued from a transport wagon five months ago. They kept her pregnant almost continuously for six years. As far as we can tell they gave her fertility drugs and impregnated her with goblin sperm to see what the child would be if it lived."

Why in the name of sweet baby Albert would anyone do that? "How did they get a gob's spunk?" I asked. I couldn't imagine a goblin would just give it up.

"The old-fashioned way," Dede said in a low, cold voice. "They let a goblin rape her. Repeatedly. You know she's only eighteen. She doesn't say much."

Dear God. My stomach clenched so hard it felt as though it had turned inside out. I didn't look into that cell and neither did Dede, but she placed her hand upon the door for a moment, as though the poor soul on the other side could feel it.

We went down the line. There were male halvies down here as well. The common denominator with most of them was sexual experiments. Some had been forced to endure horrific pain just to see how much they could take, their bodies forever disfigured by being made to heal in cruel and terrible ways. It was those ones – the mutilated ones – that made me realise this was real. These people – my people – had suffered horribly.

But I couldn't believe they were part of some grand aristo plot to keep us all under the Crown's thumb.

"How do you know humans didn't do this?" I asked as we returned upstairs. I wanted to place the blame for these atrocities at feet I could accept.

"We have found human workers at some of the facilities, or driving transport vehicles, but it takes a lot of money to conduct this sort of work. A lot of secrecy. It's too well hidden to be a human operation. Do you really believe a gob would work for humans?"

I couldn't believe a goblin would work for anyone they could easily eat. That wasn't the only reason I had for finding this all hard to swallow.

"You don't believe aristos would do such things."

"No," I replied, meeting her gaze with a direct one of my own. "I don't."

My sister stepped out of the lift as the gate creaked open. I followed, stopping when she did. She didn't look angry or mental, or even mildly put out. She simply gazed at me with sincerity in her wide eyes. "What are we, Xandy?"

"Sisters." When she shook her head, I caught her meaning. "Halvies."

"That's right. We're neither entirely human nor aristo. That makes us freaks to both sides. I don't think the vampires and weres like us any more than most humans do, maybe even less. We're protection and lab rats to them, and little more."

"You're basing that on a handful of halvies who have had awful things done to them."

"And on what Fee has told me of their experiences."

I snorted. "Because Fee wouldn't lie."

"She wouldn't."

"Yeah?" Dede might have grown a backbone, but she was still as naïve as a child. 'Because the night I saved her sorry arse from a gang of betties – the same night she stole my hospital records –

she was with an aristo. If she hates them so much, why did she leave with the fucking alpha?"

My sister blinked. She didn't have an answer for that one. Ha. I'd made her doubt her precious new best friend.

"We're more than a means to an end to our father," I added, even though I wasn't certain.

She gave me a sad smile. "He had to fuck a human for each of us to exist. Do you think he liked it? Do you think he made sure those women enjoyed it?"

I hadn't thought of it before. It was just how things worked – how halvies came to be. Like most, I tried not to think about my parents shagging.

Dede walked away, leaving me with my thoughts as I followed behind. When we returned to the room where my mother had been, she and Ophelia were waiting.

"How was the tour?" Ophelia smiled mockingly. "Did you stop by the gift shop?"

"I'll do that on my way out," I retorted. That was assuming they let me go. I jerked my chin towards her. "What's that?"

She glanced down at the syringe in her hand. I was suddenly wary and on guard, ready to fight if I had to. "I would like to take a sample of your blood."

"Fuck that."

Dede held up a flimsy file folder. From where I stood I could read my own name on the label. "Wouldn't you like to know why you're tested more than other halvies? Or why your medical records aren't where they should be? I don't want you to be an experiment, Xandy."

My poor misguided baby sister. I couldn't even be angry at her right then. Oh, for certain she was mad as a syphilitic monk, but that was real worry in her eyes. Worry for me.

"Plus we won't let you leave without it," Fee added.

My gaze moved carefully from Dede to Ophelia, then to my mother. I could cheerfully take on Fee, but I wasn't certain I could fight Juliet, no matter how hurt and angry I was. And I didn't know how many guards there were. There was a very good chance I wouldn't make it out of there alive if I used violence.

If I let them take my blood I could get out unscathed and still report this to ... well, someone. Val would be the best bet, or maybe Church. One of them would know how to handle the situation without Dede ending up dead or imprisoned.

Without scandal.

The only way things could possibly end up all right was if I continued to play along. I rolled up my sleeve, presenting Ophelia with the vulnerable underside of my left arm.

"Do it."

CHAPTER 7

STRAYING LATE AND LONELY

"This won't hurt a bit," Ophelia said, as she positioned the syringe over my flesh. The sharp tip pierced my skin and the vial quickly began to fill with rich red blood. My sister glanced up from her work to give me an arch look. "Just a little prick."

"Aren't they all," we said in unison, then stared at one another, unsure of how to react. Fang me, we really were sisters. For a moment I wished things were different – that Ophelia wasn't a traitorous bitch and that we had known each other before this. Blood – family – was important. It was sad that I hadn't even known her well enough to recognise her when we first met.

I didn't want to feel any regret when it came to Fee. As she slid a second vial into the tube, I turned to our mother. She stood a few feet away, watching.

"You're not mad, are you?" I asked, voice shamefully hoarse. After years of wondering if I'd succumb to the same dementia, I needed to know. Though she had to be at least half hatters to be part of this lot.

Her blue eyes clouded. "No. I might have been, though. Once."

She clasped her hands in front of her. "You have to know that I wanted to contact you. I've watched you from afar whenever I could."

Oddly enough, I believed her. Something inside me melted at those words. I was such a fool. She was only telling me what she thought I needed to hear to soften me up. "Of course you couldn't trust that I would keep your secret."

Ophelia pulled the needle from my arm and placed her thumb over the tiny hole. "*Can* we trust you?"

"For now," I replied honestly. But once I was outside these walls . . .

Ophelia stared at me for a moment, as though trying to gauge my sincerity. She looked almost sad. I wasn't fooling her. Dede and my mother maybe, but not this one. We were too much alike for her to believe I'd keep quiet.

"Here, take this with you." She handed me one of the vials of my blood.

"What's that for?"

"For you to get tested yourself," she replied, and dropped the used syringe in the small bin by her feet. "So you'll know we aren't lying about the results. Take it somewhere discreet. And for the love of God, don't tell anyone it's yours."

Her words raised anxiety in my chest. The vial was warm against my palm. I slipped it into my coat pocket. It seemed so strangely earnest a gesture that, for a moment, I actually wondered if maybe – just maybe – they really were telling me the truth, and all my convictions were horribly wrong.

"Fee, love," came a familiar voice from the door. "Are you almost . . . Oh, sorry. Didn't mean to intrude."

I turned. It was the doctor from the morgue – the one who had been in there when Val and I identified that charred body that wasn't Dede. He looked much more approachable in trousers and loose shirt. I fancied I could smell the warm salt-musk of his blood.

"Nothing to be sorry for." I forced a smile. I felt stupid knowing he'd been in on the deception. It was exactly the boot to the arse I needed to get out of there.

"Xandra."

I paused on the threshold and turned my head to meet Dede's gaze. I didn't speak. I simply waited. Finally she spoke. "Thank you."

The four of them stared at me. I held their fate in my hands and we all knew it. I could turn them in and distinguish myself, or I could keep my mouth shut and protect Dede, and possibly condemn myself. One way or the other, I had to find out the truth. Who could I trust?

"Don't thank me yet," I said, and walked out the door.

I took the Met to Covent Garden – one of London's "neutral" zones that catered to aristos, halvies and humans. It seemed the logical choice of destination when I wasn't ready to return home.

Once I was certain I hadn't been followed – fairly easy when on foot and sniffing for the scents of Bedlam – I stopped at a privacy box and stepped through the bright red door. The smell wrinkled my nose. There was a glistening smear of something on one of the walls. I did not want to know what it was – though the bare breasts and spread legs staring up at me from the laddie rag on the ground gave me a good idea – and kept as far away from it as the small space would allow. Fucking pervs.

I pulled my rotary from my coat and dialled Church's number. It rang several times before going to his message service. This wasn't anything I had planned to tell him over the aether – you never knew who might be listening, even on supposedly secure connections – but not getting him irked me all the same.

"It's me," I said after the annoying beep. "Call me as soon as you're able. Church ... it's important." I pressed the button to disconnect and stared at the gadget for a moment before dialling Val as well, with the same results. Church not answering I could understand, but where the hell was my brother? He was on bereavement leave and had no social life that I knew of.

Sighing, I tucked my rotary into my pocket and threw open the door. The smells of smoke, night and exotic food greeted me – a welcome reprieve after the skankiness of the box.

I had no idea what to do and was as restless as fuck. I contemplated going to one of the city's opium dens – the smoke would mask any other scents clinging to me and calm me down – but thought better of it. I'd chased the dragon before, but I'd never really enjoyed it – it made my head too fuzzy.

An absinthe bar was out of the question. Much as I could tolerate the green fairy, it wasn't the sort of thing I wanted to imbibe in large quantities, and large quantities was what it took to get me pissed. Once there, I had to keep drinking to maintain, so I'd learned that the best stuff was a high-proof grain alcohol. Vodka, preferably.

I thought about what Dede had said about the Freak Show, and decided to go there. I hadn't been in a while, and it was a place I could find distraction. It had been opened in 1877 on the site of an old theatre, and had been run by only three generations of halvies, thanks to our long lifespans.

The building was a huge circus tent made of pink-stuccoed stone with paintings of old spectacle posters on the sides. It looked kitschy and camp, but it was one of the hottest clubs in town. A long queue stretched around the corner from the velvet-roped entrance. There were still several hours left of night and these people – mostly under the age of five and twenty – were eager to get their party on. I almost felt guilty for flashing my badge to be let immediately inside, but if anyone was in desperate need of a drink at this moment, 'twas me. A few line-waiters cursed me, but I flipped them off and crossed the threshold without a flicker of guilt. Most of them were human anyway.

Inside the big top the bar was a series of small stages and one large platform in the centre – that was where the headlining acts performed. There were tables in front of each area, and not one of them was empty. A large sign just inside the door warned – in a very sideshow script – that touching the performers was strictly prohibited, as was any form of harassment, and that any persons committing such acts would be ejected from the club immediately, and subsequently banned from returning.

Everyone was dressed for a night on the town, glittering under the dim coloured lights. I hadn't seen so many short bustled skirts or brightly coloured corsets in a long time. Aristo women generally stuck to the old way of wearing corsets as undergarments rather than sporting flashy ones over their clothes. They didn't show quite so much stockinged leg either. The gents in the club wore kilts and long trousers. Some had mutton chops, which were back in vogue, while others were clean-shaven right down to their skulls.

I must have looked like some gothic mortician in my funeral kit – a grim reminder of all that had happened since I woke up. I removed my long coat, feeling cooler and more comfortable in my halter-style corset and trousers. Plague me, but the world felt shaky beneath my feet, and yet ... yet I was oddly calm, as though some part of me had been expecting this. I had known deep down that Dede wasn't dead, so it wasn't really a surprise to find out she was into something bad. Why else would she disappear?

The things Dede had showed me were just too awful to

contemplate, and something had obviously happened to those poor people. However, I wasn't going to condemn all aristos based on the word of some human-fucker – and that was what Ophelia was.

I found a seat at a small table, near one of the side stages. On the glossy black platform a young woman in a sheer red body-stocking – with solid panels in just enough places to keep her act from being X-rated – rested her chin and upper body on the surface of a table. Her hands reached behind her on the wooden surface to grip the sides as she slowly brought her long legs up to curve over her head and dangle in front of her face.

When we were young Dede had loved to dance and do gymnastics and tie herself in knots. She should have gone on to become a performer of some kind rather than part of the Peerage Protectorate. I think she would have been happier that way. She might have avoided Ainsley if she'd followed her heart rather than expectations.

Me, I had always wanted to be RG. Though at times I felt like there was more to me – some potential I had yet to reach – but it hovered just out of arm's length. I wasn't what I was supposed to be, and I didn't know how to get there.

"Hellooo, gorgeous."

Smiling, I glanced up at the tiny Asian waitress in a magenta Marie Antoinette wig standing before me. She was dressed in a corset, short bustled skirt, fishnets and high boots. I wished I had her legs. "How are you tonight, Miss Penny?"

Penny Dreadful batted her false eyelashes, dark eyes sparkling. She was one of Val's siblings, and that made her family in my mind. "Delicious as always, duckie. The new busboy is all up in my business, desperate to sample my charms."

"But you're playing hard to get?" I guessed with a grin.

She rolled her beautifully made-up eyes. Penny was halvie, but she was also one of the most popular drag queens in all the Empire. "Of course. A lady can never be too careful. You look like a girl who wants to drink the day away."

Now would be the perfect time to ask her about horror shows, but I simply couldn't do it, not when there were so many people around. "I need a bottle of something potent, Penny my love."

She eyed me intently from beneath high drawn-on brows. "Going to need more than a bottle to fix you up, lovey." She glanced around the club, and a smile curved her red lips. "Miss Penny has found just the thing to brighten your day, gorgeous."

I followed her gaze against my own better judgement. Oh. My. God.

It was Vex MacLaughlin.

Was this a coincidence? It had to be. It only seemed strange because I'd seen him a lot over the past few days. My heart bounced off my ribs at the sight of him standing by the bar talking to a pert halvie girl. Aside from being somewhat intimidating, he was one of the most stunning examples of aristocratic lineage ever born. Tall and muscular, he had short dark hair, intense light blue eyes and a grin that showed off big white teeth.

"All the better to eat you with," Penny drawled sweetly, as though reading my mind.

I shook my head with a chuckle, and that was all it took to tear my attention away from the Scot. In addition to being a supreme fighter and fair leader, he was one of *Good Day* magazine's sexiest aristos. There weren't a lot of royal bloods who looked as good as he did.

So of course I snuck another peek at him. He held a bottle of beer in one large hand as he leaned his opposite elbow on the bar. He stopped in mid-conversation and sniffed the air. How he could pick up any one scent in a place like this was amazing, even for a were.

When he turned his head and stared right at me, I froze. Why did he look at me like he thought I'd be good on toast? Why did he look at me at all? I was a halvie, he was an aristo. He could have any woman he wanted. Did he smell Fee on me and wonder how and why? Did he know she was a traitor and now suspect me as well?

The wolf scared me a little, with his intense grey-blue eyes and rugged good looks. He had that imperious air about him that came with being alpha. He was dangerous, and could make some real trouble for me if he wanted.

Something inside me responded to that danger. My gums stretched as my fangs pushed themselves out. I wanted to walk right up to Lord MacLaughlin and sink my teeth into him.

As if he sensed that, the MacLaughlin moved away from the bar and walked toward me with long, purposeful strides, leaving the halvie he'd been flirting with blinking in bewilderment.

"Bitch," Penny said slowly. "You are my fucking hero."

My mouth was as dry as a desert. "Whisky, Penny," I rasped. "A bottle."

"You lucky sow," she retorted with a grin, as though she hadn't heard me, but she bounced off in the direction of the bar, passing the MacLaughlin on her way. He said something to her that made her laugh.

I stood up when he reached my table. Despite the trembling in my knees, I began to curtsy.

"Don't," he commanded with a bit of a wince, and held out his hand. "That's an archaic custom. I'm Vex."

I straightened and accepted the handshake. "I know who you are, my lord. I'm—"

"Alexandra Vardan," he interjected, gently rolling the Rs. "Our paths seem to keep crossing as of late. May I join you?" He gestured towards the other chair at my table.

I was wary but not stupid. "Of course."

He waited for me to sit before joining me – those aristocratic manners kicking in. A few curious patrons glanced our way, but the sky didn't fall nor did the ground open up.

As bizarre as the last few hours had been, this had to be the cherry on top of the madness. Obviously the world had gone arse-up-hatters and no one had thought to send me the notice.

"So, Xandra," he began, his low growl of a voice carrying easily over the crowd and performers, "has anyone ever told you that you smell like running through heather in the rain?"

I might have rolled my eyes if he hadn't smiled in a self-deprecating fashion that I found utterly sexy.

"Oddly enough, a fellow said that to me just last week," I replied with a grin. "Must be my shampoo."

He laughed and I breathed a little easier. Maybe he hadn't come over to eviscerate me, or question me about Fee.

Penny arrived with the whisky – a top-shelf brand that I would never have thought to ask for – and two glasses.

"Put this on my tab, Penny love," Vex commanded. I liked that he was nice to her. So many people weren't.

"You don't have to do that," I told him. "I ordered it, I can pay."

He gave me an amused glance, but I didn't spot any conde-scension in it. "That bottle of Springbank is older than you are. I know, because it was made in Kintyre by my people. Consider it a point of pride and indulge me, please."

Why not? Better his wallet than my own. I shrugged, but soft-ened it with a smile. "Consider yourself indulged, my lord."

Penny set the bottle on the table in front of us. I caught her not-so-subtle glance as she slid a crystal glass towards me. She waggled her painted-on brows – subtlety was not in her reper-toire – and patted Vex on the shoulder of his dark grey greatcoat. "When are you going to have a drink with me, duckie?"

The alpha grinned. "Whenever you command, Miss Penny."

That got a smile out of her. "Have fun, my sweeties." Then she sashayed off in a rustle of petticoats and bustle.

"I adore her," I said.

"She's rather something. Whisky?"

I nodded. He poured a glass for each of us and raised his in salute. I took a sip from mine – the whisky was smooth, with a vaguely smoky, earthy flavour.

"It's good," I said.

Vex smiled. "I would hope so." He took another drink. "I heard about your sister. I am very sorry for your loss."

I risked a glance at him and saw sincerity in his blue-grey eyes. So, maybe he didn't know about Fee's traitoresque activities. That was good, I thought. He had the look of a man who had lost someone dear himself. His words touched me, because even though Dede was alive, I would spend the rest of my life knowing she was out there, lost to me for ever.

"Thank you," I replied hoarsely, and took another deep swallow from my glass.

He leaned back in the chair, his arm hooked over the top of it. His jacket pulled taut across his bicep. I wondered just how strong he was with that build. Weres tended to be more physical than vamps, though vampires were often faster.

"I want to thank you for coming to Ophelia and Niall's aid the other night." He poured himself another shot and topped mine up as well. "The pack might have lost them both if not for you."

What would he say if I told him I wasn't so pleased with myself for saving Fee? I'd never really wished anyone dead before – except for the bastards who killed Rye – so thinking that the world might be better without Fee in it brought a sliver of guilt with it. I blamed her for Dede's leap off sanity ridge, blamed her for the mess I now found myself in. Most of all I hated her for having the last decade-plus with our mother.

"You know the Yard is looking for Ophelia?"

His flinty gaze met mine over the rim of his glass. "I've spoken to an inspector, yes. I'd like to say it's all a misunderstanding, but I haven't seen the girl since that morning. Have you?"

I couldn't be certain how much of Fee's scent lingered on me, but I also couldn't tell him the truth without outing Dede as a traitor and admitting that I had been to Bedlam. Then I'd have to explain why I was at a club, drinking, when I should be at the Yard filing a report.

"No," I lied.

He smiled, and leaned forward, bracing his forearm on the table. "I didn't come over here to talk about your sisters."

Of course he knew my relation to Fee. Her aristo father – the Earl of Blackwood – was part of the pack. Still, it unsettled me a little that he so obviously knew so much about me.

"Why did you come over here, my ... Vex?" I asked.

White teeth flashed, bright beneath the dim lights. "Because finally I've found you in a place where neither of us has a duty to perform and you don't have that old leech hovering round."

He meant Church. The two of them had something of a rivalry, but I couldn't tell if it was friendly or whether they both delighted in getting in each other's faces.

Years ago, MacLaughlin had come to the Academy to check on Rye and some other were halvies who had been sent to London to study and train. He and Church had disagreed on something and ended up physically fighting. Rye had stepped in – and got a broken nose for his pains. I think it was Church who had accidentally struck him. Regardless, the students watching had had no idea what had happened. We only knew that Vexation MacLaughlin was one – if not the only – man who could match Church in a fight.

Every girl in that class had a bit of a crush on Church, but that day we all fell for Vex as well, especially when he did the gentle-manly thing and offered Church, and the entire class, his apologies. Rye used to tease me about him – and now I was to believe that he'd had his eye on me for some time?

I wouldn't have been more surprised if Church had got down on one knee and asked for my hand. But I didn't find the old man nearly as sexy as I did the wolf across from me.

"Would you like to go upstairs?" he asked, seemingly unper-turbed by my stunned silence. "Maybe do a little dancing?"

I hadn't been dancing since Avery's birthday, when we'd all gone out and got completely sauced. We'd danced until the club closed. Even Dede had had a good time.

"Sounds fun," I replied, and let him take my hand to guide me to my feet. He carried his glass and the bottle in one hand – two long fingers twining around the neck – and held my hand with the other. I followed him up the flight of stairs near the wall to the first floor. He pushed open the heavy door and we entered a world of darkness pierced by bright lights and pulsing sounds. A man in a ringmaster costume showed us to a table in a darkened corner – apparently it was Vex's usual haunt.

Vex set the bottle on our table and drained his glass in one gulp. "Shall we dance?"

I drained my glass as well and returned his grin. "Promise not to step on my toes?"

"On my honour." He offered me his hand and I took it, liking how warm his fingers were around mine. Were metabolisms ran even higher than those of halvies. He pulled me out on to the dance floor as the DJ started a song with a thumping beat and elec-tric violin – like an orchestra on acid.

It wasn't the kind of music easily danced to as a pair, but Vex hauled me to him and began to move, gracefully matching the rhythm. His shoulder was hard beneath my hand. He was over six feet of solid predatory muscle and heat – and grin. I couldn't forget that grin.

"I keep thinking you find something about me terribly amusing," I told him as his hand slid down my spine. I shivered – just enough to embarrass myself.

"Intriguing," he replied. "Not amusing. You know, most women I meet view me either as a potential mate or a threat, but you ... I get the feeling you can't quite decide."

I arched a brow – that spastic thing again. "Humility passed you by, didn't it?"

Vex laughed – deep and sharp. A few heads turned at the sound of it. He pulled me closer so that almost every inch of us from chest to toes touched. "It's not considered a good trait for an alpha," he informed me good-naturedly. "But you're the first to point out my lack."

Most people in his immediate circle would undoubtedly be too afraid or too devoted to do anything of the kind. "I didn't mean to offend you."

"I'm not offended, sweetheart. Not at all." And then he twirled me around so fast the club continued to spin even when I had stopped. Delighted laughter spilled from me. After the night I'd had, it felt like a monstrous relief.

When my vision cleared, I found him watching me with that same amused expression, but there was a hint of curiosity in his gaze. He lowered his head, so that I could feel his warm breath on my neck. He inhaled deeply, held it, and then let it go in a rush of heat over my skin. I shivered.

"You smell good," he murmured against my ear.

'So do you," I replied. And he did – like sunlight and cloves. Was this really happening?

We didn't speak for the remainder of our dance, just moved to the music, touching and breathing each other in. He went to my head quicker than the whisky. When the music ended, he led me back to our dark table and poured another drink for the both of us.

I reached for my glass, but he stopped me, his hand cupping the side of my face so I had no choice but to turn towards him.

"Forgive me," he said. And then his mouth was on mine and he tasted even better than he smelled. My fingers curled around the open neck of his shirt, tugging at him as though it were possible for the two of us to get any closer. His hands pressed against my back, holding me tight against his chest as he slid his tongue between my lips. I hadn't been this ... desperate for a man in a long time. Either I hadn't met one who inspired this need, or I hadn't allowed myself to feel it. Regardless, the MacLaughlin turned me on something fierce.

The kiss ended too soon. He released me and reached for his glass, downing it in one swallow. Then he turned to face me. His eyes were bright, touched with wolf-gold, his expression uncertain.

"Can I take you home?" he asked, and though the question sounded innocent enough, there was nothing innocent about it.

"Only if you come inside," I replied, lifting my glass to my dry mouth. What the hell was I doing? As right as this felt, it was also setting off alarms in my head. Church had warned me away from Vex. He was tight with Ophelia. There was a very good chance he just wanted to use me.

Then he couldn't complain if I used him as well.

"Make no mistake," he rasped, fingers curving around the back of my neck as he placed his face in the curve of my shoulder and drew a deep breath. "I plan to come inside."

I shivered as that moist heat fanned over my flesh. I was so randy at that moment I could have taken him right there in the booth. "I'm ready whenever you are."

Another glimpse of his golden eyes, and then he was on his feet, tugging me by the hand to join him. We went downstairs and

I retrieved my coat. Thankfully there was no sign of Penny. I couldn't face her raunchy pleasure on my behalf.

Outside the night had cooled, the breeze sweet. The shiny black Swallow pulled up in front of us. The valet climbed out and handed the keys to Vex, who slipped him a generous tip in return. My escort opened the door for me and I slid inside.

Moments later we were thundering through the streets towards Wellington. When we reached my place, he parked out front, seemingly unconcerned that someone might notice his shag-mobile.

The drive had only served to increase the tension inside me. My knees shook as I climbed the steps. When Vex pushed me against the front door and kissed me thoroughly, I thought I might literally combust on the threshold. Regardless of each of our motives, there was no denying we were honestly hungry for one another.

I managed to unlock the door. He was right on my heels as I stepped inside. No sign of Avery – good. She must be at Emma's. I jabbed at the alarm with clumsy fingers, trying to ignore the fact that Vex's own fingers were already loosening the laces of my corset. It unhooked at the front, but it seemed so much more . . . *wicked* to have him unlace me.

I ran upstairs, the wolf giving chase. My room wasn't too bad, only a pair of stockings and bloomers on the floor. He didn't seem to care, and neither did I. In minutes we were both naked and he . . . he was *so* very impressive with his clothes off. He seemed equally enamoured of me, which was arousing in itself. Nothing like seeing worship in the eyes of a lover to make a girl forget her flaws.

Vex flashed a grin in the darkness as he braced himself above me on my suddenly small bed. I reached up and ran my thumb over his bottom lip, over the smooth white of his teeth.

"All the better to eat you with," he said, and I knew he had heard Penny at the club. I didn't even have time to blush before he slid down my body and made good his word.

CHAPTER 8

IN THE COMPANY OF COURTESANS

When I woke up the next day I was alone.

I wasn't surprised. In fact, I was a little relieved. I wouldn't have to explain anything to my sibs, and I wouldn't have a gorgeous distraction keeping me from doing what needed to be done. Besides, Vex MacLaughlin was out of my sphere. My job was to protect his kind and his job was to produce more halvies, get married and hopefully beget fat, healthy aristo babies.

He hadn't asked me anything about Fee or Dede, or Bedlam. We hadn't talked much at all. Maybe it really was a coincidence that he'd come for Ophelia in the park. Maybe he really was interested in me.

Right. So interested he had to sneak out without saying goodbye.

I threw on a black velvet kimono and ran my hands through the bird's-nest tangle of my hair before leaving the sanctuary of my room. I should shower – I had the smell of sex and wolf all over me – but I was hungry and didn't mind being distracted until after breakfast.

The delicious aroma of fresh hot coffee rose to greet me as I went downstairs. With it came the equally appealing scents of French toast and fried sausage. My mouth watered and I walked into the kitchen to find Val at the stove, Avery, Emma and Vex at the table.

Fang me. He was still here?

Everyone looked up at my arrival. Val barely raised a brow, but Avery and Emma looked as though they were practically bursting for want of details, while Vex ... he gave me a look I felt right down to my bones.

He rose to his feet and came around the table to me. One strong arm went round my waist as he gave me a quick hug. "Can I get you a cup of coffee?" he asked.

I shook my head. "You don't have to do that. I can get it."

He grinned. "Consider it payment for all the embarrassment my being here will no doubt cause you," he said in a low tone. We both knew there was no point in whispering when our companions had acute hearing – and were shamelessly eavesdropping.

I slipped an arm around him. He was so big and tall, and smelled surprisingly good for a man who had yet to shower. "I'm *not* embarrassed." Perhaps that was a small lie, but I wasn't embarrassed about him, more of what my siblings might get up to.

"Good." He kissed me and gently shoved me towards the table. "I'll get you a cup."

I would rather have stayed with him, but I sucked it up like a big girl and made the walk of shame to the table. My sister looked at me with such disbelief that I couldn't help but chuckle. I sneaked a glance at Vex and caught him smiling. I suppose I could take some ribbing if it meant my brother and sister stopped thinking about Dede.

"I assume you've introduced yourselves," I commented.

"Of course," Avery retorted, expression slightly affronted. "His lordship helped me and Em carry in groceries this morning."

"After which Avery immediately rang me," Val added with a grin. "Told me to come straight away. I thought there were children – or at least puppies – in need of dire rescue."

Avery pinkened as we all laughed. "Well, it's not every day a marquess comes to call." Or the alpha of the entire UK werewolf contingent. Vex just happened to be both.

"I should hope not," Vex said with a grin, placing a mug of steaming coffee in front of me. "My pride would be deeply wounded."

I raised a brow at the same time as I raised my mug. "We wouldn't want that."

He winked at me and I grinned. This wasn't the first time I'd brought someone home, but it was certainly the most surreal. It felt . . . comfortable, and it should have been anything but.

Vex helped Val bring three large platters of food to the table. Along with the sausage and French toast there were fried tomatoes, bacon and scrambled eggs, potatoes and ham. A halvie diet needed a lot of protein in it, and this morning I found myself craving the savoury fried meats and creamy eggs. It wasn't just a craving – I *needed* it.

Half-bloods have huge appetites, but my ravenous hunger was matched by Vex's. I watched him fill his plate three times with egg-soaked fried bread and sausage, drenching both in sweet syrup. I think he drank an entire pot of coffee. And through it all he was polite and open towards my family. He asked Val about work – which I believed was genuine interest because he didn't ask about the hospital break-in at all – then enquired as to how long Avery and Emma had been together and when they had met.

"Speaking of meetings," Avery began with no attempt at subtlety as her wide gaze flitted between Vex and me. "How did you meet my sister, my lord?"

"Vex," he corrected before shooting me a warm glance. "I first noticed your sister some time ago, but hadn't the nerve to approach her until last night."

My stomach flipped over. He had to be joking, hadn't he?

"Really?" Avery echoed my doubt, and were it not for Vex I would have pinched her.

The werewolf laughed – that deep bark I'd heard the night before. It rumbled through my entire body. "Really."

There was something odd in his gaze. He seemed sincere, but there was a glimmer of regret as well. It disappeared in a flash, but I knew I hadn't imagined it. I had no idea what had caused it either. To be honest, I didn't want to think too hard about it. Why ruin a perfectly good afternoon with paranoia?

After breakfast, Emma insisted on doing the washing-up, and Vex announced that he had a meeting with the Queen later that day so had best be on his way. I walked him out.

I turned to face him, to tell him all the usual things one said when saying goodbye to someone they'd shagged, but I never got a chance to speak. Strong arms closed around me, lifting me clean off the floor so that my toes brushed against his shins. For a moment I thought he might devour me, and I was prepared to die with a smile on my face. He kissed me hard and good and hungry – and it didn't feel like goodbye. It felt more like "to be continued".

Good, because in addition to being the first man in my bed for quite some time, he was my only link to Ophelia outside of Bedlam.

"What was that for?" I asked when we came up for air.

He set me down, but didn't let me go. "Because you feel like home, and I'd rather stay with you and your family than drink bottled blood out of Queen V's china cups." A slow smile curved his lips. "I suppose that sounds like romantic drivel from an old wolf."

Throat tight, I shook my head. There was nothing old about him. "I think it's the nicest thing I've ever heard."

Vex stroked my cheek with his thumb. "I would like to see you again."

I nodded. "My schedule's open." Bereavement leave tended to have that effect.

"Dinner tomorrow night?"

I was half disappointed he didn't want to get together tonight and half exultant because tomorrow wasn't that far away. "It's a date."

"I'll ring you to make plans." He kissed me again before slipping on a pair of dark glasses that would protect his sensitive eyes from the sun. Weres didn't have the sun issues that vampires did, but they were still nocturnal creatures, weaker in the daylight.

The door clicked shut behind him. Not even ten seconds later, Avery, Val and Emma pounced on me. Who would have thought my love life would displace Dede's "death" as topic of choice? That was fine by me; at least when I answered their questions about Vex I didn't have to lie.

After the interrogation was over, I dressed and then went downstairs to the cellar, where Avery and I trained and worked out. Being stronger than humans was well and good, but as halvies we needed to keep our bodies and our skills honed. It was something I took very seriously as part of the Royal Guard, even if I was on forced leave.

Val was already there, beating the sand out of a punching bag with his bare fists.

"Doesn't the Yard provide a gymnasium for you lot?" I asked.

He stopped punching long enough to glance at me. "I've been told to stay away from work for the remainder of my bereavement leave."

"Ah." His situation was the same as mine, and he didn't like to be idle any more than I did. I suppose spending too much time in our heads was a family trait.

I held the bag steady for him, putting my own weight behind it to give him more exercise. "Val, there's something I need to talk to you about. That girl who broke into Prince Albert—"

"Ophelia Blackwood, your sister, I know."

"Well, yeah, but—"

"You saved her from a betty attack later that night. I saw the park surveillance footage. It's all right, Xandy. You're not guilty by association. It's not like you and she have been hanging out, and even if you had been, it's not as though she'd make you privy to her plans."

"No." But she had – sort of.

He swiped the back of his arm across his brow. "I know she's one of MacLaughlin's. The Yard's already spoken to him, otherwise I might be suspicious of the two of you suddenly making a connection."

"Suspicious how?" I didn't sound *too* defensive.

"You know how the vamps and weres are – neither bunch trusts the other. MacLaughlin is the only one who ever dares challenge Her Majesty. Add that to the fact that he was one of the last people seen talking to Dede before her arrest and … well, if I hadn't watched his interview myself, I'd wonder why he'd suddenly developed an interest in our family. If he had something to do with Dede's death."

I swallowed, my mouth suddenly very dry. "Albert's fangs, Val. Way to destroy a girl's ego." I sounded caustic, but inside I was twitching. He'd outgunned even my own suspicions. Was Vex a traitor too? Why hadn't he mentioned talking to Dede before she "died"?

What had I fallen into? I thought he could give me some info on Fee. Thought maybe he intended to use me for the same. I hadn't quite thought about the fact that there might be something darker behind his interest.

If I told Val what I knew, I could walk away from it all and let him take it to the Yard, but then I'd be brought in for questioning, as would Vex. Bedlam would be raided, and four people with whom I was connected would be arrested.

That wouldn't look good for me, or the rest of my family. There were more people at stake here than just me and Dede. I had to do this the right way. I had to find out just what exactly was going on.

Val frowned. "Are you all right? I'm sorry, Xandy. You must think I'm a complete git. Of course MacLaughlin is with you because he wants to be with you."

I forced a smile. "Just thinking about Dede. No worries. Enough talking. Let's spar."

Fighting with him was a fabulous focus. I had to concentrate on not getting my arse kicked, so there was no room for Dede or anything else – not even Vex.

Afterwards, sweaty and bruised, I hugged my brother and ran upstairs to shower. Things seemed so much clearer when I was clean. While I was getting dressed, my rotary rang. It was Mrs Jones, apologising for calling, but she'd had someone enquire about Dede's flat, and would it be possible for me to come round and start tidying up? She'd gladly help me if I needed it. Since I had nothing else to do, I told her I'd be by in a bit, and for her not to worry, I could take care of it.

I disconnected with a shake of my head. Mrs Jones had always been friendly, but hadn't she told me Dede had paid up until month's end? Couldn't wait to get the dead halvie's stuff out and some new tenant in. Fucking humans.

I finished dressing in trousers, black shirt and grey corset, put my hair up, slipped on my high black boots and buckled them, and then grabbed a black frock coat from the wardrobe. It was a good thing I liked black, else this mourning shit would make me feel like a bloody crow.

Dede had better appreciate me maintaining her thoughtless ruse. Why pretend to be dead? Why not be a traitor *and* openly alive? She said someone had tried to kill her, but I wasn't sure I believed that any more than I believed her child was alive. The fact remained, however, that *she* believed both things with all her heart.

Before departing my room, I took the vial of blood from the pocket of the coat I'd worn the night before. It was still whole, the glass cool against my fingers. I made a fist around it; debated whether or not to toss it in the bin.

"Plague it." I shoved the vial into my pocket. As an afterthought, I strapped on the Bulldog, using a holster that slung low on my hips and fastened round my thigh. I couldn't wear the shoulder harness because of the tight fit of my coat. I felt a bit like one of those American gunslingers with the weapon so close to my fingers.

Downstairs was empty as I strode through the foyer to the door. I grabbed the keys to the Butler and a pair of dark goggles, and walked out into the late afternoon. The summer sun was high in the sky, warm and bright.

My first stop was the Prince Albert Hospital – the same place Fee had broken into. I needed to see my friend Simon. I didn't trust my half-sister, but her advice about taking the blood to someone I trusted was sound. Simon was the only person I would trust with something like this.

"What have you got for me, gorgeous?" he asked when I walked into his domain of mass spectrometers, centrifuges and various other bits of equipment I couldn't name. It was clean and discreet and that was all I cared about.

Simon was a tall, lanky halvie from up Birmingham way. Nerdishly cute, he had floppy brown hair that fell over his forehead and pretty blue eyes over which he wore stylish spectacles.

I offered him the vial of blood. "Can you do a work-up on this for me? All the bells and whistles."

He took the vial and held it up to the light. "Anything for you, luvvie. Whose is it?"

"Mine," I replied ignoring Fee's command not to tell.

He shot me a quizzical look. "You all right, darling?"

"I'm fine. I think. I need this to be just between us, Simon. Seriously."

He looked concerned, but thankfully didn't press. "When do you need the results?"

"Soon as possible. There's a triple espresso in it for you."

"Now you're just talking dirty. I don't have much going on, I'll make it my top priority."

Relief put a grin on my face. "Thanks, Simon. I knew you'd come through."

A smile tilted one side of his mouth, but his gaze retained a glimmer of worry. "Ring you when I have the results."

I turned to go, then stopped. "What do you know about the records theft the other night?"

He shrugged. "Nothing. No one here is saying much about it. Were your records amongst the ones stolen too?"

I nodded. "Yours?"

"You know it, though not like mine have anything good in them. I reckon they were after one halvie in particular. Maybe two. It throws suspicion if they take a bunch of other random ones."

His words sent a shiver of unease down my spine. And I'd given Vex a hard time about his ego. Mine wasn't much weaker. Why did I instantly assume that my records were the ones they were after?

Because Fee had waved that file in my face like a red scarf in front of a bull.

"You watch too many procedurals, Simon."

He laughed. "Got to have some excitement in my life. Call you in a few days, love."

I thanked him and told him he was my favourite labby, and then left the building. I was a little nervous about the outcome, though I was fairly certain there was nothing special about my blood. Still, if Ophelia was to be believed, someone had mucked about with my medical records, and I wanted to know why. Was I one of the experiments Dede had gone on about? Or maybe, Ophelia just wanted to have something to hold over my head so I wouldn't go outing their little rebellion to the authorities.

There was no point in getting all mental about it until I had the results. My grip on sanity felt tenuous at best, so why step on my own fingers?

I made the trip to Whitechapel in record time. The flat was just as it had been during my last visit. Mrs Jones had left boxes outside the door for me, along with a large roll of tape. She was in quite a hurry indeed.

I tossed my coat on the sofa and put two of the boxes together. One was for things I'd take with me. The other was for donations. If Dede wanted any of it back, she could drag her arse to the charity shop. I certainly wasn't risking my own neck to take it to her. I was in too deep as it was.

Why couldn't I have just believed she was dead?

I went through her ACs and VCs. A lot of them I already owned, but I took some anyway and some of the extras for Avery and Val.

Someone was going to have to come and collect her furniture. Was betraying your country worth leaving your life and family behind? Obviously it was, because Dede had done just that.

I had tried to wrap my head around it long enough. No more. Instead I popped a cylinder into the player and turned the volume up. I was so taking her audio system home with me.

It was because of the high volume of the music and my subsequent singing along that I didn't hear footsteps approach the door. In fact, I didn't know I had company until the door of the apartment swung open. I whipped the Bulldog out of its holster and levelled it at the intruder.

Churchill froze on the threshold, watching me as warily as if I was a wild animal.

"I hope you're not planning on using that thing," he joked.

Safety on, I slipped the handgun back into place, snug against my hip and upper thigh. Then, as I turned the volume down, "Apologies, sir. Reckon I'm a little on edge."

He nodded and stepped inside. "I should have announced myself. Obviously it would be difficult to hear me over the music." And my caterwauling along with it. But if Church hadn't wanted me to hear him, it wouldn't have mattered if I'd been sitting here in stone silence, I don't think I would have known he was there.

When I didn't say anything, he remarked, "You sounded rather chipper."

That came across as vaguely censorious. Or maybe I was just paranoid. After Bedlam and Val's remarks about Vex, the ground was a little unsteady under my usually sure feet. I put a photograph of me, Dede, Avery and Val in the box of stuff to take home. "I considered wailing and gnashing my teeth, but it's not a good look for me."

He chuckled, and I relaxed a little. "Rumour has it that you were quite chummy with the MacLaughlin at Freak Show last evening."

I paused over the box. "If rumour has it then it must be so." I forced a smile to soften the words, but I had no intention of discussing my personal life with Church. What I did want to discuss was the things I'd discovered at Bedlam, but that wasn't going to happen.

And why wasn't it? This was my chance to tell him everything and wash my hands of it. Keeping quiet would only make things worse. Yet here I was, keeping my own counsel. Church would not excuse Dede for being part of the group who had killed his friends and family during the Great Insurrection. He wouldn't forgive me for keeping it from him either.

I opened my mouth to speak . . .

"Grief can lead to poor choices, Alexandra. I do hope you will be careful in your dealings with the marquess." A deep furrow cleaved the flesh between his brows. "I hate to think of what he'd do to an impressionable girl like you."

Dealings? Impressionable? "I didn't ask him to do my taxes, Church. We had some drinks and danced, that's all."

His gaze locked with mine and I noticed his jaw was tight. "You left with him."

It was on the tip of my tongue to tell him just how little I liked this condescending attitude when a particular flicker in his eyes stopped me; made my stomach clench.

Was Church jealous? Fang me.

"I did," I replied, placing another photo in the box. "And that's really none of your business, sir." I tried to keep my tone even, but I was starting to feel like the whole world was going barking mad. Thoughts of confiding in him disappeared as my defences came up.

Church looked as though I'd slapped him. "You're right. It isn't any of my business with whom you spend your free time. I thought our years of friendship gave me the right to speak freely with you. I see now that was an error, my apologies."

I sighed and reached for another photo. "Martyrdom doesn't

suit you, old man. I appreciate your concern, but there's no need for it. You don't like the marquess and I respect that, but I do, so you need to respect that in return."

He opened his mouth as though to argue with me, but closed it just as quickly. "Fine."

The word must have left a poor taste in his mouth, given his pinched expression. I smiled, for a moment forgetting all my questions and suspicions. "What brings you to this part of town, Church?"

He looked about the flat. "I got your message. It sounded important. I thought we could chat face to face, and I could help you put Dede's affairs in order."

I hesitated, a statue of Danger Mouse in my hand. Right. I had called him. Didn't seem like such a smart move with hindsight. "That's not your responsibility. Not like she was with the Academy or RG."

"No, but she was Peerage Protectorate, and I'm on the board. Plus, as a friend of the family, I'm here to do all I can for you in your time of need."

Twenty-four hours ago I would have believed him without question, but paranoia made me suspicious – and Church had trained me to be that way. Did he suspect Dede had faked her death? I had told him my own theory; had he followed up and discovered the truth about Bedlam?

No. If Church had found out about Bedlam, it would have been raided by now.

Unless he knew I'd been there and he was trying to protect me. *Fuck.*

"That's very good of you, sir." I was a better actress than I thought – not a hint of falsehood in my tone. "Thank you for your concern, but I have the situation in hand. I'm sorry for the dramatic message. I was feeling . . . out of sorts."

He picked up a bobble-head doll that sat on a shelf by the door and studied it. "Dear Alexandra. You wouldn't ask for help even if you needed it, would you, you stubborn, stoic girl?"

My brow twitched but didn't arch, thank God. Stubborn maybe, but stoic? Did he know me at all? "No," I admitted. "Probably not. Can I get you anything? I think there's tea in the cupboard."

He held up a broad hand. "Please, do not trouble yourself. I'm off to the Devonshires' later this evening and have several pressing things to take care of before then."

I stared at his hand. No doubt that lack of fine bones made him stand out amongst his own kind even more. Did he blame his mother for it, as I blamed mine for my moments of madness?

I reckon I couldn't blame her any more. Seeing as how she wasn't really mad, it was a useless exercise. All nuttiness was completely my own.

"I'll probably spend most of the night here," I volunteered. "Not like I have anything else to do."

He lifted his chin as he pinned me with a frankly questioning gaze. "You would rather be at work than spend this difficult time with your family?"

"I would rather be at work than alone with my own thoughts, sir." That was true – and more of a confession than I should have given. Then I added, "Grief and idle hands do not mix."

I thought Church might take his leave now, but he didn't. Instead, he came closer, leaning one elbow on the box of things I'd planned to take with me. "You went to Bedlam last night. Might I ask if that had anything to do with why you rang?"

He did suspect something. "I wanted to have my own private memorial to my sister. And afterwards I suppose I felt rather sorry for myself." I busied my hands with putting more items in the boxes, so that I didn't adopt a defensive posture. Wait a moment ... "Might *I* ask how you knew where I was, sir?" And how had he known where to find me now?

I felt him watching me as I worked. "When Avery told me you hadn't returned home with her, I checked your locator chip. I was concerned for you."

Concerned for me maybe. But he'd definitely been concerned as to what I'd been up to. I made a mental note to dig out my old displacer. We'd used them when we used to sneak out to go clubbing. Basically they fooled the transmitters beneath our skin into thinking they were somewhere else, so if a parent or Academy employee tried to check up on us they'd think we were somewhere much more suitable than the truth.

I hadn't used my displacer since joining the RG because I thought the tracker a good idea given the danger of the job, but now it seemed more like an invasion of privacy than a safety precaution. "You could have rung me instead of spying on me."

Church smiled slightly. It was an expression I'd always thought of as calming; now it struck me as falsely placating. Damn Dede for making me question him! "Don't be like that, Alexandra. I don't mean to pry."

That both mollified and chastised me. "Beg pardon, sir. I'm not myself at present."

He straightened and patted my hand with his own much larger one. "No offence taken, my dear. If you do not require assistance I will leave you to your unfortunate task. You will let someone come by and take away what you do not keep, won't you? You won't try to do everything yourself?"

It was a kind sentiment, and I tried to see it as just that. I nodded. "I will, promise."

"Take care, my dear girl." Then he cupped the back of my head with his palm and kissed me on the forehead. My throat tightened, my eyes burned. It was all I could do at that moment not to fall down at his feet and admit everything, beg his forgiveness and his help.

But I held my tongue and knees firmly in place, and didn't even dare to breathe until he was gone, door closed behind him. Then, my shoulders sagged and I drew a deep breath into my lungs.

I was hungry.

All the boxes Mrs Jones had left were filled and taped up in the middle of the living-room floor. I'd packed almost all of the cylinders and knick-knacks from the open area. I'd need more boxes for the bedroom, loo and kitchen. I'd have to rent a van to take everything I wanted to keep.

I grabbed a packet of crisps from the cupboard and ate those before climbing on to the Butler. There was an Indian restaurant I liked near Drury Lane, and since I didn't feel like going home, I went there instead. As soon as I sat down I realised that I was the only person at a table alone. Everyone else was there with someone, or a table full of someones.

I ordered food, and when it came I ploughed through the basmati, naan and rich butter chicken in record time. I followed it up with a sinfully delicious dessert and left the restaurant sated.

I went next to St James's, to a gorgeous sprawling building of pale stone and tall columns. It looked like a palace, but was actually the most prestigious brothel in the Kingdom – Courtesan House. I had spent much of my early life there, and had visited often through the years afterwards, but as I stood outside the gate, I hesitated to push the button that would alert staff to my presence.

What did I hope to accomplish with this visit? Was I looking for truth, absolution or something else? How many times did I have to pick this scab before I could be satisfied with the scar? Nothing I might find in this house would make the last few days any better or make any more sense. I should just turn on my heel and go home. Later, if Avery and Emma were around, I'd order pizza and we'd share a bottle of wine.

I pressed the button.

There followed a crackle of static before I was asked to identify myself. I'd no sooner said my name then the gates began to open with a clink and the whisper of well-oiled hinges.

Finely crushed gravel crunched beneath the thick soles of my boots as I walked up the drive. As children, those of us who lived here would run down to the gate and stare out at the world beyond. Sometimes there would be human children there, mocking us because we could only gaze out at their wonderful world. Occasionally we were taken out on trips, but halvie children were vulnerable and there were humans who were not above killing what they perceived as a monster, even if it was a child. Our world was this place until we were old enough to go to the Academy, and then that became our world until we'd proved we could defend ourselves. What happened after that depended on aptitude and choice.

Returning here was like coming home again, and a combination of dread and elation unfurled in my stomach. I'd been back but a handful of times after my mother was taken away, and the anxiety of that memory clung to this place like the stench of a rotten tooth.

It was a long walk up the curving drive that cut through the pristine lawn with obsessive precision. Beautifully manicured trees were placed in exactly the right places so as to be aesthetically pleasing without seeming completely pretentious. An air of respectability clung to the place even though it was essentially a whorehouse – a very pricey one that was run by the Crown and open to aristocrats only, but a whorehouse nevertheless.

Some of the human children used to like to remind us of that, call our mothers vile names and talk like we were dirty and inferior to them because our mothers had been paid to have us – as though that made their love less real. Naïve as we were, we didn't understand how they could possibly hate us for having an entire house of maternal love and attention. I was a teenager before I realised that humans simply hated us; the circumstances surrounding our births was just a convenient excuse.

There was a black wreath on the door, its ribbons whispering in the slight breeze. The noise of the city was a muted hum, easily ignored. I was captivated by those ribbons and the lilies woven into the wreath with them. I'd never thought; the entire house was in mourning – for Dede. This was the worst time for me to show up asking questions.

I turned on my heel, prepared to sprint back the way I'd come, but the door opened and I was stopped by a familiar voice.

"I do hope you weren't planning to leave without saying hello."

Wiping the grimace from my face, I turned. I didn't have to force a smile; it came readily. "Is this a bad time, Sayuri?"

Val's mother was matron of Courtesan House. She was incredibly tiny, with smooth skin and the barest of lines around her dark eyes. She wore her thick black hair up in the Gibson style, little tendrils hanging around her fair cheeks. She looked like a Japanese doll, in a long white gown with black flowers embroidered along the hem and cuffs of its full sleeves. Her hands were clasped at her cinched waist.

Her head tilted ever so slightly over her left shoulder. "It is never a bad time to see you, child. Come inside."

She didn't have to tell me twice. I could knock her halfway to Whitby but I would never dream of defying or arguing with her.

That I loved her was a testament to just what kind of woman she was. She was human, pure and true, and I loved her regardless. I loved all the women of this house who had cared for me when I was a child, and even now as an adult. In my mind they transcended their species, as though courtesan was its own classification. I supposed it was – in a way. Not every human had the right mutated genes to birth a half-blood child.

I jogged up the shallow steps and right into her open arms. I felt big and clumsy as I folded myself around her, but there was steel in her spine – more so than I feared there was in mine. It was easy to see why my father had chosen her to carry his firstborn, and her beauty was only part of it.

"How is Lecia?" I asked as we crossed the threshold, Sayuri's arm around my waist.

The little woman shook her head, a firm set to her mouth. "A mother's grief settles into the soul, tearing it into little pieces so that she will never be the same again."

This was the Sayuri I had always known. One moment she could be sharply succinct and the next almost poetic in her verbosity. My own mouth remained silent. I was so angry at Dede in that moment for putting her own mother through this. She would argue that her mother would rather she was dead than a traitor, but I'd bet my fangs that Lecia would prefer to know that her daughter hadn't killed herself, that she was alive.

We walked into the matron's office. Sayuri closed the door behind us and gestured to the plush sofa. "Sit."

I did as I was told. She rang for tea, and a few moments later I had a hot cup of Darjeeling and several sugar biscuits – the fat, soft kind that had so much flavour they made your mouth sigh with every bite.

"You didn't come just to check on Lecia or say hello to an old friend, did you, Xandra?"

I dunked a piece of biscuit in my tea. "You were here when they took my mother away, weren't you, Sayuri?"

She went still – even for her. It was only a moment, but I noticed it. "Yes."

This was the first time either of us had spoken of it to each other. She had to know I'd come asking questions one day.

"Was it because she was hatters or to get rid of her?"

Sayuri shifted in her chair. This was the most discomposed I'd ever seen her. "I don't believe I am the one you should discuss this with, Xandra."

"If not you, then who? Not like I can ask my mother." Of course that was a lie, but she couldn't know that.

Sympathy flashed in her eyes, but I refused to feel guilty about it. I didn't know if I could trust my mother or my father to tell me the truth, but Sayuri loved me, had cared for me. She was the one person I knew who was incapable of lying.

"Juliet was unwell," she said slowly. "Leaving the house was in her best interests. It was in the best interests of everyone who lived here."

I shook my head. "I don't remember her being mad."

Her dark gaze locked with mine. "I never said she was mad."

Right, she was "unwell". I didn't push it, because I saw something in her eyes that stopped me: fear. She was afraid to tell me.

"What is it, Saysay?" I had the big guns out now, using the name I'd called her as a child.

She shook her head. "I made your mother a promise that I would never, ever tell you what happened. I have no intention of breaking that, whether you can speak to her or not. You'll have to talk to your father if you want the truth."

But would he tell me the truth? Would my mother?

"I just don't understand the big mystery," I confided. "All I want to know is why she was taken to Bedlam."

The matron tilted her head as she set her cup on its saucer. "It's been twelve years. Why now?"

Yes, smartarse, why now? I couldn't tell her it was because dear Mama and I had been reunited. "Dede's death has made me nostalgic, I suppose."

More guilt stung at the softening of her features. "You poor girl. Yes, of course it makes sense. How insensitive of me."

"You're the least insensitive person I know," I admitted, in one of the rare honest moments I'd had since I arrived. "I don't want you to break your promise, no matter how much I want to know the truth. Just ..." I sighed, tears suddenly burning the back of my eyes. "Just tell me it wasn't because of me."

I hadn't realised just how afraid I was, how terrified the recent barrage of cryptic comments and bizarre revelations had made me – terrified that somehow I was to blame for everything awful that had happened to the people I loved. It was foolish – and the height of narcissism – but I had to own up to it if I ever wanted to get my head out of my arse.

Sayuri rose from her chair and came to me, sitting down on the sofa next to me and wrapping her slender arms around my shoulders. I sagged into the hug, embarrassing myself by actually letting the tears flow. But if I couldn't cry in these arms, I couldn't cry anywhere. The scent of flowers and spices enveloped me, a familiar aroma that made me think of safety and security.

"Sweet girl," she murmured against my hair. "Of course it had nothing to do with you. She loved you. She still loves you. You are not to blame."

I accepted that, because I needed to believe it, and it was the closest thing to the truth I was going to get.

The next afternoon, Vex kept his promise to call and asked if I wanted to meet him at Freak Show that evening for a drink and then dinner. Of course I said yes, and immediately went to my wardrobe to find what I could wear for our date.

After selecting an outfit, I tried to keep busy for the rest of the day, but after working out, I didn't have much to occupy my time except for my thoughts – which by now I'd established to be an exercise in self-pity.

I didn't want to think about Dede any more. I didn't want to think about my mother or how my life had gone arse over tits. If I had someone to spend time with – go shopping or have coffee – I wouldn't be stuck here with nothing but my own mind to amuse me.

I didn't have any friends, not really. Until now I'd never thought I needed any, but it would be nice to have someone I could meet for drinks or maybe go clubbing with. I used to do that kind of thing with Avery and Dede, but now Avery was practically married and Dede was a traitor.

And I still had my head up my arse.

So I returned to Dede's to pack up the remainder of her things. The apartment was neat, but one of the boxes I'd packed before wasn't where I had left it. Someone had been in here, poking about. Some of Dede's Bedlam friends? It was reason to be alarmed, but I couldn't manage much more than annoyance. I did not need this added shit. It was Dede's problem, not mine. Cold but true.

I spent a handful of hours packing, then called a removals company and made arrangements for them to come in and take the boxes and the furniture away to storage. I'd figure out what to do with it all later.

It was time for me to go. I only had a couple of hours to get home, change, take my supps – which I'd forgotten *again* – and leave to meet Vex. I left the apartment and locked the door behind me.

In the corridor a scent assaulted me like a faceful of warm chocolate. The roof of my mouth tingled and saliva rushed over my tongue. What was that incredible smell? It was rich and earthy, with a faint salty copper tang.

Blood. It was blood. The realisation crashed over me like a wave, bringing shame and horror with it. What was wrong with me? I never used to crave blood like that – never wanted it so badly. Now twice in a matter of days I'd been overwhelmed by the need to bite and drink. It had to be stress – that was the only explanation I could think of. I pressed my forehead to the cool whitewashed wall and waited for the craving to pass, gums aching as I fought to keep my fangs from extending.

A man came up the stairs, gave me an odd look and then continued on to his own flat. It was him that I had smelled. Him that I had wanted to take a bite out of. He was fortunate that I was disgusted not only by my own desire, but by him as well, else I might have tackled him to the floor.

My knees were trembling as I made my way down to the first floor. I fished a packet of crisps out of my pocket and stuffed them into my mouth by the handful. That would take the edge off until I got home. I'd get some real food and take my supplements. I'd been too lax about taking them lately.

Once home, I took my supps, grabbed two slices of cold pizza from the fridge and devoured them while I ran a bath scented with vanilla oil. I was much more myself once I slipped into the hot, sudsy water.

Afterwards I dried off, rubbed cream into my skin, put on some make-up and pulled on snug violet trousers, white tank and black velvet corset. High-heeled black boots gave me extra height and I topped it all off with a velvet choker and leather frock coat. My hair was coiled into two artfully messy buns on either side of my head.

Oddly enough, I was a little early as I approached the entrance to the club. Just as I walked past an alleyway someone grabbed me. A very strong someone. I reached for my dagger but they pulled my arm behind my back and slammed me face first into the side of the nearest wall. The brick scraped my cheek as I struggled.

"Why did you do it?" a voice hissed in my ear.

Ophelia? "Do what?"

She wrenched my arm higher. I ground my teeth, swallowing the grunt that desperately wanted to crawl out from between my lips. "You know what you did."

"Honestly, sis," I growled against the brick. "I don't have the slightest idea of what the fuck you're talking about." But she was seriously pissing me off.

The pressure on my arm eased a little bit and I took advantage of her hesitation. I pushed against the wall with my free hand, shoved myself backwards and cracked the crown of my head into her face. She released my arm and I whirled around with a round-house to her chest, knocking her to the other wall.

Ophelia touched the back of her hand to her lip – it was bleeding. When she looked at me her eyes glowed yellow in the dim light. The wolf in her had come out to play. Shit. The predator in me responded by unsheathing my fangs, extending them from my itching gums. That bloodlust I'd felt earlier came rushing back. At least this time I understood why I felt it.

We dived for one another, colliding like snarling cats. Fists and feet flew – some connected and some didn't, but each of us was in it to win, possibly to kill. And I had no idea why.

She hit me hard in the face, and I retaliated with a kick intended to get her in the stomach but caught her in the thigh instead as she managed to move out of the way. She smashed me in the skull with a brick. I staggered back, world spinning as my head rang like Big fucking Ben. Ophelia grabbed me by the throat and squeezed. Blackness threatened to take me down.

"Why did you do it?" she demanded. "He'd done nothing to you. Nothing."

"Didn't . . . do . . ." That was all I managed to say before I was robbed of oxygen and started gasping for breath.

Something took hold of me then and reared up in the darkness flooding my mind. I loosened her grip and sucked air into my starving lungs as I lunged forward, slamming against the side of the building. My fangs scraped the warm skin of her neck before I managed to regain control. I threw myself backwards, shoulders smashing against the opposite wall of the alley.

Panting, fighting for calm, I leaned against the wall to keep from falling to my knees, and looked up at Ophelia, who slid down the wall to sit at the bottom of it, elbows on her knees, forehead against her fists. She didn't seem to notice that I'd almost ripped her throat out. I'm not sure she even realised how close I'd come to seriously hurting her.

Against my better judgement, I went and sat down next to her on the cold dirt and stone. I touched my head where she'd hit me. Thankfully it wasn't bleeding. "What happened?"

She lifted her head and looked at me with real anguish in her eyes and a stony tightness to her jaw. "Raj." Her voice was rough and raw.

"Your human?" I didn't know how else to phrase it.

She nodded. "He went out earlier today and didn't come back. When I rang him, he didn't answer. Finally I went looking for him."

I didn't like the direction this conversation seemed to be headed. "You found him?"

She nodded and ran her hands over her hair. "Yeah. I found him." She sniffed and turned her head towards me, hand cupping the back of her neck. "He's dead."

CHAPTER 9

I AM NOT AN ANIMAL

"You think *I* killed him?" The woman had bollocks the size of Big Ben.

"No," she replied, but my relief quickly expired, "I thought you'd turned him in so someone else could kill him."

My jaw dropped. Never mind that I would have thought her capable of being just as vengeful.

"Because I'm just a vindictive bitch, or because I'm so misguided in my perception of the world?"

She thought about it. "Both."

If she hadn't been so obviously pained by the loss of her lover, I might have thought she was trying to be funny. "Where did you find him?"

Ophelia laughed – that bleak, hoarse bark of grief. "Traitor Lane. They carved 'Insurgent Meat' on his face." Traitor Lane was where they'd marched the captured insurrectionists to the gallows. "Well, I'm certainly delighted that you thought I'd put someone else to the task rather than do it myself." I stopped there, biting my tongue to keep from saying more – words that would be tactless and cruel given the situation.

My sarcasm barely registered with her. "It seemed rather convenient, given your recent appearance at Bedlam."

I shot her a wry glance. "Right. Because I'd turn in a human rather than you."

"Fair enough." She wrapped her arms around her bent knees. "Dede said you don't like humans. I thought you'd done it to punish me."

"Most halvies don't like humans," I retorted, leaning back against the wall. "Ophelia, if I wanted to punish you, I'd punish you. They would have raided Bedlam if I'd given you up."

She seemed to consider that. "Why haven't you reported us?"

"I have no idea," I replied, as honestly as I felt able. Dede's remark that I'd be suspected of being a traitor as well was of little consequence. "I suppose there's been just enough bizarre shit going on that I'm not one hundred per cent certain which way is up."

"I felt that way at first too. Then Mum showed me the truth."

"How long have you been with her?" Why was I doing this to myself? Did it really matter?

"Little more than a year."

"That's it?"

"That's it. Until then I thought she was lost to me, same as you."

Same as me. Was she trying to butter me up? "So what? She found you, fed you her vague history of Bedlam's secret citizens, and you signed up?"

She shot me a droll look. She looked just like our mother but with blue hair. "By the time she rescued me from the facility the aristos kept me in I didn't really need much convincing. Even before that I wasn't partial to vamps. In Scotland we have quite a different view of Buckingham Palace than you Londoners do. Victoria tends to treat the pack like we're dumb hounds begging for scraps."

Did it make me a small person that I envied her for feeling like she was part of the pack? Every were in the UK was accepted into the pack, including were halvies. As a vamp halvie I was well treated, but I was well aware I wasn't one of "them" as far as the aristocracy was concerned.

Maybe that was why I'd been so attracted to Vex – he didn't treat me as though I was below him.

"What about Vex?" I asked, feeling suddenly – oddly – protective of him.

She regarded me warily. "Vex is it? What of him?"

I ignored her dig, and cursed myself for using his Christian name. "You swore fealty to him."

"To him and the pack, yes. And I meant it."

I wanted to ask how much he knew about her treasonous activities, then decided better of it. I didn't want to find out, coward that I was. "You don't think being part of a traitorous group might be seen as a betrayal of that oath?"

"I've never betrayed my alpha, and I never will. The monarchy, however, betrayed us a long time ago." She held up her tattooed arm. "I have the number to prove it."

I frowned. The brick at my back caught at my coat – little annoying snags. "What did they do to you?"

Ophelia shook her head. "Nothing I feel like sharing with you. I wouldn't want it to come back and haunt me later. And don't pretend you're above doing just that. You and I aren't that different."

I shrugged, and winced when my coat rasped against the wall. It better not be ruined. I loved this coat. "What would happen to those poor halvies in the underground cells if Bedlam was raided?"

"I don't know. Maybe they'd let them stay. Maybe they'd

lobotomise them. Or maybe they'd be tried for treason as well, hard to say. Regardless, they've already suffered enough."

That was at least one point on which she and I agreed. "Dede's already hurt enough people with her *death*. This kind of scandal could destroy my family."

"Destroy the Duke of Vardan, you mean."

"And his children – my brother and sister."

"Ever stop to consider that maybe your father deserves a little hurt?"

I bristled. "Ever considered my boot in your face?"

A mocking gleam lit her eyes. She didn't look all that broken up for someone who had just lost a lover. When Rye died, I was a mess. I cried for three days before anger took hold. Either my maternal sister went straight for rage, or she was an unemotional bitch.

I knew which one of those had my wager.

"Your family's your biggest weakness," she informed me – as though she had some great insight into my inner workings. "Someone's going to use it against you one day."

I smiled – an ironic twist of my lips. "Someone already did. Dede knew I'd find her. Hell, she might as well have left a trail of breadcrumbs for me to follow."

Speaking of which . . . "How'd you find me?" I asked.

"Your tracking signal," she replied. "The RG isn't the only bunch to find those things useful."

That was it. I was finding my fucking displacer and I was going to do it quick. I didn't want the Bedlamites following me any more than I wanted Church watching my every move.

"So . . ." She looked me in the eye. "Can we trust you?"

"I haven't decided yet." That was as honest as I could be.

My sister didn't look at all surprised – or worried. "You could always join us."

I laughed bitterly as I shook my head. "Not going to happen."

"It will," she insisted, so certain of it I wanted to slap her – or ask what she knew that I didn't. "There's too much honour in you for it not to."

Right, because she knew so much about fucking honour. "Five minutes ago you thought I was a murderer."

She shrugged. "You still could be for all I know." Her eyes were hard. "Honour's relative."

"Right." I slapped my hands against my thighs. She was mad as a sack of cats. "Well, I have somewhere I need to be. I'm sorry for your loss. Don't come near me again."

I jumped to my feet and started for the mouth of the alley.

Suddenly she was there in front of me, blocking my way. "Xandra, wait. Look, I'm . . . thank you."

That was as close to an apology as I was going to get, and I was glad of it. If she went all emotional on me I'd probably go mental. As it was, my response came in the form of a terse nod.

She ran a hand over the back of her neck. "You want to grab a pint or something?"

She might have asked me if I wanted to go to the moon I was so bloody gobsmacked. "No." It came out wrapped in a laugh of disbelief. I wanted to add, "You fucking nutter."

Maybe I was naïve – or conceited – but she appeared genuinely disappointed by my rejection. Guilt nudged me right below my breastbone but I ignored it. I didn't know her, didn't like her and couldn't afford the association, even if she was family.

"I am sorry about your boyfriend," I said – lamely – and slipped past her out of the alley.

I hoofed it to Freak Show, brushing the dirt from my coat as I walked. Fortunately the scuffle with Ophelia, and that damned brick wall, hadn't mussed me up too badly. I didn't want to have to explain my appearance to Vex.

There was a longer queue in front of the club tonight than there had been last time. It was fairly early in the evening for such a crowd. The sounds of live music thumping from inside explained why.

"Hey, there's a queue!" a voice protested as I walked to the front. The halvie at the door wore a bright yellow corset that matched her hair and warmed her caramel-coloured skin. Short bloomers showed off mile-long legs with garters. A gauzy bustle cradled her hips to fall almost to the ground. She towered over me in five-inch heels.

She sneered at me, full lips parting to reveal a hint of fang. "I don't have to let you in, you know. Just because you've got that badge don't mean you're privileged." Her accent was cockney – a very human way of speaking. Most halvies born to official courtesans were raised in a fairly posh, if not physically challenging environment. This one hadn't the skills to be Protectorate, Yard or RG, so she spent her nights tossing rowdies out on their ears.

And now, for whatever reason, I was going to get some of the blame for that.

"Actually," I replied, about to rub a little salt in, "it does make me special – top five per cent of my class and all that, which you already know. I'm not asking you to cater to my whim, or even play nice, but I'm meeting the MacLaughlin in ten minutes, and I don't think you want to be the reason I give him for being late."

She either wanted to puke or to job me – I wasn't certain which. Regardless, she moved aside so I could cross the threshold. I forced a smile and a sweet word of thanks.

"What is it about you that antagonises everyone you meet?"

I froze. People milled around me in the swathes of light that punctuated the dark. Slowly, I turned.

"Did you follow me?" I demanded.

Ophelia shrugged. "This was the closest place to get a drink."

My ego didn't quite believe her. "Right. Enjoy, then." I turned to make my way through the club.

The crowd was mostly halvie and human – not an aristo in sight. Having to deal with a gathering of humans set my teeth on edge, despite the club's no-violence policy.

I went to the bar rather than the tables, as that would give me the best view of the door when Vex arrived – and the best view of the club if a human or six decided to get rowdy. The ebony wood gleamed with polish and had several high stools along the length of it.

I hopped up on to one of the stools, which resembled a taller version of an eighteenth-century chair. The bar was designed to be an elegant mishmash of eras, but the upholstery's various designs complemented each other in a way that made the whole thing work.

The skeleton of Joseph Merrick stood in a glass case against the wall beside me, adding a little cover from possible attack. There had been great debate over the Elephant Man in his time. A small band of aristos had wanted to make the attempt to turn him, to see if the blood would cure him, but a human doctor stepped in and convinced Merrick to refuse. Said it would be a degradation.

Staring at the twisted, distorted remains, I thought of what Ophelia had said when I was at Bedlam – that even amongst freaks I was freakish.

"What'll ye have?" the Irish barman – human – asked.

I ordered a hard cider and tossed a handful of pound notes on the bar when he thrust the frosty bottle towards me. I turned to find Ophelia there – again.

"To family," she said, clinking her tankard against my bottle. Something in her tone gave me pause.

"Are you taking the piss?" I asked.

Another of those bollocks shrugs of hers. Fang me, I wished I could get drunk.

My rotary chirped that I had a digigram. I pulled the device from my pocket and checked the screen. The message was from Vex, informing me that he'd be a few minutes late. Brilliant. I was stuck with Ophelia for a little while longer.

"Are you trying to make trouble for me?" I asked. "Or are you just doing a rotten job of spying on me?"

She choked. I whacked her on the back – hard. She pitched forward, coughing, and shot me a glare. "I think you just broke a rib."

I scowled at her. "You must also think I'm mentally deficient if you believe for one sweet minute that I'm buying any of this family shit."

The band finished their set, and for a moment a heavy silence descended over the place as the two of us regarded each other with equal amounts of animosity. Then twin sisters Maisie and Grace took the spotlight to juggle, dance with and swallow fire. Maybe Fee and I should get up there and throw knives at one another.

Penny sidled up to me as Ophelia continued to brood. Had I truly injured her? More guilt added to the pile. Why didn't she just sod off and leave me alone?

"Dearest, you look scrumptious as always," Penny told me, tossing back glossy red ringlets. It was a different wig every night for Penny. "A little dusty, though. You here for that gorge alpha again? I heard you two left together the other night."

Out of the corner of my eye I saw Ophelia turn her head ever so slightly, listening to Penny's bright rambling. I closed my eyes – not because I was embarrassed, but because my private life wasn't any of my sister's business.

"I'm meeting him in a sec," I admitted.

Penny squealed. "I'm taking you out to lunch so you can tell Sister Penny all about it!"

I smiled and told her to ring me, and then she flitted away like the glorious butterfly she was.

"Come with me," Ophelia said over the music that accompanied the fire-dancing siblings – an industrial number with harpsichord added in. "There's something I want you to see."

I should decline, but I had to admit I was curious. After this surreal experience, how could I not be? Besides, I had some hope that maybe whatever she wanted to show me might shed light on this whole fucked-up situation. "All right, but make it quick." And discreet.

She arched a brow. "I won't make you late for the alpha, don't worry."

"I won't," I retorted, holding her gaze. What I did with Vex and vice versa was none of her business.

Her lips curved into a mocking smile that I'd dearly have loved to chew off her face. "Let's go."

I drained the remainder of my cider and slipped off the stool to follow after her like a good little puppy.

She led me out of a side door and up a flight of red-carpeted stairs to where the balconies and other rooms were. We continued down the hall almost to the very end, stopping in front of a door with a small red heart painted on it. The heart looked as though it was bleeding.

How appropriate that she'd brought me to a room for bleeding hearts, given the trouble I was courting for not reporting her and everyone else I loved who had turned their back on their queen and country. As a member of the Royal Guard I was sworn to protect the Crown, yet here I was in the company of someone who would see the monarchy destroyed.

If I was found out, not even my father could save me from execution, or at least a lengthy prison sentence in New South Wales. In this situation, the juice – as Dede was once fond of saying – was not worth the squeeze.

Yet I did not turn away. Part of me was forced to admit that I wanted to see where this led, because I might be loyal but I wasn't stupid. As wrong as I thought Dede and her Bedlam crew were, I had seen just enough lately to make me wonder if perhaps there wasn't something terrible going on. I wasn't prepared to blame the entire aristocracy for it, or even all vampires, but if halvies were being experimented on, I needed to stop it.

Ophelia turned the knob and pushed the door open. "After you."

I hesitated on the threshold. The room was dark save for a soft glow coming from one wall. I took a step, and once I saw that Ophelia was with me, I moved deeper into the room, turning to face the dim light.

What I saw snatched the breath from my lungs. It wasn't a light at all, but a two-way mirror looking into the adjacent room. We were alone on this side, but on the other there were at least half a dozen vampires, and they were feeding on half-bloods.

More than just feeding, actually – given the state of undress and, uh, *arousal.*

"They have to be humans with dyed hair," I whispered hoarsely. I'd always been told that aristos didn't feed on halvies because it was so close to cannibalism. A little bite during sex was all right, but to feed was taboo. This was more than little love bites. Blood ran down the chest of one of the halvie women. I recognised her as the hoity bitch who'd given me a hard time at the door.

"They're not," Ophelia replied, shattering my frail hope. "It's a regular occurrence here. Halvies sell themselves as blood whores. I hear our blood is like an aphrodisiac to aristos."

I swallowed – hard. That would explain all the writhing going on in there – and why I was able to spy on it from in here. It was a frigging voyeur room, just like they had at some of the fancy brothels around the city.

My opinion of Freak Show dropped a little for it having such a set-up. Apparently it wasn't enough just to showcase freakiness; they also dealt in it. I made a note to ask Penny about missing employees and patrons when I got her alone.

"Still think they're the good guys?" Ophelia asked, close enough that her breath skimmed the ridge of my ear.

I shuddered. "Drinking halvie blood might be wrong, but there's no law against it unless the donor's unwilling. I don't see any of these putting up much of a fight. It's kinky and skanky, but that doesn't make those aristos evil."

"But it does make them liars." She folded her arms over her chest. "Makes you wonder what other lies they've told, doesn't it?"

Slowly, I turned to face her. Her faulty logic didn't warrant such a smug expression. "You brought me here to . . . *this* just to prove a point?"

Her legs were braced in a defensive manner. "Pretty much, yeah. You're so fucking blind to them. You probably think Vex is in love with you or something."

"Don't you judge me, *human*-fucker. A human who was just murdered, might I remind you, and *this* is what you decide to do with your evening?" I pointed at the mirror. "And do you have a problem with your alpha? Because I'm pretty sure that was the wolf who came to your rescue the other night after I saved your thankless arse."

Her spine stiffened. "I would die for the MacLaughlin, but he's still an aristocrat. They fuck halvies, but they don't love them. I would have thought Dede's affair with Ainsley would have taught you that."

I could have slapped her for using Dede's pain in such a flippant manner. "Aren't you sweet to care?"

"Originally I'd planned to kill you, so I'd say educating you instead is an act of mercy."

Mercy? "You think you could end me, wolf girl?"

Lupine gold brightened her eyes. "I know I could."

I snorted, stood up straight and put myself right in her face. We were almost perfectly nose to nose. "No," I said softly. "We both know you *couldn't*." The one thing I had absolute confidence in was my ability to fight.

Ophelia blinked. I felt rather than saw her back down. She'd driven me to that strange, calmly violent place where I could have ripped her heart out and then had tea. My hands wouldn't even shake.

"I meant what I said earlier." My voice was cold – detached. "Don't come near me again, or I will end you. Do you understand me, traitor? I'll fucking kill you."

Then I walked out of the room, leaving her staring after me. I had been absolved of whatever guilt or regret I might have felt for her. We might share a mother, but we weren't sisters.

Vex and I ended up at a quiet, low-key restaurant. I didn't want to remain at Freak Show, where Ophelia might spy on us. We sat there, eating, drinking and talking until almost dawn.

He seemed to genuinely like me, which was good, because I genuinely liked him, despite having been warned against it.

"How well do you know my sister?" I asked.

Vex's gaze lifted to mine over flickering candle light. The air between us smelled of rich coffee, warm sugar, spiced vanilla and the subtle musk of two bodies attracted to one another. "I was wondering when we'd get to this."

"To what?" I might as well have batted my eyelashes I sounded so innocently surprised.

His mouth tilted on one side. He seemed to find me terribly

amusing when I wasn't even trying. "When you'd start asking about Ophelia." He took a sip of coffee. "I've no desire to have her hanging over our heads, so here you go: I've known the girl her entire life. She's part of my pack and under my protection. A couple of years ago she was abducted. I searched for her and never found her. Several months ago she returned to us. If I ever find who took her I'll rip their hearts out. Yes, I know about PAH and why she was there, but if that gets back to your chief inspector brother I'll deny it, and you and I will become those clichéd ships that passed in the night."

I stared at him. He certainly was direct. "Whose records was she after?"

Flame reflected in his grey-blue eyes. "Whose do you think?"

"Mine."

He grinned. "I've forgotten how arrogant youth can be. It's not always about you, Xandra."

It wasn't said as an insult, but it stung a little. Relieved me too. "So it's just a coincidence that you were one of the last people to speak to my sister Dede before she was taken, then Fee stole my records, and then you hit on me at Freak Show."

Now he was the one who looked stung. "Drusilla and I discussed the weather and you. The nonsense with Ophelia might have brought you within my reach, but sleeping with you for any reason other than wanting you is not a level to which I would stoop."

No, I realised. He'd hire someone to get information, or to sleep with me for that matter. I felt a little guilty about hoping to get information out of him now that he made it sound so tawdry.

Still, I couldn't help but think he knew something I didn't. Then again, if he didn't know about Ophelia and Bedlam, he could very well say the same about me. We barely knew each other. Trust would come if this thing between us progressed.

"I didn't mean to offend you," I said. "I've been a little ... off recently."

"I expect you have, and I'm not offended, but you should have a little more confidence in yourself. You're an attractive woman, and I am after all just a man."

I snorted. That was like saying Big Ben was just a bell.

He leaned across the table, eyes flashing lupine gold. A more intelligent woman would have moved back, or at least flinched. I stayed where I was, so that we were almost nose to nose.

"I'm courting you," he announced, words wrapped in a growl. "I haven't courted anyone for more than fifty years. I don't even care if that makes me sound like a fucking antique, so drop the self-deprecation, get a leash on all the reasons why we shouldn't do this and just admit you want me too."

A part of me wanted to offer him my throat at that moment. It was such an instinctive thing, I actually had to stop myself from doing just that.

Plague the mess my life was in at the moment. How often did a girl have a man like this fall into her lap? He was like a school-girl fantasy brought to life. He'd probably end up being more drama than he was worth, but at that moment, he was an extremely good thing. He was right. I should have confidence in more than just my ability to hurt people.

"All right," I murmured. The air around us vibrated with tension – the good kind. I thought perhaps he might throw money on the table to pay the bill and drag me out of the restaurant, or at least to the loo, for a quick shag, like in the pictures. Instead, he leaned back in his chair and went back to his coffee. The tease.

The tension eased, and I picked up my fork and went back to tackling the two desserts that sat between us on the table. He'd left me most of the crème brulée. As disappointed as I was not to be ravished, it was nice to chat. Finally, a conversation that wasn't rife with drama. He had a lot of interesting stories to tell. When I asked about the Great Insurrection he said, "I don't want to ruin the evening by talking about that bloody day."

I understood. My only frame of reference was what I'd read in my history books, seen on the box or heard from Church or my father, and even then the two of them never relayed anything personal.

"Do you know anything about halvies selling their blood to aristos at Freak Show?" I asked later, as I ripped open packets of sugar and dumped it into my third cup of coffee.

"Fuck." Vex shook his head, expression tightening. "You saw the room, didn't you?"

I nodded, appreciating that he hadn't lied. "Have you ever been in there?"

"Once." He lifted his mug. "I didn't stay long."

I stirred my coffee, not quite meeting his gaze. "Have you ever been on the other side of the glass?"

"Christ, no." He didn't sound offended, though, which was lovely. "Feeding isn't a spectator sport as far as I'm concerned."

I managed to look him in the eye. "Have you fed from halvies?" Obviously wolves had to be more careful with their bite, but it was possible for them to take blood without doing much harm. Anything else was often treated by law as attempted murder.

Faded eyes met mine without flinching. "Yes."

He didn't offer excuses or apologies, and I liked that. He simply sat there and let me do with the information what I would. I smiled. "Well, you are ancient, so I reckon odds were in your favour." Especially since he'd been around long before such things were considered taboo.

Was I making excuses or simply being open-minded?

He laughed at that. "It's a wonder I don't crumble to ash I'm so decrepit."

My grin grew as I popped another bite of creamy goodness in my mouth. "I'll make sure I carry a broom from now on."

Finally, we finished eating. Vex paid the bill despite my insistence that I could cover my portion. He was old-fashioned that way, I supposed. We walked outside. Instead of getting into his motor carriage, Vex insisted on walking me to where I'd parked the Butler earlier. He even carried the box of pastries I bought from the dessert case.

"Thank you for tonight," I told him as we stood beside the motorrad. "It was lovely."

A faint smile curved his lips. "I don't think lovely's a word with which I've ever been associated. Thanks." The smile faded. "Xandra . . . certain parties seem to have an extraordinary interest in several halvies, and you're one of them. Your sister Dede is another. I'm trying to suss out why."

I frowned. Where did that come from, and why was he telling me this now? "There's nothing special about me."

He crossed his arms over his chest, the leather of his long coat pulling taut across his shoulders. "Don't be daft. You're a very unusual woman – in the best sense. The old man wouldn't have set his sights on you if you weren't."

"Church?"

He nodded. "He's always taken a keen interest in you."

"He saved my life."

"Did he." It wasn't a question, but not quite a statement either.

"I don't think I like what you're saying." I moved to pull away, but he reached out and grabbed my hand.

"You don't have to like it." Vex's gaze and grip were firm. "You just have to be smart and careful. You owe yourself and the people who care for you at least that much." I could have reacted badly to such darkly spoken words, but they had the opposite effect – they convinced me of his sincerity. This was a man who had a reputation for being heroic in every sense of the word. He had fought in the Great Insurrection and was a favourite of Queen V, despite being a wolf. He could very well be working on Victoria's behalf. For all I knew, Ophelia could be a spy he had planted in Bedlam.

What did that mean for Dede? I stopped my imagination there – wild speculation wasn't the answer.

"Apologies. I feel as though the ground is shifting beneath my feet."

"I don't think it's going to get any steadier. You have my support, for what it's worth."

I met his gaze. It was open and frank. There was nothing about him that suggested I shouldn't trust him. And yet, he was still holding out on me – I could feel it. I reckoned he felt the same about me. "Thank you."

We stood there a moment until he checked his pocket watch. "I have to go. I'm following up on some information. I'll ring you when I get back from Scotland?"

It took me a second to realise he was asking permission. Big bad alpha wasn't certain if I was still into him. Cute. "You do that, my lord."

He kissed me – rather possessively I thought, all weak in the knees – and stood there watching as I drove away. A girl could get used to such chivalry, even when she could take care of herself. I drove home with an odd sense of contentment in my stomach, despite the feeling that Vex had made me feel like I'd dropped even further down the rabbit hole.

I ate the pastries – glazed and still warm – on the sofa, and washed them down with three cups of piping-hot tea in front of the box while watching three quarters of the latest *Mr Jones* series – a programme about a time-travelling alien who continuously saved the aristocracy from threat of annihilation in very confounding and amazing ways.

I hated having to be on bereavement leave. Right now I could be working, at a party or a ball, or maybe the theatre. Too much time alone equalled too much time in my head, and that was not a good place for me, even on the best of days.

What was I going to do about Church? He had seemed strange the last time I saw him. He didn't want me to trust Vex. Vex wanted me to trust him. Dede wanted me to keep my mouth shut. My mother wanted my blood. Ophelia wanted . . . well, who the hell knew what that hatters bitch wanted? Why weren't my records in my file? Who had them? What was so special about me that those details needed to be hidden?

My brain was starting to hurt from all this pointless thinking. Thinking did nothing. Action was the only thing that would truly yield results.

After taking my empty dessert box to the kitchen and dumping it in the bin, I toddled – yes, toddled – off to bed. My kit was strewn across the carpet as I undressed, moving between the bedroom and the adjoining loo. Dawn hovered on the horizon and I was exhausted. I grabbed a light cotton shift to sleep in and pulled it over my head.

Face scrubbed and teeth brushed, I climbed between the soft, cool sheets with a sigh, eager for thoughtless sleep. I heard Avery come in as I burrowed into my pillow. A few minutes later her soft footsteps came into my room.

"Xandy? Are you awake?"

"Barely," I replied, lifting my head. "What's the matter? I thought you were staying at Em's."

"I reckon she deserves a reprieve from my weeping and wailing." She was smiling, but there was a wealth of sadness in her tone – and her expression. "Thought I'd come home and see how you're holding up."

She was breaking my heart. "I'm . . . all right." When she

lingered in the doorway I knew the question she couldn't quite bring herself to ask, and peeled back the blankets. "C'mon, then."

The relief on her face was devastating. If I saw Dede again I was going to be sorely tempted to kick the little brat's arse from here to Brighton for putting her family through this awful, cruel charade.

Halfway across the floor my sister stopped. "Ow." She lifted her foot and pulled something free of it. "Found your earring."

I hadn't been wearing earrings tonight, but when I did, I always took them off and set them in my jewellery case on the dressing table. "Let me see."

Simultaneously she slid into bed and handed me the earring. The faint light coming in through the windows was enough for me to study it fairly closely. It was one of mine, but it only took a second for me to realise where I'd seen it recently.

In Dede's ear at Bedlam. She had been here. Why? It couldn't be a coincidence given my run-in with Ophelia. I'd thought it had been dodgy, the way she insisted on hanging about.

I didn't want Avery to see my reaction – neither the surprise nor the anger – so I rolled over to place the earring on top of the night-stand nearest me. "Thanks."

I rolled back on to my side to find her facing me – an almost mirror image, complete with hand beneath her pillow.

"I can't believe I'll never see her again," Avery whispered, her voice breaking slightly. There was no question who she was referring to.

"I know," I replied, because it was the only thing I could say at the moment that was true but wouldn't reveal all. Hopefully she'd think my hollow tone was from grief and not the fact that it was all I could do not to jump out of bed, go find my sister and come aboard her like a cinder that's found its way on to the rug from the fireplace.

I stayed awake for a long time after I knew Avery was asleep. I watched her, admiring how peaceful she was. I envied her ignorance, even her grief, which I was abysmal at faking. I thought I would prefer that pain to the truth, and this gut-gnawing rage that wanted to take my head clean off my shoulders. There was only one thing that could be done about it. I was going to have to go back to Bedlam after all.

It would be rude of me not to return the earring.

Righteous indignation and hurt kept me awake for longer than I cared to admit. The sun was on its steady rise by the time I finally fell into a deep and oddly peaceful slumber. I didn't stir until half past three. Avery had already got up, the spot in my bed where she'd slept long cooled. Yawning, I stretched and sat up, the smell of bacon and fried bread coaxing me from my little nest.

And then I remembered that Dede had snuck into my house – for whatever reason – while Ophelia followed me to Freak Show to make certain I didn't go home and catch Dede in the act. And accused me of murder.

A girl simply could not ignore such offence. It meant going back to Bedlam, but it would be worth it to use Ophelia's head to alleviate some aggression. Besides, it wasn't as though the place held any fear for me any more; my mother obviously wasn't hatters. The whole lot of them were mad, to be sure, but not in *that* way.

But first – food. I'd go to Bedlam later. Let the filthy bastards think they'd fooled me.

I pulled a kimono over my shift and padded barefoot down the stairs, following that heavenly scent. "When did you learn to cook?" I demanded as I approached the kitchen, only to find it wasn't Avery at the stove at all, but Emma. Avery was at the table reading a copy of *Good Day*.

"My mother," Emma replied with a wide grin. "Good morning, sunshine. Hope you don't mind me barging in."

I smiled back. "Sweetie, you can barge in whenever you want if you promise to cook something while you're here."

She laughed, and Avery glanced up from her reading with a small smile. "Oi, don't be flirting with my girl."

"And you're lucky to have her." I went to fetch a coffee mug from the cupboard. "Any good gossip?"

"Actually . . ."

Something in her tone made me pause in the middle of filling my cup. Cafetière in hand, I turned to her. "What?"

She flipped a few pages back and turned the magazine so I could see it. I moved closer, still clutching the cafetiére.

Staring up at me was a photo of me and Vex taken outside Freak Show. I hadn't even noticed a flash bulb. It was the night I'd first met him at the club. We were looking at each other like hungry . . . well, wolves. Beneath the picture was the caption *Sought-after bachelor Lord Alpha "Vexation" MacLaughlin leaves Freak Show with Royal Guard Alexandra Vardan. Is the Duke's daughter what's keeping him from courtesans and a mate?*

"I spend one night with him and I'm to blame for the fact that he's held off on marrying and breeding? Fuckers." I tossed the magazine aside.

"It's a good photo of the two of you," Avery commented, picking the damn thing up again.

"They said it themselves, he's sought-after." Emma offered me a plate piled with eggs, meat and dough fried in bacon fat. "And you're the first woman he's been seen with publicly for a long time."

"Every straight single bitch and halvie in the Kingdom is going to *despise* you." Avery actually grinned as she said it.

"Brilliant." I topped up her coffee and poured my own, then sat down at the table with my breakfast. "Lovely way to start a relationship."

"Ooh," Emma cooed as she joined us. "Relationship, is it?"

I rolled my eyes as she and Avery snickered. A few mouthfuls of heaven later I was no longer annoyed with either of them. "Move this woman into the house," I demanded of my sister. "I want her to cook all the time."

They laughed, but I caught the look that passed between them and felt a little stab of envy. There were times when I wanted someone with whom I could communicate with just a glance. Someone to snog and snuggle with. Halvie guys tended to avoid me, as my reputation as a scrapper preceded me. It wasn't as though I was constantly getting into fights; it was just that I always won when I did. Things had changed a lot over the years, but men still tended to avoid women who could bosh them senseless.

I'd have to fight fairly hard to best Vex, I realised, then pushed the thought aside. Two dates didn't make us soulmates. Wanting to trust him and naïvely wanting to believe he was on my side didn't mean we were meant for each other.

We made small talk as we ate, the three of us avoiding the topics of Dede (thank God) and my love life (thank fuck). I had just finished my second cup of coffee and my third piece of bacon-flavoured bread when I heard my rotary ringing. I had left it on the tallboy in the foyer when I came in this morning.

I jogged out to answer it, my heart skipping a beat when I saw that the number slots on the front had Simon's digits in them. I pressed the button to answer immediately. "Hullo?"

"What kind of shit joke are you trying to pull on me?"

I flinched at the volume and bitterness of Simon's tone. "I don't know what you're going on about."

"Don't give me that bollocks. The blood you brought me."

"What about it?" My heart was dancing an Irish reel. I wondered if perhaps my mother or Ophelia had tampered with the sample, but I'd seen them take it from my vein – had accepted the vial immediately with my own hands. They couldn't have done anything to it.

"You're going to make me say it? Drag my humiliation out a little longer?" He was really angry.

"Simon, I'm not having you on. Now please tell me what you found out so I can be as confounded as you are."

He hesitated, wondering whether or not I was on the up and up, no doubt. "Are you certain this is your blood?"

I knew I should lie. "Yes. As certain as I can be."

"Well, someone made a mistake somewhere, because I don't see how it could possibly be your blood."

My heart drummed hard. "Why? What's wrong with it?"

"It's not halvie," he replied sharply. "Love, if this is your blood you shouldn't even exist."

CHAPTER 10

CURIOUSER AND CURIOUSER

"What?" I demanded. "Of course I exist."

Cold rage overcame the panic fluttering in my chest. Fucking Ophelia. She had done this. There was some kind of mistake.

"I'm coming over," I told him.

"You'd better," he agreed. "I want to draw a sample of my own."

"Be there as soon as I can." I pushed the button to end the call. Fang me. My hands were shaking.

My sister and her girlfriend looked up as I entered the kitchen. Avery's pleasant expression faded almost immediately. "Everything all right, Xan? You look pale."

I nodded – big fat liar that I was. "Dede's landlord," I lied. "Wanted to know what to do with Dede's things. I told her I'd come by."

The look on her face made me feel like shit. It also made me want to strangle Dede. She was the one who'd got me mixed up in this mess. What fucked-up reason did Ophelia have for swapping my blood?

"Do you want me to come with you?" The fact that she asked proved that she wasn't up to the task.

"Nah, I can take care of it. I'll donate what we don't keep to charity."

"She would like that," Avery remarked quietly.

No, I wanted to say, she wouldn't, which was exactly why I intended to do it.

I kissed Avery on the forehead and said see ya to them both, then I ran up to my room before heading out. In my bedroom, I opened the door to the large walk-in wardrobe and flicked the light switch.

There was a small box marked "MUM" that had a few toys in it, some children's jewellery, a plastic barrette, photos and a couple of items of hers that I'd been given when she had been hauled off to Bedlam. I removed one of the photos – a shot of the two of us at the Courtesan House on Christmas Eve. I might have been five years old. My mother looked very much like she did now, which made me wonder if they did cosmetic surgery in Bedlam.

I put the photo back in the box and replaced the lid. No time for walking down memory lane, even if the box marked "RYE" tempted me like the proverbial snake in the garden. Instead I opened the one that read "ACADEMY: YEARS 10 & 11". Inside were medals and ribbons I'd won, papers I'd written that had got good grades. A photograph of me and Churchill sparring – he'd beaten the crap out of me, of course. It was an exam and I got the highest mark in my age group. In any age group, actually. The only other person to come close had been Rye in his tenth year, beating me by two points. By the time I finished my final year I had set a new record – better than Rye's. As far as I knew, no one had topped me yet.

But this photo and reminders of my failure to reach my full potential weren't why I opened this box. I dug down through notes from the few friends I'd had, more photos and programmes for school tournaments. I didn't even stop to look at the card my father had given me upon graduation.

There at the bottom of the box was the object of my search. It was a small, nondescript box that looked like it could be a rotary or AC. In reality it was a displacer, and it would keep anyone who might be monitoring my whereabouts from seeing where I was.

Really, if Ophelia had been smart she wouldn't have told me how she found me last night. But then if I'd been smart I would have realised she was up to no good. I didn't want her – or Church – knowing where I was.

I put the box back, gathered clothes and headed to the shower. A little while later I was dressed in snug black trousers, camisole, tall boots and black corset jacket that flared out and fell almost to my knees in the back. The device went into a pocket of my trousers, while the others ended up housing my rotary and watch. I tucked a few pound notes in with the displacer and slipped the lonsdaelite dagger inside a sheath in my right boot. I left the Bulldog behind.

Despite my frantic hurrying I'd lost an hour searching for the displacer and getting ready. It was that time of day when the streets and motorways teemed with humans coming home from their tedious jobs – whatever they were – and most halvies were getting ready for theirs. We were outnumbered by the humans, and it occurred to me then that I should know more about them. They kept the city running – electricity, plumbing, trains … And we simply assumed they were controlled. Cowed. Some even assumed the humans liked their situation.

I knew differently now. There was rebellion brewing. The barest stirrings of it could lead to war. Was the aristocracy any more prepared to take on the humans than they had been in '32?

Fang me, but that was a fight I wanted to be part of. My entire life I'd been taught that humans were the enemy, that every last one of them wanted to see aristos and halvies wiped off the face of the earth. How could Dede and Ophelia be so certain that when the day came their human comrades wouldn't turn on them? After all, we were just dirty half-bloods, right? My hands tightened on the steering bars.

It took me twenty minutes longer than it should have to get to Simon's office at the hospital, even with the advantage of being able to weave in and out through the mass of cars and carriages, buses and trolleys.

I parked the Butler in the first available spot I found and practically ran through the front doors. I hurried to the lift and punched the button for the lab, which was one floor down. The doors slid open to reveal a corridor much more sterile than the prettily painted lobby and waiting area I'd run through upstairs. Here the overhead lights cast a slightly greenish tint along the whitewashed walls and tiled floor. They flickered above me as I walked.

It was quiet down here. The thick soles of my boots were silent on the polished floor, making nary a squeak as I set out at a brisk clip to the left. Simon's office was a small space just outside the lab that used to be a storeroom. I knocked on the door and turned the knob, not bothering to wait for permission.

The door swung open. Simon wasn't there.

But he had been.

I entered cautiously, wishing I'd brought the Bulldog regardless. A quick assessment of the room and I didn't bother pulling a weapon – I knew I was alone. I couldn't smell, hear or sense another body nearby. The heavy smell of smoke lingered on the air, as did the aroma of coffee. A cup on the desk had been knocked over, spilling latte all over the papers there. The chair lay overturned on the floor, Simon's jacket still draped over the back of it.

A cigarillo burned in a crystal dish – the kind old grannies put barley sugar and peppermints in. It had been deliberately left to drown out all other scents, reinforcing the fact that Simon hadn't left voluntarily. I knew that just as certainly as I knew I wouldn't find any trace of my blood in the lab. I knew these things because there was a smear of blood on the wall behind the desk. I also knew without touching or tasting it that it was still warm.

And that it was Simon's.

I did look for any information that might pertain to me – in both Simon's office and the lab itself. Once I told the techies that Simon wasn't in his office and that there was blood on the wall, they'd filed out to investigate for themselves and call the authorities. That left me with just a few minutes on my own, but that was all I needed.

There was no trace of me in the lab, and the smoke obliterated anything that might have been left behind in the office – everything but that awful smear on the wall.

Simon could have fallen and hit his head. At this very moment he might be upstairs getting stitched up. But I knew that wasn't so because others in the lab would know about it. If the blood on the wall had been thicker I might suspect that he'd been shot, but I hadn't smelled gunshot residue – the smoke couldn't conceal that – and there wasn't any splatter. I called his rotary to see if he answered.

He didn't. No surprise there. Was it a coincidence that he had disappeared – violently – after contacting me? I didn't think so, which meant that one – if not both – of us had some kind of surveillance on our line.

Fang me, could Simon have truly been taken because of me? My blood? Why? It made no sense.

Unless I was an experiment, like Ophelia had suggested at Bedlam. The thought sent my heart pounding. This was not the time to go full-on hatters.

How was I going to find out the truth about me now? An awful, selfish question given the circumstances, but I thought it regardless. More importantly, what was it that people were taking such extreme measures to keep me from finding out?

My search for answers was yielding nothing but more questions, the most important of which was where was my friend? There was a chance Simon's disappearance had nothing to do with me at all, but in that case I'd expect to find the results of his tests in his office, or on his computer, and there hadn't been anything at all. The Yard didn't find anything either – nothing that they cared to share, and usually they did share with RGs.

They wanted to talk to me – officially. While I waited, itching and squirming in my own skin, I took a walk down the corridor, sniffing for traces of Simon. If the peelers hadn't found anything it was unlikely I would, although at the exit I thought I caught a whiff of myself, which is an unsettling sensation when you're not expecting it.

There was a drop of blood on the floor. This had to be where they'd taken Simon out of the building. I pushed the door open and walked through, careful to avoid the blood.

Outside in the back lot the smell disappeared. Plague it all. Why couldn't I catch one bloody break?

I went back inside and waited a few more minutes. Once I had given my statement to Inspector Granger from Special Branch – and she had expressed her sympathy over Dede's "death" – I left the hospital and tore off in the direction of Bedlam, weaving in and out of traffic as recklessly as I dared without attracting undue attention. I held tight to my anger, because that kept me from dissolving in a fit of guilt. I had no idea anything would happen to Simon when I brought my blood to him, but I felt responsible for his disappearance.

When I arrived at Bedlam, I parked the motorrad around the corner and hurried through the wrought-iron gate and up the path. It smelled like rain and the waning day was grey. I'd probably get soaked on the way home.

The asylum loomed before me like a house in a gothic novel – as though it was a living, breathing creature of darkness. I had the absurd thought that it would swallow me alive once I crossed the threshold.

Obviously I still had a few issues with the place, but right now, it just pissed me off.

I swept through the front door like the heroine in an American action film, all butch swagger. The guards stiffened at the sight of me, reading my body language as a threat. I smiled. I wasn't in the mood for their shit.

"Do you have an appointment?" one asked, his hand hovering over the pistol at his hip.

"I don't need one." I started to pass by them, but one stopped me with his palm against the top of my chest – just above my breasts. I glanced down at that hand, so large and brown against the pale bit of skin peeking out of my coat.

"You're going to want to move that," I told him, raising my gaze to his. "And not down."

I gave him credit for not smirking, but he didn't remove his hand. "No appointment, no pass."

I wrapped my fingers around his wrist, still smiling.

A minute later, as the alarm the other guard had set off rang in the west wing, Ophelia came tearing around the corner looking ready for a fight. I stood just inside the hounds, the two guards unconscious on the floor at my feet.

"Hello, sunshine," I said cheerfully, stepping over the legs of the guard who'd put his hand on me. "Miss me?"

"You might have called," she informed me – rather peevishly I thought. She was wearing a long purple frockcoat over her grey trousers and black corset. The coat matched a bruise on her jaw. My handiwork, I reckoned. "Now who's going to deal with visitors?"

I shrugged. "They'll be awake soon." A moan from behind me proved me right. "See, one's coming round already. Take me to Juliet."

Ophelia's blue eyes glittered. "Say please."

Good Lord, we really were sisters. I found myself smiling at her in a demented fashion. "Pretty please."

I had the pleasure of seeing some of her bravado waver. She wasn't a stupid girl; she simply didn't trust me any more than I trusted her. She did, however, know that I was spoiling for a fight, and that I had the undoubtedly lucky advantage of being slightly unhinged.

The second guard began to come round as she watched me. The first sat up slowly. Ophelia glanced grimly at them before jerking her head back. "Come on then. I'll take you to Mum."

I despised her right then. I blamed her for a lot of this – even the shit that had nothing to do with her. It was convenient and made me feel better. She could call Juliet "Mum" without a second thought, while I felt as though I should ask permission, even though I would rather razor-blade my own tongue than admit that I wanted to have such familiarity with the woman who'd borne me.

"You know they can track you here," she muttered.

"Taken care of."

She glanced at me – warily. I wasn't about to tell her about the displacer, just in case she decided to put a silver bullet in my brain and cut off my head.

My half-sister didn't seem to like having me walk behind, so

I fell into step beside her. Our strides matched almost perfectly, as did the slight swing of our arms. Neither of us spoke until we reached a set of double doors near the end of the west ground-floor corridor, behind which I could hear the muffled sounds of sparring. Ophelia opened them – with a bit more of a dramatic flourish than I thought necessary – and gestured for me to enter.

Across the threshold was what must have been a dining hall or ballroom at one time – a really large space. Whatever it had been, it was now a gymnasium and training room for their treasonous rebellion.

On a large tumbling mat my mother – looking better than a woman her age ought in pink spandex – sparred with a large man. They weren't using any particular school of martial art, but rather seemed to incorporate whatever suited them. Arms and legs spun and struck with impressive speed and force. They weren't fooling around.

It took me perhaps two seconds to realise that my mother moved entirely too fast to be a normal human. Why was that? If she had visible sores I'd suspect her of being a betty, but she looked far too healthy.

Then her opponent struck a particularly effective blow and knocked her back several feet. Being a courtesan didn't give her any more strength or speed than a regular human. The strike should have laid her out. My mother didn't even fall. She came at the man with a snarl.

A freaking snarl that sent a shiver down my spine. Albert's fangs – the hits just kept on coming.

I didn't need to see the gold sheen to her eyes to realise the truth. My mother was a fucking werewolf.

I've never fancied myself one of those people who, early in Victoria's reign, might have been described as having an over-abundance of spleen, or an imbalance in their humours, but I'd had a lot of things happen to me in the last couple of weeks and there was a bubble of near-hysterical laughter stuck to the back of my throat. Since the treatment for hysteria was basically vibrator-induced orgasm until one was too weak and too sore to "fuss about" any longer, I held the laughter in check. I liked the big O as much as the next girl, but that really wasn't what I needed right then.

Although I couldn't quite say what I did need at that moment. So I sat down on a chair against the wall and ground the heel of my left hand into my forehead, elbow digging into my thigh.

I'd never heard of a courtesan being turned before. Courtesans were for breeding, not turning. I had to think that more of these women would have been changed into full-bloods if it was that easy, but perhaps then they couldn't breed halvies. Obviously my mother had been turned after I was born. By whom? And why was I just finding out about it now? Was her turning part of the reason my blood was supposedly being monitored? Was it because of her aristo-friendly genes that I was considered odd? She was more than just a carrier if she could be turned.

"You all right?" It was Dede who asked. She'd come in just a few seconds ago.

"Do I fucking *look* all right?" I demanded, glaring at her as she stood over me.

Her lips twitched. I think she was enjoying this. "You look like you're about ready to toss your pot."

What she lacked in eloquence she made up for in accuracy. I was feeling a little sick. That feeling intensified as my mother approached – her opponent dismissed. Juliet had a concerned and slightly horrified expression on her face. I watched as the gold faded from her eyes.

"My dear girl. I never meant for you to find out like this."

That would indicate that she meant for me to find out eventually.

"When?" It was all I could think of – the only thing that seemed important at that moment.

My mother placed her hand on mine. Her skin was almost hot compared to the chill of my own, but then werewolfs ran a little hotter than the rest of us. "When I was pregnant with you," she replied softly. "Three months."

Now I knew why she had given up being a courtesan after I was born. She had to. *Fang me*. "That's why you wanted to check my blood, to see if it did anything to me." And it was why my blood looked weird to Simon. I'd have markers that belonged to vamps, halvies and weres.

Her expression was grim. "Yes."

"Who was the were who did this to you?"

"I don't know. It was dark, and my senses were human then. I never saw his face, and afterward . . . our paths never crossed."

I had the feeling she would have killed him if they had. "Why didn't you have me tested when I was young?"

"Your father did, but he told me there was nothing to worry about."

I met her concerned blue gaze in surprise. "Vardan knows?"

She made a choking sound as she chuckled humourlessly. "He found me after the attack. For all I know he could have instigated the whole thing."

I glared at her. "He would never." How could anyone take such a risk with the life of the woman carrying his child?

A thin blonde brow arched. "Such misplaced devotion. You don't know His Grace like I do, my girl. After I was bitten I told your father I would have to have an abortion as the law dictated. He wouldn't let me."

My spine straightened. "He didn't want to lose his child."

"He wanted to see how you'd 'turn out' – as he put it. I assume that's why he continues to monitor your blood."

I laughed. I couldn't help it. It was as though I had the lead role in some bizarre panto and didn't know my lines.

Ophelia kicked my chair. "Don't you get it? You've been a lab rat your entire life. They've been studying you."

I shrugged. "If I was that much of a freak, wouldn't they know by now? Wouldn't *I* know?"

"It would be in their best interests to make you think you're normal."

I winced. "I suppose you'll find out when you get your test results back."

My mother dabbed at her damp brow with a towel. "Didn't you take your own vial for testing?"

More laughter – just a chuckle this time. I leaned back and rubbed a hand over my eyes. If I didn't laugh I just might become what my father liked to call "a watering pot". "Right, here's the kicker – my blood and the bloke who tested it have gone missing. It looks like there was a struggle. That's why I came here. I thought perhaps you lot might know something about it, but you don't, do you?"

I looked up at my mother, so young and beautiful, her pale brow marred by a frown as she shook her head. She looked worried, and I wasn't comforted by the fact.

I looked from Juliet to Ophelia and back again. "No one else knew."

My sister spoke first. "Did you talk to this man on your rotary?"

"Yeah. Someone obviously overheard his end. That or I have a huge coincidence on my hands."

"You said there seemed to have been a struggle?"

I nodded, shoving my thumb and middle finger along my aching brow. Headaches were rare amongst halvies, but I was working on a good one right now.

"You need to get a new rotary," my mother said. "Don't tell anyone about it. Use it only in emergencies or to call us."

"You think someone tapped my phone?"

"Either yours or that of your friend."

Albert's fangs. I really was in an American action film. Any minute now some bald man would pop up with a machine gun and call me a motherfucker. Why hadn't I thought of the tap being on my end? I was paranoid about everything else.

I was starting to feel a little shaky. I took a sealed packet of supplements from my inside coat pocket with the intention of swallowing them – maybe with a biscuit.

Ophelia snatched the packet from my hand. "Yeah, don't do that."

I watched as she tossed them in the bin against the wall. "Oi! I need those."

"No you don't," she replied, "they make you weak. They contain pharmaceuticals that suppress reflexes and instincts. I can give you proof. God knows what else they put in yours." My supplements would not be the same as Avery's or Val's, and we were always cautioned never to take another halvie's supps unless we absolutely had to.

Bloody hell, was there anything in my life that was right side up? I sucked in a deep breath. Just because they told me these things didn't make them true – I had to remember that. But the easiest way to find out was to stop taking the supps and see what happened.

And the next time I saw Vardan I'd ask him about my mother becoming a were.

My father had a good reason for keeping this from me – just as

I knew Church had his reasons for concealing the truth as well. Maybe everyone under this roof was one of the bad guys.

But what if they were right?

My mother must have seen my confusion, because she chose that moment to take pity on me. "Go a few days without the supplements and see how you feel."

"I feel like tearing someone's throat out when I don't take them."

The corners of her lips tucked in a grim parody of a smile. "That will go away. It's withdrawal. It may get worse before it gets better, but you'll be all right. You won't be a wreck for long."

Speaking of wrecked . . . "I almost forgot." I smiled brightly at Dede and Ophelia as I stuck my hand into my coat pocket. "Next time you want to search my house, just ask."

They both protested, but I tossed Dede the earring Avery had found. Her cheeks flushed dark red as she caught it and realised what it was. "Sloppy," I told her.

She looked me dead in the eye. "You would have done the same."

"Sure I would have, but I would have made certain I didn't leave any trace of myself behind." I glanced at Ophelia. "And I wouldn't send in a distraction."

She stiffened and met my gaze but remained silent. She wasn't sorry either. I tried to remember that she had just lost someone she loved, but even that didn't make me feel charitable towards her.

"What were you looking for anyway?"

"Information on what happened to Raj," Dede replied.

"Right, because I turned him over to the . . . the what exactly? A secret organisation of aristos that I'm somehow privy to?"

Dede lifted her chin. "To Church."

I'd come close to turning her over to Church. "Why would I do that?"

She shrugged. "Everyone always thought there was something between you two. You worship him and its plain he has a thing for you. He always gave you good grades."

I stepped forward, temper raised to a point that it threatened to blow the top of my fool head off. "I earned those grades, you selfish cow. I am not fucking Church."

"No," Ophelia jumped in. "Why settle for a low-level vampire when you can fuck the alpha."

My fist whipped out and caught her in the jaw – opposite the bruised side. "Now you can have a matched set," I snarled. My mother stepped forward and wrapped strong fingers around my wrist, forcing my fist down. "I wish the three of you would stop acting like feral cats tossed into a sack. And I wish you wouldn't talk like you were born in a gutter. Did you not learn any decorum at Courtesan House?"

The three of us each lowered our eyes in shame. Juliet continued, "Trust has to be earned and rightfully given by all of us. Alexandra has reasons to be wary of our cause just as we will be wary of her, but the lies and subterfuge stop here."

I arched a brow. "Is that so?"

Her expression was fierce as she sharply dipped her head. "You need to sort out for yourself which side you're on. All I ask is that you be as careful in the company of aristos as you are with us, and extend to us the same discretion you offer them. Find out for yourself what they're keeping from you and why. Meanwhile, give us a chance to prove ourselves."

I couldn't really argue with that. If this insurrectionary lot proved to be full of shit, I could always turn them in, or at least set Special Branch on to them. There was a part of me that wanted it to end that way, and another part that hoped for all the wrong reasons that Dede wasn't a traitor.

"Agreed," I said, rising to my feet. "Anything else?"

Ophelia stepped up – big surprise. "You really don't know anything about Raj's murder?"

I shook my head. "I wish I did." I meant it. "Either you've got a traitor in your ranks" – what did one call a traitor amongst traitors? – "or someone's on to you. Whichever, you're not safe." I might not like what they were up to, but I didn't want to see any of them killed, especially not Dede.

And not myself.

I turned to my mother. Now I knew why she looked more like an older sister. "You'll let me know when you get the results of the blood work?" If it had just been the two of us, I would have told her what Simon had said about the vial, but I wasn't keen on giving Ophelia more "freak" ammunition to use on me. And I didn't want them to see how responsible I felt for Simon's disappearance.

She nodded, her expression soft but honest. "I will." And then she gave me her rotary number – which I memorised because she wouldn't write it down. "As soon as you get a new one, let me know so I'll be able to contact you."

I shouldn't have done it. If I was caught . . . but it didn't matter. I had to follow this through. No turning back now. For better or for worse the traitors were all I had.

CHAPTER 11

SURPRISES, LIKE MISFORTUNES, SELDOM COME ALONE

Amazingly, the next two days passed quietly as I tried to distract myself from wondering if there was indeed something drastically wrong with me thanks to my mother's metamorphosis – didn't Bedlam have their own laboratory? – and if poor Simon was alive. I considered calling Val, but my brother was likely to ask questions I didn't want to answer. Plus, I didn't want him to get into any trouble because of me.

Fortunately, Vex was back from Scotland and proved to be a delightful diversion. I'd given up the supplements and Ophelia was right – it was hard. I kept to home because I could smell the blood all around me, and wanted to punch anything that got in my way. It was like a horrid case of PMS but I wanted to eat people instead of chocolate. No wonder they gave us the supplements. It would be bloody hard to concentrate without them. How did aristos do it?

The night before, while in bed with Vex, I bit him – with fang.

He seemed to like it, and God knows I did. We were both a little like animals at that moment and he tasted like heaven on my tongue – warm and alive.

"I'm sorry," I told him afterwards, wiping a spot of blood from his neck. The wounds had already begun to heal, thanks to his metabolism. Normally the vamp enzymes in my saliva would cause blood to thin rather than clot – not dangerously so, but just enough to make feeding easier.

Broad shoulders shrugged as he grinned at me. "Didn't hear me complaining, did you?"

No, I hadn't. Still, didn't he find it weird? He had to know most halvies didn't go around biting people. He must wonder why I'd stopped taking the pills all halvies were prescribed and mandated to take.

"Ah," Vex said. "There you go."

I glanced up at him. "What?"

He shook his head. "I thought I had you this time, but you just slipped away on me again."

I really was a shit. "I'm sorry. I've been so distracted lately."

He merely nodded and pulled me close, so that my head nestled against his warm chest. "You miss your sister."

I did, but Dede took up less and less of my thoughts as of late. I didn't want to be a freak, didn't want to lie to people I cared about – or worse, suspect them of conspiring against me. The more I thought about the things I'd seen and heard at Bedlam, the more I doubted my own perceptions of right and wrong. I needed an anchor.

"I gave someone a sample of my blood to analyse and now he's missing," I blurted, hesitantly raising my head.

Vex went still. "Who?"

"Simon Halstead."

"The kid the Yard's looking for?"

I nodded. "He disappeared after he rang me to say he had the results of my blood work."

Storm-blue eyes locked with mine. "What did he say?"

"Nothing." I wasn't about to reveal everything. I wasn't that mental. "I went to meet him and he was gone. There was blood on the wall."

A deep scowl cleaved his brow. "Xandra, I want you to be careful. Very careful. Do you understand?"

"Not in the least," I replied honestly. "I don't understand much of anything any more, so you're going to have to give me a bit more than that."

Vex lifted himself up on his elbow. I shifted so I could better look at him. "You remember how I told you that there were certain parties interested in other halvies – including you?" When I nodded, he continued, "There are seven that I know of. Three out of those seven half-bloods are missing. Disappeared without a trace."

Cold raced down my spine, chilling each vertebra. "And the other four?"

"One's in Bedlam, one's dead, one is going about his business as usual and the last one is you."

Fang me. "Is the dead one my sister Dede?" I don't know why I asked, only that I had to ask it.

His expression changed. Resignation flashed in his eyes. He didn't want to trust me any more than I thought I should trust him, but for some reason we did trust one another. "I think we both know Dede is the one in Bedlam."

If he'd confessed to wanting to wear my underwear I couldn't have been more shocked. "You knew?"

He nodded. "Fee told me."

"Why didn't you tell me?" I knew he had been keeping things, but I hadn't expected this. It . . . hurt. And it irritated me.

"Because I didn't think it was a good idea. I'm still not sure it was."

"You could have told me." I couldn't help wondering if maybe I'd been used after all.

"The dead one is my son," he said suddenly, effectively punching my anger in the face.

I sat up. "Your son? But you've never . . . Have you?" Everyone always talked about the fact that Vex had yet to get married, had yet to produce any halvie offspring.

"She wasn't a courtesan," he replied, voice low and rough. "She was part of a family who had worked for mine for decades."

"She had plagued blood." I was master of the obvious, because that was the only way this sort of thing happened. Somewhere in that woman's family tree was a noble bastard – probably more than one. "What happened to her?" I really didn't want to know. She might still be out there. Fuck. Vex had a kid.

"I don't know. Her family abandoned her for having a half-blood. She left the boy with me and then fled the country. Duncan – my son – never forgave me for the fact that he was an outcast."

Halvies without registered courtesan mothers were considered odd, but they were hardly outcasts. My brain took a leap: the hospital records Ophelia stole. Whoever 'they' were, they were interested in us because we aren't the same as other halvies. "He was different?"

Vex nodded. "He looked like a half-blood, and had all the markers of one, but he could transform into a wolf."

"Albert's fangs." I gaped at him. "That's incredible." And up until recently I would have said it was impossible.

"He was." He smiled – it was both sad and sweet, and it broke my heart. "He disappeared shortly before his eighteenth birthday. Three weeks later his body was found in an alley in Whitechapel. They'd used silver on him. They'd . . . done things."

I thought of the halvies in Bedlam. "Experiments?"

"Aye. He must have put up a fight. The wounds that killed him weren't medical, they were defensive. They shot him full of silver and cut off his head."

Oh fuck. The thought of Vex having to see that made my stomach heave. I put my hand on his arm. This revelation made up for not telling me he knew about Dede and then some. I'd been making this whole mess just about me, and it was about so much more. Realising that made me feel as though I wasn't so alone. "I'm so sorry."

He nodded, the sadness in his eyes gone in a blink, replaced by something hard and cold. "I swore I'd find the bastards who took him. I'd been told it was humans, but something didn't smell right. I let it go because I felt guilty, but then I'd catch wind of halvies disappearing. I saw some of the ones in Bedlam. When Ophelia told me about your sister's situation, I let her steal Duncan's file. She took a stack so it wouldn't be so obvious what we were after. I wasn't surprised to discover yours was one of the flimsy ones."

"My sister?" One thing at a time. My brain couldn't keep up. "Dede?"

Another nod. "She believes the child she had with Ainsley is similar to Duncan."

I closed my eyes. *Oh Dede. You poor demented . . .* Wait. My default with Dede was to assume she was hatters, but what if she really wasn't? What if she was right? That in itself sounded completely mental, but so far the world was spinning backwards on its axis, so why not entertain the notion? That I could think of, Vex had no reason to lie. I couldn't keep telling myself that everyone telling me these things were hatters and go ignorantly on my way.

Fang me. What if Dede had been telling the truth and we all treated her like a demented idiot?

I'd think about that later. "Why weren't you surprised to find my files missing?"

"Because you're different. You're not quite a half-blood. You're not aristo, though. Your scent is a combination of wolf and vampire, and something wild. I don't know what you are."

Well that made two of us, only he didn't seem all that worried about it. I was. His son was dead, and he knew Dede wasn't. He knew more than I ever could have imagined.

"You know about my mother."

He nodded. "I'm not with you because of her – or any of this."

I wanted to believe him. I really did. Time would tell. I didn't think I was in any danger from him – not physically – and it seemed we had a fledgling trust going on. I had confided in him more than I had even in Church. I didn't want to be wrong about him, but I wouldn't put all of my faith into him just yet. Still, he'd told me things I never could have found out on my own, and that was reason to keep him close.

That and I wanted him close. I didn't consider myself weak, but being with him made me feel stronger, and I needed that right now, whether it was real or not.

I had to find out about Dede's kid. I had to do a lot of things. But first I had to eat. My stomach let out a low growl that sounded vaguely feral. I was starving – so much so that Vex looked tasty in ways that weren't just sexual. "Breakfast," I said. "We can talk while we eat."

"I'll cook," he said, sliding out of bed. "It's one of my many talents."

I chuckled and tossed back the blankets. I knew he was trying to lighten the mood. He was probably wondering if he'd revealed too much to me.

"I suppose you learned to cook while trying to charm a kitchen maid?"

"You're right. Mary MacConnell." He pulled on his trousers. "She was a fine little thing."

I slipped into a purple satin kimono. "And how long ago was that?"

"Eighteen fifty-seven, before I even knew I was plagued." The smile disappeared from his face as the glaze of a painful memory slid across his eyes. He reached for his shirt, which was tossed over a nearby chair. "That was the same year my brother Robert died."

Fang me, but he'd lost a lot of people he'd loved. Near-immortality had its misfortunes. "What happened?"

"Apoplexy – that's what they called it back then. I suppose it was a brain haemorrhage or the like. He died and I became the heir. I was the first wolf in our line, you know."

I stared at him. "Your brother was . . ." I couldn't quite make the words come out.

A small smile curved his lips as he pulled the fine linen over his shoulders. "Human, aye. I'm one of the few aristos who remembers where we came from."

His smile was teasing, but I felt shame at his words all the same. "I didn't know aristos could have human children." Then again, I hadn't known that an aristo and a human carrier could produce a full-blood.

"Well, we were all human at one time. It took centuries of plague waves to make us what we are. Human births were much more common in the beginning, but then more of us changed and our human relations aged and died. These days a human child being born to full-blood parents is more rare than a goblin. It's not like our diets are conducive to carrying healthy human babies."

"No, I suppose not." Why had I never heard this before? Not even in school were we taught about the humans who came before aristos – who gave birth to aristos and in turn were sometimes born to them. This knowledge unsettled me a little, though it shouldn't have. But I was even more disturbed by the fact that I had never once wondered about it.

I was trying to put the thoughts from my mind when there came a noise at my balcony – a scratching sound, like claws on glass. Vex and I exchanged glances and I moved towards the doors. He stepped in front of me, putting himself between me and whatever was outside. I peered over his shoulder as he turned the handle and opened the door.

It was something worthy of an old skit-based comedy production – or rather, it would have been were it not so terrifying.

A goblin stood on my balcony, shielding its eyes – already covered by bright magenta sunglasses – from the candlelight inside the room. Its paw slowly lowered as it realised the light wasn't much brighter than that inside its den. It was wearing a cloak and a wide-brimmed hat.

Vex growled low in his throat – a rumbling, menacing sound that made the hairs on my body stand up and take notice. He didn't attack, though, which said much for his control over his inner predator. Most people would react to a goblin with fear or violence and get themselves killed.

The goblin bowed. "The MacLaughlin. Lovely. Xandra lady – I have words for you by order of my prince."

It was female, and obviously found Vex easy on her protected eyes. Scowling, I moved in front of him. His hands gripped my shoulders, as though trying to push me through the floor like a tack.

I regarded the goblin much like a mouse regarded a hungry tom. "It must be important for the prince to send you cobbleside."

She nodded, the light from the room glinting on the numerous golden studs piercing both her tufted ears. "Something was

left in the tunnels, something that reeked of the Xandra lady."
Her accent sounded vaguely Welsh, though it was difficult to
tell when she spoke in that stilted English the gobs seemed to
favour. "The prince says you should know. You should come."
And then she stepped back as though she expected me to follow
immediately.

"She's not going with you," Vex informed her through clenched
teeth.

The little goblin – she only came up to my chin – gazed up at
him and smiled – baring her immense fangs. "Hers to decide,
wolf."

"I have to get dressed," I told her. This wasn't a ploy to get me
into the tunnels – no goblin would be so obvious, nor would they
come this far above ground, to a private home, to hunt. No, if the
prince had sent this goblin to collect me, then he had something
I needed to see.

The hirsute woman bowed her head, turning in such a way that
her cloak opened, and I could make out the slight curve of her
breasts. A pink nipple peeked through the fur. That was something
I couldn't unsee, no matter how much I wished it.

I closed the door, relegating the fiend and her bits to the dark.
I turned and immediately grabbed my underpants from the floor,
where they'd landed earlier that evening.

"What are you doing?" Vex demanded as I shoved my feet in
and wriggled the silk up my legs.

"I'm going with her," I replied, snatching up my undershirt.

"Are you mental?" he demanded.

I pulled the thin garment over my head. "Quite, but that doesn't
change the fact that the prince sent her here. The goblin prince,
Vex. Don't you find that strange? Intriguing, even?"

"Aye, it's a fucking marvel, but that doesn't change the fact that
it's dangerous!"

I flipped my hair out from beneath the straps of the tank before reaching for my black-and-white-striped knee-length trousers. "I've dealt with the prince before. I'll be fine." Oddly enough, I believed it.

He turned the air blue with his curses as he began buttoning his shirt. He shoved the tails of it into the waist of his trousers before reaching for his boots.

"There's no way I'm letting you simply walk off with a fucking goblin." He pinned me with a look that reminded me he was alpha for a reason. A look that also told me that once this current situation was over, I was going to have to explain just how I had "dealt with the prince".

"Fair enough," I replied, and meant it – on all accounts.

When we were dressed, I opened the French doors again. Leaving this way, I had less chance of disturbing Avery. The goblin was still there, sniffing the night. "Your house reeks of sex," she said conversationally.

Sweet baby Albert. A flush rose to my cheeks. "Is that a problem?"

She met my gaze without guile or innuendo. "The thing what unites us all, Xandra lady. No problem, never."

A philosophical goblin. Who would have thought? I supposed you didn't survive and become the efficient predators they were without some manner of intelligence. They only sounded uneducated.

Before I could think of a response, she'd vaulted over the side of the balcony. I strained my ears and heard the grass below rustle as she landed. Vex followed – I suppose to make certain I wasn't alone with the goblin for even a second – and then me. I landed with nothing like the goblin's grace, but stealthily enough that I got my pride on. She gave me a nod, like a teacher approving of a student's first attempt.

She led us through the shadows, blending with the darkness behind buildings and deepened by gardens. Perhaps five or six minutes passed before she ducked between two houses, the space barely wide enough for Vex to move through sideways. At the end of this narrow alley was a square grate set into the ground. Thick plumes of grass kept it almost completely hidden from sight, and the reinforced iron top gave it a formidable appearance. It would take several very determined humans to open it – determined and stupid.

The goblin lifted the iron with relative ease, and immediately disappeared into the hole without a word. I made to follow her, but Vex stopped me. "Me first," he said.

I might have rolled my eyes if it weren't for the fact that I found his protectiveness a little sexy and endearing. I've *never* been treated as something delicate – and I didn't think that was how I was being treated now. It wasn't that Vex doubted my ability to protect myself; he would simply rather that if one of us got hurt it be him.

It was rather lovely knowing that he was putting my welfare before his own.

As soon as he started down the ladder secured to the subterranean wall, I followed. Our hostess immediately climbed back up to pull the grate closed. I could have done it if she'd only asked.

A little ambient light found its way down to us, but it was going to get very dark very quickly – too dark for me or even Vex to see well. Obviously the goblins had prepared for this, because there was a soft click and the light of a very small hand torch made an oval in front of us.

Vex reached back and took my hand in his, guiding me. "Where are we going?" I asked.

"Little way," the goblin replied, before taking a left turn down another corridor. It was like an underground labyrinth. Had the goblins carved these tunnels and fortified them, or were they from the London of years ago? I'd hate to be left to my own devices down here.

Eventually we came upon what looked like a tiny Met station. On the track was a small cart with an engine in front.

"Is this the old post rail?" I asked – with what I'm ashamed to say sounded like awe in my voice.

Ahead the goblin nodded. "City wanted we plague to be happy, so left us trains. Get in, please."

At least she was mannerly. Vex and I joined her in the red cart – it was a close fit. Our companion didn't have the odour I associated with goblins. In fact she smelled almost good to me, like warm fur with a smoky hint of incense.

"What's your name?" I asked, tired of thinking of her as "the goblin". I was curious too.

She shot me another glance – one I'd seen a lot in my life. It was the look people gave me when they didn't know what the blooming hell to make of me. "Elsbeth," she replied, and then surprised me by adding, "Born of Norfolk."

I had to clench my jaw to keep it from dropping. Norfolk was rumoured to have been the first dukedom ever bestowed in the Kingdom, and to think that this abomination descended from it . . . well, it made it that much harder to think of her – Elsbeth – as just a monster.

All goblins were of aristocratic birth, though they considered themselves something more. That they were monsters was what made them frightening – disgusting – but underneath that fur and sharp teeth beat hearts more plagued than mine had ever thought of being. They were mutations, simply put. The same as halvies.

"I think we might be related," was all the intelligent response I could muster.

Beneath her muzzle I thought I saw a hint of a smile, but she said nothing. I wasn't as afraid of her as I had been. Maybe that was because I had Vex with me. Or maybe it was because I was more afraid of this thing that was so important a goblin had come above ground to fetch me.

The rest of the trip passed in relative silence. From what I could tell, we were headed north-east – away from the den beneath Down Street station. Eventually our cart stopped and we disembarked, following Elsbeth on foot down another track. Just as I had thought – we weren't far from the Prince Albert Hospital stop.

"Left it to be found, they did," Elsbeth told us as the faint scent of train, dirt and decay reached my nostrils. "Reeking of Xandra lady and death."

She hadn't mentioned death earlier. "What is it?" I asked. My voice had a slight tremor to it. A suspicion had already begun to take root and I prayed that I was wrong.

"Left for us to dispose of," Elsbeth continued, as though she hadn't heard me. "For the plague to hide."

She stopped walking and I was brought up short behind her. Out of the shadows came half a dozen goblins, one of whom was the prince.

"Xandra lady," he said by way of greeting. "Your prince regrets, yes. Greetings, wolf."

And then he did the damnedest thing. He took my hand in one paw and patted it with the other. I shivered but didn't snatch my hand away. "Come."

I walked beside him for maybe ten or twelve feet – Vex, looking tense, close behind, with the rest of the goblins closing ranks. We stopped next to what looked like a bundle of rags, but when the light of the torch made the journey from end to end, I knew it wasn't rags. Rags didn't wear loafers.

The prince nodded at another goblin, who came forward and

turned the body over. I knew before I saw the face who it was, but the lifeless eyes that stared up at me drove a spike of dread right through my heart.

Simon.

When the gob ... when *Elsbeth* had said that Simon's body had been left for the goblins to hide, she meant that he'd been left for them to eat, effectively getting rid of the evidence. He would simply be one more missing person in the vast necropolis of London.

It made me think of all the bones I had seen in the plague den. Most of those were from the Insurrection, or scavenged, rooted out of plague pits and ancient graves, but how many of them were from murder victims tossed down here like garbage and blamed on the goblins? It was an easy and efficient way to dispose of a body. It was what would have happened to Simon if the gobs hadn't caught my scent.

There was blood on Simon's lab coat – my blood. Not much, but it was there. Perhaps from his tests, or maybe there had been some left over, I dunno. It was enough that the goblins had smelled it and identified it, and for that reason I was glad. I was still afraid of them – would be a fool not to be – but they could have just eaten him. Instead, they'd risked coming above ground, where some human might have tried to be a hero, to find me.

Simon hadn't been dead for long, and judging from his injuries he'd been tortured shortly before being killed. I knew this because the wounds hadn't been given a chance to heal. They'd stabbed him through the heart with a silver blade – it was still in him.

"He was killed because of me." I glanced at the prince. "This is my fault."

The prince regarded me with his one eye. It was a gaze full of knowledge, predatory yet sympathetic. "Because of you, yes. Fault of you, no. Many secrets is your life."

"That's one way to put it," I agreed. "Could you smell anything on him?" My own senses were so overwhelmed by the scents of the underground that I didn't trust myself to sniff out more subtle odours.

"He stinks of the blood."

"My blood stinks?"

A soft bark – laughter. "*The* blood. The fanged ones killed but did not feed." His muzzle wrinkled. "Tried to hide their stink."

Nothing could be hidden from a goblin nose. I almost imagined I could smell the strains of the plague, the Prometheus Protein that made up the vampire bloodline, but it was only my imagination desperately wanting to assign blame so that I could assuage my own.

"You're sure?"

He shot me a look of indignant arrogance. Of course he was sure. He *knew*. Fang me. Vampires had done this. Christ. A tear slid down my cheek. Poor Simon.

Soft fur touched my face – the prince was wiping my cheek. I froze, fear making steel of my spine as I waited for my throat to be ripped out. Claws brushed my skin but didn't scratch. Gentleness from a goblin? Why the hell not, seeing as how fucked-up everything else was. "He was your friend?"

I nodded, and he patted me on the shoulder with that same paw – it was a strangely soothing gesture. "The plague will not take him. The plague will honour your friend and put him where he will be found, not lost."

I swiped the back of my hand across my cheek. I was not going to cry for Simon, I was going to find who'd done this and make them pay for it. "You will?"

A resolute nod followed. He turned to the others. "Take the meat to St James's Park for the mice to find."

Good God, and I thought I was bigoted – and harsh. Meat, of course, was what goblins called any food source, but hearing that term applied to my friend turned my stomach, even though it wasn't meant to offend. And mice ... well, that was a charming term for humans. Mice and rats didn't cohabit, and those of the plagued blood thought of rats as our mascot, if you will. Like the Americans and their eagle.

"Thank you," I said. "I owe you a great debt." I felt the gravity of those words as I spoke. Indebted to a goblin was not a position in which I wished to find myself, but there was no way around it.

The prince shrugged. "I think not, but if pretty would like to bring tribute another day, that would be good."

I was getting off easy and smart enough to know it. "All right."

Two goblins picked up Simon's body and made their way down the track, their eyes covered by dark glasses. A lump pressed against the walls of my throat, choking me. I had failed him. I hadn't been careful, hadn't taken all of this seriously enough, and he had paid for it.

Well, I was taking it rutting seriously now.

The prince bowed his head to me and disappeared into the dark. The others followed after him, leaving Vex and me alone. We found the exit and quickly escaped cobbleside. From there he hailed a hack that returned us to my place. Good thing Vex had a few quid in his pockets, else we would have ended up walking.

"Come," he said when we were inside once more. Avery wasn't home. He took me by the hand and pulled me into the kitchen. "I'll make us something to eat."

He was quiet while he cooked and so was I. What was he thinking? Was he wondering what the hell he had got himself into? Was he, like most people I had cared about, going to leave or be taken away?

Poor Simon. He'd said my blood was different. But the prince had said it smelled normal. Whatever my defect, it had no scent and was worth killing to keep secret. What the bloody hell was it?

I was pulled from my thoughts when a plate was set on the table in front of me. Steam rose, bringing the most delicious aroma to my nose. Saliva flooded my tongue.

I looked down at the thick steak, seared on the outside but undoubtedly red and juicy within. Vex had fried potatoes and eggs to go with it, and added toast that was such a beautiful shade of brown I was almost reluctant to butter it.

"I think you might be the perfect man," I told him.

He chuckled and sat down across the small table from me. "I doubt that."

I picked up my fork and hesitated. He was being so good. "Vex . . ."

"Eat first," he commanded. "I can wait for an explanation – but you will give me one." There was no anger in his eyes, just simple determination. I had no problem with that. He had come into the tunnels with me. We were in this together now, so I owed him at least an explanation. And my frayed nerves told me that if I held on to all of this any longer I'd blow an artery in my brain.

We ate in silence. It was so unbelievably good. I soaked up every last trace of yolk with my buttery toast and slumped back in my chair, sated. Vex had already finished and sat with an arm hooked over the back of his chair, legs stretched out, waiting for me to speak.

And so I spoke. I told him about Dede going missing and how I'd gone to the goblins for information. I told him how she'd been taken to Bedlam – which he already knew because of his association with Ophelia. I told him that I had seen the halvies in the cells, and that I'd been told I was different. I went on about giving Simon my blood – even though I'd already told him some it before. I told him I didn't know who I could trust, that I didn't think I even knew myself any more.

Afterwards I fell silent, gnawing on the side of my thumb as I waited for him to say something.

"You need to get someone else to take your blood," he said finally.

"Ophelia kept a sample to test."

He nodded. "Good. I'll check with her. Don't use your rotary or house line for discussing any of this."

"I've taken care of that as well – now. That's how I reckon *they*" – I made quotes with my fingers in the air – "found out about Simon."

"You're no doubt right." His expression was grim. "Promise me you'll be careful. If the people who took Duncan are involved, they won't hesitate to kill you."

An image of Simon's corpse flashed in my mind. The marks on him ... there were worse things than being murdered. "What about you? How deep are you in this, Vex?"

He got up to pour each of us a second cup of coffee, obviously weighing how much to tell me. I think we'd both begun to realise that we'd only get the answers we wanted if we took a chance on trusting each other. "I met Victoria and Albert not long after their marriage. She was enamoured of Scotland and our people – we were a curiosity for the English back then, with our wolves. Still are, for that matter, though many vampires treat us like well-behaved dogs. I got on well with Albert. He was a good man. Smart, fair. He didn't see humans as simply a convenient food source. He wanted to do right by them."

I took my cup as he offered it across the table. "I can't imagine having that sort of sentiment for humans."

"Aye." He took a drink. "This was before your time – long before the Insurrection. Things were different then. Everything changed in the nineteen-thirties." He fell silent, remembering.

"Albert was killed by humans."

"He was killed. I'm not convinced it was at human hands, not with the finesse with which he was done in."

I frowned. "What do you suspect?"

Sharp grey-blue eyes lifted to stare at me. "He was killed by someone every bit as strong as he was. Someone he knew. He hadn't tried to defend himself."

"You don't think . . ." It was almost too horrible for me to even speculate. ". . . that *she* killed him?"

The corner of his mouth lifted. "Careful, sweetheart. That sort of talk will get you arrested. All I know is that after he died, I asked a few questions and suddenly Her Majesty wasn't so in love with Scotland any more, and my wolves became somehow inferior to her vampires. Did you know that I was supposed to be in charge of training half-bloods at the Academy?"

"No. She gave the job to Churchill instead?"

"Yeah, for all the bloody good it's done him, the bastard. He's never forgiven me for it, either. He thought it would curry favour, but all it got him was kicked down the social ladder. Makes me wonder what he did to get her to notice him in the first place."

His tone made me frown. "Are you insinuating that you think Church killed Prince Albert?"

Vex held up his hands. "I'd never dream of impugning the honour of your hero, but I notice you've not confided any of this to him."

"No." I looked away. "I haven't." Why hadn't I? Church had always been there for me. I should have gone to him straight away, but I hadn't. I hadn't wanted him to know. Hadn't wanted him to look at me differently. Hadn't known if I could trust him. I still didn't know.

But I trusted Vex, and he was a human sympathiser.

"Are you a traitor?" I asked him, lifting my chin to meet his gaze once more.

"No," came his quick reply. "I love my people and my country. I've not done anything to jeopardise that, but I will do whatever is necessary to protect them both."

I understood what he meant. I didn't mean to keep to myself what I knew about Bedlam, but I couldn't hurt people I loved. At least I knew my priorities now.

"I've been worrying this bone for a long time, Xandra." Vex's voice rumbled down my spine. "And now that you think you have blood on your hands, I reckon you won't be able to play ignorant any more. I will find out what happened to my son. I will find out why you've been singled out, and I will deal with the people responsible."

"Even if they're of the aristocracy?" The word trembled on my tongue. Fang me, why couldn't I have simply believed Dede was dead?

He flashed a slightly feral grin. "Sweetheart, I might be a wolf, but I'm a Scot first, and I've *never* trusted those English bastards."

CHAPTER 12

ADVERSITY IS THE FIRST PATH TO TRUTH

Some American fellow once said that the English people possessed "an extraordinary ability for flying into a great calm". I always found that sentiment a little ... offensive until I experienced that very sensation.

Talking to Vex about Dede, Bedlam, the past, would normally have made me nervous, and perhaps made me wonder if I wasn't hatters after all for trusting someone else with my secrets, especially someone I hadn't known for very long. Instead, I felt a strange kind of peace at having let it out. The world hadn't ended. No one had hauled me off to Newgate. I felt lighter – unburdened. I also found my desire to discover the truth for myself refocused. Maybe I didn't want to believe that aristos – vampires in particular – were behind some of these awful things, but I couldn't hide my head in the sand.

But I needed ... no, I *had* to find out what had happened to Simon. I wasn't going to have his blood on my hands for naught.

I also owed it to Dede to treat her claims about Ainsley as though they might be true.

And I owed it to Church to take what Vex said about him with a bucket of salt, just as I owed Vex the same. In fact I reckoned I owed Vex a tad more than that. He trusted me with the truth about his son, and accorded me more respect than anyone had in quite some time. Church was good to me, but he still treated me as though I were a child – to be protected and coddled.

Vex and I went back to bed after we'd talked. I needed ... something. Reassurance, perhaps? Validation? Comfort? Regardless, we had something of a desperate shag and passed out wrapped around one another. He felt warm and solid next to me, and I realised how much I had craved just that. It was a little pathetic really, my needing someone to lean on. It had been a long time since I felt as though someone had my back rather than me always having theirs.

By the time we woke up, Scotland Yard had Simon's body. This we found out from the news on the box. Missing halvies didn't garner quite so much attention, but a dead one sure did – especially on a conservative human news programme that was all too happy to report the death.

"Sick bastards," I muttered.

Vex shrugged, and I allowed myself to enjoy the sight of his shirt pulling tight across his broad shoulders. "They're afraid of us, and it's always been human nature to hate that which frightens them."

My jaw dropped. "You're not condoning this." I jerked my thumb at the screen.

Harsh laughter came in response. "No. I don't think death is anything to celebrate, but I understand why they do it. We have no idea how long our lifespan is. Humans know they have an end coming – even you will outlive most humans by an entire lifetime."

"If I'm lucky," I replied. There were Royal Guards who had lived to see retirement, but a greater number had died in service. That thought had the opposite effect on me than it should have. "I need to go back to work."

His gaze was sharp. "You're in mourning."

Oh, right. Wouldn't do to have me break protocol. Someone might get suspicious. "And it's driving me hatters. I need to be doing something, not sitting around with my thumbs up my arse."

"Do you actually do that?" he asked with a saucy grin. "Because I'd like to see it."

I rolled my eyes at him. "You're such a dog." Literally. "Seriously, I can't take much more of this."

"Then tell them you want to go back to work. Petition Her Majesty. She'll probably side with you. She continued to run the country after Albert died."

He had a point – one worth pursuing.

"I'll talk to my father; maybe he'll plead my case."

Vex leaned back, stretching his arm across the top of the sofa. "Alpha trumps duke in aristocrat hierarchy. I'll talk to her if you want."

My surprise must have shown, because he took one look at my face and chuckled.

"You'd do that?" I asked. "But then she'll know we're … friends."

"Oh, is that what they call it these days?" His grin softened the caustic edge of his words. "Call me old-fashioned, but I was of the notion that we were doing something they used to call 'dating', or, if you want to go back even further, 'stepping out'."

For what it's worth, I loved the way he said "out" in that sexy brogue of his. "Fine. She'll know we're stepping out with one another."

"I imagine it hasn't escaped her notice, given that it's already made the gossip rags."

Another valid point. There was nothing left for me to say. "Thank you."

His eyes shone with a vaguely golden sheen. "Come over here and thank me properly."

It would have been ungrateful of me to refuse, so of course I did as he commanded. Snogging was fantastic for passing time, and Vex took my mind off everything else.

I might not be ready to put my entire life in his hands, but I trusted him. Part of me figured I didn't have much choice. I had to trust someone, and so far he had been the one to share more of himself with me.

He went off to fetch us something to eat, and I went to my desk and started up my Ava. The logic engine immediately leapt to life when I flicked the power switch. I'd paid a lot of quid for the bloody thing, but I did appreciate her speed. I sat down as the main page for my Aethernet connection popped up, and typed 'DUNCAN MACLAUGHLIN DEATH' into the search bar. I hit the return key and waited.

Two seconds later I was reading a news story about the murder. I'd gotten lucky that it mentioned Vex in it as the one who found the body, because Duncan hadn't gone by MacLaughlin, but Fraser, which I assumed was his mother's name. The article referred to him as Vex's ward. He hadn't seemed embarrassed about the boy, so why not give him his name? Was it so people wouldn't know the truth about Duncan's conception? The contract between aristo and courtesan was considered a marriage of sorts, giving legitimacy to each halvie born under it. Duncan wouldn't have that.

The article didn't leave anything out, and came with accompanying photograph of a blood-soaked sheet covering a body on damp cobblestones. Vex stood in the background. The anguish on his face was all the proof I needed.

In fact, I wished I hadn't seen it.

If Ophelia had been taken for experiments, and Duncan had been killed, why had I led such a relatively safe life? Was it because I had the advantage of being half-vampire rather than half-were? Or was it just dumb luck?

Or, was it as Dede suggested and I was special? I couldn't believe that. I'd know if I was special, wouldn't I?

Vex walked in just as I finished the article. I didn't want him to see it, so I clicked on the exit box. He glanced at the screen as he set a tray of food on the coffee table. "It's all right. I know that article by heart."

"I . . ." what was the right thing to say here? "I didn't want to make you see it again. I hope you're not offended that I looked him up."

"Of course not. Can I assume you believe me now?"

There was the slightest edge to his voice. The MacLaughlin didn't like having his honour questioned. "I believed you before. I just wanted to see for myself. Everyone's been telling me to find the truth for myself, so you can't blame me." Maybe that was a little defensive, but he would have done the same thing, I was certain.

He nodded, and his shoulders relaxed. "You're right. I'm sorry, it's just not the sort of thing I'd make up."

"I'd hope not." I got up from the desk and went to him. I put my arms around his lean waist and hugged him. After seeing the article I needed contact, and I reckoned he did too. We stood there for a long time, just holding each other.

A little while later we were finishing off a huge bowl of warm toffee pudding when the bell rang. I wasn't terribly surprised to open the door and find my brother on the threshold, wearing his inspector face.

"We need to talk," he stated, brushing past me. The late-afternoon sun hit me full in the face without his body there to block it. I winced as the brightness flooded my eyes. Bloody hell, that was blinding. I quickly closed the door.

"Talk about what?" I asked innocently, as I turned towards him, blinking away the spots dancing in front of my eyes.

"Let's start with how your blood came to be on a murder victim." Slowly, the inky splodge that was my brother came into focus. He stood with his legs braced, arms folded over the dark coat of his uniform. He looked menacing.

I arched a brow. "Should I assume the victim was Simon Halstead?" Just saying his name made my throat tight.

Val gave a curt nod. I shrugged. "He was doing blood work for me."

"What sort?"

"None of your business."

His shoulders heaved as he drew breath. "Xandy, this is a murder investigation. Everything about this man and your involvement with him is my business."

"You're supposed to be on bereavement leave." I crossed my arms over my chest. It seemed I wasn't the only one in my family who needed to keep busy. "Am I a suspect? Am I under arrest? Aren't I a conflict for you? You shouldn't even be here."

A muscle in his jaw twitched. "You could be a suspect, yes. What sort of tests were you having him do, and where were you on Tuesday evening between six and eight?"

Between six and eight? That meant that whoever had taken Simon had kept him alive for between three and five hours after he called me. My stomach rolled at the thought of what had been done to him during that time. I had seen the results of some of it. Had he confided to his captors what he had found? Or had he taken my secrets to the grave?

"The tests were of a personal nature," came Vex's voice from behind Val. "And she was with me on Tuesday."

Val turned. "No offence, my lord, but the questions were intended for my sister."

Vex's spine straightened. He was a fair bit taller than my brother – and much broader. "No offence, lad, but if the Yard knew you were here, investigating a case that involved one of your family members, you'd be reprimanded and most likely suspended."

Brilliant. A pissing contest. Just what I needed. "I asked Simon to test me for any signs of mental illness," I blurted. "And Vex is right, I was with him Tuesday night." To be honest I couldn't remember where the hell I'd been that night. I didn't even know what day it was.

Dull red seeped into my brother's cheeks. He never liked discussing emotions or anything that had to do with mental health.

I used his discomfort to my advantage. "With my mother and now Dede, it's a valid concern, Val." Amazing just how easily that lie rolled off my tongue.

He cast a sideways glance at Vex as he rubbed a hand over the back of his neck. "All right, all right. Are you okay, then?"

"Yeah," I replied, shaking off the guilt. "Yeah. I'm good."

Then my brother surprised me. He turned to Vex. "My lord, would you mind giving us a moment of privacy?"

I was about to chastise him for his rudeness, but Vex bowed his head. "Of course." He turned and walked towards the kitchen. It wasn't as though he couldn't eavesdrop if he wanted.

"That was boorish," I hissed when we were alone.

"I don't care," he shot back. "What the great ruddy hell is going on? As soon as that blood on Halstead was identified as yours, I was told to leave it alone and the entire thing was given over to Aristocrat Affairs. They put Churchill in charge."

My stomach dropped. "Bugger." Those were the big guns. They were strictly aristo business and aristo-run. They answered directly to the Queen. The only good part of this news was that Church was involved. He'd be calling next, no doubt. "I take it you've gone back to work, then?"

He ignored that, dark eyes boring into mine. "Tell me you're working on something top secret. I really don't want to think you're involved in something so shady that Victoria's right hand is watching you."

"It's neither," I replied truthfully. He was legitimately worried for me, and I hated not being able to tell him everything. "Val, I don't know what's going on. Unless AA view me as a suspect, I can't think of a reason for their involvement."

"Really?" my brother challenged in a peevish tone. "You can't think of one?"

"No." I didn't feel even a little bit guilty for lying to him. AA had taken him out of this, and I was going to keep him out of it. I had already lost Dede; I was not going to lose him too.

"Bugger." Val ran a hand through his thick indigo hair. His gaze snapped back to mine. "You're certain you're not in trouble?"

I almost laughed. His tenacity made him a good inspector, but it was a pain in the arse right now. I jerked my head in a forced nod. "I'm certain."

He looked relieved, so much so that I knew I would never be able to confide in him. He'd want to fix everything – and to Val that meant abiding by the rules and the laws. I had already broken several of each. He could never know about Dede, the goblins, Bedlam, Vex – any of it.

So I pushed aside my feelings of guilt as he kissed me on the forehead, and told myself I'd lied to him for his own good, to protect him. What he didn't know about Simon couldn't get him in trouble. What he didn't know about Dede couldn't break his heart.

And what he didn't know about me couldn't get him killed.

My first night back to work was the Buckingham Palace Platinum Ball in celebration of the 175th year of the Queen's reign.

I had no illusions as to why I had been allowed to return to work. Vex had indeed gone to Queen Victoria on my behalf, and apparently Her Majesty did express admiration of my dedication to the Crown, but the simple fact remained that this celebration was incredibly high-risk as far as a human attack went. They needed all the protection they could get.

But if I was allowed back to work then Aristocrat Affairs couldn't view me as much of a suspect in Simon's murder. I wouldn't be allowed within a hundred yards of the palace if I were.

Val was there as well. He wasn't in uniform, but in evening clothes, greeting and screening the guests as they moved through the hounds, testing for silver and other weapons, even though most of the guests were halvies and aristos. There were a few humans in attendance, however – members of the human division of parliament. They'd be the ones I'd watch closely that night. I always watched them.

Val looked as surprised to see me as I was to see him. I handed him the Bulldog before I went through the detector, as was procedure. "You look nice," he said when he gave the gun back to me.

"Likewise." I tucked the weapon into the holster hidden in the bustle of my black silk gown. Regardless of being allowed to return to work, I still had to adhere to mourning dress, as did Val, who was in head-to-toe black rather than the usual black and white. "Avery here too?"

He nodded. "Came in about five minutes ago with Lord and Lady Maplethrope. Lady M asked her to accompany them tonight, said she'd feel safer. Halstead's murder's being pinned on humans, and it's got the entire peerage on edge." Like Dede, Avery was Peerage Protectorate. Viscount and Viscountess Maplethrope were her clients. From what I understood, she quite liked them, and they treated her extremely well.

"Bad form," I said with a frown. "Asking her to break mourning. They're saying humans killed Simon?"

My brother arched a brow at my surprised tone. "Who else would have done it? And I don't think either of us has the right to comment on proper mourning behaviour."

I forced a smile. "I suppose not." And then, since I didn't want to talk about Simon's death, and I was holding up the line of aristocrats behind me, "Be sharp tonight, Val."

He patted me on the shoulder. "You too."

The skirts of my gown swished around my low-heeled black boots. I had to lift them as I climbed the crimson-carpeted staircase. I was on the left bank as I ascended, rather than the right, where invited guests made their entrance. This segregation allowed me to go directly into the ballroom rather than wait to be announced. I passed Avery as she waited in the line with her lord and lady. I waved and she blew me a kiss. She wore a velvet gown so black it didn't even shimmer in the light. She would have a small arsenal in her bustle as well, and probably a dagger in her garter. Mine was tucked into my boot.

Humans. They were blaming this on humans. I shouldn't be surprised. A few days ago and I would have swallowed that story like ice cream, but I'd seen the body. I'd been there when the goblins said he'd been killed by vamps. Goblins didn't lie, but could they have been wrong?

Or were the real killers simply trying to cover their arses? I couldn't be distracted by this now. I had to stay sharp. If I didn't do my job tonight, people could get killed.

The ballroom was by no means crowded when I entered, but it was filling. Most of the aristocracy clung to the notion of being fashionably late, but they also knew better than to keep Her Majesty waiting. In less than an hour this room would be packed with not only England's highest-ranking citizens, but also many from Ireland and Scotland as well – even some from other European houses.

The red carpet that usually covered the floor had been rolled up to reveal a highly polished surface perfect for dancing. Overhead, crystal chandeliers lined both sides of the ceiling, and accompanying wall sconces contributed to the golden glow cast over the space. At the far end of the room, two thrones sat side by side beneath a gilt arch. The Queen would sit in one of them. Perhaps the Prince of Wales would occupy the other – a seat that had once belonged to his father, Prince Albert. The thrones were two items that had been saved from the fire that ravaged the palace during the insurrection.

To the left of the thrones, in the corner of the room, the small orchestra played something by a composer I recognised but couldn't identify. There would be no modern music for the next several hours – Her Majesty wasn't a big fan of anything written after 1915. Social gatherings were one of those things about which Queen V remained steadfast, and she liked them to be comported in a certain manner – hers. Though, she had conceded to having electricity installed when the palace was rebuilt.

I stood off to the side, watching the guests – dressed in the style of court reminiscent of 1887 – as they mingled and a steady stream of others trickled in. It was a river of men in black and white, the women in shades that would put a peacock to shame, corseted and coiffed.

Most of them were as devoted to the old ways as Queen V was, arriving in horse-drawn carriages, wearing pounds of petticoats, the men with mutton chops. But their homes had electricity and running water. They listened to recorded music and watched the box. Aristos enjoyed comfort as much as the rest of us, but they needed to keep some of the past with them. I think it stopped them from feeling like antiques.

Or freaks.

Their names and titles were as familiar as the back of my own hand, though some I had not heard in several years. I, along with the rest of the RG, had been briefed on those visiting from other houses across the Continent. This was an auspicious occasion, after all. Victoria was the first monarch of her kind to have ruled this long.

I checked names against faces, as did my colleague on the other side of the door. There would be Guards downstairs as well, scattered throughout the palace, patrolling the grounds, watching from rooftops and lorries parked on the street. All of us were armed, prepared to risk our lives for our nobility. Avery only had to protect her family, but every aristo under this roof was my responsibility – and the responsibility of every RG – for the rest of the evening.

"You know, you're very sexy when you're serious."

I smiled and a shiver danced down my spine at the sound of Vex's voice. "Is that so?" I asked, keeping my attention on the increasing crowd. "I'll have to remember that."

"Aye, you should." He stood beside me, and I appreciated that he took care not to obscure my view of the room. "So, are you on duty all evening?"

I nodded. "Until Her Majesty tosses you sorry lot to the kerb. Why?"

He shrugged, all predatory grace as muscles shifted beneath his black jacket. What was it about a black suit and white shirt that complimented almost any man who donned them? He even wore a cravat, impeccably knotted around his neck. An easy grin curved his lips. "I thought maybe I might squire you on to the dance floor at some point."

I hid my pleasure with a coyly arched brow. "Wouldn't such squiring set tongues to wagging?"

His gaze locked with mine – warm and seductive, with just a hint of gold in the faded blue. "I don't care. Neither should you."

Maybe it was the fact that he was a wolf. Or perhaps I was caught up in the nineteenth-century atmosphere and was having an attack of feminine delicateness, but fang me, he was sexy when he put on the alpha.

I smiled. "All right. I can take a break around one. Come and find me."

"I will." His gaze continued to smoulder. "And when this is over, I think you should come home with me."

I started. As in to his house? I didn't know why, but the invitation threw me. That said something about the amount of trust he had in me if he was going to take me to where he slept. That, or he meant to kill me. "Are you sure?"

The amusement on his face might have stung were it not tempered with genuine warmth. "I'll meet you downstairs." Then he took one of my gloved hands in his much larger one and raised it to his lips. It was official – I had time-travelled back a century. All I needed was Mr Jones and his privacy box.

My pleasure diminished, however, when I happened to glance towards the entrance – I was on duty, after all – and spied the couple who had just been announced.

"What is it?" Vex asked.

Silently I berated myself for not having hid my reaction better. "Ainsley," I replied in a low voice as my gaze followed the slim aristocrat and his petite wife. Both of them were incredibly pretty – doll-like, almost. I never understood what Dede saw in the dandy, but then she would wonder the same about me and Vex.

"Isn't he . . . ?" Vex stopped.

I glanced at him, mouth thin. "The man my sister tried to kill? Yes."

"Did he deserve it?"

I turned my attention back to Ainsley in all his blonde, blue-eyed perfection, and watched as he conversed with other guests as though he hadn't a care in the world. I thought about Dede and how she had wept for him after she lost the baby. He never came to see her.

"Yes," I replied.

"Then it's too bad she didn't succeed."

I could have kissed him for that. "Indeed. You should go and mingle."

He nodded, not the least bit offended by my dismissal. He left me with a squeeze of my hand and the promise to collect me later. I allowed myself the pleasure of watching him walk away for no longer than two seconds before putting my attention firmly back on my job, where it belonged. Just as well, because at that moment, Churchill was announced. It didn't matter that I was no longer his student; if he caught me slacking, he'd ream me for it.

Pale eyes searched the crowd before settling on me. He seemed surprised to see me, but nodded in greeting regardless. I nodded back as I switched on the small device tucked around and in my right ear. It worked in a similar fashion to a rotary, only the line was shared by every Royal Guard in attendance.

It was quarter to the hour; all the guests would be expected to be in attendance at that time, and the doors would be shut precisely on the hour. Her Majesty would make her appearance at half past. The communication device in my ear made it easy for all the RG's to alert one another to any possible threat.

One by one, all fifty of us on duty – our full ranks – reported in, letting the rest know we were on the job and accounted for. As I did before every society event, I sent up my usual little prayer/mantra/what-have-you that there would be no problems tonight.

I remained at my post by the door, watching the line of guests trickle to a few stragglers, then to nothing. Over my earpiece I heard a co-worker confirm that the palace doors were shut and secured. Everyone on the guest list had arrived and no one else would be granted admittance for the remainder of the evening.

That was my cue to start patrolling. Usually I preferred to work both interior and exterior security, but since the event was locked down, the guards were stuck doing one or the other. There were RGs outside right now who envied those of us inside, and in a way, I envied them. At least out there you didn't have to witness all the fun in which you weren't allowed to take part. I'd only get away with dancing with Vex because of who he was – not like I could refuse him.

About half an hour after we were locked in, Queen Victoria made her entrance to much applause and bowing and curtsies. My spine snapped straight like the leg of a card table when the fanfare began. A voice in my ear told us all to be on guard.

In heels she might have been five foot two, if that. The plague kept her appearance the same as it had been when she was in her late twenties, so she was fairly slim, with long, lustrous brown hair that she wore piled up on top of her head in an elegant knot. She had a round face with large blue eyes, a slightly aquiline nose and a small mouth. Her skin was so fair she looked like a china doll, though she could never be likened to one in any other way.

She was the most powerful being in the country – in the world, I suspected – and she looked like a waif. I, like everyone else, was in shameless awe of her. When she passed by, I curtsied so deeply my knee brushed the carpet. I should have bowed my head, but I had to keep a watchful eye. Queen V gave me a once over and then nodded, and I felt the recognition and weight of that condescension. Obviously she approved of my return to work and continued observation of the proper mourning rites.

Fang me, but I don't think she had acknowledged me since the day I graduated from the Academy – and then she'd treated me the same as everyone else. I noticed two of my fellow RGs glancing at me as though they were jealous. Idiots. If my new-found celebrity status with Vex didn't earn me their scorn, this would for certain. It wasn't as though I asked for it, or went out of my way to attract notice.

She walked to the back of the room, where her throne – and Albert's empty one – waited for her. Before she sat, she looked out at us all. The band had fallen silent, as had everyone in the room.

"We are very pleased to see you all tonight," she began, in a surprisingly strong, clear voice that carried throughout the hall without the aid of amplification. "On this momentous occasion, we thank you for celebrating with us and take a moment to remember those who are no longer with us." En masse we all glanced at Albert's vacant throne.

"For almost two centuries have we reigned over this vast empire," she continued. "We have seen many changes and have shared many experiences – some more poignant than others. But what has never changed is our love for our country and our people, and so let this night be a celebration not just of how many years we have ruled, but of how many years we have endured, and will continue to endure."

The applause was thunderous. Victoria was not what one would consider verbose, but she made every word count. I clapped until my palms stung and then watched her take her place on her throne. She would sit there for the remainder of the evening, giving audience to guests who wanted to wish her well, and over-seeing the proceedings. I would not speak to her. Only aristos were given leave to speak; we halvies were there to work.

Over the course of the evening I admit my attention slipped. Occasionally my mind would trick me into thinking I saw Dede, or even Ophelia, in the throng. My heart would give a great leap of terror, and I'd experience that chest-crushing paralysis, only to then realise I was a plonker. A few other times it was Vex who drew my eye. I watched him dance with what seemed like a legion of eligible ladies but in reality was probably only five or six. That low aristo birth rate really cut back on the number of debutantes each year.

My gaze jumped to Ainsley and his wife, who were also danc-ing. If Dede had indeed given birth to a fully plagued child, that would certainly be an advancement in increasing aristo numbers. Given the desire for "pure" blood, it would explain why Ainsley would pass his lady off as the child's mother.

It would also explain why someone would have an interest in unusual halvies. Why someone might want to experiment on them.

Fuck. It was like a flash bulb going off inside my head. I had to keep myself from running up to Vex, yanking him away from deb number whatever, and telling him my suspicions. This wasn't about hurting halvies, or even using them as guinea pigs. If aris-tos were truly behind these atrocities – such as letting goblins rape halvies – then it was like a darker part of the Pax. The government tried to sell monitoring human DNA as a good thing for humans, but it was simply a way for aristo-backed scientists to weed out those who carried the plague and see if they could be used for the good of all with "royal blood". This was about increasing aristo numbers.

I came back to myself in time to find Vex watching me with a

quizzical expression. I arched a brow at his mousy companion –
a full blood were who could probably eat me for breakfast. She
didn't see my look, but Vex did. He winked at me, obviously
enjoying the little niggle of jealousy poking at my spleen.

"Did MacLaughlin just wink at you?"

The sound of Church's voice snapped my shoulders back. That
was what I got for letting my guard down. "Probably he had
something in his eye, sir," I replied as I turned my head towards
him.

We stood nose to nose. How little he was. Right now his pale
blue eyes studied me as though I were an ant beneath a magnify-
ing glass – no emotion, only curiosity.

"You cannot fool me, Alexandra Vardan. I know you better than
you know yourself." I would have liked to argue that point, but he
went on. "The rumours about you and the Scots wolf are true. Tell
me, is he what brought you so prematurely out of mourning?"

I matched my gaze to his and held it there, no matter how much
the bottom of my spine seemed to writhe. "Duty to my queen and
a desire to be useful brought me out of mourning, sir. As it did my
brother and sister as well." I kept my voice low. We weren't far
from the Queen, and I didn't wish her, or those who were paying
her court, to hear our conversation.

He clasped his hands behind his back. The stance lifted his
chest, made him seem larger. "You've been different these past
few times we've met, Xandra."

"Losing a sibling changes a person," I countered. I wasn't
going to admit that being around him confused me. He had
changed. He seemed almost offensive with me – as though I had
displeased him in some way.

Such as sleeping with a man he hated. Only, this didn't feel like
a fatherly sort of displeasure. He looked at me as though I had
wounded him on an emotional level.

"Your blood was on that murdered halvie they found."

I didn't flinch, though I might have paled. It felt as though all the blood in my head had run screaming for my feet. "Are you accusing me of being involved in Simon's death, sir?"

"You must admit it looks suspicious," he commented, dodging the point.

"Suspicious?" I echoed. He never would have said these things to me before. He would have immediately asked what happened, what he could do to help. No, this was the attitude of a man who wanted to make me squirm just a little. "Is it against the law to have a friend do some blood tests for me?" I hadn't planned to say it, but what the hell.

"What manner of tests?"

I smiled – a little mockingly, I might add. "I wanted to make certain the insanity that obviously runs in both sides of my blood-line hasn't affected me as well."

"There was no indication of any tests found in his office or his computer, or on the body."

I shrugged, relieved that Simon hadn't left a paper trail. "He called to give me the results. I went to see him with some questions, only to find him gone." I didn't want to confide even this much, but this was Church, for fuck's sake. He was the man to whom I'd run with everything from a scraped knee to a broken heart. I couldn't turn my back on all of that just because fingers had been pointed in his direction, or because he was jealous of Vex.

Jealous over me.

"Were the results satisfactory?"

I met his gaze evenly. He looked genuinely concerned and I felt like a cad for lying to him. I wanted to tell him how sorry I was. "They were, thank you. Sir, I . . . " I heard something that drew my attention, smelled something that brought my fangs out fast and hard – fear.

I whirled around. The orchestra still played, the dancers continued to dance. Conversation buzzed around us, but my attention went immediately to the one thing that didn't belong.

Up on the balcony. A human with a rifle – pointed at the Queen.

"Gun!" I yelled, my voice seeming to reverberate around me. As I leapt forward, I was aware of several things at once: the music screeching to a halt, the discharge of the rifle, screams, and how sweet that human bastard smelled.

How the bloody hell could I smell him from where I was?

I moved faster than I ever had before – or at least I seemed to. One moment I was beside Church; the next I crashed to the floor, my shoulder exploding with pain as I took the Queen with me.

I sucked in air, forced myself to reach for the Bulldog hidden in my bustle. Hot blood ran down my left arm. I'd been shot. Damnation, it hurt. Felt like my shoulder was on fire. My head and stomach churned in opposite rotations.

Tetracycline. Fang me, there was tetracycline in the bullet. And the bullet was silver. It had gone straight through – luckily for me. It still hurt like hell.

"Your Majesty, are you all right?" I demanded, positioning myself so I wouldn't drip blood on her. Plague me, even my eyes burned.

"Quite," she replied, looking both shocked and relieved. "Young lady, you are most extraordinary."

I smiled despite the throbbing in my shoulder. "Thanks."

Church and my father appeared at my side. I told Vardan to look after Victoria, and then I jumped to my feet. I swayed, but just for a second. The shooter was already gone, but I could track him.

It didn't matter than a dozen RG had already taken off in pursuit. It didn't matter that Vex was shouting my name as he pushed through the crowd. I knew I could catch the bastard – that I was the only one who could. It was hubris, of course, but I was so high on endorphins it felt like kismet. Those endorphins were the only thing keeping me standing.

Hitching my skirts, I ran, following the heavenly scent – which had only grown stronger. Had human fear always smelled this delicious? And how did I know that that was what I smelled?

The others had gone up to the balcony first. That was a waste of time. If the shooter had been smart enough, and stealthy enough, to get inside, then he was smart enough to have an escape route planned – a quick one. I knew it as soon as I found it.

He had gone out through a window – there was a length of grappling cable hanging outside the glass. How had he even got in? Every staff member was a long-term employee, and had been screened before the event. Guards patrolled outside, watched every entrance and exit despite all of them being securely locked.

But one of them couldn't have been secure. Either that or someone had let the human in. One way or the other, this was going to reflect badly on my people. We were supposed to prevent this kind of thing, and one of us had fucked up – royally, to be perfectly accurate.

I swung out of the open window below the balcony, dropping easily to the ground. My shoulder seemed to be going numb, though it was probably shock. Soon my body would start repairing itself, but the drug's properties would have the opposite effect on me from what they had on non-plagued blood, and would slow the process down. It was a powerful weapon when trying to kill a halvie or an aristo, fighting our blood as though it was a sickness.

The would-be assassin wasn't far ahead. As I raced past the few halvies who had beaten me outside, I could hear him gasping for breath, the lumbering, graceless slapping of his boots on pavement. And I could smell him – like a cake straight from the oven, or a fresh cup of chai. My mouth actually watered.

My lips peeled back from my teeth as I ran, forced back by the fangs extending from my gums. I could stop, raise my right arm and put metal in the human, but I didn't want to shoot him. I wanted to take him down and rip out his throat – but I'd settle for just a little taste before turning him over to Scotland Yard.

He ran into a Met station. I followed close on his heels, dimly aware of humans stopping to stare, or cry out as I raced by – a crazed halvie bleeding like mad and waving a gun almost as big as my head. Two tourists got in my way, almost toppling me over as they stopped to take a photo. The flash momentarily blinded me, scalding my sensitive eyes. I stumbled, blinked rapidly and pushed on, spots dancing in front of me.

My prey ran below, pushing his way through the normal underground crowd. They cleared a path for me, and when the human jumped the platform, running for the dark of the tunnel, I ran too.

He glanced behind, saw me and gave a little cry of distress. The glint of metal in the darkness, and then a flash. He fired at me, but missed. Terror didn't exactly make for an accurate shot.

I reached for him. He could shoot me again if he wanted – I'd survive, at least long enough to finish him. Behind me I heard the pounding of halvie feet – at least a dozen backing me up.

The shooter fired again. Then another report – someone had answered from behind me with a shot of their own. I was sure he'd missed, but then I felt a familiar heat in my chest – or was it my back? – knocking me off balance and making me careen into the rough stone wall.

I struggled for breath and was rewarded with what felt like a building sitting on my breast. The bullet had collapsed my lung, and hadn't had the manners to go right through me. It was inside, filling me with its poison.

Poison that was taking me down much further than it ought to have. Staggering, I tried to push off the wall and take up the chase once more, but I couldn't. I stumbled to my knees. I was on the tracks, and any moment there would a train. I could feel the vibration beneath my palms.

I was going to die.

Out of the darkness came the scent of fur and smoke. Strong furry paws clutched me, pulled me up on to a ledge and further into the shadows. I heard the pounding of footsteps – someone running through the tunnel. Then more running – this time several people. I might have called out, but a paw over my mouth stopped me. It smelled of dirt and strangely of coffee.

Quickly my eyes adjusted to this new darkness. I blinked and looked around me. I was surrounded by goblins. The prince stood in front of them, eye glowing in the darkness. "Xandra," he said, "you bleed, pretty."

And then he licked his chops and everything went black.

CHAPTER 13

THE PURE AND SIMPLE TRUTH IS RARELY PURE AND NEVER SIMPLE

For a moment I hoped I was in heaven – or wherever it is my kind go when death calls. I wanted to wake to peace and warmth in a place where trying to suss out what I was didn't get people killed, and I didn't get shot by mental-arse humans.

Instead I opened my eyes and discovered that I was in hospital. The flimsy little gown they'd put me in had tiny pink piggies on it. My first thought was that I had to have been in bad shape to be admitted. My second, I'm ashamed to admit, was whether or not they'd let me take the nightie home with me.

"It's about fucking time," growled a voice to my right.

I turned my head with a smile. Vex rose from a chair beside my bed. He was still in his evening clothes, though his cravat hung loose about his neck. He looked tired, drawn and terribly gorgeous.

"Heaven's better than I imagined," I told him, my voice a rasp. I took back what I'd thought earlier about him contemplating killing me. There was no faking how wrecked he looked at that moment. It was as comforting as it was terrifying.

"Don't even joke," he chastised me, taking a cup of water from the nightstand and holding it for me to take a sip. "You scared the fucking fur out of me tonight. If it wasn't for the gobs ..." He stopped, expression grim.

I had a fuzzy memory of the prince finding me. I thought I was going to be served on toast. "If it wasn't for the gobs, what?"

He shook his head. "They saved you. I don't know how they did it, but they kept you from dying with a fifty-calibre silver bullet in your chest, and tetracycline in your system."

"Halvies aren't frail, Vex."

"Your heart stopped." His face was ashen now. "I was there. Your heart stopped and there was so much blood. The prince took you and made your heart beat again."

I stared at him. "You were there?" Wrong detail to get hung up on, but I didn't want to think about how close I'd come to dying. And I didn't want to think about the debt I now owed the prince.

"Aye." His expression told me it wasn't something he wanted to discuss.

I swallowed, and tasted something unfamiliar in the back of my throat – like a memory on my tongue. My stomach clenched, not because it was unpleasant, but because I had an awful feeling I knew just how the goblin prince had saved me.

"What were you thinking, going after the shooter alone?" demanded Vex, so angry I could practically feel the heat of it on my cheeks.

"My job," I replied, shifting against the pillows. I winced – the entire left side of my torso felt like it had been pounded, ripped apart and set on fire, which I supposed it had. "Why did you chase after me?"

"If the situation were reversed, wouldn't you run after me?"

He had a point, but I was the one trained for this sort of thing. "You could have been hurt."

His rugged features twisted in annoyance. "Please. If I hadn't followed you, you wouldn't be here. The prince wouldn't have given you to anyone else."

"Why not?" The tunnel had to have been swimming with halvies by that time.

A muscle in his jaw ticked. "Xandra, you were shot from behind."

Fang me and chew the wound. "I was shot by an RG? But I'd be certain the bullet had been silver. You've got to be joking." When I saw that he wasn't, "Who? Which bastard fired without being certain I was clear?"

Vex shrugged. "They don't know. No one's owned up to firing before they had a visual on the bastard, and once they did, they put more holes in him than a fucking lace doily."

I ignored his antiquated comparison. "No one admitted to it?" No, I suppose no one would want that on their record, or the suspension that would come with it.

He took my hand in one of his. His fingers were so warm I almost sighed in bliss. Thank God for whatever meds they'd pumped into me, because right now I was just relaxed enough that hysteria couldn't take hold.

He looked me dead in the eye, and made sure I was paying attention before he spoke. "I don't think it was an accident."

It was ludicrous. Ridiculous. Paranoid. And if it wasn't for Simon's death – murder – I would have laughed it off as impossible. But my life had been turned upside bloody down the past few weeks and I'd be mental to say anything was impossible at this point. A fortnight ago I would have claimed my mother being alive was impossible.

"Xandra?"

I glanced up. Vex wore a slightly pained expression. "What is it?"

"I think you just broke one of my fingers."

I immediately let go, staring at his hand in horror as I eased my grip. I'd left white marks on his skin, and his left ring finger was bent at a strange angle.

"Bloody hell," I whispered. "Vex, I'm so sorry."

He popped the bone back in place with little more than a grimace. "Nothing that can't be fixed." His grey gaze locked with mine once again, but there was something in his eyes I couldn't name. "I didn't know halvies were so strong."

"I didn't either," I replied. In fact I was certain I shouldn't have been able to hurt a were like that. Human bones were different; they were brittle compared to an aristo's. "Vex, what the ruddy hell is wrong with me?"

He took my hand again – brave man. "I don't know, but we'll find out."

Since I'd first started to "forget" to take my supplements I'd noticed more and more changes. Humans hadn't smelled like food before that. Everything felt . . . sharper.

Now I fancied I could hear nurses talking at their station, their voices low. I could smell the stale scent of piss from a long-ago patient beneath layers of cleaning fluids and disinfectants used in this room. And from where I lay, I could look up at Vex and count the dark individual lengths of his eyelashes.

The blood I was uncomfortably certain the prince had given me could account for some of that, but I'd noticed changes before tonight. What if the supplements that were supposed to keep me healthy, dampen those vampiric urges, suppressed the parts of me that were unusual? Ophelia had told me as much. What if I, like Vex's son, leaned more toward an aristo genetic code than normal? It would explain my reaction to tetracycline.

"You're going to be all right," Vex told me. Coming from him it really did sound like a promise rather than a trite remark to make me feel better.

I pulled off a weak smile. "I suppose if I was well and truly buggered I would have found out long before this, wouldn't I?"

His eyes sparkled. "Before you reached the advanced age of two and twenty? I expect so."

"You must think I'm such a child." I couldn't even say it was the drugs talking, because those were pretty much gone. I suppose I was feeling a little sorry for myself, as well as sore.

"Yes," he agreed with a mocking frown. "Because pain makes most people behave in a mature and rational manner."

I flushed. I'm such an idiot at times. "You know what I mean."

"No. I don't." He leaned down and kissed me. Even his lips seemed incredibly warm. "I think you're adorable – in a completely mature and aged way."

It hurt to laugh, but I needed the release. I was still chuckling – and groaning – when the nurse came in.

"Time for your medicine," she remarked, holding up a needle. If that was for pain, I was glad of it. I'd never hurt like this before, and rest would only help me heal faster.

As though reading my thoughts, Vex gave my hand another squeeze. "I'm going to go. You get some rest and I'll be back later."

"Good," I said. He kissed me again, nodded at the nurse and left.

The nurse smiled at me. "He's a fine one."

"Mm," I agreed. "I think so."

She came closer and slipped the tip of the needle into the small port on the IV attached to my arm. That was when I noticed the salt-water blue peeking out from beneath her green hair. I looked past the glasses on her nose and the dark hue of her skin. The glasses were just that – plain glass – and the warm honey tone of her skin was purely cosmetic. She was also wearing coloured contact lenses, but her nose was almost exactly like mine.

I grabbed her by the front of her uniform and hauled her against the rail along the side of my bed, my battered insides screaming in protest.

"What the fuck are you doing here?" I demanded around clenched teeth.

Ophelia pushed against my fist. "Let go of me, freak. I'm here to help you. This needle has Prometheus Protein in it."

I could feel her heart hammering against my fist. She was afraid – maybe of me, or maybe of getting caught, but it was enough for me to let her go.

"Why would I need your help?" I asked, suspicious, peevish as she depressed the plunger. By injecting me with the protein responsible for the aristo mutation, she would essentially jack my body into healing itself. The hospital staff had probably given me a watered-down version – the legal dose – already, but a concentrated shot would only make me heal all the faster.

Though there was a chance it would also make the differences in me that much more pronounced.

"Because you're not safe here," she hissed, casting a glance towards the door. Then she turned to me with a shake of her head. "I still can't believe you're shagging the alpha."

"Why?" She didn't have to sound so freaking surprised. "Did you think your liege had better taste in women?"

"No, I thought it went against your vampire-loving sensibilities." She wiped the now empty syringe with the edge of my sheet and tossed it in the sharps bin. No prints. Clever. "What's your precious Churchill have to say about it?"

"My personal life is no more Church's business than it is yours,"

I retorted, though she had struck a nerve. Everyone, even the general populace, seemed to have an opinion on my private concerns.

"I wonder what Vex sees in you?" she mused with a smirk. "I suppose it's your feral nature."

I glared at her. "Fuck off."

My back ached and itched – the shot she'd given me was working already, forcing my battered body to repair itself. "What is it to you anyway? Jealous?"

The mockery in her eyes faded. "He's a good man. I don't want to see him get hurt."

I met her gaze. If I could beat her senseless with my eyes I would, but she was sincere in her concern for Vex. She'd probably known Duncan. "Neither do I."

"Then we don't have a problem." Her smile was mockingly sweet. "Word from our human connections is that tonight's attack on Victoria was a hired hit."

"And?" I asked, knowing from the gleam in her eye that there was more.

She lowered her head to whisper near my ear. "Hired by an aristo."

I froze. I think my heart might have stopped for a second. I turned my head so that we were practically nose to nose. "You believe this?"

"I do. They wouldn't have told us at all, except the assassin was killed. And you got shot."

I snorted. "As if they care what happens to a stinking halvie."

Was that pity in her blue eyes? "There was only one intended target, Xandra, and it wasn't you. That you put yourself in front of that bullet makes you honourable, whether human, halvie or aristo."

Her words caught me so far off guard, the only expression I could muster was a scowl. "I did my job, that's it."

A teasing glint brightened her eyes. "Look at you, all humble and annoyed. You'll be famous when the morning rags come out."

I hadn't thought of that. I supposed taking a bullet for one's sovereign was newsworthy. Fang me. I was not looking forward to this.

"Good PR for the RGs," Ophelia remarked. "Mayhap you'll get a promotion."

My heart jumped at the thought. "Is there something else you wanted to say?"

The light in her eyes died. "Mum was terrified when we heard the news."

Throat clenched, I clung to my surliness. "So distraught she had to come see me for herself."

My sister's face tightened. "I had to stop her from doing that very thing, brat."

I shifted against the pillows, wincing as the healing muscle and tissue inside me protested against the movement. My gaze locked with hers, and I saw nothing but honesty – indignant at that – reflected back. "Why? She hasn't seen me for years, and you don't even know me."

She looked affronted. "You're my sister."

Something else we had in common: a sense of familial loyalty that was as knobbed up as it was commendable. I wasn't about to throw out my arms and spout poetry about the love of sisters, but I was touched.

"Thank you," I said, some of the fight draining out of me. "You can tell her that I'm fine."

"You're not fine. You were shot – twice. Once by someone on your own side. Xandra, you're truly not safe here."

"As safe as I am anywhere else. Whoever shot me knows me. I wouldn't even begin to guess who to suspect."

"Wouldn't you?" Her stare bored into mine. "Maybe you

should think on that. I have something for you." She reached into her pocket. When she brought her hand out, she offered her closed fist to me. Slowly, her fingers unfurled. In her palm was a spent slug wrapped in tissue. It was silver, with bits of dried blood on it.

"It's the one they took out of you," she explained. "The one that wasn't from the human's weapon."

"You stole it?" I could have slapped her. And maybe hugged her. "Albert's fangs, woman! It's evidence!"

"Evidence that someone tried to steal not thirty seconds after I grabbed it. I had to hide in a cupboard to keep from being seen."

I took the metal from her, careful not to touch it with my bare skin. As it was, the tissue was little protection. My thumb and forefinger began to sting. "How do you know he was after this?"

"Because when he discovered the bullet wasn't there, he made a call to someone telling them it was gone. The person on the other end was not impressed."

I set the bullet on my lap, where layers of sheet and clothing would protect me from it. What had I landed myself in? "Did you recognise the voice?"

She shook her head, her expression rueful. "It was familiar, but I haven't run with London's respectable crowd for a long time. Most of my life's been spent in Scotland."

I knew that. I stared at the squashed bullet. It was a relatively small thing, yet it had done so much damage. "Still, the human was apparently shot by every RG in pursuit. Even if I found a match, there'd be no way to prove whose gun fired it."

Ophelia arched a brow. In that moment it was almost like looking in a mirror – except for the fact that she had made her skin so dark. "I reckon you've got a real puzzle in front of you then. Oh, I have something else for you as well. From Dede."

I glanced at the door, making sure there was no one there, listening to our damning conversation. "What?"

She pulled an envelope from inside her "borrowed" uniform. "Here."

I opened the flap and pulled out several photographs – the kind taken with an Ensign "immediate" camera. The first showed Lord Ainsley and his wife.

"Did Dede take these?" I demanded, glancing up. It was one thing for her to be a traitor, but another thing altogether for her to risk herself for a bastard who never loved her.

Ophelia jerked her chin towards the photos. "Look at the next one."

I did, and the image captured made my heart skip a beat. There was Ainsley, Lady Ainsley and their son. He was a little boy of approximately four or five years of age, with shaggy blond hair and green eyes.

"Fang me," I whispered. There could be no denying the kid's parentage; he had his father's hair, but he had his mother's green eyes. He looked just like her.

Dede.

They released me at dusk. I was well on my way to recovery, had taken full advantage of the blood bank – intravenously, of course – and had made myself enough of a pain in the staff's collective arse that they were happy to see me go. No one even questioned my rapid recovery thanks to Ophelia.

I wasn't sure how I felt about her risking herself to steal a bullet and bring me those photographs. I had an easier time thinking of her as an enemy, or at least a nuisance. Thinking of her as an actual sister would complicate things. Family, I'd been told, was my biggest weakness. Ophelia was enough like me to play on that.

Avery and Emma came to fetch me. Vex had called to see how I fared and to say that he'd come round later. I needed to think of what to do, not only with the pictures, but with the disfigured lump of metal that was also in the bag with my belongings.

I didn't know anyone other than Val who might be able to test the bullet, check its markings and all that. Did I want to involve him? The Yard already had my blood on Simon. If Val was caught doing ballistic tests on the bullet that shot me – a bullet stolen from the hospital before it could even be sent to the laboratory – he could get into a lot of trouble.

Ophelia wouldn't have given it to me if she knew anyone capable of doing such tests. I had yet to hear from my mother about their own tests on my blood. Either her lab person was really slow, or there was foulness running amok in that quarter as well. Or perhaps she hadn't yet quite thought of the proper maternal way to say "Sorry, but you're fucked."

It was tempting to say sod it and stick my head in the mud and pretend none of this had happened – stop looking. But being shot had pissed me off, in addition to scaring the shit out of me. Maybe it had been an accident, maybe not. I would never feel safe at work until I knew who had done it, and I wanted to have a little chat with the twat responsible.

Or hide in the cellar and never come out again. Both had their merits.

When we arrived home, Avery insisted I rest and shooed me into the den while she and Emma made tea for the rest of us. I was glad of the reprieve. I was healed from the actual bullet wounds, but tetracycline was a bitch. I hadn't thought it would muck me up quite so badly, but the muscles and tissue down the entire left side of my back felt stiff and sore – bruised and raw. I was still a little nauseous as well. According to the doctors I would be fine the next day, when the drug was fully flushed from my system, but for the moment I had to whine silently to myself while putting on the show of a stiff upper lip.

I was lounging on the sofa like a lady recovering from a good swoon when my rotary buzzed in my pocket. I pulled it out and realised it was the one my mother had given me. The screen said I had a new message:

WE MUST MEET.

Not very cryptic at all, that. I listened to make certain neither Emma nor Avery were on their way, and quickly keyed back, TOMORROW EVE. That would have to suffice, as I wasn't going anywhere for at least the next twenty-four hours. I was going to take advantage of my sister's newly presented hero-worship of me and let her play nursemaid.

I needed a little vacation from this full-on hatters situation. I was home, where I was as safe as I could be. I was going to watch the box, eat until I felt my skin stretch, and try to pretend that things were normal for a few hours. As normal as they could be given that it appeared I had been intentionally shot.

I was prevented from fantasising about all the things that could be wrong with me by the arrival of Avery and Emma. One had a tray with the teapot, cups and plates while the other's contained sandwiches and cakes. I watched them arrange everything on the tea table with a smile.

"You two are so domestic. You should get married."

My sister and her partner exchanged glances. Avery's cheeks lit up like a Christmas tree. "We've talked about it," she murmured, avoiding my gaze.

I raised a brow and turned my attention to Emma, who looked at my sister as though the sun rose and set on her.

"Life is short," I quipped. "Best to do these things while you can."

I hadn't meant it as some "I've seen death" sort of wisdom, but obviously that was how Avery took it, because her big eyes filled with tears. "You're right."

"Ave," I began, reeking of remorse, "I didn't mean ..."

"No." She shook her head and turned to the other woman. "Emma Stanfield, I would like very much to marry you."

Aw, shit. I didn't need to see this. I didn't *want* to witness this intimate moment, but that didn't stop my eyes from tearing up. It was the pain, obviously – and the stress – making me overly emotional. I looked away and busied myself with filling my plate while they whispered, kissed and generally cooed like pigeons at one another.

Avery announced that it was cause to celebrate, and ran off to find a bottle of something, still wiping happy tears from her cheeks. I offered them my felicitations when she returned, and the three of us toasted the happy news with champagne, cucumber sandwiches and cake. The champagne mixed pleasantly with the horse tranquilizers I'd been given for pain.

We were still celebrating – the champagne long gone – when someone rang the bell. Emma went to answer, giving me a few moments alone with Avery. I appreciated it, because I got to hug her and congratulate her in private.

Emma returned with our guest – my father. Avery leapt up to greet him, but when I went to rise from the sofa, he stopped me. "Stay where you are, my dear." It was clear that he intended to sit next to me, so I moved my legs to give him room. He seemed happy – more chipper than I'd seen him for quite some time. His eyes were bright, his cheeks rosy. Avery must have told him her news. My sister offered to open more champagne, but he refused.

"How are you feeling?" he asked, patting my legs through the blanket I'd draped over them.

"Fair to middling," I lied. This was without a doubt the worst wound I've ever sustained. "You?"

"The pain of seeing you injured notwithstanding, I am exceedingly well this evening."

"I noticed," I replied, feeling the infectious pull of his smile. I cast a grin at Avery. "Betrothal giddiness abounds."

"There is that," Vardan replied. "And there is this." With a great flourish – the kind all dramatic people seemed to possess – he pulled an envelope from his jacket pocket.

"I met Her Majesty before coming here. She asked that I give you this."

Hesitantly, I reached out and took the envelope. I had no idea what it could be, but my stomach danced with anticipation. I broke the royal seal and removed the paper inside.

I wasn't certain when my hands began to tremble, or the rest of me for that matter. I didn't know exactly when the words began to blur or my heart started to pound so hard my still-healing wounds hurt.

"Xandy?" came Avery's concerned voice. "What is it?"

I looked up. I couldn't quite see her through my bleary eyes. "It's a royal summons. I'm to be knighted."

"Is this good news?" Vex asked, sitting at the bottom of the chesterfield, his arm stretched along the back. "Or bad?"

He was the only one to ask me that question – and he'd waited until we were alone to do it. My father had left hours ago, and Avery and Emma had departed shortly after he arrived – and after my sister made him swear to look after me. She and Emma had run off to celebrate their engagement. To be honest, I was glad to have them gone so Vex and I could talk.

"I don't know," I replied, glancing at the summons on the coffee table as I picked absently at the chenille throw over my legs. "This should be the happiest day of my life."

His gaze was incredibly wise – and non-judgemental. "My mother used to say there's no such thing as 'should'. *Is* this the happiest day of your life?"

I hesitated. "No." It was the truth, and I couldn't decide how I felt – guilty or angry. "It's not."

He lifted his fist and rested his temple on it. "Why's that, then?"

As if he didn't know. "Mostly because someone I know shot me in the back. There's something wrong with me and a friend of mine is dead because of it."

Vex watched me for a moment, his expression vexingly unreadable – hence one reason for his name, I suppose. "That doesn't change the fact that you took a bullet meant for Queen V."

I rolled my eyes. "Fine, but you must allow that the distinction is diminished by circumstances."

His lips twitched. "Aren't you a fancy talker?"

"I am educated, you know."

"I never would have assumed otherwise." His expression sobered. "I'm not suggesting a commendation will make everything better. But Xandra, this is a big deal – something you should enjoy and be proud of. Everything else can fly the fuck off."

"Now who's the fancy talker?" I teased, but I appreciated the sentiment. I really did. He was right – this was a big deal and I should enjoy it, regardless of all else. "Thank you."

Vex smiled – a little half-grin that made my libido wish I was in better condition physically. Alas, I was a mess and so none of that for me. In any case, this sitting and talking together felt more intimate – somewhat unsettling and naked, but good.

Vex made some sandwiches and found a couple of bottles of ginger beer in the fridge. He brought it all in on a tray with two big bowls of warm treacle pudding for after. My mouth watered.

"You're very domestic for an alpha," I remarked as he set the tray on the table and offered me a plate with a huge sandwich on it.

"Would you rather I thump my chest a few times?" he asked with an amused expression. "I don't have to prove myself. I already know what I'm capable of, and so does the pack."

"And now I know you're capable of making a brilliant sandwich," I said as I swallowed a bite of bread-embraced heaven.

"An alpha's job is to take care of his wolves."

"I'm not a wolf."

His gaze lifted to mine – direct and certain. "No, but you're still mine."

His gaze was so intense I couldn't hold it for long.

"Your scent has changed," he went on, seemingly oblivious as to how his remark unsettled me. He wasn't that blind though. "You smell wild – like the wind and the rain. It's subtle, but different."

My attention wandered to the large plastic bottle on the table. Avery had left my supplements, with orders to take them. Prescribed for me and me alone. Medication could change the way a body smelled, couldn't it? I took the bottle and dumped a large white pill out into my palm.

"You have labs and all that in Scotland, right?"

Vex wiped his mouth and smiled. "Telephones and flush toilets too."

I offered him the pill. "Would you find out what's in this for me?"

He didn't even blink as he took it. "What are you thinking?"

"I don't know what to think." That was probably the single most honest, revealing statement I'd made in days. "But right now you're the only person I trust to help me and not get yourself killed."

Vex cupped the back of my head in one hand, long fingers parting the tangle of my hair. "We'll figure this out, you have my word. I won't let anything happen to you." Then he kissed me.

It was the sort of kiss that made a girl feel like she couldn't draw breath – and not care. And just when I thought I might pass out from a lack of oxygen to my brain, I heard something – and it wasn't blood pounding in my ears. Suddenly my hearing went all sensitive-like and I heard the sound of claws scraping at my front door. Vex must have heard it too, because we both stiffened at the same time. And when he lifted his mouth from mine, a growl escaped.

"Is that what I think it is?" I whispered. Now that I was listening, I heard a pinging sound – like breaking glass.

Vex's expression was dangerously grim. Yellow light reflected in his eyes. "Goblins."

He didn't seem surprised as he rose to his feet and left the room. I followed after him – slow and stiff. I'd just entered the foyer when he opened the door. The exterior light was out – that must have been the breaking glass I heard – and standing in the darkness was the goblin prince, wearing a red-tinted monocle over his good eye, and a velvet frock coat across his broad furry shoulders. He looked like he was auditioning for "Gob in Boots".

He bowed at the waist in a very old-fashioned gesture. I was surprised to see that his fur looked groomed and shiny. I sniffed, and smelled the clean scent of earth and grass.

"MacLaughlin. Lady. Might your prince enter?"

I would have refused had he not saved my life. This was the second goblin to show up at my house in the last week – and at the front door, no less! At one time I would have thought the prince had come to kill me, but now I knew that if the goblins wanted me dead I'd be dead by now. In fact, the goblins were the only ones I was reasonably certain did *not* want me dead at all.

That went against every horror story I'd ever heard about them.

"Come in," I said. I didn't want anyone who might drive by to see a goblin on my step. As he crossed the threshold on slightly canine legs, I continued, "Why are you here?"

"We needed to see that the wolf and the lady were fine. Needed to talk."

I frowned. Should I be grateful or alarmed?

Vex bowed his head in a show of respect. "I am well, prince. As dictated in the Plaga Carta, I offered my humble apologies for the spilling of goblin blood in the tunnels last night."

My frown deepened as I looked from one to the other. "What the ruddy hell is this?"

They both turned to me, but I kept my gaze on Vex. It wasn't well lit in here, but it was still bright enough that the sight of the prince in my home unsettled me. He looked so familiar, yet alien at the same time. A nightmare from childhood.

"It's the law," Vex explained. "When a member of one aristocratic race spills the blood of another, the leaders of the two sides get together and express their regret. It's meant to keep the three races from going to war."

Because no one wanted to go to war with the goblins.

"But how did you spill goblin blood?"

To my surprise, the alpha's expression turned slightly sheepish. "When the prince tried to take you from me, I . . . bit him."

My spastic eyebrow syndrome kicked in, jerking both brows straight up. "Bit him?"

The prince nodded, with a grin that made the bottom of my stomach clench. "Almost let his wolf out. Drew blood. Most impressive, the MacLaughlin, protecting our pretty lady." Then his amber gaze locked with mine. "Shall we accept the wolf's truce?"

Why the bleeding hell was he asking me? "Of course," I replied, resisting the urge to add "shit for brains" at the end.

The goblin smiled – without showing teeth. It made him look almost cute, like a sweet mutt, the sort that wagged its tail at everyone. "Good words. There is no harm, wolf. Did the sickness take you in?"

"Not for long." Vex shoved his hands into his pockets, but there was a tension to his spine. I knew he could attack at a moment's notice if necessary. However, I didn't reckon it would be.

"Sickness?" I asked.

"Goblin blood makes everyone but other goblins ill," Vex informed me casually. "It's like drinking acid."

"But . . . " I stopped myself. I'd almost said that the prince had given me his blood and I was fine. But that couldn't be what had happened, if it was so terrible. The shape I was in, it would have done me in for certain.

Wouldn't it?

The goblin watched me with his one keen eye. "Yes, pretty?"

I shook my head. I wasn't going to ask a question I might not want answered. "Nothing." I was suddenly very hungry, and tired. I needed to get back to that sandwich. And I knew there was something afoot. "You didn't come up cobbleside just to check on Vex. You gobs have ears everywhere; you would have known he was fine. Why are you here?"

"Mayhap your prince worried for you. Wanted to see you well."

The sincerity in his raspy speech surprised me. What had I done to earn the respect of the goblin prince? I wasn't certain I liked it, but it beat having him eat my face, so I would learn to be fine with it.

"I'm doing quite well, thank you." Then I remembered my manners. "And thank you for saving my life."

His ears – battle-scarred as they were, folded down as though

I had literally patted him on the head. "My honour. I also came to give the Xandra lady this." He held out his paw. In the centre of it was an old spent bullet inside a tiny plastic bag – the sort with a press seal on the top. The idea of a goblin using such a bag amused me, but I didn't make it to a smile.

That bullet was silver – no wonder he had it in a bag. It was tarnished, but it was the same size and shape as the one taken out of me.

"What is it?" I asked, arms over my chest. No way was I touching it just yet.

"The metal what took mine eye," the prince replied. "Many years ago. Silver burned – made sure no eye ever grew back."

It said a lot about his strength that he'd even survived it. "Why are you giving it to me?"

"We are certain it is twin to the one which shot our lady in the dark."

Slowly I loosened my arms, and reached out to pluck the little bag out of his palm. My mouth was dry. "Who shot you?"

Both the prince and Vex watched me closely. I knew I had to be white as chalk.

"It happened when I saw the young Xandra lady and tried to touch the wonder. Then pain. Much pain." His voice was even scratchier than before. "It was the Churchill."

CHAPTER 14

NOT SINGLE SPIES BUT AS BATTALIONS

No fucking way had Church shot me. Not on purpose.

"*You're* the goblin that attacked me?" Old fear – foolish now that I had already decided I wasn't so afraid of him – came rushing back. I remembered that moment, when I fell to the ground, fur and snarls surrounding me . . .

I growled. Both Vex and the prince started at the sound. It was just as much of a surprise to me. I sounded brilliant, and bloody frightening, but when the hell had I developed that particular ability?

"Did not attack!" There was so much vehemence and indignation behind the goblin's words that for a moment I forgot my fear and my anger – forgot that I could growl. One clawed finger pointed at me. "The Churchill made violence. Your prince would never hurt the Xandra lady."

This went against everything I'd ever been taught about goblins. Since that seemed to be the way of things lately, I wasn't entirely sceptical. And if he wanted to hurt me, he could have ripped me apart the night I braved the den. "So what then, you were just trying to say hello?"

He shrugged, shoulders lifting beneath the thick fur. "What else?"

"Indeed," I replied drily. It was unquestionably a suitable explanation for one of the defining incidents of my life. "Why me?"

The prince lifted his hands – paws – pads up. "Your prince was drawn to the child pretty. Never seen anything like you, with hair brighter than blood."

Anger tore through me, filling me with the urge to snap at him, all spit and fang. "I thought you were trying to kill me."

"Thought what the Churchill *told* the child to think." Indignation drew his spine up straight – we were eye to eye. "The plague be not as bad as taught."

"You eat children," I fired back. "How is that not bad?"

"Meat is meat. Blood is blood. It is good."

"Right. That's it. Out." I stormed past him to yank open the door. I didn't care that he could disembowel me in the span of a heartbeat. Truth be told, I was feeling a little itch to do some ripping of my own.

The door came right off the hinges, leaving me standing there holding it by the handle. The heavy wood hit me in the side of the face, knocking me backwards. As I twisted, the entire left half of my body felt like a thousand hot pokers had been shoved into it at once.

I'm fairly certain I cried out – though pain has an odd way of making one *un*certain. One thing was irrefutable – the fact that I fell to my knees like I was some sort of Roman soldier in battle, holding a bloody door for a shield.

Vex was immediately there beside me, checking on me with his gentle hands. The prince carefully relieved me of the door, and set it back in its place.

"I'm good," I told Vex as the pain subsided to just this side of bearable. Fang me, but that hurt. I'd probably ripped stitches.

What the hell had just happened?

"Where's your medication?" he demanded as the two of them helped me to my feet.

"Living room."

He had no problem leaving me with the goblin as he went to fetch the pain meds. Obviously he trusted the beast.

"Your prince can help," came a whispered rasp.

I turned my narrow gaze to his. "How?"

He offered me a bottle from the pouch he wore over one shoulder. It looked like blood. "Drink."

"I don't trust you."

Intense yellow eyes locked with mine. "We have done nothing but help the Xandra lady. We never will hurt our pretty." As his fingers – or were they claws? – wrapped round mine, he squeezed gently but insistently. "The plague serves you."

"What kind of blood is it?" What I wanted to ask was why the goblins appeared to be so loyal to me, but my mouth couldn't seem to find the courage to form the words.

He removed the cap. "The best kind."

I was right – he had given me blood before, but it hadn't been his. Couldn't have been. It had to be a vampire, or maybe werewolf.

Regardless, one sniff and I knew it was the right thing to do – that it would make everything better. It was like chocolate and cake and chai – everything rich and delicious. I heard Vex returning from the living room, so I tipped the bottle and took a deep drink.

Sweet baby Albert, it was fantastic. Earthy, with a hint of something like cinnamon and clove. It filled me with warmth, causing a tingling in the areas where I hurt the most, as though healing them. It was.

I looked at the prince, ignoring whatever Vex was saying. "It's working."

The goblin smiled that awful smile. "Said pretty was special."

Vex grabbed me. "What the rutting hell did you just drink?"

"Blood," I replied. I didn't tell him what kind.

"No more nasty vampire pills," the prince ordered. "No good for the Xandra lady."

"You're lying down," Vex commanded. To the prince he said, "We're going to have a chat."

I didn't argue. The blood had made me a little ... giddy, almost as though it was an opiate. I felt light-headed and warm. The pain had lessened, and though it wasn't totally gone, it was all right. I could almost ignore it. Vex put me on the chesterfield and covered me with a blanket. He took the bottle from me. I reached for it, but then it was gone, and I closed my eyes, savouring this feeling. I could hear Vex and the prince talking. I think they left the house, because their voices were muffled. I couldn't focus enough to concentrate on what they were saying, but I knew I was the topic, and Vex sounded angry.

And then I faded into oblivion and nothing else mattered.

The bullets matched.

I didn't want to believe it, but there was no denying they came from the same gun, despite having been fired more than a decade apart. Vex and I studied and compared the two of them under a duoscope – a wooden box divided into two halves, with viewing lenses on both. We put a slug into either compartment, switched on the interior light and then examined the spent silver simultaneously, magnified.

We reached the unfortunate conclusion the next morning, after I woke up in my bed to find him sleeping next to me. The last thing I remembered was hitting the chesterfield after getting stoned on the blood the prince had given me.

I felt amazingly good for someone who had very nearly died. I suppose I owed that to the prince as well. I hoped he wasn't keeping a tally, because I didn't want to think about what he'd want in return.

I went downstairs to get breakfast – my stomach was growling like a rabid wolf. I had a craving for steak, crispy on the outside and bloody in the middle, with eggs and toast. I wasn't going to be a master chef any time soon, but I could stumble my way around a kitchen all right. I made enough for Vex as well, because I knew the smell would wake him.

And I was right. I'd just sat down to eat when he walked in, all scruffy and mussed. He kissed me, loaded his plate and joined me. After we'd eaten, and consumed a pot of coffee, we compared the bullets in the duoscope he'd had delivered after I fell asleep the night before. I had to. I couldn't stand the anticipation any longer.

Discovering that they matched almost made me lose my breakfast.

"There has to be an explanation," I said. "He couldn't have known he'd shot me."

Vex looked dubious. "I don't see how a man like him could make such a dangerous mistake." Something in my expression made him add, "But perhaps you simply got in his line of fire."

My chest hurt. "Maybe. This just doesn't make sense." Church loved me. I was uncomfortably certain of that. He had changed towards me over the last few years, but he would do anything for me. He would never hurt me.

Never. But my fingers shook.

The alpha rolled one of the slugs between his fingers – gloved to protect him from the silver. "Neither does the fact that he carries silver bullets. He can't have to subdue goblins that often."

"Precaution?" Val had silver ammo in case he had to take down a halvie in the line of duty.

"Could be." Vex straightened, and rotated his shoulders. "If he was trying to kill you, he wouldn't have left the bullet behind."

I barely met his gaze. "Ophelia said someone else tried to steal it."

His mouth went grim. "Might have told me that a wee bit sooner. I'm sorry, sweetheart. Churchill shot you, and only he can tell you why." He jerked his thumb towards a huge arrangement of roses I hadn't seen before sitting on the hall table. "Seems he feels broken up about it."

I hadn't smelled the roses because other bouquets had already been delivered before I arrived home from hospital. This one was by far the largest, and made up of every colour of rose I could think of. It was a little much, to be honest.

"The sentiment of a sorry man," I murmured, leaning in for a sniff.

"Or a guilty one." Vex ran his hand down my arm. "It had to have been an accident."

He was right. What else could it be? That Church knew my secret and was prepared to kill me because of it? That made no sense at all – not when "they" had kept me alive for so many years. Obviously there were people out there who knew the truth about unusual half-bloods, and they hadn't come for me yet.

But they had told Dede her baby had died so Ainsley could raise him. And someone had killed Vex's son. I had a nephew I would never be able to know, a nephew who would never know his mother.

Mortifying tears burned my eyes and spilled down my cheeks. Poor Dede. Poor Vex. Poor me. Church was my mentor, the measure against whom I held myself in almost every aspect of my life. He could not have hurt me on purpose.

Vex gathered me to him and held me while I had my cry-out. I let it go on a few minutes and then pulled myself together. It was surprisingly easy. What was all the fuss? The world was a clusterfuck of illusion. Nothing was new; I'd just had my eyes opened to it.

I was not about to go mental just yet – I'd done a bloody good job of keeping a grip on my sanity thus far – but how much more could my world be turned inside out before I finally cracked?

"What do you need me to do?"

"Find out what's in my supplements." I hugged him. "And be here when I need an incredibly broad shoulder to go hatters on."

He kissed my forehead. "I can do that." His brow was knitted as he stroked my hair. I didn't know what to make of his expression, or the weight of his gaze as it drifted over my face. It was as though he was looking for something just below the surface of my skin.

"What?"

He smiled. "Nothing."

"Liar. Regretting getting involved with me, aren't you?"

Vex's smile faded as a hint of gold lit his eyes. "If I didn't want to be with you, I wouldn't be here. You leave my thinking to me, all right?"

I should have been at least a little cowed by his tone and posture, but instead it awakened an answering aggression in me – a welcome change to having my head up my arse. I found that growl that had come out of me last night and used it again.

Gold bled through Vex's gaze. A low rumble came from his throat. Fangs lengthened in my mouth, gums tingling. I ran for the stairs as though I'd never been injured, my wolf close at my heels.

Afterwards I had carpet burn on my palms and knees and a wreck of a bedroom to straighten, but it was worth it. I felt more centred than I had in a while. However this mess worked out, I was going to be all right. I had to be.

"You're going to Bedlam, aren't you?" Vex asked as I got dressed. He was sprawled on the carpet, naked. Most of the scratches I'd inflicted had already healed, leaving nothing but traces of blood behind. God, he tasted good. I could suck the very marrow from his bones and still want more.

My stomach twisted. I turned from the dresser and dropped to my knees beside him, fastening my mouth on a bite on his shoulder that hadn't yet healed. I sucked, pushing against his warm, salty flesh with my mouth, shuddering as his blood slowly coated my tongue. Vex shuddered too, and wrapped his arms around me, holding me close as I licked the wound clean.

"You're such a bitch." He chuckled against my hair.

I lifted my head, caught between humour and mortification. "I reckon those supplements kept me from wanting blood."

"Let's find out what else they did." He kissed me hard on the mouth and rose to his feet. I stood as well, and we dressed side by side. He kissed me again before leaving and made me promise to ring him later.

I left shortly after he did, pulling on my driving goggles, manoeuvring the Butler out into an early twilight brought on by a sky full of grey clouds. It was only seven o'clock, but felt later. I steered the motorrad around a carriage pulled by four matching horses. In the distance, Big Ben clanged out the hour. Lights were just beginning to come on as darkness crept over the city. It wasn't bright enough to hurt my eyes, but not dark enough to make me feel invisible. The wheels of my motorrad bumped over cobblestones, then smooth asphalt. The ageless elegance of Mayfair bled into taller buildings made of glass and steel, and lights that blazed with a garish glow. Vehicles thundered past me, and on the walks pedestrians hurried home as darkness came early. Were they as afraid of night as aristos were of the dawn?

When I arrived at the asylum, the guards didn't try to stop me. I suppose they were still smarting from the last time we tangoed.

Ophelia met me in the west wing, ground-floor corridor. Even though the plush carpet muffled her steps, I'd heard her coming long before I spied her. Another aspect of not taking the supplements? Or the prince's blood? I noticed a slight bruise peeking out from beneath the top edge of her corseted waistcoat.

"You all right?" I asked as she approached. "You look a little knocked about, and you smell like blood."

She hesitated, and gave me a look that went beyond wary. "I'm fine. Just a bit of a scuffle. Mum's in her office."

My sister didn't walk in front of me – as though she was afraid of offering me her back. She didn't seem too keen on ambling along beside me either. I fancied I could smell her uncertainty about me, and it went straight to my head like petrol.

I smiled when she drew back. What was wrong with me? I'd always enjoyed getting under people's skin, but this was excessive. I wanted her to be afraid of me.

She was pale as she held the door to our mother's office open for me. It was clever, the traitors of Bedlam actually running the hospital

"Is everyone here part of your movement?" I asked.

Ophelia slid a wary glance my way. "Those who need to be."

That wasn't much of an answer, but I didn't have time to press it. My mother greeted me with open arms, but her embrace was ... cautious. A werewolf – a "made" aristocrat – was leery of me.

"I assume the results of my blood tests came back."

Juliet released me. Once again I was struck by how young she appeared. She also seemed tired. "Yes."

"Well?" I looked from her to Ophelia and back again as the two of them shared a glance. "The two of you are all knots and tangles. What is it?"

"Perhaps you should sit," Juliet suggested, gesturing to the velvet sofa. She looked knocked about too. Had she and Ophelia been fighting? What could have happened to make them go at one another?

"I don't want to sit," I argued petulantly. "I want to know what's wrong with me. Right. Fucking. *Now*."

Both mother and daughter flinched, but Ophelia stepped back. It was then that I noticed the handgun beneath her coat. I had left the Bulldog at home – again. My trusty dagger was in my corset as usual, but wasn't there a saying about bringing a knife to a gun-fight? And did my sister plan to shoot me? The few times we'd met, I'd never noticed a firearm, so why was she toting one now?

"You are right," my mother allowed in a gentle voice. "You deserve to know everything. When you were born looking the same as any perfectly healthy half-blood, I assumed you had not been affected by my having been infected."

"But you were wrong," I offered when she didn't seem to know what else to say. Fang me, but she looked as though she'd rather take a bath in liquid silver than tell me what the ruddy hell I was.

She looked away. "Yes." A rueful sigh followed. "When Ophelia showed me that you were one of the halvlings with missing paper-work, I knew I'd been right to worry when you were young. And now that I've seen the results of your blood work, I know what my becoming a wolf did to you."

The look she gave me was pleading, as though she wanted me to fill in the blanks so she didn't have to tell me the truth.

An elastic band seemed to snap inside my brain. My father was a vampire and my mother was a werewolf. Those two things didn't mix – not successfully. I valued family and those I cared for above all else. I was stronger than I should be. Had more accurate senses than I should. I could be feral at times, had an acute sense of smell and had started to crave blood.

Albert's fangs, how could I have been so stupid? How could I have not put it together sooner? No wonder the goblin prince had been curious about me.

Church was wrong. I didn't have the senses of a goblin. I *was* a fucking goblin. My mother's transformation had mutated me inside her womb. It was a miracle I survived.

Or a cruel joke, depending on how I looked at it.

"Did you know?" I asked. "When I was younger, did you suspect?"

My mother shook her head. "I wondered, but no, I didn't know, not for certain. I think your father . . . Vardan had suspicions."

Rage gushed up from deep inside me. I felt betrayed and hurt. I wanted to deny the truth even though I knew it in my bones. I thought I'd always known.

Fangs, massive and alien, tore free of my gums so violently that I tasted blood. My nails broke out of their beds, lengthening and sharpening before my very eyes until they were curved like claws, black and sharp. The real me was coming out to play.

"*Jesus Christ*," Ophelia rasped, her eyes huge in her pale face. My own face felt stretched, as though my skin couldn't contain my teeth and bones. My eyes were sharper – I could see the individual beads of sweat on her brow. I could smell it too – and her fear. It rolled over me in a wave of pleasure, so sweet and deep – better than chocolate or orgasm or any sweet memory – and she did nothing to control it. Everyone knew you were dead if a goblin got a taste of your fear.

I lunged, snarling and drooling, and took her to the ground with ease. She screamed all the way down, pushing at me with strong hands. I was stronger. When she went for her gun, I grabbed that hand and squeezed, shivering in delight when she screamed even louder.

I knew it was wrong, and I didn't care, didn't even try to gain control; it felt so *good* to let it all go. I opened the gaping maw of my mouth even wider, feeling the cool delight of saliva drip on to my lower lip.

I tore into the flesh of my sister's shoulder as if it was no more substantial than a pub-fried chicken wing.

And God help me, she tasted *good*.

CHAPTER 15

I BEHELD THE WRETCH – THE MISERABLE MONSTER WHOM I HAD CREATED

I woke up with my hair clotted with blood and the remnants of a nasty gash healing on my scalp – I felt it when I lifted a hand to massage away what I thought was nothing more than a bit of a headache. My fingers came away sticky.

"What the . . . ?" I muttered and opened my eyes. I regretted that move instantly. Someone had positioned a goose-neck lamp over me so that its light glared directly into my face.

"Fucking hell!" I cried, clenching my eyelids shut. Light continued to pulse and dance behind them, even though it was dark inside my head. It hurt – those glowing orbs smashing off the sides of my skull.

"You okay, Xandy?"

I didn't open my eyes again. "What is this, Dede?"

I heard her come closer – felt her presence hovering nearby. More goblin genes kicking in, I suppose.

Fang me. I was a goblin. They ate *children*, for Christ's sake! They were practically animals. And yet they'd been good to me. I had never witnessed a goblin acting like a monster. In fact, aside from Vex, the prince had treated me with more respect and kindness than members of my own family. What did that mean?

"We needed to make sure you wouldn't fly off the handle when you woke up," she explained. "The light was my idea."

"Turn it off."

"Can't. Sorry, but you hurt Fee pretty bad."

Shit. Ophelia. "Is she all right?" The words stuck in my throat.

"She will be. Fang me, Xandy, you could have killed her."

Instead of making me contrite, the censure in her tone had the opposite effect. "I wanted to kill her."

"Oh." Disappointment dripped from her tone. "I guess that's what goblins do."

I snorted, pressing a hand over my eyes to create a comforting shade of black beneath my lids. "I've always been a goblin, Dee." My tongue tripped over the words. Admitting it out loud was ... difficult. "I've never killed anyone before – not with my teeth, at any rate." I could still taste my half-sister's blood on my tongue, faint but agonisingly delicious. I should feel sick about it. I didn't.

Blood was blood. Meat was meat. It was all good, right?

"I've never seen you like that before. I've never been as afraid of you as I was when I saw your face covered in Ophelia's blood."

My stomach turned ever so slightly. I reckoned I felt a little guilty after all. The thought was strangely comforting. "So you smashed me over the head and carried me down to the cells."

I could almost imagine her frown. "How do you know we're in the cells?"

"I can smell it, hear it." Now I knew what I was, it was so much easier to tap into these awakening senses. I'd dampened my hearing and sense of smell a long time ago. It was just a matter of paying attention now. "We're below ground. It's the worst place you could have brought a goblin. Anyone would know that." I'd wager she stiffened at that jibe.

"I reckon it will hold you well enough."

"Turn off the light, Dede."

"No."

I sighed. "My head hurts" – that was almost a lie, as it was healing rapidly – "I'm calm, and I'm sure you have a weapon loaded with lovely silver bullets, so turn off the light."

"Juliet said . . . "

As she spoke, I reached up to where I knew the light was, and crushed the bulb with my bare hand. It burned like a bastard, and I caught little bits of hot glass in the face, but at least it was reasonably dark.

Dede gasped. I sat up, pushing the now useless object of torture out of my way. I shook off the splinters of glass before opening my eyes. There was a dim lamp in the far corner, giving off just enough light that I could see perfectly and my eyeballs didn't feel like they were being skewered.

"What time is it?" I demanded.

My sister sat as far back as she could in a rickety chair, her knees drawn up in front of her like a shield. Protection from me. As though her thin little legs could stop me. She didn't even have her gun pointed at me. Her fear awakened the goblin in me, but it sickened the part that was still her big sister. "It's ten o'clock in the evening."

So I'd been out for a while. "I'm leaving." Avery would wonder where I was. Vex too. There were probably messages from both on my rotary.

"You can't leave." She jumped to her feet, tried to position herself between me and the door as I stood.

I stopped. "Are you telling me I'm a prisoner, Dede? Are you choosing Bedlam over me?"

Her wide jade eyes filled with tears, but she kept her chin up, bless her poor fucked-up heart. "I don't want to. Please don't make me."

"Move, dearest." Being locked up in Bedlam was a cut too close to the vein for me. I had to get out of there. Ophelia was going to be all right and I was grateful for that, but I couldn't stay here after what I'd done, knowing what I was. I had to go home, to my last scrap of normality.

To my surprise, Dede stepped out of my way, and I crossed the worn Morris-print carpet to the door.

There was no handle or knob, just a smooth length of titanium-reinforced steel.

"Told you there was no leaving."

She sounded a little too smug for my liking. Obviously she thought she was right, but I remembered looking at these cells last time I was here. I stepped back, lifted my leg and sent the door flying with one good kick. The bones in my foot and shin shuddered in pain, but it faded to a dull ebb in half a second.

I shot my stunned sibling a triumphant glance. "You put me in a cage designed to hold halvies, but I'm not a halvie, Dede." With that perfect bit of melodramatic dialogue delivered, I walked out, carefully stepping over the fallen door. In the corridor I could hear the growing agitation of the halvies kept down here. I had scared them, all these pitiful creatures.

I paused in front of the door of the cell where the girl who had been raped by goblins was kept. Was I just another of "their" halvie experiments? Just who the bloody hell were they? Aristos?

Yes. If ever there was a time for me to wake up and smell the tea brewing, it was this moment. No more excuses or blindfolds. I was a goblin and my father knew it, or at least had suspicions that his child was a mutant, a monstrous birth defect.

But I didn't look like one. That was why I had been allowed to live as I had. Watched. Studied. Simon had been killed to protect the secret. It would be such a scandal if the truth got out.

I was like Duncan MacLaughlin after all, only I had my father's rank to protect me. And Churchill. He had kept me close. No need to lock me in a cage when they could just take my blood and watch every move I made.

Dede chased after me, and caught me at the lift. "I really don't think you should go home right now."

"Worried I'll hurt someone else? Relax, I'm in total control of myself." And I had things to do. People to see, such as Churchill.

"I am worried, but you also have blood all over you."

I paused. "Fine. I know you have at least one shirt in your cupboard that belongs to me."

We got into the ancient lift together and rode up to the first floor. There were a few halvies and humans milling about. They all looked at me as though they'd cheerfully slit my throat but were terrified to try. It wasn't a pleasant sensation, and I felt for the dagger in my corset. It was still there. Thankfully no one had the bollocks to take me on, or perhaps they'd been ordered to give me a wide berth. I didn't care. I had a reputation as a skilled scrapper before this. That made sense now too. As did the blood the prince had given me. It wasn't vampire or werewolf – it had been goblin blood. It hadn't made me sick because it – or a mutated flavour of it – ran through my own veins. I was a goblin, but unlike any other goblins I knew of.

Just what was I capable of?

Gobbing out had put everything in clear, cold perspective. Little things from the past tallied up – my strength, speed, senses ... I was a freak who shouldn't have made it outside of the womb. If I didn't do something, and word of that got out, someone was going to kill me.

Dede's room was almost exactly above my mother's office. She gave me a clean shirt – one of mine, just as I suspected – and I used her loo to clean up. No wonder her insurgent mates had looked at me that way. My hair was a wild tangle of vivid red, and my pale face was covered in the rust of dried blood from the nose down. Similar stains marked the front of my kit.

I removed my corset – which was thankfully reversible – and then ran water in the sink to wash with. Once reasonably clean, I put on the fresh shirt and turned my corset round the other way. I borrowed some of Dede's make-up and a hairbrush. I exited the toilet to find her sitting on her bed, sending a digigram on her portable logic engine. About me? Unfortunately, goblins couldn't read minds.

"Ophelia's going to be fine," she informed me. "Luckily, you didn't rip her open when you bit her."

I swallowed hard at the bitter taste rising in the back of my mouth. I'd attacked my sister and liked it – not hurting her, but the blood. I didn't want to talk about it. "Good. Look, I'm sorry."

She arched a brow. If not for that terrible black hair, it would be like looking in a mirror. "Tell that to Ophelia."

"That's not what I meant." I tossed my bloodstained shirt into the rubbish bin by her dressing table. "I'm sorry I didn't believe it when you told me what happened to your baby. I should have been there for you and I wasn't. If you choose this place and its people over your family, I don't blame you."

Her face fell. Surprise? Anguish? A combination, probably. Now might not have been the best time for me to play the big-sister card, but I didn't know if I'd get the opportunity later. There was a good chance that I wasn't long for this world – a risk all Royal Guard and Peerage Protectorate accepted with the job; I just never thought I'd actually find myself facing the prospect of being hunted into an early grave.

I didn't want to die, but I'd prefer that to being someone's lab rat, or ending up like one of the halvies in Bedlam's basement.

"Thank you," Dede whispered, wiping at her eyes, mobile forgotten. I went to her, gathered her against my stomach and held her for a moment, stroking her hair as she cried. From this angle, I could see a little root growth, and the true copper of her hair peeked through the dull black. It made me smile for some reason, even though everything was pretty much shit.

"What are you going to do?" she asked me a few moments later. Her voice was thick and nasal.

"Eventually I'll have to try to make it right with Ophelia." I might not like her much, but she didn't deserve what I'd done. "But for now, I'm going home." It was an outrageous lie, and she believed it.

"Be careful, Xandy."

"I will," I lied again, and kissed her on the forehead. "I love you." I hugged her tightly, and was hugged back. There was a finality to it that unsettled me. It would be a long time before I came back to Bedlam, if ever. My mother might run the place, but I'd proven myself . . . unstable. And they had proven themselves untrustworthy. They were afraid of me, and that meant they would immediately make arrangements to protect themselves from me. Just in case, of course.

And really, weren't traitors the last thing I needed right now, what with everything else?

Leaving Dede was difficult, but I did it. She walked me out so no one would attempt retribution for what I'd done to Ophelia. Seemed my big sis was a tad popular in the asylum. In a fair fight I had no doubt that I could take a handful of them, but there were too many to face alone, no matter how tough I might think I was.

I walked past the glares without a sideways glance or flicker of expression. I deserved their hatred and fear. I'd done a horrible thing, and my only consolation was that I hadn't killed Ophelia. My attack on her hadn't been provoked; it had been the behavior of an animal.

That was as far as I could think about it. My head was swimming, trying to figure out what to do next. Confront Church? My father? Run to Vex? Go home and hide under my bed?

It was dark when I stepped outside – good and dark. My eyes seemed to prefer that to the brightness of Bedlam. I could see better than before, my sight sharper than a cat's. It was as though Ophelia's blood had awakened more of the goblin in me. Fucking brilliant.

The Butler was where I left it, and I climbed on. I pulled on my goggles, turned the key in the ignition and drove towards Mayfair, my mind churning over events with an eerie calm that I knew would eventually dissolve. Shock never lasted as long as you wished it might.

There was rain in the air as I drove. The moisture clung to my face and hair, dampened my clothes. It felt good – soothing. By the time I arrived at the walls of the Mayfair district, I was wet all the way to the skin and my hair hung in damp clumps around my face. The guards at the main gates didn't even blink at the sight of me. I had to swipe my badge, leaving a computer log of my visit, but that was the very least of my worries. I didn't even care that they patted me down.

I drove to Down Street and parked in front of the old station. It didn't feel so foreboding or frightening now. It was almost like coming home. I liked that it was dark, and quiet. Neglected.

How long before people started to avoid me? I wouldn't be able to keep my . . . condition a secret for long, would I? If the papers got wind of me attacking someone . . . well, details like traitors hiding in Bedlam might be omitted without difficulty, especially by a sympathetic human. Who would care about the source when the story involved the daughter of a duke?

I glanced up at the sign above the door. I wasn't about to abandon all hope, not yet. The heavy door creaked as I pushed it open. I crossed the threshold and let the door slowly obliterate what little light slipped in from outside as it closed. I gave my eyes a second to adjust before jogging down the debris-dusted stairs.

I was home.

There wasn't any merriment tonight. No one tried to give me fruit. There were no writhing humans. I wished there were. My heart hammered even harder than it had the first time I came down here. It was quiet. Where were the humans? There were miles and mazes of tunnels beneath London. The humans could be anywhere. Had they been killed? Eaten?

Would I be invited to stay for dinner? My stomach rumbled. Fuck, but I was twisted.

As I entered the great hall, I saw rows of furry bodies sitting on the floor in front of the prince's throne. The sconces filling the room touched its broken pillars and remnants of Roman habitation with a mellow golden glow that didn't offend sensitive eyes. Fires burned in hearths set into each well. The prince was in his seat of bone, reading to the gathered goblins from an old leatherbound book. I stood very still, listening to his raspy growl of a voice as he read. He read better than he spoke, and Henry Fielding's *Tom Jones* was met with eager expressions.

They hadn't noticed me come in. Or they'd been expecting me. I wasn't sure which explanation was more – or less – comforting.

I stood at the back of the room, letting the heat from a nearby fire warm my damp skin and the prince's voice push reality away for a few moments. When he was done reading, his audience clapped – the leathery slapping of paws – and when he lifted his head to look at me, every goblin in that hall turned to do the same.

I was a rabbit staring down a pack of drooling dingos. They tipped back their heads and sniffed the air, muzzles open, tasting my scent.

My mouth was dry, and I licked my lips – it was like dragging carpet over pressboard for all the moisture it dispersed.

The prince rose from his throne with that shark smile and came towards me with his bizarre gait that seemed both graceful and awkward at the same time. He didn't look as though he should be able to walk on two feet, but he did it very well. I had no doubt that he could move just as easily, if not better, on all fours.

"Lady," he greeted me. "You honour the plague."

"I haven't any tribute, Prince. I apologise."

He tilted his head to one side, amber eye watching me closely. "No need for tribute, lady. No need."

He was being so cordial – more than usual. My stomach dropped several inches. "You know. What I am, you know."

The prince tapped the ragged leather patch over his right eye. "Since lady first met the prince. We have waited years for truth to find the pretty."

I appreciated that he hadn't denied it, or outright lied. Every one of these goblins had to know what I was. Didn't they? When Avery accused me of smelling like wet goblin, was she smelling the den, or me? "Do I smell?" I asked, unable to stop myself.

"Like plague?" He seemed surprised that I asked. When I nodded, he added, "Little. Unique. Wild. Smell like . . . hope."

What the bloody hell did hope smell like? It was a nice sentiment, but utterly useless in this situation. Still, I didn't say
anything. Better not to anger him. I wasn't sure just how my being
a goblin changed our relationship, but he might see me as a
subject now rather than an equal. Who was I kidding? As far as
gobs went, he had no equal – that was why he was the prince. I
might be a goblin, but I didn't fit in here any more than I did
cobbleside.

"Now your scent is blood." His gaze brightened. "You've fed."

Fang me. Heat rushed to my cheeks while my stomach
revolted. "Yes. I'm not proud of it, Prince. I could have killed
her – my own sister."

He patted my shoulder. The pads of his palm – paw? – were
rough enough that I could hear them scratch the fabric of my coat.
"That happened not, did it? All is well."

"All is well?" I echoed, anger seeping into my tone. "I'm a
bloody freak. That is not well!"

He scowled, and for a second my heart literally stopped, I was
certain of it. "Not freak. Pure blood." As he spoke, he swept his
arm wide to encompass the hall and all its occupants, who had
now risen and stood watching the two of us as raptly as they'd listened to the prince read.

"The Xandra lady is plague's hope," he went on. "Hope to one
day see sun. To bring plague cobbleside. One day all plague will
be as pretty as you."

Good Lord, they saw me as some sort of Chosen One! I was
not going to mate with goblins. I didn't care if I was one. That
would break me for sure. Just the thought of it was enough to
make me borderline hysterical.

"I'm not your saviour."

The prince smiled – without teeth – and did not argue. I didn't
quite trust him. "One of us. Gave you dead friend as proof of

plague loyalty. Now I tell you 'twas the Churchill's scent on the dead friend."

I stared at him. "Churchill killed Simon? Why didn't you tell me this before?"

"Xandra lady would not have believed."

He was right – I wouldn't have. I wasn't altogether sure I believed it now. I always had a tendency to believe what I wanted, and despite the bullets and this admission, I wanted to think the best of Church.

"The plague has proof," the prince continued. "Surveillance of the Churchill leaving the halvie in the tunnels. Not the first he's left."

I didn't want to know that. Ophelia had said Church was involved in experiments on halvies. I just couldn't believe it, yet I'd seen the results in the dungeon at Bedlam. Goblins had been involved too . . .

I lifted my chin. "Did you know about the experiments?"

He shook his shaggy head. "Heard. Lost brethren to bastards. Never found where. One thing the plague does not know."

So halvies weren't the only targets. The people behind those atrocities better hope the goblins never found them, if the expression on the prince's face was any indication.

They would keep records of their experiments, right? In case one happened to yield favourable results.

Like me.

I needed proof, or no one would ever believe me. The entire world thought my mother went hatters, my sister too. They'd believe it of me in a heartbeat. But if I could prove that these things were happening, then I just might survive this.

I'd start with Church. If he was involved – and I had to face the fact that he was – then he might have copies. There must be something linking him, surely?

I'd thought he loved me. Cared about me. I respected him more than I respected my own father. Hell, I thought of him *as* a father. The thought of him betraying me . . . it made me angry. So fucking angry. Anger was good. I could work with anger. Anger kept my head out of my arse.

"I have to go," I told the prince. Then another thought occurred to me. "Is there any way for me to get to Churchill's without using the streets?" Even without the Butler, I was a familiar sight around these parts. Being spotted in Down Street was one thing, but I didn't want anyone to remember seeing me around Churchill's tonight.

The prince nodded. "Your prince will take you."

"I'm not your responsibility. You don't have to take me."

He looked affronted. "Xandra lady is my responsibility. The prince is her servant."

If he'd turned on me and bitten off my nose I would have been less surprised. "You are the prince of goblins," I informed him softly. "You serve no one." No, that wasn't completely true, since the leader of each race – Vex for wolves, the Prince of Wales for vamps, the Prime Minister for humans, and the goblin prince – technically answered to Queen V, but the goblins had always been a bit of a wild card that way.

Would I still be knighted when Her Majesty learned what I was? Right now, it wasn't much of a priority.

"Nice words," the goblin replied in that crackling tone that made him sound like a prepubescent nightmare. "But untrue. Come, lady. Follow your prince."

"You really are my prince," I said as we began to walk. "At first I thought you were simply arrogant."

I walked on the side of his good eye, so I didn't miss the glance he shot me. "Not arrogant. Certain. Hmm, maybe a little arrogant."

Was that humour?

"Do you eat all the bodies they toss down here?" I asked as we left the great hall and began to walk deeper into the den. A broken bone – a femur – lay against one wall. I'd be lying if I said I wasn't a little nervous. I'd be stupid to forget that this was one mass grave.

"Meat is meat," he replied, as he had the other night at my house. "We cannot hunt far. Must take what is offered."

"Why not cats and dogs?"

"Would pretty rather eat cat or human?"

"Human," I replied immediately. Fang me, but I was a monster too. The idea of eating a poor little cat . . .

He must have read my expression, because he nodded. "Much we consume is carrion, but the plague won't hunt what cannot fight."

"You're goblin. Nothing can fight you."

He barked low – laughter, I realised. "Now who is arrogant?" He gestured to the leather where his eye had been. "Some things can fight."

That took the mood down a notch or two. "I'm sorry. He shot you because of me."

"The Churchill shot because he was afraid for the girl. No apologies for love."

I snorted. "He shot me too." Although I still clung to the hope that it had been an accident.

His fingers curled around mine, rough and warm. He squeezed – like a father might, like my mother used to. "Worry not. The plague will protect. Plague is family."

Right. Not sure how I felt about that, so I kept my mouth shut. I held his hand for a bit, though. It was comforting, strange as that might sound. Creepy, too.

"I'm supposed to be knighted," I said. I wasn't sure why I told him this. "I should be celebrating."

"The lady cannot be knighted." He said this with such gravity I sighed. His concern for my safety was too overwhelming. I couldn't even respond.

We walked about a quarter of a mile, perhaps a little more, before the prince pushed on a door concealed in the stone wall. It slid open to reveal another tunnel – an old service route perhaps. Sewer, or waterway. Light from the street above slipped in through the manhole in the roof. The prince squinted at it, but seemed otherwise unaffected. It didn't bother me, but then I spent most of my time above ground.

I could hear traffic, rather than the deep rumble of trains. There were few motor carriages in Mayfair, though certain aristos did own them. Here, the streets bustled with carts and coaches, and smelled of horse shit and hay.

"Here," the prince said, pointing to a rusted ladder bolted into the pitted brick wall. "Up to Berkeley Square."

"Brilliant." Church lived in Berkeley Square. "Thank you. For everything." Some part of my brain resisted being grateful, insisting that goblins were the root of all my troubles, but I hadn't time to feel sorry for myself. Maybe I'd do that later. Right now, I was simply keenly aware that the prince had come through for me every time I needed him, and even when I hadn't.

He amazed me by bowing over my hand. "Have a care, lady. Pretty blood could start a war if spilled."

I swallowed. "You would go to war for me?"

"All the plagues in Britain would fight for the lady."

"I wouldn't want that." The idea of it made me sick. A goblin attack would decimate the city. It would be like setting sharks on a tank of seals.

He patted my shoulder. "Then do not die." This was followed by that terrible grin, only instead of shuddering, I smiled back. Then I climbed the ladder, opened the manhole cover enough to make certain I wasn't going to get trampled by a team of horses, and exited to the square.

Old-fashioned street lights lit the pavements and gardens. They weren't gas-operated any more, but like most aspects of the past, the aesthetic was kept. The street was lined with mansions – some original, some new, and the rest memorials to those who were long gone. These houses had no entail, their owners being the last of their line, and were never rebuilt. Over the last twenty years or so, a few had been razed. Some foreign and lesser aristos had begun to build homes on the land – all in an architectural style at least a century old. It probably didn't look much different than it had prior to '32.

Church's house was one of these newer dwellings. He had a family house in the country somewhere, but Mayfair was where he spent the majority of his time. His house was a lovely cream stone building that seemed incredibly large for one person to live in, but I supposed he planned on marrying one day.

If anyone would take him. Many aristo women would see it as marrying down to attach themselves to him.

I approached the house from the back. I scaled the stone wall and crept along the top of it until I was in jumping distance of the house. The grounds would be protected by alarms, as would the house itself, but I knew how to get in.

I jumped from the wall and sailed through the damp night to the balcony. I caught the balustrade and hauled myself over. The French doors were unlocked, letting me inside easily. Of course, once I was in, they shut and locked automatically. I had less than thirty seconds to disarm the alarm before an armoured unit of RGs arrived to riddle me full of holes. Quickly I crossed the carpet to the panel near the main door. I punched in 1-9-1-8-5-4 – Church's mother's birth date – and breathed a sigh of relief when the tiny red light stopped flashing.

This was Church's bedroom. It was neat to the point of obsessiveness. I would find nothing pertaining to me here. The old man kept his life in neat little compartments. I would be business, and therefore all information about me would be in his office, where his best security was housed.

I eased open the door to the corridor and peered out. Empty. As far as I knew, he didn't keep many servants, and that would work in my favour. Chances were that I wouldn't be seen at all. Slowly, I stepped out and ran down the hall. The thick carpet muffled my haste until I reached the door to his study.

He purposely kept his office on a higher floor so it was more difficult to get to – and so he would stand a better chance of saving things if we ever had another insurrection. I'd laughed at him for being paranoid; now that I knew insurgents were out there, I realised he was only being smart.

There was another alarm panel here on the cream-coloured wallpaper. This one had a keyboard of letters. I punched in LEONARD – Church's middle name – before using a hairpin to turn the tumblers in the old-fashioned lock. The alarm had to be turned off before the door could be opened. I knew all of this handy information because I'd seen him enter it enough times. I was surprised he hadn't changed it. I supposed he didn't see me as a threat. Maybe he thought I was too dumb, or perhaps he thought I'd be afraid.

Or maybe I was doing exactly what he wanted me to.

I opened the door. The lamp on the desk was on, so I didn't have to switch on the other lights. This was the tricky bit. I might know how to get around his alarms, but I had no idea where he kept his valuable documents.

Then I spotted it. It was a painting he'd purchased in Germany by some insipid painter named Adolf. He liked it because he said it was so very human. I never understood the appeal of a country church scene. It wasn't as though we lacked for those in England.

I crossed the room to the painting and pulled on the frame. It came away from the wall on hinges, revealing a safe behind it. A little too easy, perhaps, but then this was the one thing I did not have the code for.

I tried Church's birthday, and his mother's again. I tried the date of the Great Insurrection. I searched his office for clues and tried any and all combinations I could think of. I wasted half an hour doing this. Had I sneaked in here for nothing? I could not leave empty-handed. I'd sit behind that fucking desk and wait for him to get home if I had to. I was not leaving without answers.

In a fit of what I supposed was arrogance, or simply futility, I tried my own birthday. The door to the safe swung open.

What the bloody hell? This was too wrong. Fortunate, of course, but so very unsettling. I shook the creep off my skin and removed a ledger and a stack of files from the interior of the safe.

The files had names on them – some I recognised and others I did not. I stopped when I found one that read VARDAN, ALEXANDRA ELIZABETH. It was at least two inches thick, and worn, as though someone had gone through it on a regular basis.

I opened it. A photo of me taken earlier this year for my RG badge was clipped to the inside cover. These were the documents that my hospital files lacked. On top were pages that made very little sense to me, with all their medical jargon, but it was clear that they contained blood-work results. My throat tightened at the sight of the name at the bottom of the results – and the smear of blood across it.

Simon Halstead.

CHAPTER 16

MORALITY, LIKE ART, MEANS DRAWING A LINE SOME PLACE

At that moment I thought my heart might give up and stop beating, it was so completely broken. It hurt. Fuck me, it hurt so bad.

How could Church have this information unless he was the one who killed Simon? The suspicion had occurred to me, but seeing this made it real, not just paranoia.

Quickly I sorted through the rest of the folder. There were photographs of me from birth right up to a few weeks ago – candid photos. I hadn't even been aware of being photographed. Every injury was noted, every event – including the date of my first period. Perv.

But more importantly, there were the results of all the blood tests Ophelia had asked about. They monitored everything about me, including the fact that I seemed perfectly normal despite my "tainted" blood. On one sheet, in red ink, it was written that I "responded well" to the supplements, which were designed to "inhibit" any potential goblin behaviour.

That would explain why things began changing when I stopped taking them.

There was more – so much more I couldn't process it. I couldn't take it all in – it was too much.

There was a digital processing machine on a sideboard near the heavy wooden desk. I went to it and scrolled through my rotary for Vex's number. I dialled the corresponding digits on the face of the machine, and began feeding pages into the slot. I didn't bother with photographs, just the pages that seemed important. Church's set-up was state-of-the-art and incredibly fast, but it still took a good quarter of an hour to send it all.

I should have taken it all home and sent it from there – that would have been the smart decision. If I'd done that, I wouldn't have been at the machine when Churchill walked in. I hadn't heard him over the digital processor. He was that quiet, and I was that distracted.

"Good evening, Alexandra."

I jumped. Before I did anything else, I jabbed the buttons to erase the transmission history so he wouldn't see where the pages had gone. Then, without any pretence of trying to lie my way out of the situation, I slowly turned to face my former mentor.

The sight of him, all sharp and dapper in his evening clothes, made me both sad and angry. "Hullo, Church. The party at Chesterfield house let out early, did it?"

He stripped off his gloves. "What are you doing here?"

I held up the file. "A little light reading."

His shoulders slumped a little. He looked younger, boyish almost. It didn't suit him. "I wish you hadn't found that."

"You're not even going to attempt to deny it?"

"Deny what, my dear?"

"*This*." I shook the file at him. "Aren't you going to tell me it's all a misunderstanding?"

Hands in his pockets, he moved towards me. I took an instinctive step back – right into the sideboard. "You're not stupid, Alexandra. You've read it, were obviously smart enough to copy it. What could I say to make you doubt your own eyes? I'd have to lie, and I so hate lying to you."

"You've done a good job of it the last couple of decades."

"Yes, well . . . that was necessary."

"Necessary for who?"

"For you, of course." He seemed surprised I would even ask. "All I've ever done is try to protect you."

My jaw literally dropped. "You shot me in the bloody back!"

Church sighed. "To keep you from catching up with Victoria's would-be assassin."

Fang me, he wasn't even going to deny that either. "Why? You shot him too. Thankfully you did a better job on him than me."

"Yes, well I didn't want you dead. I regret you were as badly injured as you were. Still, the prince took care of you."

I stared at him. Had I heard him correctly? "Did you . . . were you involved in the assassination attempt, Church?"

He smiled at me. "My dear girl, if I was, do you think I'd admit to it? Besides, you ruined that plan, didn't you?" His gaze sharpened.

He *had* been involved. An icy-hot sensation spiked down my legs to pool in my feet. I had adored this man. Part of me still did, despite the fact that I didn't know the real him at all. "What purpose could possibly be served by the death of the Queen?"

"Hypothetically?" he queried with an arched brow. "Change. The Great Insurrection should have been a well-learned lesson for aristocrats. We are the superior race, yet we hide away like rats. We throw bones to the humans because they outnumber us and we don't want another rebellion. Victoria refuses to see that another revolution is coming. Aristocrats should be strong, inspiring. Instead, we let half-bloods defend us. Once we were glorious, fearsome creatures. Now, they write romances and make foolish teen films about us. Is it any wonder the humans seek to overthrow us?"

"Killing the Queen would only give humans that much more power." Bedlam would love it if Victoria had been killed. That sort of tragedy would weaken the aristocracy.

"Prince Albert Edward would unite us as a whole."

"The Prince of Wales knows you tried to kill his mother?" This was becoming a kind of paranormal melodrama.

He shrugged. "I didn't try to kill anyone." Did he think I was wearing some sort of listening device, recording his words? "But even you must admit we need change, Alexandra. You, and others like you, are key to that change."

My heart squeezed into my throat. "There are others like me?"

"Not quite like you, no. Not yet." He smiled – a mysterious little twist of his thin lips. "But there are other unique half-bloods out there, contributing to the betterment of our kind."

I thought of the cells in the basement of Bedlam. I thought of Vex's murdered son. "Are these halvies willing participants in this plan of yours?" Christ, this was too much. "Church, how can you be a part of this?"

The sharp jut of his cheekbones flushed. "If not for me, they would have put you in a cage years ago."

"Is that supposed to make me feel better? How long have you known what I am?"

"Since the prince tried to grab you. I couldn't let anyone find out the truth."

"Why not?" I demanded. "What did I ever do to deserve such *condescension*?"

Church blinked. "You're my special girl. You always have been." He came forward, and I edged to the left, closer to the door. "You must know I'd never let anything happen to you."

"Other than shooting me in the back."

"None of this would have happened if you hadn't gone looking for Dede. Where is she, dear girl? Poor mad Drusilla. She needs help."

At one time I would have confessed everything to him. "She's dead."

He cocked his head to one side. His perfectly groomed and pomaded hair didn't move. "We both know that isn't true. She wouldn't leave the child."

The metaphorical knife twisted in my chest. "Did you do that?"

The gleam in his eyes turned sympathetic. "Everything I do is for the good of my kind, Alexandra. Dede could help us increase our numbers. If aristocrat and half-blood matings can produce viable births, think of what that means. The human side is negated, and a half-blood is already of noble blood. Studying half-bloods, especially those with unique characteristics, we can continue on."

Bitterness flooded my tongue. "So we're just lab mice to you, then?"

"Not you. You're so much more."

"I'm a goblin."

"You are more than one of those monsters. Alexandra, you're a miracle!" He suddenly became animated – like an old automaton wound up for the first time in decades. "You have all the advantages of being fully plagued without the defects that goblins suffer. You are the beginning of something wonderful for the aristocracy. You are hope."

That was the second time someone had referred to hope in relationship to me. The first time had been the goblin prince.

I opened my mouth, but Church cut me off. "You are going to be the salvation of the aristocracy. You and me."

Oh, fang me. He was not hinting at what I thought he was, was he? He was. I could tell from the pervy way he looked at me.

"Church . . ." I licked my lips. "I don't think of you in that way. You've always been a father to me. Besides, I'm seeing Vex."

His face darkened. Perhaps mentioning Vex hadn't been the smart thing to do, but I wasn't exactly thinking clearly right now. "Do you think he loves you as I do? I've spent your entire life preparing you for this moment. I have moulded you into exactly what you are supposed to be. I won't lose you to some barbaric wolf."

"I'm not yours to lose." In all the years I'd known him, I'd never thought of him in a sexual manner. Sure, I'd crushed on him when I was young – all the girls had – but that had gone away. I had idolised him, not lusted for him. He was more my father than my father ever had been. The idea of him putting his hands on me . . . it turned my stomach.

"How is Vex anyway?" he enquired with false sweetness. "Did he find anything useful in the hospital files? Is he any closer to discovering what happened to his son?"

I stared at him, unable to conceal my shock – and fear. I couldn't even open my mouth. I knew now without a doubt that he had been involved in Duncan MacLaughlin's death.

Church smiled – gently. "You should tell Ophelia to be more careful in her choice of bed partners."

Her murdered human. Raj. Had he been a spy for Church?

"Why'd you kill him?" I asked. "If he was feeding you information, he was useful."

"Did I say anything about killing him?" His eyes narrowed. "The good doctor and I had an agreement, but he had a crisis of loyalty and refused to tell me where Dede was. He also refused to give me further information on the leaders of the insurgents, such as where they hid when not in Bedlam. I decided to terminate our business arrangement after that."

So he knew Bedlam was involved, but not that it was traitor HQ. And he knew that Dede was alive, but not where she was.

Good. My estranged family members were safe for now. At least I could tell Ophelia who had killed her lover. Maybe then she'd forgive me for almost killing her.

"It won't look good for you or your alpha, fraternising with insurgents, Alexandra."

Ah, so now he was going to use Vex to try to manipulate me. "It won't look good for you, Church, when people see video of you dumping Simon's body, or when they discover that the bullet that almost killed me came from your gun. I'm still the daughter of a peer."

"When they find out you're a goblin, they'll hate you too much to care. I could have protected you from that. I still can."

His words hurt – not just because they came from him, but because they were true. "And once it gets out that you're experimenting on halvies, you'll be arrested, peer or not. I took copies of your research." Good of me to remind him of that.

"Ah yes, and sent them to . . . " He moved past me to check the machine. "Vexation MacLaughlin. Too bad about that."

Ice formed in my stomach. I'd erased the transmission log, but not the last number called. "What do you mean?" Vex couldn't be part of this. He just couldn't.

Churchill removed his rotary from his inside coat pocket and dialled a single number before holding the device to his ear. "It's me." His cold grey gaze locked with mine. "Kill the wolf."

Vex could not die. Not because of me.

"I wish it didn't come to this," Church lamented, tucking his rotary into his pocket once more. "But you give me no choice. I'm not going to let that bastard take what I've worked so hard for. What is mine."

I was included in that. Bastard made me sound like a bloody possession, or a reward of some kind.

I dived for the door, but like any good opponent, Church saw that coming and put himself between me and escape. I barely had time to brace myself for the fist that flew towards me. It caught me on the jaw – the bone cracked from the impact. I flew back, but caught hold of a bookcase. It smashed to the floor, spilling leather-bound editions around me, but at least I was still upright.

My old mentor looked surprised. "Don't fight me, Alexandra, you can't best me. I'm a one-hundred-and-thirty-eight-year-old vampire who learned to fight a century before you were born. What are you?"

"Your best student," I replied, savouring the taste of blood in my mouth as my throbbing jaw began to heal. "And one pissed-off goblin."

He started at that, and I took the opportunity to launch myself at him, pulling my dagger free from my corset. As much as I wanted to pummel him into oblivion – and maybe rip out his throat – I didn't have time for this shit. Vex was in danger. So when Church lifted his right hand to block me – meaning to strike with his dominant left – I veered to his right and came up under his elbow with a quick slash.

The ends of his cravat fell to the floor as crimson blossomed and bloomed against his snow-white collar. His eyes widened and his fingers wrapped around his throat. I hadn't killed him – I would have to take his head clean off for that, and I hadn't time. He hadn't expected me to use a blade. He always taught us to use our bodies as weapons, and hadn't known about my dagger. I wondered if perhaps my mother hadn't feared something like this might happen when she gave it to me.

As he slumped to the floor, gurgling, I wiped the bloody blade on my trouser leg, shoved it back in my corset and took several steps backwards. I cast the old man the briefest of glances as I took off at a run. Going through the house would take too long, and there was a chance I'd catch more trouble. Church had already cost me enough time. Instead, I hurtled through the right-hand window overlooking the street. Glass exploded around me, slicing at my clothes and skin, catching in my hair.

I expected to hit the cobblestones hard – and most likely with my head. I landed on my feet, in a crouch, just like in films.

Just like a goblin.

My skin stung where glass had pierced it, but I ignored it – it would heal soon enough. I took off running towards Curzon Street. Vex was either still at Chesterfield House or on his way home. I had to find him before Churchill's men did.

I ran fast – faster than I'd ever imagined moving. If I thought about it, my feet tangled, so I stopped thinking and just ran. All that mattered was finding Vex. I passed carriages and cars. People yelled at me as I sped by, but I ignored them all.

On the corner of Charles and Curzon Streets I heard snarls and angry voices. I turned right and ran towards the sound. I knew it was Vex. His wolf spoke to that part of me that came from my mother's altered blood. I made a noise low in my throat that came out as a loud growl. Fighting with Church hadn't brought out my goblin side – only pissed it off – but it was here now, in gleeful anticipation of spilling blood.

Of protecting what I thought of as mine.

I didn't fight it, I let it come. I wanted it to come. It didn't hurt so much when my fangs broke through, thick and sharp. The claws stung, but I didn't care. I could feel the bones of my face changing. My fractured jaw protested, but gave in, making room for my canine teeth.

It was five on one. Five young vampire and halvie combatants, armed to the teeth, against Vex, who had shifted into a form somewhere between man and wolf. He should have looked hideous, but I thought he was the most beautiful thing I'd ever seen – because he was still alive. A sixth attacker lay on the ground, dead. His throat had been ripped open.

Vex glanced at me as I came to his side. His eyes widened, but that was his only reaction. He knew me by scent, and I supposed he was more concerned with staying alive than with what I looked like.

How did Church plan to explain the death of the alpha? Murder was a serious offence, but killing the leader of the wolves would cost him his own life. I had no more time to think about it – thankfully – when one of the halvies charged me. She hesitated for a moment when she saw my face, and that was all the opening I needed. I jobbed her between the eyes, remembering at the last split second to hold back. I didn't want to kill her, and there was a good chance I'd do just that if I hit her as hard as I could.

She went down with appalling ease for a halvie. If Church had trained this lot, the old man was losing his edge. Another halvie came for me and I knocked him down as well. It took a bit more effort, but not much. All I had to do was slam my skull against his and he crumpled like a puppet with its strings cut.

That left three vampires. I recognised them as lesser peers. One was the offspring of a baronet. Another was a baroness, and the third was the son of a viscount. Part of Churchill's plan for aristos to aspire to be the "glorious" creatures they used to be?

Given the dead body already on the ground, I knew Vex didn't share my reluctance to kill. In fact, the way he was toying with the baronet's kid I thought he was going to kill her as well, but he stopped at rendering her unconscious. She was bleeding, but she'd heal.

That left us one apiece. Fair odds, until the baroness pulled a pistol from beneath her bustle.

"That's not exactly sporting," Vex said, his voice a guttural growl that made me shiver – and not entirely in a sexy way.

The vampire glanced at him before returning her attention to me. "I know you. You're Vardan's. What the hell are you?"

Fair enough question. One I'd ask myself were the situation reversed. "Me," I replied with a shrug. I mean, really I was little bit of everything, wasn't I? "But just so you know, the goblin prince promised that the goblins would go to war with anyone who spilled my blood, and that includes Churchill's lackeys. Perhaps the question you should ask is whether or not I'm worth dying over."

Her face went stark white. The pistol turned to Vex.

"Uh-uh." I wagged a finger at her, silly with power. "Hurt him and I'll take it personally. Don't you think the old man's brought you enough trouble for one night? You can either beg the alpha's forgiveness for being a stupid cow, and hope he has mercy, or you can die. Or you can take your chances with the goblins. Either way, I'm pretty sure your life's going to be a lot shorter than you'd planned."

The pistol lowered. Beside her, the son of the viscount wiped blood from his mouth with the back of his hand and said, "I hear St Petersburg is lovely this time of year."

"We could still kill you," the baroness argued. "The goblins wouldn't have to know."

I laughed, and called her bluff. "Go ahead and shoot me, then. See how long it takes before the prince rips out your liver."

She swallowed and tucked the gun underneath her bustle. "Will you let us go?" she asked Vex.

He looked more like himself now, save for the blood around his mouth and the wildness in his eyes. He glared at her as though he would dearly love to taste her blood as well, but being alpha, he was as much ruled by politics as bloodlust. She had asked for mercy, and she was a vampire.

"Leave," he commanded. "If I see your face again, I'll rip it off your skull."

The vampires didn't need any more encouragement. "Give my regards to Rasputin," I called as they slunk into the shadows and disappeared from sight. The Russian aristocracy didn't much like to talk about the Mad Monk. Not aristocratic, he wasn't entirely human either. Maybe he was like me. Regardless, he was a scary son-of-a-bitch.

"I'm going to regret that," Vex commented drily when we were alone.

"Maybe," I replied, "but better that than finding out Church got it all on video." There was only one dead body on the ground, and it was a halvie. I hated to think it, but a halvie death wouldn't stir up quite so much trouble. People expected us – I mean halvies – to die. Self-defence was a valid excuse for killing.

"Churchill's behind this?" Gold glowed in Vex's eyes. "I'll tear his fucking head off."

If anyone could best Church, it was Vex. And quite possibly me, though he'd probably fuck with my head so bad I'd cave in.

"Let's get out of here," I suggested. "We can talk about it at home."

We climbed into his motor carriage, leaving the body for the unconscious combatants to deal with when they woke up. There would be traffic along soon as more of the party at Chesterfield house let out. I was surprised no one had stumbled upon us as it was, but then this wasn't the route most would take. Church would have known that.

A short while later we were in the monstrous tub in Vex's bathroom, up to our shoulders in hot soapy water. We sat at opposite ends. I stroked his calf while he rubbed my feet.

"So Churchill planned to kill me because he's in love with you?" The documents I'd sent him had been printed and were on his bed, where he'd tossed them before running the bath. He'd made copies as well, smart man.

"He doesn't love me." I groaned with pleasure as his thumbs dug into the ball of my foot. This bath had been a glorious idea – to get us clean and to soak some of the tension from my muscles. "He sees me as a means to an end."

Vex nodded. "Marrying you would increase his social standing, and if you produced full-blood children he would be seen as a saviour to the aristocracy. Victoria would probably overlook the fact that your mother was once a courtesan."

Of course Church would be seen as the saviour, rather than me. Wanker.

"And the fact that you're a goblin."

My head jerked up. "You knew?" He couldn't have read it – he had barely glanced at the pages.

He shrugged. "I had my suspicions."

"Why didn't you say anything?"

"Would you have believed me?" He gave me a kind smile. "It was something you needed to find out for yourself, especially since I wasn't one hundred per cent certain."

"And it doesn't . . . bother you?"

He ran a big hand up my leg. "To be honest, I find it kind of sexy."

Smiling, I leaned back against the porcelain, warmed by the water. "Really? You reckon it's sexy to date someone who could decide to eat you?"

His lips tilted lopsidedly and his eyes began to sparkle. "You can nibble on me whenever you want. Do I get to eat you too?"

Blood rushed to my cheeks – and other places. "Well . . ." My words turned into a squeal as Vex grabbed both my ankles and jerked me through the water towards him. I had to hold on to the sides to keep from going under. He caught me around the back with one arm and hauled me up so that I straddled him, our chests pressed together. One move of my hips and he'd be all mine.

I hadn't realised it through all the anger and hurt, but I desperately needed someone. I needed him. He was the one thing I felt I could depend on. Church had made me doubt him – even if it was for just a second – and I felt like shit for it.

"What would you have done if you'd arrived at Curzon Street and they'd got the better of me?"

"I would have killed them all," I replied, honestly.

That was the end of our conversation. He wrapped his arms around me and pulled my head down to his.

Water was all over the floor by the time we climbed out of the bath. Vex had food and wine sent up and we had supper in his room, where I told him everything that had happened, including my suspicions that Duncan had been experimented on, and my certainty that Church had known about it.

I expected him to fly into a rage, but instead he just looked sad, and I realised I was seeing him as a father whose pain for his son was greater than his rage. I didn't know what to do for him, so I put my hand over his and sat in silence with him.

A little while later I spoke. "What do I do, Vex? All I have against Church are the papers I copied and my own interpretation of events. It might be enough to start an investigation, but it's not enough to put Church away. He's the one who shot Queen V's assailant, so he's in her favour at the moment, despite me taking the bullet. And I still don't have all the answers I want."

"You may never," he cautioned. "Make no mistake, though – one of us is going to have to kill Churchill. If not sooner then later."

"I know." I didn't want to think about it. I didn't want to think about any of it.

"My people and I are here for you, whatever you need."

"Wolves and goblins," I said with mock pomposity. "I must be the shit, what?"

He didn't even crack a grin at my false bravado. "You need to be careful. Christ only knows who else is involved."

"Do you think I should go public with what I am?" The thought made my stomach drop.

"It would make it harder for some to get to you, but would make you a target for others . . . " His gaze locked with mine. "Unless you asked the prince for protection."

I ran a hand through my hair – it was a tangled mess. "I'm not sure I want to broadcast my freakitude. And I'm not sure I want to embrace my inner goblin. Fang me, I wish I had never stumbled upon any of this."

"If you hadn't, you might have played right into the vampires' hands. Your mother and your sisters would be dead. Look, you don't have to do anything right this minute. Think about it and figure out what to do after the knighting ceremony. You'll be a lot harder to get rid of with a title attached to your name."

I flopped back on the bed. "Ever since I was a kid I wanted to be knighted, and now that it's happening I can't even fucking enjoy it."

Vex reached over and took my hand. He rubbed his thumb over my knuckles. "Enjoy it now. You're safe here, and you don't have to worry about anything while you're inside these walls. Concentrate on some happiness."

"My God, I love you." As soon as the words left my mouth I knew how they sounded. I would have said the same to Avery, or even Emma, but it wasn't to a sister or a friend, it was the man I was sleeping with.

He laughed – a loud bark I felt right down to my toes. "Relax, sweetheart. I'm not going to bolt for the Highlands just because you said the 'L' word. I know what you meant."

My face burned, but I was so relieved. And a titch disappointed.

What had I expected? That he'd declare undying devotion to me now and for ever? Bollocks.

I watched as he lifted his hand to my face. He stroked the pad of his thumb between my eyebrows. "Don't frown, lass. I'm not making sport. I care about you too. I wouldn't be here if I didn't."

He lay down beside me. I moved so he could slide an arm beneath me and pull me close against his chest. It was amazing, the restorative powers of a hug and a snog.

Afterwards, we went to bed, though dawn was still a couple of hours away. I was bone tired, but not ready to go to sleep. "Tell me what it was like early in the plague. I want to know what it was like to not have rotaries. Do you remember when the first motor carriage was built?"

"Aye, I had one," he replied, and proceeded to tell me all about it – and how he could run faster than it drove. He told me about parties and events I'd only read about in my history textbooks. His voice and the stories gave me a sense of grounding, as though the entire world hadn't shifted beneath my feet.

I fell asleep to the sound of his voice describing what it was like to be a wolf on his estate in Scotland, where he had acres to run with his pack, and until I woke up the next afternoon, I forgot to be afraid. I forgot everything.

I hid at Vex's until the evening of the knighting ceremony. Avery was pissed off that I didn't come home and let her help me get ready. She thought I was at Vex's so I could get a regular shagging, not because he was worried that Church might come after me – which surprisingly hadn't happened. Vex told me to invite her and Emma over for dinner beforehand – as if I could eat with my nerves the way they were.

That was another thing – I had realised that after attacking Ophelia, I'd lost my usual hearty appetite. It returned earlier today, and I wondered if blood sustained me better than actual food. A bit of a disturbing thought, though my stomach growled cheerfully at it.

It was good having my sister there, and Emma too. They helped me get dressed and do my face and hair. Vex had pack business to attend to, so I enjoyed the company. Avery and her chatter made me feel normal again. Like maybe everything was going to be fine after all.

"I wish Dede could see you," she whispered after pinning the last lock of my hair in place.

Tears threatened, but I blinked them away. "I wish she was here too." And I did. I would give anything to go back and somehow change it so she never got mixed up with the insurgents. Hell, I'd go back and make sure she never got involved with Ainsley. He was the one who'd ruined her life for her. I'd like to go back and change things for both of us.

"But I'm glad the two of you will be there," I told them, putting on a smile.

"Val should be here any minute, if he's not already," my sister informed me. Her lips curved despite her watery eyes. "You look so beautiful, Xandy."

I stood up and hugged her. "Thank you. So do you." She wore black because she was still in mourning for our sister who wasn't really dead. Emma too, which I thought was quite sweet seeing as how Dede was no relation to her.

I, however, was not wearing black. I was wearing a dove-grey silk gown that was subdued enough to please Her Majesty, and shiny enough to please me. It had a boned bodice embroidered with birds in a darker grey. The skirt was layered, and pulled up in the front to reveal a feathered petticoat beneath. The shoulder straps were wide and left my arms bare, so I tugged on matching gloves that came to just above my elbows. I had boots dyed to match, the heels of which were hourglass-shaped and inset with onyx stones.

Avery had curled and pinned my hair so that it was a huge, elaborate thing adorned with feathers that matched my dress. I wore Tahitian pearls in my ears and around my neck, and I'd done a full face, complete with false eyelashes.

Oh, and I had my gun in my bustle – just in case. And my dagger in my boot.

I hadn't been so well turned out since graduation from the Academy. I'd lost my virginity that night. Hopefully tonight would prove more satisfactory than that one had.

We went downstairs and found not only Vex waiting for us, but Val too. I gave my brother a good hard hug. It felt like forever since I'd seen him. He looked tired, but otherwise well, and the solid black of his clothing suited his colouring.

Vex had gone all out as well. His thick hair was neat, his jaw freshly shaved. He was dressed in black and white – the standard evening attire for the aristocracy – but instead of trousers he wore a formal black kilt with tall, thick-soled boots.

"You look fetching," I told him. "Sexy knees."

He grinned. "Thank you. You don't think I'll overshadow you?"

I rolled my eyes and took his arm. "I reckon my ego can take it."

The five of us took Vex's carriage to Buckingham Palace. The ceremony used to be held at St Paul's, but the Queen didn't like to leave the palace much – not since the Great Insurrection. She had people come to her whenever possible, and since the cathedral was in the more human part of the city, it simply wasn't safe.

The Royal Guard was out in full force when we arrived. I recognised all of them, and it took me twice as long to get inside because they all wanted to congratulate me. My chest ached with gratitude. I missed my colleagues. I just wanted to get back to work and back to normal as quickly as possible.

I knew that wasn't going to happen. Tonight, however, I was going to pretend.

The night lit up with flashes as we walked into the palace. Certain reporters from aristo-friendly papers were allowed to photograph particular events. They were subjected to intense security measures, and only allowed so far into the palace, but apparently they thought it was worth the chance to catch a glimpse of the aristocracy. Their papers certainly cashed in on it. Humans might hate us, but a lot of them were fascinated by us. I suppose it had always been that way, even before the plague.

Inside, we were met by my father and his countess. She smiled tightly at me, but her blue eyes were flat and cold. I was surprised she was even here, but it wasn't for me. She was here for Vardan, and for the press outside.

My father hugged me. "I'm so very proud of you, Alexandra."

Two months ago I would have melted at those words. I would have teared up. Now ... well, I felt somewhat empty. He knew what I was, and he'd let them take my blood and ply me with drugs to keep me looking and acting the way he wanted me to look and act. Any extra interest he'd ever had in me was no more than the attention a child paid to a science project.

"Thank you, Father." I turned to his wife. "Your Grace, how lovely of you to come. You look very well this evening." I only said it to force her to speak, and even then she merely thanked me. Cow.

We went into the ballroom – where I'd been shot just a short while ago – and were shown to our seats. There were two other honours being bestowed this evening, and my knighthood was last.

Out of the corner of my eye I saw Churchill enter. He met my gaze almost immediately, as though he'd been looking for me. I glared at him, but he smiled serenely and nodded in greeting. I noticed he wore a red cravat, and knew without doubt that he'd done so to intentionally remind me of slitting his throat. He was a bit twisted that way. He was a bit twisted *every* way.

I wouldn't say it to anyone, but I was a little afraid as I looked away. Churchill wasn't a man who gave up. He wanted me as his wife or dead, and he wouldn't stop until he had succeed. I would never marry him, so that only left him one choice. I wasn't sure I could kill him if the opportunity arose. I suppose I was a little twisted too, because part of me still loved him.

He sat a couple of rows ahead and to the left of me. Was he here just to make me squirm? He couldn't actually believe I wanted him here. But then, my wants wouldn't matter, would they? He was here because people would talk if he wasn't.

Vex squeezed my fingers. I squeezed back. He might seem relaxed, but I could feel the tension in his muscles where his arm pressed against mine. We couldn't even enjoy sitting together – and him wearing a skirt with probably nothing underneath.

I barely managed to pay attention during the ceremony. I didn't care about the other people being honoured. It wasn't that I was completely self-absorbed; I just kept waiting for Church to jump up and shoot me in the head with a tetracycline-filled bullet. No wonder the one meant for Victoria had hurt so much – goblins were much more susceptible to the drug, and to silver. And I'd gone through life thinking that neither of them was that big a concern.

Finally it was my turn. My knees trembled as I rose and walked to the front of the room, where I took my place before the tiny Queen. She smiled at me – no teeth, of course – and told the room full of people how I was being honoured tonight because I had "bravely and selflessly" put her safety before my own. I had risked my life to preserve hers, and therefore my service to Crown and country was to be rewarded with a knighthood. She then asked me to kneel. I did so, on the padded cushion that had been provided.

She lifted a large, gleaming sword and placed it on my shoulder. For a second I had a vision of her lifting the bloody thing and taking my head clean off my shoulders with it.

Queen V had just started to say the words to complete the ceremony when a commotion rose up in the crowd. My spine went rigid. This was it. This was when Churchill would make his move. My right hand eased behind me, slipping beneath my bustle to curve around the Bulldog . . .

"No!" came a familiar rasping voice. "The Xandra lady cannot be knighted."

I closed my eyes. This was worse than Churchill making a move. Way worse. The crowd buzzed loudly with incoherent conversation. Shouts rang out, followed by a growl.

"Silence!" Victoria commanded, her voice filling the room so clearly and strongly my ears rang. "Prince, what is the meaning of this intrusion?"

I turned my head and saw the goblin prince approach. He was the damnedest sight, with his fur neatly groomed, wearing a frock coat and cravat. He did not bow to the Queen. He did not defer. He approached her as an equal, and with a scowl that made him look like a rabid hell hound.

"Not a dame," he insisted, as though the mere idea was a personal insult against him. "Cannot be. *Will* not be."

"And why is that?" Victoria asked in a voice so cold my blood froze.

"Yes," I murmured. "Why is that?"

The prince heard me and met my gaze. "Because Xandra lady is a queen. Our goblin queen."

CHAPTER 17

TO THE DEAD WE OWE ONLY THE TRUTH

I was *what*?

I staggered to my feet, the movement sending Victoria's sword clattering to the carpet. Neither she nor I bothered to look where it landed; we were both watching the prince, but while Queen V looked infuriated, I was stupefied.

I'd been outed.

"Is there anything else I need to know?" I demanded of the prince before turning to my paler-than-death father. I tried to ignore the stupefied crowd. "Anything else that's been conveniently kept from me? Because I'm pretty topped up on surprises."

The Queen shot me a narrow glance. "Calm yourself, girl. Prince, whatever do you mean, she is your queen? She is obviously *not* a goblin."

Now it was about to get interesting. I could deny and earn the prince's disapproval, or I could face the truth – put it out there so no one else could be hurt because of it.

Fuck me, but sometimes I hated having even the smallest degree of honour. "Actually, ma'am, I am," I informed her. My voice carried much more than I'd intended, and the gathered audience seemed to gasp in unison. I grimaced.

Slowly, the Queen turned towards me, blue eyes hard as stone. She might be tiny, but she was one scary bitch. "And just when did you discover this interesting biological fact?"

"Recently." I cleared my throat to get rid of the squeak in my voice. "I don't know anything about this queen rubbish, I assure you."

The prince turned his one eye on me. "Told the pretty she could not be knighted."

"You didn't tell me why. I thought you were concerned about my safety."

He turned back to Her Majesty, lip curling back from his fangs. "Queen trumps dame."

Victoria hissed at him.

"I am not your queen," I insisted. Any minute now I expected the two of them to go for one another's throats. "I can't be."

"For years the plague has waited for one to lead us to rightful place. Xandra lady is the one. The plague has worked with blood queen, but now we have our own." He knelt before me, head bowed. "The plague serves our lady and no other."

Oh *Albert's bloody fangs*. Everyone under the aristocratic blanket – even humans – had a leader who then deferred to Queen V. But the prince had just essentially told our sovereign that she no longer held their allegiance. I did.

"Quite," Victoria agreed, turning those stony eyes of her on me. I could see that her fangs had come out – tiny and dainty but razor sharp. I entertained the notion of showing her my own. That was what this was all about, wasn't it? Dominance. The prince had placed me above him, so now Queen V saw me as a threat. "It seems you are indeed the goblin queen, Lady Alexandra."

And she was not happy about it.

Historically speaking, the monarchy of England did not like it when things didn't go their way. They especially didn't like it when another queen showed up and threatened their Divine Rule. Someone tended to lose a head, such as Lady Jane Grey or Mary, Queen of Scots. But it wouldn't be me, not today. The goblins had claimed me, and anyone who took a swing at me had better be ready to take on the entire plague.

So this was what power felt like. I didn't want it, but I was glad of it. I'd been shoved into this position by circumstances I'd never invited, but if being the goblin queen kept me alive ...

I turned my head to see Churchill's reaction, but he wasn't in his seat. Where the ruddy hell had he gone?

I put my hand on the prince's shoulder. "Get up. Please. I'm not comfortable with you bowing at my feet." Then to Victoria, "I didn't know anything about this."

"That makes two of us," she replied tartly. "We are not amused by this debacle."

"You think I am?" I arched a brow. "Your Majesty, my entire life has been turned upside down."

"We will discuss this in a more private setting at another time, *Your Majesty*." Oh, she was very pissed off. Brilliant – because I so wanted another enemy, just to balance things out.

I met Vex's gaze. He smiled. For a moment I thought I might actually survive this.

"There will be a meeting of the faction heads on Monday," Queen Victoria imparted. "MacLaughlin, you will attend, as well as the prince and his new queen."

The prince's muzzle wrinkled, pulling back from his glistening teeth. He snarled low in his throat. I shivered at the sound – as did three quarters of our audience.

"Our queen does not take orders from a leech." Right, gobs thought themselves the superior race. That meant they saw me not only as their queen, but as *the* queen. Furry bastard wasn't going to keep me alive; he was going to get me fucking killed.

To my astonishment, Victoria swallowed. Resentment glittered in her eyes when she turned to me. "Your Majesty, are you free on Monday to attend a meeting of the faction heads?"

I wondered what she'd do if I said no. "Yes. Monday is fine."

She smiled coldly – revealing fang. "Excellent." She turned to leave, effectively dismissing us all.

"Churchill's caught a traitor!" a voice yelled.

Perfect timing. The outburst took all the attention off me. Maybe I'd get to sneak out without the press jumping on me. The prince had to know a way out; after all, he'd got in somehow.

Wait. A traitor? My stomach sank as my heart began to pound. There were only two traitors I knew of who might risk capture to see me knighted.

Much of the audience surged to their feet, scrambling in the direction of the voice. I forgot Victoria and the prince. I went to Vex. "I need to see who the traitor is."

He nodded, but asked no questions. "Let's go, then."

We pushed our way through the throng. It was much easier than I'd anticipated, since people gave me a wide berth.

A hand came down on my arm. "Alexandra . . . " It was my father.

I shook off his hold. "Later." I had no time for him now. There was nothing he could say that would make this better or excuse his part in it.

A shot rang out as we reached the door. I shoved Earl Spencer out of my way. He flew like rag doll straight into the Duke of

Devonshire. I really had to come to terms with this new strength.

Outside the air smelled of humidity, gunpowder and blood. I paused on the steps to search out Churchill, and found him partway down the walk, standing over a body. Flashes went off in a bizarre strobe effect, illuminating the scene with wince-worthy brightness. I caught a glimpse of flat black hair on the ground, and then I saw the traitor's face.

Oh, fuck. No. *Nononononono*. I hitched up my skirt, and ran. My heart struck hard against my ribs, as though desperate to break free. Camera flashes blinded me as I fell to my knees so hard the impact rattled my bones.

"She's a traitor," Churchill said very loudly – so that all the reporters could hear. "She even falsified her own death to ingratiate herself to the insurgent cause."

Familiar green eyes stared up at me, glassy and pained. "Xandy?"

I gathered her up in my arms, not caring about my dress or anything else. "It's all right, Dede. You'll be all right."

Church had shot her twice with silver bullets filled with tetracycline – both in the chest, very close to her heart. I bit my wrist and offered her the blood, hoping to buy her a little time until we could get her to hospital, but as soon as she drank, she began to cough and gag.

I was a goblin, and my blood was toxic. Fuck. How could I forget that?

"Hold on," I told her, cradling her against my chest as she spewed fresh blood all over the silk of my gown. I looked up, and saw Ainsley watching in horror. His son – Dede's son – stood beside him, clinging to Lady Ainsley's skirts. "Call for an ambulance!" I shouted.

"Ainsley . . . " Dede whispered. She'd turned her head and was now looking at her child. I watched a slow smile curve her bloody lips. "Beautiful boy."

Tears streamed down my face as I tried to wipe the blood from hers. "Beautiful just like his mum," I whispered.

She looked at me, and I could tell she was slipping away. The antibiotics and the silver were killing her. My blood was killing her. Her lips parted. The diamond in her front tooth caught the light and sparkled with pink wetness – blood. That damned stone had started this. If not for that I might have thought she was really dead and I wouldn't have gone after her. This might never have happened if not for me not being able to leave things alone.

Her fingers closed around mine. "Just wanted to see him. I wanted . . . to see you get . . . your dream."

I swiped at the tears on my cheeks and smeared her blood on my skin. "I'm so sorry, Dede."

"I'm sorry too," she whispered. "I . . . " And then she was gone. Just like that, my baby sister was dead, and I was left holding a shell. For a moment, everything went quiet. I looked up and saw easily a hundred faces staring back at me, all of them still and silent. It didn't last. A flash went off, followed by another, and then the shouting started up again.

The ambulance came. They took my sister out of my arms. I didn't try to hold on. She was gone.

Suddenly Vex was there, helping me to my feet. He put his coat over my shoulders, and I shivered at the warmth. I hadn't realised how cold I was. So cold. Dede's blood soaked my front, stained my skirt and hands. I turned my head and saw Avery and Val. Avery was sobbing in Emma's arms, and Val . . . our poor brother just looked shocked. Of course they were shocked – they'd thought Dede was already dead. Our father looked stunned as well. He was pale and shaken. I didn't fool myself that it was fatherly love. It was scandal. One daughter a goblin, another a traitor – this would affect him socially for the rest of his days. A mark on the Vardan name.

Good.

I let Vex lead me away, despite the people calling my name. Scotland Yard was there. They were friends with Val, they'd look after it all.

But where was the bastard who'd shot my sister? I searched the crowd and finally found him, beside his carriage, talking to a couple of Yard constables. He met my gaze, and what I saw in his made something inside me howl with rage.

He looked sad, as though he felt actual remorse for what he had done. As though he hadn't had any choice but to kill her. He'd done it to keep the truth about her son secret. He had done it to ingratiate himself with Victoria. She'd never believe now that he was behind the attack on her, not when she saw me as her enemy. No doubt he thought this would keep me in line as well, that I'd back down and keep his secrets.

He thought wrong.

I don't quite know how much time passed before I was able to go after Church. I let the rage fester inside me until I felt like I might explode, though I kept it contained while I spoke to the inspectors.

I avoided my family as best I could. It wasn't that difficult, as they were all in shock and staring at me like they didn't know me any more. In fact, even the press gave me a wide berth. Being a goblin was going to have some perks after all, it seemed.

Shit. The whole world was going to know I was a goblin in a few days. News like this wouldn't be confined to just London, or even England. Pretty soon my freakishness would be broadcast on an international level. I couldn't even begin to fathom the ramifications.

Meanwhile, my furry kin had made themselves scarce. The prince had no issue with ruining what should have been the single most important night of my career, but he didn't want to stick around for the aftermath.

My career. This was going to be the end of it. Only halvies could be Royal Guard. I'd have to give up my badge, my gun. My life.

I turned to Vex, who had stayed by my side the entire time. He was the only one who had. "I need to be alone."

"Are you sure?" he asked.

I hated lying to him – he was so *good*. This was going to affect him as well. What would the pack think of him sleeping with a goblin? How long would it be before he was forced to walk away? "Yes."

"Because if you're going after that fanged cunt, I want to be with you."

I brought my hand up to touch his face and stopped – I was still covered in my sister's blood, though it was sticky and cold now. "I don't want you involved." It wasn't just a matter of revenge; it was politics.

His mouth thinned, but I knew he understood. He understood probably better than I did. "Be careful, and call me if you need me."

I nodded, gave him back his coat and slipped away. I made certain Church saw me.

There was a tunnel beneath the palace that had both an interior and exterior entrance. It was an escape route for Queen V should there ever be another attack on Buckingham Palace. As a leftenant in the RG I was one of the few people outside the aristocracy who knew where these entrances were located. It was how the prince had managed to get in and out. It was also probably how Church had smuggled his assassin inside.

The external door was within the palace gates, so I didn't have to be concerned with the press following me. I found it relatively easily, though if I hadn't known where to look I would have missed it, as it was concealed within a false section of the exterior wall. It was unlocked, just as I had expected. In London, doors that led underground were usually kept easily opened, with the assumption that anyone who chose to use them was taking their life into their own hands. The goblins might not come up to hunt very often, but anything that walked into their territory was considered fair game.

But I didn't have to worry about that any more, did I? Now people had to worry about *me*. Imagine the fear I'd inspire as a goblin who could walk in the daylight, who could grab a child whenever I wanted.

I paused just inside the door as it closed behind me. How long before an angry mob of humans showed up at my door with torches and pitchforks? How long before the Bedlamite insurgents, or the vampires, or the weres, decided I needed to be put down?

Let them come, a little voice in my head whispered. *You have some of the most terrifying creatures in history behind you. You're one of them.*

But right now I had more important matters at hand.

Stone stairs led below ground. I jogged down one flight, turned and then took another. I didn't stop until I reached the small platform lit by a solitary light. It was the abandoned mail rail. Extra lines had been installed around Mayfair after the Great Insurrection, so as to provide an escape for aristos in the event of a future attack. Vex and I had travelled on just such a line when the goblins found Simon.

Poor Simon. Had Churchill shown him any compassion before executing him? My friend had died so he couldn't reveal my secret, but it had been revealed anyway. Church hadn't figured on the prince coming above ground to claim me. Now his plans of secretly using me to secure the future of the aristocratic – specifically the vampire – nation were ruined.

Thank God.

I slipped the Bulldog from beneath my bustle. The blood on my hands had mostly dried, but was still a little tacky on the metal. Did the old man know I could hear him, even though he was silent as a cat? Probably not. I'd always thought him so quiet; now his footsteps sounded as clumsy as a human's as he came down the stairs.

I held the gun close to my skirts, out of sight, and waited.

"I thought I might find you here."

At the sound of Church's voice, a wave of sorrow washed over me. I turned to see him standing a few feet away, the gun in his hand pointed straight at me.

"And I knew you'd chase me," I replied wearily. "Why'd you kill her, Church? Just to hurt me?"

"She got herself killed. She should have stayed in hiding."

"You knew she'd want to see me and the boy."

"I thought she might, yes. Predictable, your poor sister. I saved her the torture she would have got in Newgate. We both know death was the best thing for her."

"She was guilty only of faking her own death, nothing more."

"She aligned herself with traitors, my dear. I've already given Her Majesty all the notes from my investigation into Drusilla's activities. I'd been watching her for some time – not long after she was first approached by Ophelia Blackwood and her traitorous followers."

Ophelia? So Church didn't know everything, then. He didn't know Bedlam was their primary hideout and he didn't know my mother led them.

I didn't try to hide my disgust. "I suppose all of this buys you much of Victoria's favour, doesn't it?"

"There's an old saying about joining that which you cannot defeat. She'll favour me for weakening her enemies. She'll favour me even more if I fix the problem you now present."

Of course this was how it was going to go. I smirked. "Oh, Church. Are your affections that fickle that you'd toss me over with so little regard?"

"I've loved you since the first day I met you," he replied, and my heart leapt in surprise. "You have always been extraordinary, but now the world knows what you are. They will hate you and fear you. I can't protect you any more. I'd rather see you dead than in a cage."

This was not what I had expected to hear. I hadn't expected to see genuine remorse on his face. "Am I to understand that as the man in charge, you couldn't protect me from that?"

"I'm not in charge of those experiments, my dear. The responsibility for that is higher up the food chain than my lowly self."

Well, wasn't that just fucking marvellous. Exactly what I wanted to hear. "You'll start a war with the goblins." I had the satisfaction of seeing him pale at that.

"I can take care of the goblins. We should have fire-bombed their den a long time ago."

My stomach cramped. I'd always hated goblins. Like everyone else I'd been terrified of them, but now that I had a connection, now that I knew I was one of them, the thought of them being wiped out was horrible. Aside from Vex, they were the only ones who accepted me. The prince had done nothing but help me – though it would be a while before I could forgive him for announcing my goblinness to the world.

I'd changed so much in the last few weeks I barely recognised myself at times.

Church raised his pistol. "I am truly sorry it has come to this, Xandra, but you are my responsibility, and if I don't deal with the problems you've made, it won't go well for me. You either align yourself with me, or we end this. Now."

So it came down to me or him. Fair enough. It was an easy choice on my part, albeit a painful one. I hated him, but part of me still loved him.

"I used to look up to you," I told him. My voice was shamefully hoarse. "Every man I've ever met I've compared to you."

"Even Vexation MacLaughlin?" His tone was bitter. Mocking.

"Even him. Although I have to say, he wins hands down, Church. You're pathetic. Pitiful, even. I feel sorry for you. You'll never be good enough, you know that, don't you? They will always see you as less than them."

Flushed, ruddy and dark, he pulled the trigger, but I dived out of the way of the shot – right into one of the mail cars. It was what I'd hoped he'd do. I needed him angry and vicious. It was the only way I could go through with what I had to do.

I pivoted my body and whipped my own weapon up to shoot out the light. The small room exploded into darkness as I struggled upright. I could see in the blackness – not quite perfectly, but better than before; better than Church. I reached into the front of the train and shoved the lever that set the little engine in motion.

Church jumped into another car as the train began to pull away. He wasn't far behind me, and blindly coming closer. I aimed my gun at him – right between his lying, traitorous eyes. I could end him and avenge Dede right then and there.

But I wanted him to see it coming.

I flicked the safety and shoved the Bulldog into the bustle holster. I was fairly certain Church wouldn't have heard the sound over the noise of the little train. This thing had to be one of the originals from 1927. Though it had seats installed for Her Majesty and her entourage, the engine hadn't been refurbished.

Church had almost reached me – the train wasn't very long. I had my calves pressed back against the engine car, my feet firmly planted on the swaying floor.

We were travelling fast enough that a breeze ruffled my hair. It felt nice, despite the smell of dust and dirt, and old machine. And Dede's blood. I couldn't forget that. Not even for a second could I forget that.

For weeks I'd fought to keep a tight hold on my sanity, and now ... well, I'd let go of that the moment my sister died in my arms. Whatever I was right now – goblin, halvie, freak – sanity played no part in it. I was full-on hatters and it felt right.

Church had his gun in his left hand when he reached me. I grabbed his wrist and twisted hard. He actually cried out when the bones snapped. The pistol clattered to the floor of the car. A half-blood never would have had the strength to hurt him.

I released his arm and caught him with a right hook. His head flew back, but he didn't fall. He came back with a right of his own that struck me hard on the side of the head. I'd forgotten that the old man was ambidextrous.

We went through a section of tunnel lit by another solitary light, and I caught a glimpse of him twisting his injured wrist into proper alignment. I bitch-slapped him, and we plunged into darkness once more. He knew exactly where I was now, however.

I blocked his next swing, but was totally unprepared for his skull smashing into mine. Stars exploded in front of my eyes. Bloody bastard. Wanted to play like that, did he?

I brought my knee up, and was rewarded with the feeling of his bollocks squishing like ripe plums against my leg. He doubled over, and I gave his nose the ball of my hand, smiling as cartilage crunched. If the blood on my hands had still been wet, I would have smeared his face with it just so he would have to wear it and smell it as I did.

I could have done more damage, but I wasn't trying to kill him. I was merely playing.

A glance over my shoulder and I saw that we were almost at our destination. I pulled the handbrake just as Church straightened. The train screeched to a halt, sending him stumbling once more.

"For a vampire, you certainly are a clumsy twat," I sneered, before vaulting over the side. Bits of brick and broken glass crunched beneath my heels. There had been a light here once, but it had been busted a long time ago and never replaced. On the opposite side of the track, an old oil lamp in a sconce cast a weak glow on the rusty fresco painted on the wall beside it. Next to the painting was a door. I ran to it, pulled it open and ran down the dark stairs.

I stopped at the bottom and listened, waiting for Church to give chase before continuing.

"I'll get you, you fucking goblin bitch," he snarled. All pretext of caring was gone. Good. I needed his hate. Needed to see him for what he really was. He might have thought he loved me, but I was just a stepping stone in his ego's quest for social elevation.

I laughed. I'd really pissed him off if he'd taken to swearing. "Brassed off that I got the better of you? You're the one who taught me to fight." With that I scampered away, running through the dark as sure-footed as any cat. A brick whizzed past my head.

"Try throwing with the hand I didn't break," I called over my shoulder, adding a hefty dose of mockery to every word.

I ducked into another doorway – this one roughly forged, chipped away by decades of use and disregard – and waited with my back flat up against the rough wall. The air smelled of dirt and fruit, smoke and fur.

And yes, a hint of pine. A torch burned in each corner of the hall, illuminating little pieces of life the Romans had left behind. If I looked long enough, I'd probably find bits of an actual Roman too.

Church burst into the hall just as I snapped my arm straight out.

His throat connected hard with my forearm, sending shock waves all the way to my shoulder. He fell back like a cut tree, hitting the dirt floor with a loud thud. That had to hurt. He'd heal quickly, but for a few minutes he'd have one hell of a concussion.

I bent down and grabbed his ankle. The bone was sharp beneath the silk of his sock. His shoes were Italian leather, now scuffed and dusty. It took a surprising lack of effort on my part to drag him towards yet another doorway – this one a large, uneven hole in the wall. He swore at me, and struggled, but was too stunned to put up much of a fight.

He'd gone down so much more easily than I thought, and it wasn't because he wasn't a good fighter. He was. It was just that I had the advantage of being stronger, and hadn't underestimated him as he had me.

I dragged him into the middle of the floor and dropped his foot. I kicked him hard in the thigh before moving out of striking distance. I watched as he slowly came round and sat up. Cautiously he pushed himself to his feet, weaving slightly.

He looked like hell, his ginger hair mussed, his evening clothes ripped and dirty. Blood was smeared across his upper lip. He looked wild and furious, and very surprised that I had stopped running.

He wasn't stupid. He knew I was up to something. He regarded me as though I was a wild animal, one he was concerned might bite.

"What is this?" he asked.

"This," I replied, holding my hands out from my sides, "is the great hall, and you are an uninvited guest." At the sound of my voice, goblins began to emerge from the shadows, their furry forms seemingly made from the same darkness.

Church tensed at the sight of them, and turned to flee whence he came, only to find the way blocked by gobs.

"I believe you know the prince. You shot him a long time ago. You let me think he'd tried to hurt me."

"He jumped on you." Church faced me once more. "Anyone would have done the same if it happened to a child they loved."

Bitterness blossomed in the back of my mouth. "You killed Simon. You killed my sister."

"I did what I had to do for you. For the sake of this country."

Maybe that was what he told himself to justify his actions, but I hadn't been a consideration, not really.

"You did what served you best," I corrected him. "And now I'm going to do the same."

His gaze darted around the room before locking with mine once more. "Is this the moment in our drama when I ask what that is and you shoot me in the head?"

I smiled. "Not quite." Maybe some day I would be sorry for what I was about to do, but right now I couldn't think of anything that would give me more satisfaction, despite the consequences.

I turned to the goblins gathered around us, starting with the prince. "I am your queen," I began, not the least bothered by the crazy-arsed smile I got in return. I was a little crazed myself, after all. "Each and every one of you is now under my protection, as I am under yours. Every one of you is my responsibility, and my charge."

"And your servant," the prince amended, with a bow.

I inclined my head at him. "As your queen, I have brought you a gift, and ask only that you take it, here and now."

"What is it, our lady?"

I held my hand towards Church. "Meat."

My former mentor's face drained of all colour as he realised what I'd just done – what he had allowed me to do. "Alexandra, you can't do this."

I whirled on him. My fingers crooked, itching to gouge the lying eyes right out of his fucking head. "Yes. I can." And then to my newly adopted subjects, "Eat him."

The goblins converged like a fluid mass – a single unit. The prince led the charge. Church tried to escape, but only made it two steps before the prince was on him. He swung his fist, but the goblin deflected the blow – and then lunged.

He grabbed Churchill by the throat with his teeth. The still sane part of me – and it was a little part, but loud nevertheless – didn't want to watch, but I refused to look away. This was my responsibility. My choice.

I made myself watch as blood spurted from my former mentor's neck. Forced myself to look as the rest of the goblins converged. His screams rang in my ears, and I knew I'd hear them in my dreams for a long time to come, along with the sound of tearing flesh and rending bone.

He stopped screaming just when I thought I couldn't take any more, when the taste of bile burned the back of my throat along with my own screams for him to just hurry up and fucking die. When that silence fell, it was a terrible one, for it was filled with the quiet sounds of meat being ripped from bone, along with the contented growls of feeding goblins. I watched as an older goblin handed a piece of what looked like liver to a younger pup.

The prince came to me, muzzle wet. He went down on one knee before me, lifting his arms in offering. In his hands was Churchill's heart. "Tribute, lady."

I stared at it for a moment; the bloody mass of muscle continued to throb, too stubborn to stop. It mocked me as it pulsed – even though it had been ripped from his chest, it refused to give up.

My fingers reached for it. It was warm and slick as my hand closed around it. I felt it beat against my palm. Once. Twice. I snarled low in my chest at the insult, and lifted the bloody organ to my mouth, squeezing it hard.

I stopped it from beating once and for all.

CHAPTER 18

TRUTH IS THE BEGINNING OF EVERY GOOD THING

"Are you sure you want to do this?"

I looked up from a box I'd just set on the table. Vex stood in the doorway, two stacked cardboard cartons in his arms. "Too late now. I've signed the lease."

My wolf set the boxes on a nearby chair. "You think you'll be safe here?" He glanced around at the somewhat shabby surroundings, which I planned to restore to their former glory. The house was in Leicester Square and used to be a public house.

"Safer than I will be in Mayfair." My new house was neutral territory, and while humans lived in the area as well, I was better prepared to defend myself against humans than aristos. And half-bloods. I wasn't one of them any more.

Victoria had made it clear that I shouldn't live in what she considered her neighbourhood. Well, my father had strongly suggested I move, and since both Val and Avery were pissed off at me for not telling them about Dede or my secret, it seemed a good idea to relocate. I didn't mind – not really. This way my siblings couldn't be used against me, and couldn't keep an eye on me either. Emma would take care of Avery.

I didn't know if my siblings were more loyal to me or my father, and right now my father was the enemy. I hadn't told him, or Avery and Val, where I was going, and they hadn't asked. I think Val and Avery were afraid of me as well. Maybe afraid *for* me too. It was a dodgy situation, and it hurt, but it was for the best while I sorted myself out.

"Did you hear that Parliament has declared Churchill a traitor?" Vex asked, carrying in more boxes. I hadn't even noticed he'd left the room. Everything was still a little surreal, and I was still a little too self-absorbed.

At the mention of Church, my knees trembled slightly. When it had been leaked to Special Branch that there was evidence of illegal experiments in Church's private office, they'd searched the premises and found the files. It was also circulating in the scandal sheets that he had been in on the plot to kill Victoria. The Crown didn't comment on the murder attempt, but a statement was released expressing "Her Majesty's shock and disappointment" over such a favoured subject committing such "vile" deeds.

"I did hear something like that," I replied, opening a box of books that would soon find a home on the floor-to-ceiling shelves in my library.

I was the one who'd alerted Special Branch, and leaked the story to the press. Not only did it draw attention away from me, and Dede's death, but it destroyed Church once and for all.

It also covered my tracks. No one suspected Church to be dead. Popular opinion was that he had left the country, as many personal items were missing from his house.

Those items belonged to the goblin prince now, as did Churchill's spine. The rest of his bones had been incorporated into the throne being built for me in the plague den. I wasn't in any hurry to sit on it, but sooner or later I would have to.

"Do you know anything about it?" Vex asked.

I glanced up. I trusted him with my life, but I didn't want him to know anything that might get him into trouble one day. Still, I'd had enough dishonesty and deceit to last the rest of my days. "Yes."

He paused, cradling a ceramic temple elephant in his big hands. "Did you kill him?"

"You already asked me that." I shoved some paperbacks on to a polished shelf.

"Tell me again."

I met his gaze. "I didn't kill him." It wasn't a lie.

Vex frowned. "I don't understand why the hell not. After what that bastard did . . . I would have torn his heart out."

Someone else did that for me. I swallowed. I should feel remorse, or at the very least, disgust. I felt nothing.

"He won't be coming back," I whispered.

Vex's head jerked up, but there was no censure in his eyes. No revulsion. I was fairly certain he had a good idea of what happened to Church in the tunnels. "Good." He checked his watch. "We should get ready. It's almost nine."

A familiar ache blossomed in my chest. "Right. I just have to change. You brought clothes with you?"

He nodded. He'd been my shadow these last few days, with me whenever I needed him, and sometimes when I didn't. I didn't mind his presence. Vex was one of those rare people who was content with his own company. If I needed time alone, he'd wander off and give it to me, but he always seemed to know when to come back.

We showered together. He ran his soapy hands all over me – but it was more soothing than sexual. He took care of me but didn't coddle. I leaned into his touch as though I could absorb some of his strength through my skin.

I was empty inside. The spot Dede had occupied was hollow and raw, as though cut away with a rusty blade. The loss of Avery and Val stung but wasn't as crushing. They would come back eventually; Dede would not.

After drying off, I put on a little make-up, re-pinned my hair and slipped into black trousers, corset, boots and a black velvet frock coat Dede had given me for Christmas last year. Vex dressed in head-to-toe black as well. We looked like a couple of crows as we exited the building.

My hair was still candy red, but my eyes had taken on a ring of gold around the Vardan green, and my skin was paler than it had been before. The supplements were completely out of my system, allowing the me I should have been to fully emerge. I'm not sure what I thought of her, but I was all right with her for now. Some of the new impulses and behaviours were strange and a little . . . disconcerting, but I no longer worried about my sanity or what people thought of me. I was still trying to suss out whether that was good or not.

I looked around, keen gaze searching for any sign of an assassin waiting to strike. There was nothing. Either I was being lulled into a sense of security, or I was truly was safe. For now.

I was goblin, but still looked half-blood – except when hunger or rage got the better of me. Two days ago a halvie doctor had approached me about allowing him to perform some tests on me. I admired his nerve, so I let him walk away rather than break both his knees. I told him I wasn't interested, but I'd call if I changed my mind. He seemed surprised, as though a lab rat like me ought to jump at the chance to run through another maze.

"Have you spoken to your father?" Vex asked as we climbed into the Swallow.

"Not since he suggested I move." I leaned back against the soft leather seat. "I reckon his loyalty is with Queen V right now, just as it always has been. He'll want to patch things up with her and separate himself from his abomination of a child." There was not a smidgen of self-pity in my tone, thank you very much. Just fact.

"Nothing from Avery or Valentine either?"

I shook my head and sighed as he started the engine. "Nothing." The boxes of things that had arrived at my new house yesterday had been accompanied by a note from Emma expressing love and regret, but not from my sister.

Warm fingers came down on my leg for a moment before moving to put the motor carriage into gear. "I'm sorry."

To my horror, my eyes began to burn. Thankfully, no tears leaked out. "It's all right. They'll come round."

"Whatever you need, you have me and my pack."

I don't know what I'd done to deserve him, but I was eternally grateful to whatever made me go to Freak Show that night when Vex and I met. Once, in the wee hours, I'd entertained doubts about him, wondered if he was only after what I could offer him politically, but I'd quickly pushed them away. "Victoria won't like that." But Vex had made it clear at our little "faction" meeting that he was with me. The queen hadn't liked it, but she didn't make a fuss. She was a crafty old bird. I had no doubt she had already started making plans for me.

"Victoria can fuck herself."

I smiled. "Can't imagine anyone else wanting to do it." We laughed together, and for that moment I felt better than I had in weeks. I missed my family, and I missed Dede like a severed limb, but there had been some truth in what Church had said that night in the tunnels. Dede had been somewhat mad – ever since they took her baby away. She would never have Ainsley or their child, and it would have destroyed her. That didn't excuse what he had done, and it didn't make me feel one ounce of remorse for taking him to his death. Some people had to die, and Churchill was one of them.

But I would not forget that I had a nephew in Mayfair. If it was the last thing I did, I'd make certain the world knew who his mother really was. One day. For Dede.

There was no church service this time. We went straight to Kensal Green, where armed RGs protected the gates. We had to show ID to get inside. The look on the guards' faces when they recognised me would have been hysterical if they hadn't been so . . . afraid. Vex growled low in his throat – just enough to make them both flush with embarrassment and shame. "Go right in, Alpha, Your Majesty."

Majesty. Yeah, right. It was bad enough the gobs called me that.

"I suppose I ought to get used to people treating me like I'm a monster," I remarked as Vex and I walked hand in hand towards the Vardan crypt.

He squeezed my fingers. "You're not a monster."

Tell that to Churchill's heart. I didn't say anything, just squeezed back. Sometimes I dreamed about Church, all the things he used to mean to me. I'd remember dragging him into the den, handing him over like he was nothing more than . . . meat. Those were usually the times I woke up screaming, covered in sweat, shaking. The times I woke up crying were the times I hated him most.

There was a small crowd at the crypt – my father, Val, Avery and Emma. Emma actually came over to say hello and give me a hug, God love her. There were a few other people there – Dede's mother and some of her good friends from the Peerage Protectorate – but that was it. No one else had been allowed to witness the interment of the Duke of Vardan's traitorous daughter.

And the rags had declared her a traitor. Before I'd had him

killed, Churchill had indeed built quite a case against her. Even I had trouble picking out the lies in it.

I hugged Lecia, but didn't speak. What could either of us say? Nothing that we wanted anyone to hear. We would talk later. Maybe then I'd know what to tell her about her daughter.

Avery didn't look at me, but I knew she wouldn't. She'd cave if she did, and she wasn't ready to accept or forgive. I'd do the same thing. Val nodded curtly. He was going to stay cold much longer than Avery; it was his duty as eldest to plague me with disappointment for as long as possible, just to make certain I was properly contrite.

The vicar said a few words, but I didn't listen. He hadn't known Dede and he didn't care. My attention was captured by another group of people a few hundred feet away. They were gathered around an old stone angel that had chipped wings, and pigeon shit on its serene face. I wouldn't have given them a second thought had one of them not had familiar salt-water-blue hair.

My gaze flew to the woman beside her, her face concealed by a black veil. I could tell by the height and the blonde hair peeking out from beneath her hat that it was my mother. I nodded to her – ever so slightly – before turning my gaze back to Ophelia. She wore a partial veil as well. I didn't even wonder how they'd got past the guards.

My sister looked good – healthy and strong. There wasn't a blemish on her smooth, pale throat to show that I'd ever tried to rip it open. We stared at each other a moment – her warily, and me with remorse. I'd never meant to hurt her.

Then she inclined her head, and I did the same – a truce it seemed, at least for now. I was irrationally happy to have it, despite the fact that I still didn't like her all that much. But I'd take her disdain over fear any day.

It started to rain, and the vicar ended things shortly afterwards.

Everyone filed out to face the reporters, who wanted to wring every last drop of scandal out of my sister's death. And me. They wanted me too. They would have to wait.

I stepped into the crypt, up to the shelf where a casket containing an impostor had once sat. Now, it was empty except for a tall, ornate urn. They'd burned her – there was a cruel, yet symmetrical, irony in that. I put my hand on the base, feeling the cool porcelain beneath my fingers. "Goodbye, Dede," I whispered, throat dry.

Not a single tear came. Now, when I wanted to let it out, cleanse my soul or whatever, I couldn't summon a goddam cry for her.

The Bedlam crew was gone when I emerged. Probably didn't want to risk being seen. I wanted to blame them for Dede's death, but I couldn't be bothered. Dede was dead because she'd wanted to see her kid – and me. No, she was dead because of Church. I wasn't going to martyr myself for his sorry dead arse.

He would never have a grave for people to visit. He would never have rest so long as I had his skull to gnaw on. I'd see to that. Was that mad? Yes, and I didn't fucking care.

Vex and I walked to the exit. It had taken us longer to get here than the funeral lasted. The guards had lifted their collars against the weather, but I liked the water on my skin. It made me feel clean. And the darkness made me feel . . . safe.

I watched my family climb into my father's carriage as Vex and I approached his. Reporters yelled at us. Flash bulbs stung my eyes. I could make them all piss themselves with a flash of fang and a snarl, but I'd still end up on the front page. I didn't need to show them the monster. "You all right?" he asked.

I nodded. "Fine."

"Xandra, how do you feel now that you've finally buried your sister?" a reporter asked, thrusting a microphone in my face.

I glanced at him. Just a little weaselly human with big bollocks. *Finally?* "Like I've just buried my sister," I replied.

Vex put himself between me and the reporter. "Piss off," he snarled.

"Y . . . you can't hurt me," he sputtered. "Queen Victoria signed a treaty prohibiting aristocrats from harming the press."

I smiled. "But I'm not an aristocrat."

His face went white, and he scurried off like a mouse.

Vex turned to me. "I think you like being a goblin."

"I think I want to get the hell out of here before the rest of the vultures attack." There was a barricade, but there were only two guards, and many more humans and halvies. Pretty soon they'd mob us.

We climbed into the Swallow and set off for home. I wanted to be in my own space. I wanted this all to die down so I could take stock of my life and start living it.

And I needed to prepare myself for the chance that the Queen of England might come hunting for my head.

My house was cosy when we stepped inside, the mellow lighting giving off a warm glow. Despite the unpacked boxes and furniture that still needed to be arranged, it was beginning to feel like home. A safe place. I hadn't realised how much I'd longed for this until now. All my life I'd fussed over Val and Avery and Dede. I'd made them, and my career, the focus of my life. I'd been all about pleasing other people, trying to win approval.

The only approval I needed now was my own. I intended to set about earning it. Apparently I had no problem with murder, so that was a good thing. Where did I stand on the goblin issue? They still bloody terrified me, but not in the same way. They were no danger to me – at least not to my person. And they had a sense of honour that I found both bizarre and fascinating.

But I hadn't heard from the prince since he gave me tribute. I had to admit to feeling a little . . . neglected.

"Xandra, what's that?"

I turned from hanging up my coat. There, on the table in my parlour, sat an antique hatbox with a card on top of it.

"No bloody idea," I replied, moving towards it.

Vex stopped me. "Let me."

I opened my mouth to remind him that I was as strong as he was – maybe stronger – and then shut it again. I liked that he wanted to protect me, and he seemed to like doing it. Why not let him? It was nice to know I had someone looking out for me.

Gently he lifted the top off the box. When nothing exploded, I peered over his shoulder to see another box inside. This one was covered in rich dark blue velvet. My wolf picked it up and inspected it before carefully opening the lid.

My jaw dropped. It was a crown. Hand-carved, intricate and ornate, it was one of the most beautiful things I'd ever seen. It was also quite possibly the most disturbing.

It was made of old metal and old bone. More to the point, it was carved from a skull. A vampire skull. Someone had fashioned it, embellished it. And then it had sat in the underside for a long time. I hoped it wasn't as old as it looked, because that would make it ancient.

Vex stared at it, his expression a mirror of how mine felt. "Read the card," he suggested.

I took up the envelope and ripped it open. The card inside was heavy stock, the penmanship on it perfect and scribed by a quill and ink. I read it aloud: "For the Xandra lady, Queen of all the Plagues of Britain. A coronation present from your humble servant, the Prince of the Goblins." I slid my gaze to Vex. "I reckon they haven't forgotten about making me queen, then."

"Aye, and they plan to hold a coronation." Incredulity brightened his rugged features and twinkled in his grey eyes. "Victoria's going to blow a gasket."

I smiled at his wicked laughter. I shouldn't invite trouble, but maybe this country needed a little. It certainly needed a change. "Should I try it on?"

He lifted the crown from its velvet bed. "Only if you promise to leave it on. I always wanted to get off with a queen."

His humour was exactly the right thing to ease the ache in my heart. Dede wouldn't want me to wail and moan over her, which was just as well, because I didn't think I had it in me.

"Mind you show me the proper respect," I informed him, "or I'll have your head."

He grinned – all wolf. "You can have the head, and the rest of it too."

I rolled my eyes as he set the crown on my head. It was a perfect fit, as though it had been made for me. I turned to look in the mirror hanging in the hall. It looked good too. What did it say about me that bone seemed to suit me?

"It's macabre," I murmured, raising my hand to touch it. So much work had gone into it. "And pretty."

Vex's arms came around me. "*You're* pretty." He kissed my temple. "I'd like to take you upstairs and make you forget everything for a few hours, show you what happens when two royals get naked. What do you say to that, Your Majesty?"

I turned in his arms and wrapped my own around his neck. Right now, it was just the two of us. I'd worry about the rest of it – Victoria, my family, Bedlam, the goblins – tomorrow. I set the crown aside and rose on my toes to bring my mouth closer to his as he lowered his head. I smiled.

"I say God save the Queen."

UNDERSTANDING
THE ARISTOCRACY

The following has been taken from the text Here There Be
Monsters: An Evolutional History of the Aristocracy in Europe *by
Drs Jackson and Agrafojo.*

Origins

Yersina pestis, the causative bacterium of the Black Death, contains
genetic material that is released when the bacteria die off in
response to attacks of the human's immune system. In cases with
high enough fevers bacterial DNA can be incorporated into cells that
are actively dividing (in most cases this means sperm and embry-
onic tissues).[1] Thus after every wave of plague more carriers of this
genetic material would be present in the human population.

This genetic material causes the production of a special

---

1 This occurs as a result of a process called transfection, facilitated by heat shock
proteins induced by high fever.

regulatory protein called the Prometheus Protein that has two major functions. The first of these is to increase stem cell production across the body. Stem cells routinely travel throughout the body from difference storage pools. They have two major capabilities: they can repair injured tissue by replacing the damaged cells or they can produce new, healthy tissue that the body has an increased need for. The second function of the protein is to initiate the regenerative/transformative reactions that give enhanced humans, vampires and weres their special abilities.

The Enhanced Human

A person with one copy of the genetic material would have more stem cells and be considered quite robust, able to fend off diseases and infirmity and often live to a ripe old age, but otherwise appear as perfectly normal *Homo sapiens*. If two such robust individuals produce children there is a one in four chance that a double dose of this recessive regulatory gene will occur.[2] Double-dosed individuals will either be vampires or weres. The determination of whether such a double-dosed person is born a vampire or werewolf is caused by multi-genetic interactions.[3]

The Vampire

Vampires have greatly enhanced regeneration. First this means that they will have a lifespan much longer than an average human and, once adults, will always be in prime physical health. Second, wounds incurred by a vampire, if not immediately fatal, will heal. These wounds will heal completely, leaving no scars, in a matter of hours or days where a human would be incapacitated for weeks

2 Cell DNA always contains two copies of a gene: one from the mother and one from the father.
3 Tendencies towards throwing a were versus a vampire will run in families.

or months. Third, due to the regenerative capabilities of the vampiric condition, vampires are immune to disease and *most* toxins. Finally, the regenerative properties of the vampire would allow enhanced speed and strength.

Vampires also have limited transformative abilities, specifically the extension and retraction of teeth and nails. The stem cells can extend and retract parts of the jaw and nail beds to effect this change.

Homo feralis – *The Were*

Weres have greatly enhanced transformative powers, allowing them to modify their limbs and tissues to take on animalistic capabilities (claws, fangs, four-legged stance, thick pelts, etc. ....). In addition, the transformation allows them to generate large amounts of muscle tissue, making them exceedingly strong and quick. The transformation also increases the number of olfactory nerves in the nose to improve scent detection, increased numbers of rod cells in the retina of the eye for enhanced night vision and increased auditory nerve hairs to make hearing more acute. Weres are immune to all but the most deadly diseases, but are susceptible to quick acting poisons. Weres remain hale throughout their lifespan and appear to age more slowly than the average human.

Coming to the Light

To recap, the Prometheus Protein is responsible for both the superstimulation of stem cell production and directing where and how those stem cells react. There are three variations of the Prometheus Proetin: PPv in the vampire, PPf in the were and PPr in *H. robustus*. The Prometheus Protein variants are light sensitive in the vampire (PPv) and, to a lesser degree, in the were (PPf). When light interacts with the vampire Prometheus Protein (PPv) in the skin it creates reactive oxygen, causing blistering, massive skin trauma and abdominal pain. This process also destroys the affected Prometheus Protein.

The were variant of the Prometheus Protein (PPf) has a slightly different molecular geometry and is less reactive with light. Thus the were experiences are more along the lines of a sunburn. Continued exposure to sunlight will slowly deplete a were's PPf levels, which will in turn slow the production of stem cells and further limit their ability to transform. The confirmation of the protein in *Homo robustus* (PPr) is non-reactive to light. It should be noted that projecting a strong ultraviolet or full spectrum light onto either a vampire or were would have the same effects as exposing them to sunlight.

It's in the Blood

Vampires and weres can extract both stem cells (from all human subspecies) and Prometheus Protein from living blood. They can utilise the increased resources to supplement their enhanced abilities. The stronger blood (i.e. blood with Prometheus Protein in it) the greater the boost in their abilities. Ingested proteins are effective for about week or until utilised.

Vampires, with their razor-sharp retractable fangs, are capable of extracting blood without considerable lasting damage to their donors. Weres, on the other hand, are messier. It should be noted that neither vampires nor weres *need* to drink blood unless they are over using their abilities or are mortally injured.

Silver Lining

Silver toxicity in the average human is well documented. After absorbing a very large amount of silver, whether ingested, injected or inhaled, a toxic reaction resulting in death will occur within hours.

In human blood, silver is carried by albumin, a blood protein, until excreted in the urine and stool. In *H. robustus*, the process is identical as PPr is non-reactive with silver. In vampires silver prefers to bind to the PPv protein over albumin. This binding is reversible, but will temporarily inactivate PPv for a few hours.

During this period the vampire does not produce additional stem cells and cannot activate their regenerative and transformative abilities (they are effectively *Homo sapiens*). The silver-bound PPv, however, is protected from the photoreaction induced by sunlight, making it possible for vampires to function in daytime during this short period of time, though they are more vulnerable.

In the were, silver is attracted to the PPf, it preferentially and irreversibly bonds to it. As it takes three to four weeks for the body to break down all of the silver-bound PPf and replace it with new, healthy PPf, weres are effectively *Homo sapiens* for this extended period. In addition, metabolic breakdown products of the silver-bound PPf cause a systemic inflammatory reaction. This produces "Silver Sickness" a syndrome presenting a flu-like weakness and fever during the recuperative phase.

Methods of silver delivery are many and varied. From most efficacious to least they include:

- Injection of liquid silver via hypodermic needle directly into bloodstream
- Inhalation of atomised silver vapour by the lungs
- Ingestion of silver filings, salts or liquids
- Liquid silver coated blade or electrically charged silver blade (which will electroplate a wound!) Note: weres struck by silvered weapons will scar blue. Vampires do not scar
- Topical preparation (facial creams, etc. . . . .)
- A silver bullet that stays in the body and continually releases small silver particles

I wish the goblins would come and take you away

When vampires mate with other vampires the resulting offspring always inherit two copies of the v modifier gene, resulting in another vampire. Similarly, two were parents will always produce a were child with two copies of the f modifier gene. If, however, one parent is a vampire and the other is a were then a vf modifier gene hybrid is a result. This hybrid is commonly referred to as a goblin. In addition to cross subspecies mating, in rare cases a male vampire or were can have temporary changes in the sperm due to an environmental factor which changes the v modifier to f or the f modifier to the v respectively.

A goblin pregnancy is a tremendous drain on a vampire or were mother's body as it requires a great deal of Prometheus Protein and stem cells to sustain the infant to term. Once born, a goblin inherits all the benefits and limitation of both subspecies. Their bodies contain a full complement of both PPv and PPf proteins, effectively giving them twice as much as any vampire or were. They have the vampire's remarkable longevity along with tremendous regenerative properties. Their transformative capabilities are so strong that they never appear fully human, usually opting to remain in super-enhanced hybrid states which are incredibly strong and fast. Due to their double complement of PP they also have the ability to shift more often than any were.

Goblins inherit the vampiric sensitivity to sunlight and given the increased amounts of Prometheus Protein in their bodies even moonlight is toxic. Like the were parent silver is toxic, negating all enhancements granted by the Prometheus Proteins, which are necessary to sustain goblin life. If they survive they suffer from extreme Silver Sickness and they effectively become bedridden humans for months. Goblins are the most efficient extractors of stem cells and Prometheus Proteins of all of the subspecies. They are so effective that they can extract these resources from eating flesh as well as drinking blood.

GLOSSARY

AC/A-cylinder – audio cylinder. A small metal tube used to store music and other electronic data.

aether – slang for airwaves, usually applied to telephone, telegraph and video communications not broadcast over private channels.

Albert's fangs – a "curse" seen as taking the late Prince Consort's name in vein . . . er, vain.

aristocrat – collective term for vampires and werewolves, particularly those of noble birth.

box – television.

Britme – electronic service provided by Britannia Telephone and Telegraph where people can leave a voice recording for the person they're trying to reach via stationary line or rotary.

bubonic betty – a human who injects aristocrat blood to gain enhanced senses, strength and speed.

cobbleside – above ground.

courtesan – a human woman employed by the aristocracy to breed half-bloods. These women are plague carriers, able to carry full-term, healthy pregnancies.

digigram – electronic text-based message sent between wireless devices and logic engines.

digital processing machine – device that scans and transmits documents' digital files.

fang me – being "fanged" means being used for food by an aristocrat – a practice beneath most halvies.

job – to hit or get violent with. Associated with the violence often attached to halvie occupations: "He really did a job on that human"; "She jobbed the betty hard in the kidneys."

halvie – a half-blood. Half vampire/were and half human.

hatters – derived from "mad as a hatter". Slang for crazy, insane.

horror show – illegal spectacle at which vampires or weres consume a human or halvie victim for the audience's titillation.

huey – slang for human.

logic engine/log en – electronic device that stores and processes information and allows for many kinds of digital communication over the aethernet.

meat – goblin term for anything warm-blooded, and therefore edible.

Met – name given to the Metropolitan Underground Railway.

mice – derogatory goblin slang for humans. As mice and rats don't cohabit, neither do the plagued and humans.

motor carriage – modern carriage propelled by an engine rather than horses.

pay post – receptacle for money in exchange for a place to park a motor- or horse-driven carriage. The proceeds go towards paying government expenses.

Pax, the – name given to the law that all humans must be registered and DNA tested as children to determine whether or not they are plague carriers. Used to prevent unwanted plagued births. This same law gives tax breaks to human families with only one child – even more breaks for those who have none.

plague, the – responsible for the Prometheus mutation that made vamps and weres, and goblins. Also the term used by goblins to describe a group of themselves. The London plague is used to refer to all the goblins in London.

privacy box – tall red box that affords the user privacy to make a wireless call or anything else that strikes his/her fancy.

rotary – portable wireless telephone. Has a rotary dial.

rut – vulgar, but slightly more polite than "fuck".

tango – halvie slang for a fight.

underside – underground.

VC – video cylinder. Used to record and play back video, such as films.

Yersinia – from *Yersinia pestis* – the bubonic plague. The name of the goblin city.

ACKNOWLEDGEMENTS

This book started out as a project just for my own enjoyment – a "what if" moment that took hold of my brain and forced me to write the sort of story I wanted to read. However, no book makes it to publication by itself, so there are a few people I must thank. While researching, I discovered the music of the fabulously talented Emilie Autumn, whose *Opheliac* CD could have been a soundtrack for *God Save the Queen*. Thank you for the inspiration! Also, a big thanks to all the "Muffins" on Emilie Autumn's forum, who gave me hope that there just might be an audience for this book.

I also need to thank my agent, the amazing Miriam Kriss. Without her support I don't think *GSTQ* ever would have happened. Miriam, I adore you and thank you from the bottom of my heart. I know you have my back not only as an author, but also as a friend. That's a rare combination and I hope you know just how much you rock. Thank you for all the butt-kicking and hand-holding!

Next I need to acknowledge my publisher, Orbit, and the

incredible people I work with, especially David Young, Tim Holman, Devi Pillai, Anna Gregson, Alex Lencicki, Lauren Panepinto and Ellen Wright – and others too numerous to name. Your enthusiasm and support for this project has been so fantastically overwhelming that I simply cannot articulate my gratitude. You are all fabulous, especially those of you who are British and indulge my inner Anglophile.

A big shout out to "plague masters" Eric Jackson and Emilia Agrafojo, who are not only fabulous, but who actually sat down and figured out how the mutation of the plague happened. They gave me science to back it up, making it so real I forgot the idea came from my head (and theirs!) and not a textbook. It has footnotes! They have incredibly rockin' big brains that I would kiss if it wasn't so unhygienic.

I want to thank my family and friends for being so patient when I'm full-on mental, especially my husband, Steve, who puts up with more than he should and supports me through all the craziness. Sometimes I forget that I wouldn't have made this journey if you hadn't been with me every step of the way.

And finally, I want to thank everyone who buys this book. I write because I have to, but I'm published because of you. Thank you!